BANGERS

Gary Phillips

BANGERS

KENSINGTON PUBLISHING CORP.
http://www.kensingtonbooks.com

DAFINA BOOKS are published by

Kensington Publishing Corp.
850 Third Avenue
New York, NY 10022

ISBN 0-7582-0382-9

First Kensington Trade Paperback Printing: October 2003
10 9 8 7 6 5 4 3 2 1

Printed in the United States of America

If the crimes of men were exhibited with their sufferings, the stage effect would sometimes be lost, and the audience would be inclined to approve where it was intended they should commiserate.

—Thomas Paine, *Rights of Man*

BANGERS

CHAPTER 1

Bruno "Cheese" Cortese swung away from the scarred maple bar in the Code 7 cop hangout, a draft beer in one hand and a vodka gimlet in the other. His sturdy six-three frame crossed the sawdust strewn floor in his size fourteens in evenly-spaced, surprisingly light steps for a man of his heft. Ben E. King sang "I Who Have Nothing" on the juke, below the din of the place.

"There you go," he said to his date, placing the martini glass before her. He sat close to the handsome woman at an oval table. Someone had carved into its worn surface a crude cartoon of a skull wearing a policeman's hat.

"Cheers, again," Madeleine Jirac responded, clinking her drink against his pint. She had light-colored eyes and thin, well-proportioned lips. The dark-haired woman was dressed casually in slacks, and was golden-hued from an afternoon session on a tanning bed.

"No doubt." He leaned over, and they kissed.

"So, Bruno," she smiled as their lips and tongues parted, "you think that Immanuel Kant would be a political consultant, a hack working for somebody like Mayor Fergadis, if he were alive today, huh?"

The crow's-feet at the edges of Cortese's eyes became pronounced as his mouth crinkled into a half-moon. " 'Out of the *crooked timber of humanity no straight thing can ever be made.'* Now, a guy who has that kind of outlook, what else could he be suited for?"

"Wouldn't want him wasting time teaching, now, would we?" Jirac sampled some of her drink.

"Smart-ass."

She watched him over the rim. "You like it."

His beeper vibrated before he could formulate a retort. Going out with a woman smarter and older than he was kept him alert. He clicked off the beeper without looking at its screen. "Gotta batter up, baby."

"No cowboying, right?" Her blunt fingers touched the back of his veined hand.

"Never." He got up, bent to kiss her again as he rubbed her back. "I'll call you later, okay?"

"You better."

He finally took a sip of his beer. Then Cortese walked through an archway toward the exit. He rolled his shoulders like he always did to get loose, to work the tension from his neck down into his arms and lower regions. It was a habit from his days of high school football at St. Brigid's, where he was a running back and made all-city one year. Peripherally he glimpsed someone in a corner booth, and had to look directly to make sure.

The man he'd spotted, sitting underneath a wall of photos ranging from cop tournament poker games to darts, pretended he was more interested in the frizzed dirty-blonde he was huddled against, and that he hadn't noticed him. Cortese knew that wasn't so, but what did it matter? He snorted a laugh through his nose and went on through the arch.

The exit was at the back of the hallway, where the bathrooms and an office were located, too. Andre, the head bartender, came out of the washroom and they nodded at each other.

Plastered on the rear door was a monochromatic poster warning kids of the dangers of drugs. The waiflike teenage girl staring out from the announcement had a hand-drawn word balloon attached to her mouth stating, *Discount blow job for cops.* Cortese leaned a shoulder against the door as he simultaneously pressed against the release bar. He went outside to the usual tableau of busted-up crates and plastic trash bags found behind countless taverns, fast-food stands, and restaurants across the city.

He paused and put a hand to an ear as he cocked his head into the humid night air. The theatrical actions were unnecessary, for the moaning was steady and audible. Another half-moon materialized on his face as he trudged to where he knew the sounds originated. He stuck a toothpick in his mouth and went across the warped blacktop of the back lot. To the rear of this a series of stone steps older than Joan Collins led up to a tier of brush and dirt paths. The paths wound their way into Elysian Park and part of Section D of Dodger Stadium.

"Goddamn, Rafe," Herlinda Delarocha murmured pleasurably. She was bent forward, her hands gripping a rusted pole. The woman's panties were halfway down her spread thighs, and her jeans collapsed around her Doc Martens boots. The pole she held onto went upward to a dilapidated wooden overhang that was part of a small building on the back lot that once, many decades ago, had housed city fire hydrants and now was used as a storeroom. A lone floodlight, barely giving off illumination, washed the lovers in cream yellows. There was a pair of handcuffs snapped around the woman's wrists.

Cortese worked the pick in his teeth. He leaned on the corner of the shed, watching the two for several beats, listening to their rough lovemaking. Then he said, "We got to hook and book, pardner."

"Can't you see he's busy, cheddar dick?" Delarocha said hoarsely. "Can't you see I don't give a fuck?"

"*Cabrón.*"

"Ho."

"All right," Rafael Santián grunted. He ceased and straightened up behind Delarocha. "You two ought to take that act and get a radio show." He stepped back, shook his now limp penis, and hiked up his boxers and jeans.

The pretty young woman stood erect and glared at Cortese. "What you lookin' at, mothafuckah?" She was a tall Latina with pronounced cheekbones and a teardrop tattoo in the corner of her heavily mascaraed right eye.

Cortese flicked his toothpick at her exposed leg.

"Bastard," she flared.

Cortese ignored her. "The Gargoyle has landed, Saint."

"Righteous." Santián stepped from around Delarocha as she

hitched her clothes around her wide hips. Patting her on the butt, he said, "See you later, Linda." He started to step away with Cortese.

"Yo." Delarocha rattled the cuffs still keeping her bound.

"Leave her ass like that," Cortese chided.

"Be cool, Cheese." Santián tossed a key to the woman. "Sorry about that."

"That's okay, baby, I know you got to run off with your bunghole buddy and fight crime and shit." She undid the cuffs.

"What a mouth," Cortese remarked.

"Don't she, though?" his partner observed admiringly. They turned to leave again.

"Ain't you gonna need these?" Delarocha held the cuffs and key aloft.

"Keep 'em." His back to her, Santián waved his hand dismissively. "We got plenty."

"I'll save 'em for next time, honey," she chortled. The weak floodlight gleamed on her darkly lipsticked mouth lined in black. She puckered her lips and blew Santián a kiss.

He looked back at her upon hearing the smack and grinned.

"I don't know what you see in an eightball chick like her." Cortese idly scratched his muscled belly.

"I'll pick my own route to ruin, padre." Santián was an inch shorter and not as wide as Cortese. Where his partner was built like a slumming WWE wrestler, Santián had the body of a baller. He was solid but lean, with bulked up triceps and biceps. The two ambled side by side around the corner of the Code 7 to the parking lot. Santián beeped off his Malibu SS's alarm and unlocked the driver's-side door.

"Hey, guess who the fuck was playin' slap and tickle inside?" Cortese sat on the passenger side of the cherry '72 Chevy.

Santián juiced the ignition, and the big-block 420 rumbled alive on the first crank. "Who?" he asked, unlatching the emergency brake.

"Mr. Motto and some hard-lookin' white trash broad I've seen somewhere before."

Santián had backed the car up and then got the shifter into first. Wearily he said, "You know Ahn is a 1.5-er, Cheese, a Korean-American born in Korea and raised in America."

Cortese grinned. "Whatever, Mister PC. Anyway that fuck carried on like he hadn't eyed me, but we both know we peeped each other."

"Maybe McGuire's got him working twenty-four-seven since she decided to run for mayor. If she can get some real dirt on the squad, her handlers must figure that's good for a ten- or fifteen-point boost in a dead heat."

"Who's doing her campaign?" Cortese had rolled the window down and gazed into the side mirror.

"I heard she's been meeting with that slick prick Pablo Pastor."

"She's going for the nuts, that's for sure."

"Don't she always?"

They drove along. "What's up with Curtis?" Cortese asked, to break the silence as they passed Eisenhower Park.

Grooves appeared in Santián's brow. "Man, that kid's gonna kill me quicker than the goddamn Crazy Nines. If it wasn't for hoops and girls, he'd have no reason to be going to school."

"I guess I shouldn't crack about chickens and how they always come home to roost, huh?"

"Have I mentioned lately just how funny you are, mothafuckah?"

The two laughed softly. Santián sped through an intersection against a light turning red. In less than fifteen minutes, the Malibu was rolling through the core of the Venice Heights section, a dense twelve-miles-square area just west of downtown. The Heights—or V-12, as the gang members called it—was like a lot of neighborhoods that had gone through various ethnographic transitions over the years. There was still a Greek restaurant that did overflow business during the week. But the tailor shop next to it had been replaced in the last three years with a *carnicería* complete with a full-scale plastic bull statue on its roof.

There were also leftovers of the black businesses that used to populate the landscape. To be sure, the staple of African-American mom-and-pop outlets, the three *Bs* of barber, beauty, and barbecues, were not as plentiful these days anywhere in L.A. But the West Texas Palace of Savory Meats, a rib-and-hot-links joint of citywide fame, was still owned and operated by a family who'd been around since Santián had been a kid.

"The Lanciliers." Cortese nodded at a seven-story building of a design from the Beaux Arts era. Behind the structure the cross-town MTA subway train thundered along the elevated tracks.

"And there's Big T." Santián made a left and guided the car toward a haphazard row of cypress trees alongside an auto parts store. He parked and the two alighted from the vehicle.

"Z'up?" Santián addressed Theo "Big T" Holton. He was an imposing black man a little over six-one with a wide beer-truck carriage of a body. He was always in a rumpled suit with one of his stingy-brim hats jammed over his cube of a head.

"My crackhead snitch says Villa snuck back into town from El Paso last night. Says this meet has something to do with the Nines and the Baja cartel settin' up a new thing." He took off his hat and scratched at his graying, short-cropped thatch.

Santián got the Malibu's trunk open to reveal several 870 semiautomatic shotguns and zippered duffel bags. "About what?"

"Nobody 'cept them locos up there in Lil Puppet's crib"—he pointed at the apartment house—"know for sure. But me and Ronk figure it's tied to what went down three days ago. The police chief of Juarez, across from El Paso, was driving back from mass in his supposedly bulletproof Suburban."

"The chief was cut down by heavy-duty ordnance a short two blocks from his headquarters." The new speaker was Barry "Ronk" Culhane. He was Holton's running buddy, a naturally slender individual who maintained a serious regimen of weights and bulking powders. His face was bristling with whiskers, and his thinning blond hair glistened with a recent application of Rogaine.

"And Villa was made as one of the shooters?" Cortese racked the twenty-gauge he'd removed from the Malibu's trunk. Culhane shook his head vigorously. "Not a positive, no. But we understand our boy was down there to have a face-to-face with Rosario Del Fuego."

Santián processed the information. Rosario and his maniacal brother Felix ran the so-called Baja cartel. In reality, the cartel was not headquartered in Baja. But the legend went that the two brothers engineered the assassination of a key member of the Columbian Cali cartel in a Baja whorehouse, thus solidifying the rise of their drug empire. "And he did this hit on the police chief on orders from the brothers?"

"The El Paso cops have issued an all-points for him," Culhane added.

"So let's go ask him," a fifth man spoke. Alvaro Acosta was in his dark blue patrolman's uniform. The younger man's black hair was cut military-precise, and the brown skin of his face was unblemished.

"Okay, Mister Eager, we will." Santián shut the trunk, then reconsidered and extracted two mini Astro walkie-talkies out of one of the duffles. He also clipped a shell carrier onto his belt. He used his back pocket for his two-way. He handed the other one to Culhane. "Let's be cool and cautious," he said.

Ronk Culhane took the instrument and sniffed the air. "Smells like testosterone."

Holton displayed a gap-toothed grin. The other three gave quick nods. Acosta looked on, impressed. This was where he belonged.

"Okay," Santián began, "Lil Puppet's apartment is on the fourth floor, that corner with the blinds drawn," he pointed. "There's a side exit piled high with debris, so they ain't goin' out that way, *¿que no?* Ronk, you take the initiate 'round back and come in through the laundry room. Us three will take the front."

"Do we need a warrant?" Acosta said, a worried expression contorting his face.

The four glared at him as if fungus was spilling out of his ears. "We have probable cause," Cortese reminded the new man. "We are in pursuit of an alleged cop killer. We have an eyewitness who saw Ramón 'Gargoyle' Villa enter said domicile on or about twenty-two hundred hours. Said domicile is home to one Chester 'Lil Puppet' Ochoa, who is out on parole and who cannot consort with specifically named individuals."

"Villa being one of them," Acosta piped in.

"Now you gettin' with the program." Holton slapped him on the back. "Don't let that high-yella twist McGuire get you all knotted up. We're righteous." He took his shotgun in both hands and shook it. "The streets belong to us."

"Fuckin' A," Ronk said.

The team walked in a diagonal across the wide thoroughfare of Westlake Avenue toward the front of the Lancilier Apartments. A late model Passat drove by, the driver honking at the men.

"Our fuckin' fan club," Cortese said, waving at the driver.

"Don't underestimate the power of the public, my friend," Santián quipped.

"Especially if it keeps the dogs off of us," Holton put in.

The team split up as they got nearer. Culhane and Acosta trotted toward the rear along a narrow passageway alongside the apartment building. The trio arrived at the glass-paneled front door with a brightly lit vestibule beyond it.

"Hold this, Sarge." Holton handed his shotgun to Santián. He then extracted a lock-picking kit and removed the proper tools: a pick and a tension wrench. He bent and went to work. "You'd think," the big man muttered, "that these old locks would be easy. But Yale really knew how to make 'em back in the day."

"You got to get some new hobbies, Big T," Cortese joked.

He got the door unlatched. "My only hobby is justice, son," he said in mock solemnity, straightening up.

Santián handed the shotgun back to the detective. He took the lead and plunged into the building. There was fresh paint on the walls, the latest gang pictographs having been brushed over by the tenants. In the main hallway was an elevator, but these cops knew from experience that it seldom operated. The three got to the stairs in the rear and began to ascend beside the old-fashioned banister.

Not too far from the Lancilier, Linda Delarocha also ascended a set of stairs. These were wooden steps in need of repair that ran outside the rear of a two-story structure along a hilly street called Santa Ynez. She got to the top and opened the screen and inner door letting to an austere and clean kitchen.

" 'Bout time," her mother, Lucía Delarocha, said. She was pouring juice into a glass. The woman, still a looker, who'd recently turned forty, set the carton back on the shelf and closed the refrigerator. Outside, a clean-burning bus rumbled by.

"I got held up." The daughter lifted her year-old son, Frankie out of his high chair. She made a face at him and he squealed happily.

"Sure you did," her mother remarked knowingly. She drank her juice and placed the glass on the cracked tile of the counter.

"Let's not throw drama tonight, shall we?" Linda Delarocha went though the kitchen's swing door carrying her son, her mother following. The two entered a small dining room with a built-in sideboard and leaded glass cupboard.

"Look, Linda, I made a lot of mistakes when I was younger, huh? About the only thing I did right was have you when I was seventeen. But I ran those same streets you're running now."

Her daughter bounced Frankie on her hip. "Yeah, yeah, ain't I got a job, Mom? Hell, I'm supportin' your ass now that you decided to go back to school and all." She jerked her head at the pad of paper and math book lying open on the dining room table.

Lucía Delarocha folded her arms. "You know what I'm talking about, Linda."

"You ain't tryin' to bang him, are you, Mom?" She put Frankie down, and he scooted around in a circle over the thin rug.

"Keep it up, funny girl. But I know men like your boyfriend, the great Saint Santián. Thinks he's got it all covered, the smooth *barrio jefe*." She paused, a faraway stare composing her pretty face. "But hombres like him, dudes who live for the thrill, burn too hot—and not just themselves. And what do you think is going to happen when his wife finds out about you two?"

"That's why you got to keep it on the down low, Mom. 'Cause you like to gossip too damn much."

"You trying to avoid the issue, Linda."

Her daughter twisted her mouth and momentarily looked sideways toward the ceiling, as if calling on supernatural intervention. Her son gurgled, latching onto her leg and trying to right himself. "I know what I'm doing," she finally said.

"I used to say the same thing," her mother said, "and look where I am today."

"Don't say boo, motherfuckah." Holton had the shotgun leveled on the Crazy Nine who went by the name Boney. The apartment's front room wasn't large to begin with, and was particularly cramped with all the bodies shoved into it now.

"Yo, homey, you ain't got no right." Lil Puppet's rangy frame was encased in khaki shorts and a *Number 8* Kobe Bryant Lakers jersey. He was sitting on the end of a corduroy-covered couch. The arms had numerous black stains from extinguished reefer blunts.

"What, you taking correspondence law classes?" Ronk had his Beretta 92FS out, his eyes darting all over the room. He and Acosta had already prowled through the rest of the apartment.

Gary Phillips

"Where's Gargoyle?" Santián demanded of his captive audience.

"Who?" Another Crazy Nine member named Hazy contributed.

"You smokin' so much kronik you gone simple, ese?" Santián moved a step back to better take in the four gang members they'd huddled together on the couch and made to sit on their hands. The metal security door that led out to the hallway had been quietly opened by Big T. Then the cops busted in the inner wooden door. This perfected "can opener" technique had been done in under a minute.

Hazy gave Santián a baleful glare.

"Look," Santián continued, "we know his cocky self waltzed into this building earlier, and he ain't got no *hinas* up in this muhfuh, so where did he light to?"

Of course, all he got was stony, sullen silence.

"Oops," Culhane said, sending his left foot, clad in a cowboy boot, out stiffly into the stacked stereo equipment on a low pedestal. The unit crashed to the floor, its components skidding.

"Bitch," Lil Puppet hollered. "You better replace that with the money you steal from your hoes."

Acosta quickly looked at Ronk Culhane, who now stood over Lil Puppet. The unshaven officer scratched his cheek with the barrel of his handgun. "The only thing I'm gonna replace is your asshole for my foot."

Santián zeroed his officer with a look, and he backed off. "Here it is, almost the weekend," he said to the quartet, "and you slack-dick *pendejos* don't want to spend all that time locked up . . . no pussy, no reefer, no forties."

Lil Puppet squirmed to get shoulder room. He was bunched in between Hazy and the fourth Crazy Nine member, a young man called Serenade. They called him that because he never had much to say. Lil Puppet jutted his head up at Santián. "You the one been on the dank, Saint. Ain't nobody seen—"

There was a creak, and Lil Puppet involuntarily stopped himself. "Like I said," he started again, louder, "Gargo—"

"Shut up," Santián commanded. The five squad members stopped breathing.

"Where'd that come from?" Cortese whispered.

There was another creak, and Santián looked up at the peeling ceiling. He was pointing with his shotgun when the first shot boomed. It flew through the ceiling, billowing a fine trail of plaster dust.

"Shit," Big T swore.

In a heartbeat there was another shot. This bullet caromed off the light switch, and suddenly the room was dark. Only the weak bulb from the hallway burned. And by then everyone was scrambling and yelling.

"Ceiling, crawlspace," Santián admonished. Seeing Acosta aiming over his head, he clamped a hand on the younger man's arm. "There's a floor above us, remember?"

"I'm sorry, Sarge," Acosta said, chagrined.

Another shot was let loose, and somebody yelped.

"Mothafuckah clipped me," Hazy screamed. "Watch what the fuck you're doing, Gargoyle," he barked angrily.

"Shut the fuck up," Lil Puppet warned.

Another body hurled itself in the gloomy light, tackling Ronk, who'd backed up against Big T. The three went down, arms and legs tangled.

One of the other gang members was up and running. He bumped into Santián, who was crouched against the doorjamb, knocking him over.

"I got him," Acosta said, taking off down the hall after the mute Serenade. He was a runner and worked out regularly at the track at Cal State L.A.

"We got to get upstairs." Santián grabbed Cortese's arm, tugging on him. "You two watch these clowns," he called back.

"I need an ambulance!" Hazy blared.

"Who the fuck cares?" Big T responded, instinctively ducking his head as he did so.

Cortese took the fire exit, and Santián trotted toward the staircase. "I'm bettin' he comes out on the fifth," the sergeant said over his shoulder.

"Yeah, a trapdoor or entry into a closet." Cortese banged the metal door open and took the steps two at a time up the stairwell.

Outside, Acosta was pumping after Serenade across Westlake. Two older women were walking across the street; one had a laundry basket perched atop her head as they conversed in Nahuatl, a Mexican Indian dialect. The quiet gang member dashed by, upsetting the woman and her basket. Clothes sprouted into the air as if shot out of a cannon.

"*Con permiso,*" Acosta said as he ran past the two dazed women. He wasn't going to shoot the kid in the back. He knew he'd be within policy if he did—a fleeing suspect and all that. But what kind of street cop would he be if he couldn't chase down one sorry-ass glue sniffer?

Back in the stairwell, the enclosure smelled of urine and stale sex—the Nines were known for standing quickies with their women pressed against the cinder-block walls. On the next level Cortese paused, listening at the door, then creaking it open cautiously with the barrel of his shotgun.

"Cheese?" Santián hissed.

"It's me," his partner responded.

Santián was at the opposite end. He slid slowly along the hall, his back against the rough-hewn wall. There was light, and it made him nervous, made him a target. A latch was released, and an apartment door began to open just ahead of him. Santián leaped and crashed into the door with his shoulder. The door swung violently back on its hinges. The body behind it fell to the floor inside the apartment.

"Mrs. Ruíz," Santián said between gritted teeth. His shotgun was pointed at her prone form. She blinked rapidly up at him.

"*Sagento Santián,*" the middle-aged mother of four said. "I only wanted to see what all the noise was about."

"You know better than to stick your head out when you hear gunshots," he replied in Spanish, taking the shotgun off her. He helped her to her feet. She was a big-bodied woman with a face much younger and thinner than her years.

"You're right, of course, but you've done so much to help the old neighborhood, we can do our part."

"Keep down." He went back into the hallway, closing the door behind him.

Cortese was several steps down the hall, and each man glared at the other, their crook radar on full alert. There was another sound, and they tried to locate its source. Then came a bump, and something smacked against the wood panel in one of the doors. Briefly Santián closed his eyes, attempting to direct his hearing. There, again, maybe a knee or elbow hitting the wall, and below it, something else.

He snapped his lids open and jerked the barrel of the shotgun at apartment 16. The door faced out from the wall opposite, some four yards away. Cortese frowned at him, and Santián put a finger across his lips. He crept closer. Then the door flew open, and he fell on his side, ready to pump off a round.

"Oh God, shit, please, please don't shoot me." She had reddish-brown hair and was dressed in capri pants and a snug sweater top cresting above her navel. She was maybe nineteen, and Gargoyle Villa stood behind her, one hand yanking back on that lustrous hair, the other with the muzzle of his S&W pressed against her temple.

At the cold end of the rear of a parts place on Oak, Alvaro Acosta moved with trepidation. His 9mm felt reassuring in his hand. You could do all the dry runs you wanted, play out the scenarios of what to do given X, Y, or Z situation. But when it counted, when your life was maybe on the line, your training damn sure better become as automatic as your reflexes.

Not too far away the sounds of nighttime traffic went by and from somewhere a radio broadcast *norteña* music. But Acosta had to move such recognitions deep inside a section of his brain not needed at the moment. Everything else had to be geared for survival. His thick-soled Red Wings crunched trash beneath his feet, and he paused. His $170 wool uniform seem to chafe him all over. Serenade had run back here. This was a passageway between two buildings of similar design, with low profiles and brown-bricked facades. It was dark, and there were numerous bulky shapes denoting stacked crates and whatnot. Down the way, spanning the length of the gap was the gleaming metal of a chain-link fence. If Serenade tired to climb over, he'd see his silhouette move across its surface like a giant spider treading its web. But where the fuck was he?

"That's a chump's play, man." Cortese had his piece settled on the two forms half in the doorway and half in the hall.

"Drop the iron and back the fuck off," Villa demanded. His asymmetrical skull-like visage was a contrast to his free-weights-developed upper body—"swolled up," as they said on the streets. "Yo, like you mothafuckahs can't hear." He clicked the hammer on the gun into place to underscore his intent.

"Oh, shit . . ." The young woman's cheeks were wet from tears.

"Keep quiet." The gang leader pulled on her hair, causing his hostage to wince.

"You know you ain't getting anywhere, homey." Santián was on his feet, crouched back against the wall. His shotgun also held steady.

"I ain't playin', Santián." Gargoyle's lilting voice, like Mike Tyson's, belied his physical appearance. He moved himself and the frightened teenager along the hall toward the stairs.

"This ain't smart, Gargoyle." Santián took a few steps in his direction but stopped as the gang member pointed the gun at him.

"All is forgiven, huh?"

Cortese inched closer, holding his breath. Get a shot—*turn the girl to the right, you fuck, and I got a shot.*

"We just want to talk, man."

"Bullshit, Santián," Villa challenged. "You mothafuckahs are gonna make sure I don't see no arraignment."

"Shit . . . shit . . ." The young woman was shaking.

"You got to let her go, brah." Santián could see but didn't dare look directly at his partner. If he could keep Villa's attention on him, then maybe they had a chance. "Kidnapping is a serious charge, my friend."

"And catching a case for a cop killing ain't?" Villa snorted, and turned his head at Cortese's motions.

"Don't try and be slick, Cheese."

Cortese became immobile, eyes wide.

"We got to work this out, homey. We can't let you walk out of here with the *chica.*" Santián had a new plan. He was standing right where he needed to be. There was no being cute, so he wasn't going to try to communicate his next actions to his partner.

Villa slobbered on the weeping girl's cheek. "Fine, ain't she, Santián? Young and firm." He tapped one of her breasts with the fist holding the gun. "I guess we got the same tastes, huh?"

"You right, brah," he said in a relaxed tone, as if discussing a baseball score. "These *hinas* 'round here—" Without a hint he simply and rapidly brought the shotgun to hip level and took out the light almost directly above Gargoyle's head. Tiny glass particles could be heard tinkling to the floor. There was a light over the stairwell, but this part of the hall was now cast in long shadows and indistinct forms.

Simultaneously the young woman screamed, and Gargoyle Villa popped off a couple as he was tackled. Santián had hedged that Villa would instinctively shoot at him, thus giving Cortese an opportunity to take the fool out. He'd thrown his shotgun from him. And he'd dived left rather than right—the direction he'd been facing—in an effort to escape harm.

Santián was groping, feeling a twinge in his ankle. He collided with a falling body.

"Hey, you got *me*," Cortese proclaimed.

"But you got Villa right?"

"*Cabrones,*" the gang chief swore, attesting to the fact that he was indeed in their grasp.

Santián tried to right himself, but he stumbled and went over the girl, who was prone on the floor. If she was shot, there'd be hell to pay for their ramrod tactics. There was a moan, so at least she was breathing, if temporarily.

"Where's the grip?" Cortese boomed. "Where the fuck is his grip?"

"Knock his ass out, Cheese," Santián snapped, also panicking as to the location of Villa's gun. He put a hand down into something firm yet yielding.

"Hey!" the young woman said.

"Sorry," Santián muttered, finally leveraging his body upright. He jumped over her and joined Cheese, who was wrapped around Villa. They were like two wrestlers trying out new moves, neither getting the advantage over the other. Santián waited for his opening and brought his foot down heavily on the neck of the gang chief.

"*Pinche hoota.*" Serenade swung the piece of two-by-four, smacking Acosta dead on the forehead.

The uniform staggered back, white starbursts exploding behind his corneas. He heard more than saw the Crazy Nine take off from the recessed doorway he'd been crouching in. Acosta was in overdrive, pistol up, shooting-range style, left hand supporting the gun hand.

"Freeze, ass-wipe," he heard this voice like his father's say. Blood was seeping down into one eye, and for some damn reason he could taste grapefruit juice in the back of his mouth. Serenade was heading for the mouth of the passageway. Acosta's shirt was clinging to him, and he did the slow squeeze, as if his finger were a prehensile tail. "Yo!" he hollered.

Serenade did a circular twist of his body, as if he were going for a layup. His upper torso whipped around, his head already looking back at Acosta. But that was not what the cop was watching. There was something dull in the right hand, and it was pointed at him.

"Fuck!" he heard his dad's voice say as if from under five feet of water. The bullet left his gun. His arm spasmed, but he was already triggering a second round. Serenade's body finished turning around, then flopped over backward, the back of his head hitting the cement hard and loud.

All the sensation in Acosta's face was gone, and it only returned when he reached up to wipe the wetness out of his eye. He staggered toward the prone form. A bunch of translucent bubbles had formed around the corners of Serenade's mouth. His left hand was weakly grasping for invisible rope in the air.

"Hold still," Acosta croaked. He ripped his shirt off and pressed it onto the sucking wound. He heard footsteps and looked up to see Culhane bursting through several shadows congealing at the end of the causeway.

"R.A. is coming," Culhane said, indicating that an ambulance had been summoned. The seasoned cop took in Serenade with a brief, cursory glance and looked at the right hand. Acosta followed his gaze to a wrapped Ziploc bag of methamphetamine tabs. That was the dull object in his hand.

"He was gonna throw it, the idiot." Acosta couldn't feel his face again. "He was trying to get rid of his dope."

"Third strike," Culhane noted. "He already done time for assault. He might catch two strikes for this beef—one for assaulting you." Culhane pointed at Acosta's head. "And the third for the yayo."

"But . . ." Acosta began, searching the other man's countenance for the words, the right emotions.

"It's a righteous shoot," Culhane emphasized. "We're just gonna make it more so." He took hold of Acosta's arm and got him up. Serenade was staring at infinity. Culhane gently shoved Acosta toward the front of the passageway. The ambulance's siren got closer. "You take care of the crowd, hear?" Culhane took the two-way out of his back pocket and buzzed Santián.

"Big men," Villa riled them. The side of his mouth was red from having been walloped by Santián's boot.

"Keep talking shit," Cortese replied, giving the gang leader a nudge with the butt of his shotgun.

Santián had stopped walking and had his back to the stairs, talking low to Culhane. He then clicked off the two-way and returned it to his back pocket. Cortese looked back at him, but his partner's expression was unreadable. They continued descending to the street.

Villa's hands were now cuffed behind his back as they marched him and the rest of his homies down to the sidewalk. Big T lined them up. Two black-and-whites had arrived, and their uniforms were busy securing the perimeter. Right behind that car the royal blue Impala belonging to Lieutenant Kubrick swooped in, too.

"Thank you, Mr. Santián, thank you," the shaken young woman repeated. "You guys saved my life." She started to sob softly again.

Villa made a derisive sound and rolled his eyes.

"It's okay, Mary, it's fine now." Santían patted her shoulder as she leaned into him. He didn't dare look over at Cortese lest both men crack up. Nothing like danger to get the gratefulness going or the legs open.

Kubrick was a medium-sized man with an overhanging brow that he made up for with probing, intense icy blues. He'd beaten back prostate cancer and was a convert to jogging and an almost meat-free diet. He'd come up through the ranks. He wasn't a pogue, a supervisor who didn't know the streets. Kubrick knew where a few bodies from devious deeds were buried around town. Santián came up beside his commanding officer, who strode toward the passageway. Kubrick deadeyed the EMTs going about their tasks.

"The rollout team's gonna be here in less than five minutes." His voice was gravelly and the words, as always, delivered in his flat inflection. "You talk to Acosta?"

"No, Culhane was on the scene here after helping Big T corral the others. He apprised me of the shooting over the two-way. Me and Cheese had our hands full with a hostage situation with Gargoyle inside the building."

Kubrick glanced back at the young woman, who was now being attended by one of the emergency techs. "I see." He allowed a slight smile to linger, then resumed walking over to the shooting scene. "Culhane, Acosta, over here, now," he ordered the two, who were hovering near the body of Serenade. Culhane came over. Gingerly, with two fingers, he carried a snub-nosed .38 upside down by its ridged pistol grip.

Santián walked back toward the Lancilier Apartments. Civilians were milling around, some whispering to each other as he went past, some making sure he overheard them.

"The garbage men been busy again."

"That's good."

"*Sí*, Rosa, that's that fine-ass Saint," one giggled to the other. "What is he?"

"His mom's Salvadoran and his dad was black—Dominican I heard."

"Mothafuckahs get away with too much shit," another said.

"Somebody ought to deal straight up with them clowns," another concurred.

Santián kept going, a knot working its way up his spine. It was going to be a long night. The fun was just beginning.

CHAPTER 2

Constance McGuire swirled her coffee in its sixteen-ounce steel travel container. Slowly, as if the taste of the brew were a foreign concoction to her, she brought the spout to her lips and took a swallow. What was it . . .? After one in the morning and this was like maybe her eighth or ninth cup since getting out of bed at 6:20 A.M. Then why the hell did she feel so goddamn beat down?

McGuire bit dead skin off one side of her lip—she knew the answer. The five men who were in various states of posing, going on with their masquerade of being conscientious cops, were a big part of the reason.

"I'll stay on the piece," her investigator, Judd Ahn, said, standing next to her.

"It'll be as cold as a pawnbroker's smile."

"You never know," her investigator quipped. "Everything leaves a trace." He took off his black-framed glasses and massaged his lower jaw with his squarish fingers. "The garbage men are not impervious."

"They think they are."

"I'll go corner Acosta again—see if how he tells me the way the shooting went down is too consistent with the version he related to me less than an hour ago." Ahn had put his glasses back on and now had his notepad and a pen out.

"Present?" McGuire indicated the black-and-gold-leaf Cross pen he was lightly rapping against the pad's spirals.

"For services rendered," he quipped, and started to walk away.

McGuire playfully tapped him on the back as she, too, moved off, making a direct route to Santián. He saw her coming and turned his back to the ADA, talking to some *reina* who was holding a compress to her forehead. She couldn't be more than twenty—all leggy, long hair, with breasts a music video hoochie would envy. McGuire huffed, *Saint Santián, always helpful to the besieged citizenry.*

"If I could have a moment of your time, Sergeant."

He deigned a half turn, then resumed his conversation with the young woman. "Now, if there's anything I can help you with, or you just want to talk, don't hesitate, okay?" He handed her a business card. Inscribed in arched Gothic letters was the word TRASH. Centered beneath the acronym was its meaning: *Tactical Resources Against Street Hoodlums.* To the left was the die-stamped gold, silver, and blue detective's shield with his phone numbers underneath that. To the left of the card was the unofficial TRASH logo: a grinning skull with an eye patch and with a cocked watch cap pulled low on its bare dome, smoking a cigar. Instead of crossed bones, a rendering of a T-handled Monadnock PR-24 baton—"banana knocks," they were affectionately called—and a shotgun formed an X below the skull.

"I just want to thank you again, Mr. Santián. I know everybody thinks we all bang in the Heights, and push our children to the park while drinking a forty or smoking a blunt. But I'm trying hard to get out of here, make something of myself." She held herself, though it was balmy. "I don't want to think what could have happened if that *puta* Gargoyle had—"

"Then don't think on it too much. Put it behind you; the bad stuff is always past. You're going to be a success, Mary." Santián touched her paternally on a shoulder. "You make sure you keep up with your studies at fashion school."

"I will." She kept her wide eyes on him as she put the card in her back pocket.

Earnestly he shook her hand.

McGuire displayed her ID. "Young lady, would you mind sitting over there? I'll have a few questions for you in a while."

"I, uh . . ." She glanced at Santián for guidance. He smiled as if he were a rector advising one of his parishioners. "Just tell what you know, Mary." He and McGuire walked several paces away. "What can I do for the district attorney's office, Ms. McGuire?"

"If you're through gettin' your mack on, playah." She had more coffee. It was bitter and unadorned, as she liked it.

"We defused a hostage situation, tonight, Ms. McGuire—apprehended a badass wanted for a cop killing, and prevented a known felon from harming civilians." Santián put a hand to the back of his neck to work the kink there. "How many papers did you shuffle today, Connie?"

McGuire did a riff on her metal travel container with her short, unpolished fingernails. "I'm on the streets a lot, Santián. That's how I learn a few things now and then."

"Now and then, huh?" the two were standing under a stand of date palms, whose fronds shifted lazily in the warm breeze.

"It would seem." Briefly she glanced at the other member of her inner circle, Phenias Washington. He was the only white man she'd ever met with that last name. Like her, he was an assistant district attorney. Unlike her, he'd been assigned to the team whose job it was to be at officer-involved shooting scenes to corroborate the officers' version of events—or in some cases, to highlight inconsistencies and maybe forward their findings to the inspector general. McGuire had asked for the assignment when DA Chris Stevens had reinstituted the rollout post on his most recent election.

"We gonna go 'round and 'round the maypole, Ms. McGuire? 'Cause we got a suspect to interrogate."

Over Santián's shoulder, she noted Washington starting in on Ronk Culhane. The cop torqued his shoulders in a defensive gesture, and his face got that "Why don't you eat shit and die?" cast. But Washington wasn't called the stone cutter for no reason. He was methodical and didn't rattle.

"I merely want to get your version, Sergeant."

Santián held back a sarcastic comment. He told her the sequence of events leading to the shooting by Gargoyle and the arrest he and Cortese made. He finessed how they'd gained entry to the building, saying simply that "a resident going out" had let them in. If need be, he knew Mrs. Ruíz could be counted on to back him up.

McGuire interrupted him as he got to the standoff in the hallway. "Why didn't you call it in and wait for the hostage negotiating team?"

"You think Gargoyle was gonna simmer down long enough for us to radio that in? Come on, Ms. McGuire, we had a volatile situation on our hands. Not only was it all the way live in the hallway, let's not forget we had two officers downstairs watching the other Crazy Nines."

"Who were secured, and Culhane took off after Acosta."

"To assist a fellow officer as he should."

He finished with, "As to what happened outside in terms of Officer Acosta's pursuit of Enrique "Serenade" Perez, it went down within policy."

McGuire responded, "You weren't on site."

"I know my men."

"I want a copy of your report faxed over later this morning, understand, Sergeant?" She turned her pad so he couldn't read it, and pretended to be making a notation to herself. Everybody played their own kinds of mind games.

"Naturally." Santián stifled a yawn.

"I'm sure I'll have some more questions for you."

"Always a pleasure."

They parted, and McGuire sought out Mary Sandoval. She was sitting on a stoop; two older women hovered near her, talking.

"Excuse me," McGuire interrupted, "if I could have a few words with you?"

"I don't know what else I can say," Sandoval said irritably. "I want to rest."

"Yes," one of the woman said in Spanish, placing a hand on her hip. "Can't you see she's been through enough?"

"Why you always in the news talking bad about TRASH, huh?"

The other one, with curlers in her hair, stood, her hands gesturing as she talked. "They do a lot of good in this neighborhood, lady."

Blotting them out, McGuire continued, "Please, Ms. Sandoval, this won't take but a few minutes, and it is important." Off to the side, Culhane could be heard yelling at Washington. Lieutenant Kubrick stepped in between the two men. "Ms. Sandoval?" she repeated.

"Fine," the younger woman relented. She got up, and the two walked toward the middle of the street. French barricades cordoned off the area.

McGuire took down the young woman's particulars on her notepad, then said, "I'm not out to trap anyone, Ms. Sandoval. But I have a job to do, too."

"Look," the young woman responded, pointing a black-enameled nail, "all I know is, I'm sitting down on my couch watching *The Bachelor* when I hear the gunshots—muffled-like, ya know? As you can imagine, gunshots ain't unusual around here, right? So I'm like, on edge, right? Next thing I know ,there's this shouting and I hear something coming from the bedroom. Now I'm like, freaking, right? I don't know what to do; then this Gargoyle comes running out of my bedroom, holding a gun and hollering." She clamped her lips from stress.

McGuire's next stop would be inside the building, to check out the scene. Conversationally she said, "You live in that apartment by yourself?"

"With my aunt—she works at Green Memorial." Sandoval jerked her head in an easterly direction. Greenie, as it was called, was one of the city's oldest and largest public hospitals. The facility served Venice Heights and adjoining working-poor enclaves. McGuire's ex-husband had done his residency there.

The ADA refocused. "And then he took you hostage?"

"Hell, yes," Sandoval emphasized. "By then I heard the voices in the hallway, and Gargoyle was hella worked, ya know?"

"You know Gargoyle?"

"Come on, lady, who doesn't know him, living around here?"

"Do you feel the police officers handled the situation appropriately?"

"I'm alive, ain't I? Can I go now?"

"Sure." McGuire handed her a card. "I may have a few more questions for you."

"Whatever."

A half hour later, after checking locations in the building, McGuire and her coworkers clustered around her city-issued Grand Am. She shook her travel cup, regretting being out of fuel.

Washington began. "Culhane's story is, Acosta takes off after the one called Serenade as Gargoyle is blasting at them from the crawl space in the ceiling."

"Prove his worth to the squad," McGuire opined.

Ahn picked up the narrative. "Acosta gives chase and eventually follows Serenade between these two buildings. I went over there. It's wide, dark, and fenced off at the far end.

It actually has a name, Culver Lane, and there are several loading docks facing onto the alley.

"Acosta," Ahn went on, "is creeping along, and gets jumped by the kid. The Nine whacks him with a plank and takes off, toward the front of the alley."

"Hits him with the board?" McGuire asked for clarity.

"That's right," Ahn concurred.

"And he doesn't produce this gun until he's at the head of the lane, huh?" Washington asked the question on all their minds.

"So it would seem," Ahn answered. "Acosta is shaken, but who wouldn't be after shooting a man to death?"

"He's been in the department how long?" McGuire asked.

"This is his second year," Ahn consulted his notes. "He said his captain had put him in to be on TRASH about three or four months ago."

"Promotion or demotion?" Washington wondered.

"He was at Wilshire Division; I'll go over there and see," the investigator said.

McGuire added, "And we don't know anything about the gun yet?"

"If it's a throw-down, you know Culhane isn't stupid."

Washington folded his arms.

"And if it was planted, you think he did it?" McGuire said.

"That peculiar allegation has arisen before about the lad," Washington observed dryly. "But nothing proven."

McGuire nodded. Not too far away, Lieutenant Kubrick was talking with Santián and Cortese. Acosta had already been taken back to the station house to record his official statement. "Okay, Judd, you follow up with the captain over at Wilshire, and get what you can on the piece. Phenias, pull up Culhane's jacket in the morning and look at it with new eyes."

"Will do," Washington said.

The two men walked to their vehicles, and McGuire ambled over to confer with Kubrick. As she did so, she passed Culhane and Holton, who were getting into their unmarked, tricked-out late-edition Trailblazer. She was past being amazed that TRASH got away with lowering their cars and using confiscated funds to buy dubs, twenty-inch stylish rims. In the backseat sat Gargoyle. His handcuffs were linked to a ring set in the floor to contain prisoners.

"We'll have a chat with brother Villa, Saint," Culhane was saying.

"All right," Santián said, yawning. "I'll see you back at the aquarium." At Temple Division, TRASH had their one set of offices in the basement of the ancient structure. It was called "the aquarium" because the offices were sweltering in the summer and mold was festering along the baseboards.

Santián then addressed McGuire. "You have a nice night, now, ya hear?"

McGuire touched her rimless glasses, boring his back with a glare as he sauntered away. She could really use some more coffee.

Rafael Santián pulled into his driveway at seven minutes past three in the morning. Goddamn birds were up in the trees chirping and it wasn't even light yet. Like a zombie, he got out of the Malibu and sleepwalked his way into his two-story tract home set at the end of a cul-de-sac. The street was called Rio Chavel and was part of a new development called Larkhaven, in the suburb of Simi Valley fifty miles northwest of the city center.

The living room and dining room combined were bigger than the house he grew up in. He crept up the carpeted stairs. How come his sixteen-year-old son, Curtis, couldn't understand that his was a privileged life compared to how his father had come up? He wasn't expecting bowing and scraping, but a little goddamn gratitude now and then—was that so much to ask?

He went past his teenager's bedroom. A new poster had been taped to the door. This one depicted a brother decked out in combat gear and wearing a homburg. He was sitting on a throne, his ringed hand atop an ornate walking stick. There were some thong-clad honeys with their rounded butts pointed toward the camera.

There were the ubiquitous piles of money. And one of the women, in a platinum wig, controlled a pit bull snarling on a chrome chain leash. This gent's nom de guerre was Soljer X. His new hit single, from Def Ritmo Records, was entitled "Bounce Dat Ass On Up in This Mug."

Santián was too tired to laugh. He entered his bedroom. His wife, Nicole Scott, snored softly. He took his clothes off down to his

Joe Boxers and eased into bed beside her. He kissed her warm chestnut-colored cheek, and she Z'd on. He rolled over and went directly to sleep.

Alvaro Acosta entered through the self-locking door from the underground parking into the secured foyer of his box of an apartment house in the Monterey Hills section. He was dressed in his civilian clothes, carrying a small equipment bag. The young cop was only mildly surprised to see ADA McGuire sitting on the rim of the concrete planter. She was sipping coffee from a Yum Yum Donuts cup.

"Quite a talent you have there, Ms. McGuire." He pressed the button for the elevator. His head hurt, and the bandage taped to his head irked him.

She stood next to him. "Figured you might want to tell me what really went down along Culver Lane."

"My statement is accurate." The door opened and he got in the car. So did the ADA.

"You don't want to add anything?" The car jerked upward.

"Like why a guy, if he's carrying a gun, jumps you with a piece of wood? Not that I'm trying to hasten any harm to you, Officer, but doesn't it strike you as odd he didn't simply try to cap you?"

"Damned if I know. Maybe he was trying to avoid an assault with intent to murder charge. Or maybe these geniuses aren't exactly masters of military tactics."

She let a few beats go by. "Of course the point is moot—we can't ask him, can we?"

The car came to a stop. Acosta fixed McGuire with red-rimmed eyes. "No, we can't. Good night." He exited the elevator, McGuire not wanting to push him—just yet. She rode back down. Acosta entered his bachelor pad and, breathing shallowly, went inside. The thud of his bag on the floor was lost to him as he leaned against the door in the darkened room. He put his hands to his face, breathing in and out heavily.

CHAPTER 3

Mayor Allo Fergadis managed to balance the paper plate of eggs and ham with the cup of orange juice he set on it. He coveted the thick pancake Big T Holton was turning over with his spatula.

The honey brown surface of the pancake was like something off the Mrs. Butterworth's label. That pancake was gorgeous.

"Mr. Mayor?" Holton's flipper hovered over the perfect hotcake.

"I shouldn't—the diet, you know."

"A little excess balances the soul." Holton's gap dazzled mischievously beneath his omnipresent chapeau.

"Yeah," Fergadis drawled. The pancake beckoned him.

"Morning, Mayor," the new arrival said.

"Chief." The mayor dipped his head. "I guess I better adhere to some discipline, Detective, but I thank you for the offer."

"Not a problem." Holton dispensed the world's best pancake to an eager little girl who held her paper plate aloft.

Fergadis wistfully watched the kid skip off with her prize.

He and Chief of Police Benjamin Hidalgo stepped away from further temptation. Each had only one bodyguard with him today, and these two men walked several paces behind the duo. Hidalgo was in his dress blues, the other three in suits. The quartet crossed under the large overhead banner spread between two maple trees in Eisenhower Park. The banner read: *The Venice Heights Neighborhood Association Congratulates the officers of TRASH*. The association had put on this pancake breakfast as a fund-raiser to help provide monies for the local boxing club it sponsored, and for other activities such as neighborhood tree planting.

Some of the members of the Heights' TRASH unit—in total thirty-seven officers and civilian personnel—and a smattering of antigang cops from other divisions served as cooks. A barbecue had been done last year, but some of the officers got too intoxicated and boisterous and threatening. A breakfast was safer.

"Where we at on the Villa case?" Fergadis adroitly held his ham on his fork and nibbled off a corner.

"He's lawyered up, of course. Gone silent since being initially questioned by Holton and Culhane two nights ago."

Hidalgo, in his mid-fifties, had given up smoking less than a year ago. He sipped his coffee. He was tall and athletic and had played basketball and baseball for two years in junior college while studying mechanical engineering. But like his father, sister, and uncles, he had finally answered the siren song of the department. Of course, the constant nagging of his relatives had something to do with that, too.

But he was the chosen one—he was groomed and pushed and prodded to be the first Chicano police chief in the city. After a rigorous selection process, he'd achieved the goal less than two years ago.

"Who's representing him?" Fergadis finished his orange juice. He crumpled the cup into a ball and tossed it with overhand flair into a recycling receptacle.

"The Irish Witch, Ferris Heckman."

"Well, well. Now that's one woman, even if she begged me, I wouldn't put my dick in her mouth."

"Not if you don't want it bit off to the nub," Hidalgo remarked.

Fergadis eschewed further comments about the obstreperous criminal defense attorney, well known to the local pols, and a constant guest on the Sunday morning TV spin circuit. You never knew who was listening as people milled about. "Who's paying her freight?"

"Don't know for sure," Hidalgo replied, "but the rumor is that August Mercury at Def Ritmo is feeding the meter."

"Huh," Fergadis allowed. "Given that Def Ritmo has Baja cartel money in it, then we can assume that Villa definitely was the hitter on the police chief in El Paso."

Hidalgo was about to speak, but a photographer from the *Times* got the mayor's attention. The woman snapped a pic of the two beaming city leaders, then moved along.

"Or that he's got a role to play," Hidalgo resumed, "in this move the cartel is making. Our intel hazards this may have something to do with the pallet-loads of drug cash we know comes through the Southland, and solidifying conduits to set up legit businesses."

The four came upon a grouping of young women gathered around one particular portable grill. The girls were laughing and talking excitedly as if crowding the newest fifteen-minute singing sensation. Getting close, the reason for the mini-throng became apparent.

"Chief," Santián said to his boss as he used tongs to dispense Italian sausages to several queued-up teenagers and twentysome-things. It didn't take much of an examination to notice the amount of makeup each young woman had on, how much their hair had been teased, and how straight the creases in their khakis had been pressed or how tight their low-rise jeans rode.

Cheese Cortese was next to Santián, working another grill. His line consisted of two pensioners and an older woman in a shawl with half-nylons rolled down on her varicose-veined calves.

"Sergeant, Detective." Hidalgo curtly touched fingers to the brim of his cap as he and the mayor walked on.

In front of the statue of Dwight D. Eisenhower—which was weekly steamed free of graffiti, though no tagger knew who he was—a stage and stand-alone mike had been placed. Madeleine Jirac stepped to that microphone. She was one of the professional urban pioneers who had bought and fixed up one of the pleasant Victorians situated in Venice Heights two years ago. As the gang activity had diminished, coupled with property values in outlying areas rising like cake dough, smart realtors had begun to market a specific section of the Heights. They'd bestowed the title Mari-gold Valley, a name excavated from a 107-year-old planning docu-ment. Just as the Heights was mostly flat land, the only valley was the economic and racial gulf between the old-timers and the new arrivals.

But Jirac, the recently elected president of her neighborhood association, sincerely wanted to make sure the Valley was seen as part of the Heights, not separate from it. Not everyone in the block club shared that munificent outlook. She pushed those internecine machinations aside, cleared her throat, and began speaking.

"We want to thank everyone for coming out today." She let her words float out there for a few moments in the hopes that some might pay attention. "As you know, many have worked hard to rebuild this area of town. We want the city to know this is a place of hardworking families and caring parents." There was a smattering of tepid clapping. "We are not nightly news statistics, but men and women who want a decent place to live so we can send our children to the corner store, get our car fixed down the block, or come out to the park and enjoy one another's company."

She paused, several more sets of eyes now on her. "We know, too, a lot of what has helped make this a better, more secure part of town is the ceaseless work of TRASH." That got a rousing reply.

Hidalgo talked out of the side of his mouth. "She's the Cheese man's squeeze."

"She don't look like your typical cop groupie." Fergadis sucked at a piece of ham lodged in his bridge work.

"She's a professor of urban planning at Bovard."

The mayor made an appreciative face. The two men continued to wander about as Jirac brought the founder of the Venice Heights Association to the stage.

Fergadis had finished the ham and eaten half of his small serving of eggs. He threw the plate away in a plastic-lined garbage can. "Speaking of significant others, I hope our good Saint isn't wetting his wick where it doesn't belong. At least, not blatantly."

Hidalgo swallowed coffee. "I'll remind him. But I'd like to get a sense of where you're at these days, Al. The department would like to be reassured you're still foursquare behind our program. The department has been through hell, what with the O. J. fiasco, the Rampart mess, and the bullshit over the last chief's tenure."

"Benny"—Fergadis stood next to a mottled palm tree—"let's review the math, shall we?" The bodyguards stood a discrete distance away.

It was Hidalgo's turn to smile wanly.

"I got a nail-biting reelection coming up. I won by a plurality last time. And McGuire automatically has the black vote sewn up. Now, that ain't what it used to be in this town, but I wouldn't piss on it. Plus half the Latinos think her light-skinned self is one of them, given her flawless Spanish." Even an emersion class in Guadalajara hadn't improved his rudimentary handling of the language. "So if my wide white Greek ass isn't warming up my favorite banker's chair in City Hall come this time next year, then you won't have to sweat your next five-year term. Because you won't have one.

"I wish to God Chris Stevens was running, because I can beat him while I'm in a coma. But what with his fucked-up kids—one son an off-and-on addict, and the daughter makes Wynona Ryder look like an amateur when it comes to kleptomania—he's got too much baggage."

Hidalgo chuckled before responding. "I realize the law and politics aren't always a comfortable fit, Al. But we bust this scheme open, whatever it is, then people will be saying, 'Who the hell was Connie McGuire?' "

Fergadis flicked at a piece of egg on his vest. "I got this three-piece on because later I've have to make an appearance at a christening at St. Brigid's in North Hollywood. The cardinal will be there, and he's going to be on my jock again about how his priests in the parishes down here are hot to trot to push an investigation into TRASH's rumored activities. All these goddamned *mamacitas* thinking their little Juan or Joselito is simply misguided and not hardcore thugs and killers." He sighed heavily at his burden.

"Father Fitzhugh's already been down to central booking to see Gargoyle."

"The modern goddamn Pat O'Brien," Fergadis snorted derisively. Fitzhugh had started a nonprofit janitorial and painting service out of his church, called Homies Incorporated, which employed neighborhood youth.

Hidalgo added, "Effective policing isn't a cotillion, Mr. Mayor. You fought for and obtained the department's increased budget in no small part due to replicating the successes of TRASH throughout the city to quash gang activity. This after spiking murder rates."

"I'm not backing away from anything, Chief. But you learn something about finessing what was said or done after being in public office for more than thirty-five years." Fergadis leaned into the taller man. "And let's be clear, Benny, if McGuire or the *Times* or whoever as much as comes up with one of these hotshots' skivvies having skid marks on them, somebody's got to account for the dirty laundry, right?"

"Or some *bodies,* if there was such a thing to worry about. Or if the TRASH program didn't have the support of the public—the voting public, that is."

Fergadis drew in his breath and thrust his palms faceup as if haggling a price. "The people are a fickle bunch. Keep me informed on the Villa situation. Let's get a break soon, huh?"

"Of course. In fact, he's being arraigned this afternoon in Division-Thirty." Half-day Saturday courts had been instituted to clear the arraignment backlog.

The mayor made to go. Abruptly he stuck out his hand, and the chief, hesitating for only a heartbeat, then shook the other man's hand. Each smiled amicably. You never knew who was watching.

Gargoyle Villa daydreamed what his red-haired, green-eyed lawyer would be like in the sack. Ferris Heckman had a rock-hard butt from step aerobics, and he'd had to concentrate mightily not to reach out and touch it upon first meeting her. Sitting next to the barred window on the prison van, the sun felt refreshing on the side of his face. He yawned and amended his fantasy to include his baby daughter's mother, Raquel, in the sexual activity unfolding in his mind. Yeah, once he got out on bail, he had plans, yeah, buddy.

The van went under the 101 Freeway overpass and took the short hill up Macy then around the old post office annex. He'd heard somewhere that a developer was going to convert the building into one of those outlet malls.

When he was younger, Villa used to work cockfights held in a roundhouse where the Santa Fe railroad tracks merged off of Alameda. The men and women would yell and pray feverishly for their favorite *gallo* to win. The roosters danced and flew at each other, black and orange and red blurs coloring the air. Their gaffs—the spurs attached to their legs—would rip the flesh and eyes of the opponent in lightning motions. One of Gargoyle's tasks was to put water in his mouth and blow out a stream of mist on his handler's bird to cool it down.

These days, he'd heard some other big developer was going to turn the former train yard into an office complex. Every fuckin' thing changed. He snapped out of his reverie as the van pulled to a stop at the prisoners' entrance to the Foltz criminal courts buildings.

"You Gargoyle, ain'tchu?" The cornrowed brother next to him on the bench seat said. He was compact but developed, his buffed arms and chest straining the upper part of his orange jumpsuit.

"That's right."

"So yo," he intoned in a low voice as the sheriff's deputy unlatched the van's sliding door, "can you hook me up? They call me Ty. I've done some slangin' before."

Gargoyle gave him the street stare. The men were unloaded.

"Let's go, ladies," the deputy said as he rested the butt of his shotgun against his hip, barrel pointed skyward. The chained troop marched single file up the slope of Temple Street. Below street level, the other deputy stood by a metal door, keying in the code to unlock the entrance.

"Aw, come on, man," the one called Ty muttered as the five prisoners shambled forward, their wrists and ankles bound, and linked together by a steel cable. "I hear the Nines is making a move with the Del Fuegos. Y'all Mexicans got this shit in the pocket."

Villa figured it was useless to correct this *mayate* fuck and tell him he was Salvadoran. He was almost to the stairs leading down to the door.

"I'm just a squirrel in your sho-nuf world trying to get my nut on. I can move some weight all up in Nickerson."

Nickerson Gardens, in Watts, was one of the largest housing projects in the city. It was home to Crips and Ace Deuce Swans. "You gonna do all that from inside, huh?" Villa taunted.

"Naw," the other said as they shuffled forward. The door swung outward. "This ain't nothin' but a beef about some warrants, man. 'Sides, I can make it happen anywhere on the black end, Gargoyle. Really."

Villa was already imagining how he'd like that leggy lawyer Mercury was paying for to straddle his face while Raquel polished his knob. But the first thing he was going to have to take care of once he got out—and he'd been assured that he would—was tighten up whoever was making with the yak-yak. This deal was too sweet to get fucked over now by every punk coming out of the woodwork with his hand out.

The boaster was still yakking as Gargoyle put his left foot on the top step.

"Come on." The deputy shoved him, causing him to falter.

"Pinche—" Villa began, and then watched as the deputy dropped his shotgun and clutched his throat, red seeping between his fingers. The Crazy Nines leader barely had time to react before he recognized the sharp report of rifle fire. He was already turned around and trying to bolt, but held back by his tether to the other clamoring men. The second round of sniper fire caught him in the chest, dropping the gang leader gasping to his knees. The third .416 Nitro Express round entered his forehead off center and exited the other side of his cranium in a pulpy spew of bone and brain matter.

CHAPTER 4

McGuire threw the prelim report on her desk, causing other papers on her desk to flutter then settle down. "Just fucking lovely." She pressed her palms flat against the top of her head and slicked her hands back along the contours of her oval skull. She wished a trapdoor in her skull would open and the resolution to this mess would be dumped inside. The ADA knew her restless nights would be long in number. Villa's vacant eyes looked at her from the color snapshot clipped to the report. His irregular features were placid in death. She came around her desk.

"The bullets, shell casings, and rifle"—Washington glanced at his own notes—"it was a bolt-action Rigby, the Rolls Royce of rifles," he intoned flatly, "were wiped clean, no latents. The serial number was intact, though. And check this." He looked up to make sure he had the attention of McGuire and Ahn. "According to Thissen over at the lab, the rifle's barrel had been intentionally refitted slightly smaller in caliber than the diameter needed to accommodate those large rounds."

"Giving the bullet more spin and penetrating power as it was shot," Ahn surmised.

"And effectively destroying its use as phyical evidence," McGuire added. "Each successive round through the shaft gouges more metal and alters the lands and grooves. So the initial shell casings won't match up to latter ones. Though at some point the barrel would be hollowed out to be consistent."

"The rifle was discarded inside the top stairwell of the Hall of Administration across from here," Washington pointed at the window. The rollout team's offices were on the fourteenth floor in the building where the criminal courts were housed—where less than forty-eight hours before, Villa, the leader of the Crazy Nines, had been chopped down at its doors.

"And there were cops jumping all over here from Parker Center in less than three minutes." Ahn took off his glasses and peered at them as if they'd been placed on his face for the first time. "So whoever did it knew procedure, that's for goddamn sure." He plucked a tissue paper from a holder on a tea cart and cleaned his lenses.

"That could be a lot of people," Washington offered.

"Or there's a rat in the Sheriff's Department," McGuire morosely announced. She tugged the blinds to half-staff on the large window behind her desk. The glass was streaked with grime, and beyond that was a metal grill. She wasn't too worried about being a target.

"The Baja cartel's got roomfuls of money to throw around. They've been found to have bribed Border Patrol agents, DEA and ATF personnel, and local judges and cops on both sides of the border." McGuire was standing in front of her desk and her inner line rang. She reached back and put the handset to her ear. "Yes?"

Ahn stood at the side window and watched the foot traffic of city and county workers arriving to work, yet again to play their part in the clanking bureaucracy that was Los Angeles. One of those gear turners he recognized as Superior Court Judge Jill Kodama. He'd met her at several Asian Pacific Islander upperwardly mobile networking soirees. Seemed he'd heard she was pregnant, but he couldn't tell for sure from where he was. Conversations at those gatherings invariably got around to how, as Asians, they—and particularly Ahn, what with his being a 1.5er—had to get back to their roots.

He'd been back to South Korea last year with his mother. It was a country he had only superficial impressions of, having been brought to America when he was eight. His Hangul was spotty, and he wasn't ashamed to admit he preferred a bacon cheeseburger to kimchid. But damned if the pickled cabbage wasn't tasty with bulgogi, barbecued beef.

"That was Castillo," McGuire glumly informed her staffers as she hung up. "Guess what he wanted."

"I bet it's not bronze plaques of us bolted onto City Hall," Ahn cracked.

"Maybe our actual heads," McGuire retorted. "Castillo said the mayor wants me, Chris, Police Chief Hidalgo, and him over to his office in about half an hour." *Time enough to run dowstairs to Pasqua's stand in the courtyard and get more coffee,* she rejoiced.

Ahn winced. "Afterward, Fergadis will hold a press conference, where he assures the city that suspects have been identified and arrests are eminent." Walking back to take his seat, he noticed the logo of that ABC show *20/20* on the top of a fax peeking out from the bottom of one of the several stacks on McGuire's desk. Probably they were bugging her for an interview, which she hated doing. Now, what kind of candidate was that?

"Even he's not that big a grandstander," McGuire observed. "What he wants is political cover. That's why he's survived since the last days of that foxy cracker Yorty as mayor and he was on the city council. Al Fergadis wants to be able to say he's got all of us operating in sync, and that's he's made sure each of us has only the interests of the city at heart."

She went on. "No matter that he'll use whether we falter or succeed as the fuel to drive his reelection locomotive."

Ahn animated an eyebrow, and Washington, fitting his contained demeanor, remained calmly composed. Neither offered a direct follow-up comment.

"So what else do we know?" McGuire sat on the corner of her crowded desk. She checked her watch; her coffee window was starting to close.

Washington's index finger pierced the plane of the report McGuire had flopped onto her desk. "The rifle, as far as I've been able to determine, was last owned by a Cotter Smith in Nebraska. Mr. Smith died in 'eighty-seven, and the family lost trace of the thing. But I've got a man at Rigby I'm going to talk to."

"In England?" Ahn asked.

"The company is in Paso Robles now," Washington said. "I want to see what he can tell me about gunsmiths who are skilled enough to redo these barrels. Maybe backtracking that way, I can determine who last had possession of the thing."

"Judd, did you get an etch done of the handgun?" McGuire was resigned to struggling through the useless Fergadis meeting without the boost she so craved.

Ahn said, "Yeah, Thissen's fine assistant told me he put the handgun from the Acosta shooting through a electrochemical bath. He raised a partial number and some other markings that should prove useful in tracking down ownership." The investigator paused, rubbing his hand on the back of his neck. "You still of the opinion that the patrolman's dirty on this, Connie? The dude's got a spotless record."

"And he requested to be on TRASH twice before getting the assignment," McGuire replied.

"Everybody in the unit isn't trying to be a prick," Ahn countered. "There's plenty good that's been done. Lot of folks in the Heights sleeping easier these days."

"That I don't deny," she allowed. "But any group, from cops to the Congress, that operates with the degree of autonomy they do breeds cowboy fascism. People's natural inclination is to the animal, not the angel. And we have to go where the facts take us, isn't that so, Judd?"

"It is, Connie. But there's a difference in following the leads and setting traps."

"I didn't throw the piece down on the loading dock."

"We don't know if that's the case; that's all I'm saying."

"Judd, no one's asking you to work on my campaign staff. This is about our jobs and what's right. Period."

He looked over at Washington, who manifested a twitch at the corner of his mouth. "You know this isn't about your sincerity, Connie. But we should keep everything in perspective," he said.

"I am, Judd, I am." She blew air through her glossed lips and checked her watch. Fate was smiling; there was time for a jaunt to the fountain of coffee to give her the jolt she needed to deal with her boss, DA Chris Stevens, the mayor, and John Castillo, head of the police commission.

The phone rang again and it was her campaign manager, Pablo Pastor. He wanted to quickly go over the highlights of the overnight poll he'd had done. And he added, "You need to excoriate Fergadis on this shooting." McGuire sighed as she answered. There wouldn't be time for obtaining good coffee going into the meeting after all.

"Can you pick up Monica tonight? She has her computer club after school."

"I'll try, but I might have to be hot and heavy on this Gargoyle shooting." Rafael Santián negotiated the Malibu past a series of orange cones shunting him from the fourth to the third lane on the 118, the Ronald Reagan Freeway.

His wife made that disappointed sound over the cell phone. "Rafe, when was the last time you picked your daughter up from school? Did you know she got student of the week last week because of her extracurricular activities?"

"I saw it stuck on the fridge with magnets." He knew only too well not to cop a shitty attitude. Being a smart-ass would make for a longer lecture than he had patience for this morning. "And I was at her soccer game last Saturday, Jamiele. I'm not an absentee father."

"You got there during the second half," she amended. "And did you talk with Curtis?"

She was cranking it up. "No, he was already gone when I got up." In front of him a Navigator braked, and he tapped the clutch pedal, dropping into third. He picked the phone up off the seat, where he'd had to toss it to use the stick shift. "I'll speak to him tonight."

"You better, Rafe. A boy his age needs his father there for him. Who knows, between hormones and that bullshit he listens to, where his head is at these days? But he's been sent out of class twice in the last few weeks for acting up, and we need to get on this."

"I understand." The Navigator started moving again. "Hold on." He accelerated and got the car wound into higher gear again. Santián resumed the conversation. "But if I try to sit his ass down and give him the big pep talk, he'll just say 'whatevah' and step."

"Like you would."

He let a comeback slide. "It's got to be more—I don't know—natural—I guess is what I mean."

"He's not one of the homies you run up on in the Heights, Rafe; he's your son. You don't have to sneak up on him."

"And he's a teenager and he's angry at shit he can't name, Jamiele. I have been there."

"Sometimes I wonder if you've ever left it."

Be cool, baby, even and slow, just like how you bang Linda's coochie. "I better go, huh? I'll get Monica after school."

"Do you know what time?"

"Before five." All the extra school stuff let out between four-thirty and five.

"All right." But he could hear the unwillingness to get off the line simmering beneath her voice. Nicole wanted a fight, and he wasn't about to give it to her. Not at the moment, anyway.

"I'll call you later; maybe we can have lunch this week." The sensitive bit always got him a point or two.

"That would be nice."

"Okay, baby. Bye."

"Bye, Rafe."

He thumbed the Nokia off and was replacing it in the glove box when it rang again. Goddamn Nicole was going to have it her way or nobody was going to have peace.

"Yes," he said, turning it back on.

"What you doin'?"

He laughed. "My job, Linda; don't you have one to go to?"

"Yeah," she said, putting some nectar in her voice. "But I could go in late if I had to."

"Girl, you better put that burner on low."

"Really?" Linda teased. "I'm wearing your favorites today—black lace."

"The problem is, that don't stay on that long."

"Whose fault is that?"

Automatically, Santián began formulating time and distance in his head. "I better be good and get on the stick."

"That's what I'm trying to do."

"If you truly want to be of service," he snickered, "then keep your ears to the ground."

"What's that mean?"

Damn kids. "It means if you peep anything about Gargoyle getting blasted, let me know."

"So now I'm just your snitch snatch."

"It's a citizen's duty to inform the authorities when they have knowledge of a crime."

"All crimes?"

"The ones that count," he quipped. "And you know that's not how it is between us." Santián cranked his window down the rest of the way. The morning chill had given way to late drive-time heat and exhaust fumes.

"You don't believe what they're saying," Linda asked.

"They who?"

"The streets, *carnale.*"

"Uh, so what would that be?"

"Gargoyle was capped by the Ace Deuce Swans."

"They wouldn't have done it like that."

"They would if they wanted it to look like it was the Baja cartel when it wasn't."

"So we hound the Del Fuegos, and the brothers move in and take over the franchise?"

"Yeah."

"Do you know how you sound, girl?"

"Like them ballers ain't been after the Crazy Nines' shit?"

"But that's been at the beach areas in Playa Vista and Venice, not down in the hood with our Venice Boulevard," he pointed out.

"I'm just sayin', is all," Linda repeated. "But I might let you know if I hear different. Maybe."

"What do I have to do?" he urged her.

She told him explicitly, then said, "Are you hard?"

"You know I am."

"And you still can't make it over to the Playpen?"

Santián laughed deep in his chest. The traffic was heavy with big-wheelers and tankers as he got onto the 5 Freeway. "And I could walk to work from there."

"With a smile on your face."

"I got to hook up with Cheese. We do have this case to work."

"Fuck him." She enunciated each word, taking a breath in between.

"Now, now . . ."

"Just 'cause he's bangin' a professor, he's got to be all that. Always showing off by quoting some limp-dick mothafuckah who's written a book or something. I can quote shit, too."

"I'm not sure Shakira is on the same level as Rousseau," he said. Deftly Santián maneuvered his car from behind a flatbed carrying forklifts and zoomed ahead of an MTA bus.

"I know she's more about where I'm at than the other chump you mentioned."

"I gotta bounce. What about tonight?"

"Have to help Mama study for her history test."

"Not all night," he pouted.

"Oh, so now you want some?" she chided.

"Good way for both of us to unwind at the end of the day."

"Call me 'round ten, Saint."

"Okay."

"Saint?"

"What?"

There was quiet static, and he assumed the phone had suddenly gone into one of its dead zones. "Forget it," she finally said. "I'll talk to you later."

"I'm looking forward to it, baby."

"You better."

He hung up and drove on in to meet up with Cortese. Santián pulled into a visitor's parking space for Def Ritmo Records, in Santa Monica, thirty-four minutes later. Cortese's badass 1978 Camaro with the racing stripes was nearby. After Santián shut off the ignition, the Malibu's carburetor caused a momentary bout of engine knock from unburned gas.

"Tune-up time," his partner said, appearing beside him.

"One more item on the list." The two fell into sync walking across the parking lot. Santián was a half step ahead of Cortese, and each man casually let his eyes rove the area. It was a rhythm even they were no longer aware that their bodies fell into when on the prowl.

"This shit is tight," the taller man said, as the two reached the perimeter of the record label's building.

The sergeant regarded him silently.

"Jakob, Madeleine's kid, uses the word," the other man explained.

Santián moved forward. "Careful, son."

"You're not one to talk."

The two crossed the threshold. Def Ritmo's offices were in a fourteen-story building located on Olympic, near 24th Street. It was Frank Gehry meets I. M. Pei, with the architect as Ayn Rand's Howard Roarke incarnate: marvels of freestanding slabs, bisecting curvatures leading to sharp edges behind colonnades to the heavens, with all of it sheathed in muted and iridescent hues. It was tight.

A pretty black girl in a short print dress hustled past them in the lobby area. She had a silver stud jutting underneath her lower lip and was holding an armload of files like a running back, eyes straight ahead, neck tucked in. She sauntered past, and Santián leaned against the wall of the elevator bank as Cheese pressed the button.

"You been getting enough sleep?" Santián commented, noting his associate's failure to ogle the honey.

"I got a woman, a good woman," Cheese hammed in an Italian immigrant accent straight out of melodrama. The elevator came and they got in the car.

"You still looking for a store in bofunkland?" The Muzak over the speakers was a jaunty version of "The Girl from Ipanema."

"Just 'cause I'm the darkest thing those owl hoots in Bozeman will allow around there is no reason for you to be jealous," Cheese retorted.

"You counting the months?"

"I'm just glad to be having something to look forward to besides this shit." Cortese looked up at the digital number display. "What about you, Saint? You know you can't keep this up like there's no payback."

Santián said, "Nothing worse than a convert. . . . You're not gonna miss it? The juice?"

Cortese drew in a quiet breath. "I am, yeah, I am. But—"

He didn't finish as the car settled to a halt and the door opened onto a glass brick and burnished stainless steel reception area. Over the PA a Soljer X lyric came through, *"Bring me the head of Osama bin Bush . . ."* Along the walls were laminated posters of Def Ritmo artists with varying degrees of exposed skin or gangsta scowl.

Santián noted that one of the posters featured Edgerrin James, the star running back for the Baltimore Colts. His upcoming rap CD, to drop next month according to a sticker on the poster, was called *Crack-the-Back.* He was smiling broadly, an airbrushed twinkle added to his two gold front teeth.

"Is August around?" Santián had an elbow on the raised circular desk of the olive-complected receptionist with the peach-hued lips.

"He's in a meeting right now. Did you have an appointment?" She made a pretense of looking at her computer screen and leveled a wrinkled brow on the sergeant dressed in his civvies, his stone-washed jeans fashionably ripped over one knee.

"Nope, we don't," Saint admitted. Behind him, because it was a bit they'd done so often, he knew Cheese already had his badge out for her to see.

"You're out of your jurisdiction." The young woman kept her gaze on the sergeant. "Maybe you need some help reading a map."

"I know that's true," Santián agreed heartily. "You're East Indian, right?"

"What are you?"

He moved his head from side to side as if clearing his ears of water. "This and that—my father was Puerto Rican, mostly."

"Anytime now," Cortese cut in.

"So what about your boss?" Santián scratched at his unshaven cheek.

"Sorry," she said, shaking her head.

"You know we're not going away."

"Nobody said you had to." The phone rang, and she answered and transferred. "So now what?" She rested her chin on her palm, her elbow propped on the desk.

"Just peep him, will you," Cortese said irritably. "He knows why we're here, goddamn it."

"Chill, baby." Santián looked around and winked at his partner. Cortese didn't feel like being in on the joke.

"Come on." Santián picked up her headset. "Just tell him we're out here and we won't bother you anymore."

"I'm too accommodating a person," she sighed, and made the call. The line was picked up on the other end, and she talked. The young woman listened; then she put her hand to the mouthpiece. "Okay. Well, color me impressed," she remarked, continuing to size up Santián. "He said he'll be with you in just a few. What can I get you while you wait?"

The two were already in motion. Santián said, "Thanks, ah . . ."

"Charna."

"Charna." Santián repeated her name as if he were holding a delicate flower.

She fluttered her fingers at him as the two walked around a corner.

"You can't help yourself, can you?"

Santián shot back, "Can't hit 'em out of the park unless you swing, son."

"Shit."

Even if they hadn't known which doorway led to August Mercury's, a stranger could have made an educated guess. At the end of the short hallway was a set of frosted-glass doors with rosewood handles. As the two neared the portal, one side was opened from within by a tall, bulky Latino in Beverly Hills Polo Club hop-hop gear and smelling like he'd breast-stroked through gallons of Emporio Armani.

"Fellas," the greeter greeted.

"Z'up *ese?*" Without breaking stride, Santián went to one side of the baller, and Cortese the other. The latter got the other side of the double doors open as Mister BHPC turned around.

"You have something to do, right?" Santián inserted his body between the man and Cortese as he entered the office.

"August wanted me to see if you needed anything."

"People are awfully solicitous 'round here," Santián bantered.

"Must be all that Martha Stewart they be watching," Cortese jived.

Santián addressed the flunky. "Can I get a fresh squeezed grapefruit juice or kiwi-lime parfait?"

"A what?" his straight man shot back. Both his pupils were tight as drumheads.

"We're fine," Santián assured him. "We'll take it from here." He also went into the office. The reason for the delaying attempt was obvious to the two cops as they stood on the Isfahan rug.

Mercury was sitting at his desk, his hand brushing away some residue on its surface. He rubbed a knuckle against one nostril. "I knew if I told Char to keep you up front, you'd just bum-rush anyway," he despaired.

The young man had also entered the room. "Merc, you aw'rite?"

"Yeah, it's all good, Peacock. I got it situated."

Peacock regarded the two and remained motionless.

"Go on and see to those jewel pacs for the release party, okay?" The other man didn't move.

Cortese said, "We know you bad, man; your boss ain't mad at you."

Peacock looked for affirmation from Mercury and got a nod. He withdrew, backing up as he did so.

"Tough as they make 'em in juvie," Santián smirked. He checked his watch. "Having a little pick-me-up to get you started for your rough day, player? Before you slip on ya Fendi watch and ice ta bling-bling."

"I don't know what you're talking about, Rafael." He stood, brushing at the front of his DeMarco slacks. "I was merely finishing a Power Bar."

"Oh, that's what you cool guys are calling ya-yo these days?" Cortese plopped his large frame onto a leather couch.

"So let's make this quick, huh? I've got appointments to get to." Mercury was above medium height, with black hair and coarse yet compelling features that revealed his Mexican roots. He made a production of adjusting his white-jade-cufflinked sleeve.

Santián stood with his hands in his pockets. "Which drawer is it in?"

"Whatever you're going on about, you don't have probable cause, let alone you don't have a warrant. And, of course, no official standing in the city of Santa Monica anyway."

"Left side," Santián guessed, moving forward.

"Hey, you better settle down, man." Mercury came around the large desk and got in Santián's path.

The cop's eyes went dark. "How you want to jump?"

"This isn't right, the way you TRASH fucks act."

Santián put street command in his voice. "Shut up, or I'll pistol whip you in front of your bitches out front, including Peacock. Then take you over to your mama's house and do it again."

Mercury looked over at Cortese, who was dangling a leg over the arm of the couch. The other man held his arms apart, with a "What can I do?" expression on his face.

"This won't be admissible." Mercury pointed a manicured nail at Santián.

"No fuckin' kidding, Brainiac." Santián had the left-hand-side desk drawer open and extracted a black metal tin with a Chinese dragon enameled on its cover. Inside the container were the fine white granules of cocaine.

"Hmm?" Santián showed the snow to a blasé Cortese.

Mercury put his hands on his hips. "Can we get this over with?"

Unchallenged, Santián closed and pocketed the tin. He then sat on the edge of the desk near the fuming record label chief.

"Please." The sergeant held out a hand, indicating the swivel chair Mercury had been perched in when the pair had entered.

"That's okay—like I said, I have places to be."

Cortese spoke, "We know you ain't seen shit, heard shit, or know any shit." He took his leg off the sofa arm and snuggled into the cushions. "But we're under the gun, if you catch my meaning."

"And that means everybody else gets to catch hell till we break this mug open," Santián added.

"Like he said, I don't have any remote idea how to help you, Rafael." Mercury glanced over at his suit coat, neatly placed on one of his Eames chairs. "I do have to attend to my business, and if you really need to talk to me, you should contact my lawyer."

He started for his coat, and Santián scratched at the back of his head. "Now look here, Augusto, if we want, we can take you over to the Santa Monica station just to mess with you, and tell them about this coke we confiscated from your desk." He patted his pocket. "You may not know this, *mi amigo,* but TRASH has several inter-cooperation directives it's signed with various municipalities."

If he looked at Cortese, he would crack up from the line of bull-shit he was giving Mercury. But he knew Mercury to be a primping weasel, and anything that halfway sounded like it might grease him would get him to pause. He hated to have his routine fucked with.

"Maybe I should get Hec on the phone." He was between the Eames chair and the desk.

"Get Big Red on the horn," Cortese bluffed. "This isn't a bust; this is a procedure in the inquiry surrounding a murder. But you want to make it formal, go ahead."

Santián crossed his arms. "We'll turn you over to SMPD, baby. And you'll still have to answer our questions."

Mercury resigned himself to being compliant. "Look, this label is about bringing the sounds of the urban experience, from the pro-jects to the East Los flats, to everyone. I've helped many kids with jobs and opportunities to turn their lives around. So it's no stretch for me to extend a hand to someone like Gargoyle Villa, a young man who came up much like me, when I was asked to aid him."

Cortese clapped. "That was wonderful—inspiring, even." He took his leg off the arm of the couch and sat forward.

"The Del Fuegos really get their money's worth with you, don't they?" Santián uncrossed his arms.

"Rafael, Rafael," he said in mock lamentation. "I serve no one but the customers who buy our product because it reflects their lives, their wishes. Unlike some, I have not lost sight of my goals." His cover-boy teeth worked themselves into a mischievous grin.

"I ain't lost sight of nothing, *cabrón*," Santián seethed. "You think paying to rehab the rec center in the old neighborhood or giving away some overpriced Kobes makes you Zorro. But I'm out there twenty-four-motherfuckin'-seven, pounding the same streets we ran when we was kids. Only I know what I'm fighting for, Mister Mecarro. So those women who work in Miss Lady's pretty homes north of Montana can walk to the Ninety-nine Cent Store without getting hit up by some crackhead or glue sniffer your bosses get the Crazy Nines to sell their *drogas* to."

"Like it never was, Rafael," Mercury taunted.

"Like it should be. If you weren't the puppet pretending he was the puppeteer, you'd see that."

Mercury manufactured a bored expression. "If all you have are your tepid Dr. Laura observations, I'll be going. Try not to steal my paperweight on your way out."

Santián got up from the desk. "Who said we were through?"

Cortese leaned forward but didn't rise.

Mercury plucked his coat from the chair. "Go on, Rafe, thump on me. But this ain't Alvarado Street, *chucho;* this is the westside, *¿entiendes?* You two think you can bring that retrograde Daryl Gates shit in here and I'm supposed to pee my pants or start stuttering. Put a welt on me, and Ferris will not only eat you alive, but your kids will be paying off on the lawsuit." With a flourish, he slipped on his coat.

Cortese got up. Santián put his body between Mercury and the door. "You and your little crooked twat ain't all that, son. This is one case I'm here to see your slick ass catches."

"You must be getting worried, is that it, Rafael?"

Santián went to the other man, placing the tips of his fingers on Mercury's chest. "This doesn't end with Gargoyle's death. This is the beginning, and I'm going to ride you like a twenty-dollar ho."

"You better step," Mercury said.

"Or what?" Santián edged.

"Find out."

Santián let the back of his hand slide down the front of Mercury's tie, smoothing the material as it went. "Versace can't stop a bullet." He flipped the end of the tie in a defiant gesture.

"That a threat, Sergeant? Is that something I should communicate to Ms. McGuire?"

"The Del Fuegos may be cleaning house, Mercury," Cortese put in. "We're just trying to give you an out."

"Oh, of course I appreciate you looking out for my interests." He stepped around Santián. "And blow or no blow, why don't the both of you get on back to the *barrio* so you can scare the natives."

"We like it around here," Cortese advised.

"We might be around a lot. Enough that if your bosses ain't pissed with you, they might soon be." Santián pivoted and the two started to walk out.

"Say hi to your wife for me," Mercury quipped.

Santián halted in midstride, his back muscles tensing, but Cortese tapped his arm and they kept going.

"Since when did he grow another set of balls?" Santián wondered as they rode down in the elevator. He was also irritated that he didn't get to say good-bye to the lovely Charna, who wasn't at her post when they left.

"They must be on loan from Heckman," Cortese said. "Whatever the fuck is going down, everybody hooked into it must be looking to live large."

"Or scared, and just plain want to live."

"There is that, Cisco. But he and Heckman are walking on the far side of the dollar, as Ross Macdonald once pontificated. Greed makes you do brave things."

The Muzak over the elevator's speakers was a version of War's "The World Is a Ghetto."

CHAPTER 5

Judd Ahn took the brunt of the blow on his forearm like a prize fighter backed up on the ropes.

"Kung fu chink sushi-lovin' bastard," the man with the scraggly beard and longish blond hair cursed at him. He swung again, this time connecting with Ahn's jaw.

The blow made him loopy, and he felt his left knee getting gelatinous, but he clamped his teeth and righted himself with a hand on the rear fender of the soft-tail Harley of his attacker.

"Get your yellow claws off my bike!" the other man bellowed. He stepped forward and simultaneously twisted his upper body to throw an uppercut.

Ahn blocked the blow by getting his arm in and sweeping it aside as it was aimed at his head again. He countered with a jab to the biker's hanging gut. Spittle erupted from the bearded man's mouth, and Ahn could see that one of his front teeth was missing. But his dental inspection was brought up short as the man tried to get both his arms around Ahn in a bear hug.

"I don't know what the fuck you're doing here, boy, but your slant ass is going to be sorry." He brought both of them down into the dirt, raising a brown cloud of grit and earth. He was on top and trying to free a knife from the sheath attached to his belt.

Ahn yanked an arm loose and used the heel of his hand to strike his attacker in the ear, very hard and repeatedly. The biker had to deal with that, and as he reached for Ahn's hand, Ahn bucked his hips and got the man off him.

"That's your ass now," the man promised.

Ahn was on his feet and kicked him in the nose as he charged. It wasn't as good as Jackie Chan, but it would do. The heel of his Nunn Bush oxford collided with cartilage, and there was a satisfying crunch.

"Motherfuck!" the bellied biker exclaimed. Blood poured from both his nostrils, but he was far from through. He had the knife out and was advancing on Ahn. It was of the Bowie variety, and he handled it like someone who knew what he was doing. "Now what you gonna do, Jet Li?"

Ahn high-jumped over the Harley leaning on its kickstand. He then landed and kicked it over.

"You fuck," the biker groaned. He ran around his fallen prize to skewer Ahn.

But the other man had begun backpedaling.

"That ain't gonna help you, bitch. I'm'a catch and cut you," he vowed, rushing forward.

Ahn had needed the extra seconds his maneuver had bought him to clear his gun from his holster. The Colt felt awfully reassuring in his sweaty fingers.

The biker, a Vandal Viking, asked, "You some kind of cop?"

"Hell of a time to ask." Without wasting breath telling him to put the knife down or cease and desist, Ahn merely stepped inside what would have been the arc of the knife thrust and cold-cocked him upside his head with the butt of the semiauto.

The Viking's head snapped back, and Ahn rapped the breech of the pistol against the exposed Adam's apple. This got the man gagging and bending forward. Ahn brought his hands together, the pistol in between, and used the combination as a cudgel he brought down on the base of the man's neck. He sprawled forward, landing on his chin on the only patch of lawn in front of Red Dog's place.

Ahn bent and retrieved the blade. Sweat dropped off his face in a torrent, and he picked up his glasses, which had been knocked off upon initial contact.

"Man, why the fuck did you have to do that?" a voice squeaked.

Ahn had his bracelets out and cuffed the semiconscious man to the bike's lower frame. He put the knife in his coat pocket and walked to the house, tucking his shirttail in as his did so.

"Give me that." Ahn didn't wait for an answer and grabbed the beer out of Red Dog's hand. He pressed the cold can to his bruised face and entered the small house. Incongruously, the home was fifties tasteful, with a modular Gregory Ain feel to the design, though the place needed a scraping and painting, and parts of the roof lacked shingles.

Red Dog's crib was at the end of a road on a hillock overlooking part of the Santa Susana Wash in Chatsworth. It was located in the northern end of L.A. County, not far from the Ventura County line. Red Dog's isolated locale was ideal for the business affairs of the Vandal Vikings. The gang was one of Southern California's largest purveyors of methamphetamines, with distribution across the nation. And Red Dog's pad was often used as a way station in the transport of the chemicals used to manufacture the product, such as red phosphorus, freon illegally imported from Mexico, and the volatile hydrogen chloride gas.

"Man, what's with you?" Red Dog persisted, letting the beat-up screen door bang shut as he stalked inside.

Ahn took a quick look in the kitchen, in case there was another numb-nut lurking about. Satisfied, he tucked his piece away. "He's the one who came after me," he calmly said, moving back into the spare topography of the living room. He stepped over Barbara Reno, who sat on the floor against the couch. She was carving sections from a piece of watermelon with a butter knife. The melon was on a Donald Duck plate lying across her legs.

Red Dog glowered at Ahn, who sat in the only chair in the room: an overstuffed number that listed to one side. "Man, that was Panhead you jacked up, do you know that?"

Ahn put the can of beer on the floor. "What's your point?"

Red Dog retrieved his morning beverage. "He's part of the Ring, man."

Ahn tweaked an eyebrow as he used his shirtfront to clean his glasses. "So why is somebody from your precious leadership bunch here to see you this time of the day?"

Red Dog drank some of his brew. It was hard to tell when he was happy or agitated, as both states induced drinking on his part. "I don't know, man. Barbara tells me you're coming out, then shit, Panhead rides in, like, two minutes 'fore you get here."

Reno continued to enjoy her breakfast, engrossed in the doings on *The Jenny Jones Show* on TV. The segment had three priests who liked to dress in women's clothes, with the music they liked to change to when putting on their heels.

"I couldn't very well turn around, now, could I?" Ahn remarked unnecessarily. When he'd pulled up in his Jeep Liberty, he'd seen the bike and knew it wasn't the Dog's hog. He was working on a cover story as he got out, but the preparation proved to be moot. Panhead came running from the porch, where he'd been talking to Red Dog, and they'd gotten into it, the intros overlooked.

"But what the fuck's gonna happen when he comes around?" Red Dog sat on the arm of the couch, consternation etching his lined face. "I got a lot to lose here, Ahn. You can walk away, but what about me and my old lady?"

Reno turned to look at Red Dog, then Ahn. "My man is right, Ahn. He can't have the Vikings getting any ideas in their heads or we're butt-fucked for sure."

The two were right, Ahn admitted to himself. He needed to keep the Dog on the string. He'd proved to be a most reliable resource, as Ahn had the aging biker's balls in a velvet vise. "Let's make it I was from the Sheriff's Department."

"That's good," the desperate Red Dog agreed.

"Then he better be in lockup," Reno pointed with her butter knife. "Otherwise he's going to wonder how is it you cuffed him and he didn't go through the system."

"That can be arranged." Ahn rose, working out a stiffness spearing its way through one of his legs. "But I need something from you, Dog."

"What?" His head was in the fridge, rooting out another beer. Reno stuck out her tongue and licked her lips lasciviously for Ahn's benefit. He gave her a nervous glare.

"I've got a partial serial number from a thirty-eight I have good reason to believe was originally sold by a dealer named Macklin, who sells his wares to you—ah, how shall I say?—road warrior types. The partial was run through the system and came up a possible on an ATF list."

"You're funny as that I-tie Jay Leno, Ahn. You could be the next

Ko-ree-an Rodney Dangerfield." Red Dog had returned with another can.

"But you heard of him, yeah?" Ahn walked toward the wall phone that hung inside the doorway. Idly he tried to figure out who the hell was the first Korean Rodney Dangerfield.

"I have; that's so," the Dog admitted. "But you could have called that in if all you want is a piece run down. What it get used for? Some malt-liquor-head use it sticking up a Stop-and-Rob deep down in the jungle where your papa and cousins run a store? He and Reno laughed at his show of wit.

"Something like that." He dialed a number. His cell was back in his car, and he doubted its roaming range covered this area anyway. "Phenias," he said after the line connected, "I need to have a deputy roll out here to the Dog's house. Tell him to arrest the asshole handcuffed to his Harley. Book him on general principles, and I'll fill their captain in later." He listened, then, smirking, said, "I know, but I'm not having Connie scold me for that. I'll see you later." He replaced the handset.

"Must be tough working for a woman—and a black one at that. She acts like she's the fuckin' queen of the city." Red Dog pontificated once again.

"Just let me know about the number, okay?"

"Sure, sure. What choice do I have?"

"I can always tell your ex where you are, Red Dog."

The can stopped on its way to his mouth. "Stop fuckin' around, Ahn."

Of all things, Ahn had busted Red Dog for nonpayment of child support. The house, which was in his grandmother's name, was the perfect hideout. Reno took care of all the bills and had the utilities in her name. The Dog's ex-wife had taken up with a low-level IRS agent in Seattle. He was just a programmer, but all Red Dog knew was the IRS tag. He believed that one word from Ahn, and he'd be doing twenty in Mule Creek. Red Dog's only cash flow came from his part in the Vikings meth chain.

"Hey." Ahn brightened suddenly. "You'd better see about your boy before the sheriff arrives."

Red Dog got up quickly, a man on a mission. He headed for the door. He carried a pillow from the couch. "You're right, good thinking." The screen door slapped loudly, and he hurried out to see about his leader. Ahn felt sorry for Red Dog, caught up in something that sooner or later was either going to tear him apart or force him to make a decision that couldn't have a good outcome.

Reno was standing before him, her hand fondling him through his pants. "You'd better be careful how you play him, Judd. He's not that slow all the time, and you know it."

"Beneath it all, he's a trusting soul, Barbara." They kissed fiercely, their tongues exploring familiar territory.

"When you going to take me on a real date?" she asked when their mouths parted. "You feelin' me up at the Code 7 the other night with all your little cop buddies around is not my idea of four-star."

Ahn grinned, keeping one eye and ear tuned for Red Dog's return. "It's good to make excursions into enemy territory. How about Le Colonial and a set over at the Jazz Bakery this weekend—if you can get away."

"I'll see." She pinched him down below and withdrew her hand. "You talk to McGuire about me yet?"

"I've mentioned you to her," he fibbed.

Reno punched him on the arm. "You better not leave me hanging, Judd. I'm not just your undercover pussy."

"You're not, Barbara; you know that." He touched her face.

"I mean . . . " She looked up at him with her hazel eyes. "I kinda hoped we had developed something real here."

"We have—I'm not bullshitting, Barbara. We have." His own intensity surprised him.

The stomping of Red Dog's boots reached them as he tracked across the front porch. When he entered, Reno was once again sitting on the floor, and Ahn was adjusting the front of his pants, his shirt out.

"He's coming around," the Dog announced.

"Let him. It'll be more legit if he's awake when the deputies arrive." Ahn took a Polaroid from his inner pocket and handed it to his source. "See what you can find out about this piece, okay? The partial's written on the back."

"Okay." He took the photo, frowning. "So how come you didn't just phone me up or make a drop at the mail box in Reseda?"

Part of Reno's face tightened, but Ahn was sure Red Dog hadn't caught the brief tick. He said offhandedly, "I need this *tout de suite,* homey. And you know I always got to see about you, Dog. Got to make sure you're not starting to stockpile any weapons or armor-piercing rounds up here. Meth is one thing, cop-killing another. I've got to protect my side of the equation."

The Dog actually hadn't expected that detailed an answer, as such was not the usual from Ahn. He was already back in the kitchen, deciding to have another brewski or make a sandwich, or both. "Uh," he muttered. The approach of a siren pierced the silence following his pronouncement.

Ahn tucked the front of his shirt in and marched outside. The investigator was certainly glad his arousal had subsided. What the hell would the cops out here think of him if it hadn't?

The prostitute who called herself Hyacinth finished the hit on the strawberry-flavored blunt. She offered it to the man who'd given the dope to her, but he shook his head. She smiled, then undid Officer Reynaux's zipper as he lay back on the bed. Her gimmick was her build. Unlike other working girls, whose bodies went to bloat from too much fried foods, or haggard from being strung out, she kept in shape. Hyacinth pumped iron and took bulking powders. She ran photos of herself in the back of the *L.A. Weekly* and had a Web site showing off her muscularity. She even did sessions where dudes paid four hundred bucks just to worship her body. *God love a fetish freak,* she reflected. The woman did good business in outcalls, but she and the cop had something special— something she was taking advantage of right now.

The shades were pulled down, but the sounds from Occidental Boulevard down below reminded her it was only the midafternoon.

They were in the Playpen. That's what the TRASH crew called their urban assignation retreat rented under a retired cop's name.

"You sure you're not going to get a call?" She had his swollen member in one silver-nailed hand and finished her crack hit with the other, holding the fumes in. She jerked her head in the direction of his radio. He'd placed his Astro on the Goodwill-issued nightstand, her purse on top if it. His gun belt and Monadnock lay on the bed, near the headboard.

"Naw," Reynaux drawled. "I got to be back out there in 'bout forty-five, cheri; I got to help Ronk and this rookie keep hunting for this one they call Harpy."

She let out the narcotic smoke. "I know him," she said, her hand working up and down his shaft. "He's got the hook nose and the birdy eyes."

"Yeah, that's him," Reynaux gasped between soft moans. "You maybe know where he could be holed up?"

"Um," she gurgled as she took him in her mouth, the taste of him mingling with the residue of the crack. "He likes to play with those damned—what do they call them?"

"Video games?"

"No, you know, the model cars that go around this track and you have this controller." She began again on him.

"Slot cars?"

"Um-hmm."

"That went out when I was a kid. Where is this place?"

She stopped. "You want a blow job, Rey-Rey, or you want to interrogate me?"

He propped himself up on his elbows. "I might want to do both. I do have my job to do."

"I'm the one doing all the work," she teased, momentarily glancing over at her purse. She then resumed servicing him.

Lieutenant Kubrick hated tofu burgers no matter what you put on them to disguise the fact that you weren't eating meat. But the prospect of the return of his prostate cancer hovered like a shadow, forever haunting him. And the notion that he might not be able to see his daughters graduate from college was more frightening to him than any disease. So a regimen of little or no red meat was maintained, as well as dutiful helpings of saw palmetto tablets.

Today, for kicks, he'd put a few daubs of Pickapeppa sauce on his lunch for flavor. But he had to be cautious in this; otherwise there'd be a recurrence of his hemorrhoids. It was hell getting old, he mused as Holton stepped into his office.

"What up, QB?" Holton had one of his lived-in porkpies tilted back on his box head. He closed the door and leaned against it.

"Where we at on the Villa killing?"

"I made a cruise through the 'Shaw last night to look up a few contacts."

"Working that Ace Deuce angle?"

"It's worth pursuing," Holton opined. "The Ace Deuce Swans and Nines have territory that smacks up against each other, and we do know they loves to cap. There was a shooting of two Swans last night, in fact. I'm going to talk to the one that survived—he's over at Green Memorial. It's just too bad that most times their aims are so bad innocent kids wind up eating bullets, too."

Last summer's spike in the body count of black and brown youth was fresh in both of their minds. As the city became more Latino again, and as the heretofore black enclaves shrank, there had been an exponential increase in violent disagreements between the gangs, too. "Exacerbated by the fact the Nines have broken off big portions of the black crack trade across the city," he finished aloud.

Holton nodded in acknowledgment. "I figure if there's anything to it, I can shake something loose. You know how these homeboys love to brag about their hits." He splayed his hog-farmer hands before him. "But there's this other angle with this other Crazy Nine. Though I don't hear anything directly about the killing, I got hepped that this Crazy Nine Harpy was also at the courthouse then."

"How the hell did you find that out?"

"There's a chick named Myrna who's the barmaid at Babe and Rickey's Inn, over there on Leimert. She told me she was down there last Saturday with her sister-in-law to see her brother, who was being arraigned for a B-and-E. He was three guys ahead of Villa when the shooting went down. Now, Myrna, who's half and half, used to go out with one of the Nines' OGs, the one they called Uncle Fester 'cause of his bald head and creepy sunken raccoon eyes."

Kubrick's intercom on his phone buzzed, and he picked up the handset. "Okay," he said after listening, "tell her I'll be available in about half an hour. Thanks, Dora." He dropped the receiver back in its cradle. "That, of course, was a message from McGuire, wanting to have another goddamn talk with me. I understand she had a meeting with the mayor, her boss, and the head of the police commission this morning."

"She's using us to climb into office," Holton intoned as if reciting a mantra. "A few knucklehead decisions from a couple of hotheads and she keeps trying to build a fire out of sparks. The guilty are already in prison."

Kubrick pushed his fingers together but eschewed a response. He was loyal to his men as long as he could be sure they were walking the line—a broad line by his reckoning. "Go on about this Myrna."

"So she knows some of these other Nines by sight. She recognized Harpy, who tried to book after the shooting happened. The bailiffs are of course running all over the place, and stop him. At first the deputies figured one of the prisoners had a gat, and this caused more confusion. But they eventually questioned Harpy, I learned, only this doesn't show up in the official report."

"They must have lumped him under 'relatives and related individuals,' " Kubrick added, recalling what he read in the report. "Obviously the sheriffs didn't see him as no more connected than one of Villa's soldiers coming to give moral support. And like any self-respecting banger, he'd want to be gone when any shooting went down."

Holton put his scoop of a hand to his hat and pushed it forward across his graying hair. "But Myrna tells me that Harpy was never a friend of Gargoyle's. Way she understands it, when Uncle Fester was around there was a power struggle as to who would be the next one coming up. In the end Gargoyle and his clique dominated over Harpy."

"Could be they kissed and made up," Kubrick cracked.

"We're looking for him now."

"Keep me informed. What happened to this Uncle Fester?"

Holton had already risen. "He got stabbed seventy-five times while doing a jolt in Corcoran a couple of years ago."

"Because he dated a black woman?"

"No, his love of the nappy dugout just prevented him from ever being anything more than a captain. His real sin was skimming profits from their chop shop business."

"Amazing," Kubrick said. "Whatever breaks, I have to know it before McGuire."

"Like I'm gonna tell her?" Holton held a hand to his chest as if wounded.

"Right now we can't have surprises, Big T. I don't want or expect a squad full of angels, but I can't have a troop that doesn't understand the difference between aggressive policing and not being righteous." His gaze remained fixed on the wide man. "Restraint in all things is what I'm talking about."

"I'm clear. We're all clear, Lieutenant."

"Let's make sure it stays that way."

Holton touched the brim of his hat and left.

Kubrick tapped a fingertip on the file that had come over this morning. It was about the disappearance of a teenage girl named Serain Jensen. She was last seen in Culver City, but he'd been informed there were aspects of her case that Cheese Cortese could help with, possibly. After his lunch, he'd read through the file then pass it along. He took his sack lunch containing the tofu burger, yogurt, and two apples from his desk drawer. He walked to the room off the roll call that they'd turned into a makeshift lounge with a fridge and microwave. He put his burger in the microwave to heat it up and eat it before his sure-to-be-contentious conversation with McGuire.

His stomach gurgled, the acid giving him a nasty taste in the back of his throat. One more condition kicking up again. The sour taste reminded him of Ferris Heckman, and that she was filing suit against the Sheriff's Department for negligence in the death of her client. One less asshole, and she had the nerve to seek restitution for that? Like he was some kind of asset?

He left the room, leaving the microwave beeping its signal that his burger was ready. Fuck it. If his guilt was going to act up, he'd give it a reason. He was heading for the hot dog cart the Guatemalan woman ran. It was always set not too far west of the station house this time of day, at the curb on Temple. He was going to have onions and sliced jalapeños on his dog. Let some other sap eat the processed tree-hugger chow.

CHAPTER 6

Ferris Heckman, her reddish-auburn hair done in a ponytail, pushed herself through her workout on the StairMaster while she talked on the headset. "You've got to stay focused, August. This is no time for you to get rattled by that *pendejo* Santián." *Come on, you can do it; steady on, girl,* she coached herself.

"They know something's up, Hec."

"Of course," she retorted. "Villa got his head blown off." *Oh, yeah, there's the burn; come on, work it; keep those calves and biceps femoris at peak.* Shit, August was still pestering her.

"But you should have heard the way Santián was going on. I'm telling you, I was thinking about it later, and it sounded to me like TRASH had made a deal with the DEA or something like that."

"They'll be lucky if the Agency or the Bureau isn't after them. Anyway, you come to this after you coked up, honey?" she asked derisively.

"This isn't about that. I keep it even with the Valium. I've got to put in long hours around here, Hec. This isn't a stage show; I've got a big nut to clear every goddamn month."

"Fine, fine." There was no percentage in backing him into a corner about his increasing drug use and drinking. If he wouldn't listen to her, he'd damn sure listen to the Del Fuegos. She toweled sweat from her forehead. "You are calling from a secure line, aren't you, August?" She'd arranged that her phone numbers were always sent through a scrambler.

"I'm not stupid."

"I'm not saying you are, but when you get excited you are prone to . . . errors." She went on huffing through her workout, her tongue tasting the salt on her lower lip. "But I'm telling you, there's nothing that Santián or his gang that can't shoot straight are onto. Of course they want to break this case, because then that gets more of the public behind them, and the pressure eased off their activities."

She funneled in air and lowered her voice. Heckman was in the twenty-four-hour Bally's near her office. No one was immediately in her vicinity, but if there was one thing she'd learned from her daddy, the colonel, circumspection was always a sound course. He was circumspect to the point of being granite, but that was for mental dissection some other time. "We just need to play our part, August, and everything else will fall into place."

"I, I suppose you're right, Hec."

She was so tired of these pep talks she constantly had to supply. If nothing else, the cocaine was making him whiney and wimpy. "All right, then. I'm going to hit the showers."

"We're still on for the Sky Bar?"

"Yes, sweetie, I'll see you there around seven. I'm coming there from the Jag place."

"You turning yours in for another lease?"

"Not exactly," she hedged, aware she didn't want to say too much to him—over the phone or in person. "I need to take care of some paperwork for a client. Keep the seat warm for me, honey."

"You know I will, baby."

Heckman smirked. He sounded happy as a kid with an unlimited ticket at laser tag. She could always bolster his precarious psyche. What a gift. "See you then." She finished and, to cool down, did some stomach crunches. Walking past a mirror after the shower, she had to admit that her thirty-seven-year-old body was holding up pretty well. Dressed and combed, she left the facility, her large equipment bag slung over her shoulder.

She liked it that in her DKNY and Fossil sunglasses she could still make the heads of mid-Wilshire office grunts turn. An unmarked forest green late-model Impala went by on the thoroughfare, and she recognized it as one of the cars used by TRASH, because of how it was tricked out. This was not to have them blend in but to stand out, to let the peons know who was on the scene.

Bastards acted like barons who traveled the lowlands of their estate, the Heights. They did what they pleased, went wherever they wanted on their terms. "Fuckheads," she muttered on her way back to her offices in the Equitable Buildings. An older Korean woman walking by gaped at the foulmouthed pretty woman.

Ronk Culhane kept his vision in play along Wilshire as Acosta drove the Impala east. Involuntarily he touched his bristling hair. He wasn't 100 percent, but that redhead broad with the firm backside must have been Ferris Heckman. "She needs some real dick," he announced aloud.

"Who?" Acosta asked.

"Back there, we passed that ball buster, Heckman, walking. She's the one represents Mercury's record label, and came to bail out Gargoyle that night we'd nabbed him. Only he never called her, see? She just showed up."

"He'd already lawyered up when you and Big T were grilling him?" He asked conversationally.

"Yeah," Culhane uttered derisively. "All these motherfuckahs can't spell cat, but because of the goddamn ACL-Jew they all know how to holler for their rights." He clasped his hands and looked heavenward in supplication. "Praise de Lawd."

Acosta slowed, approaching the light at Berendo. "So you guys didn't get any hint, nothing about what's going down?"

Culhane stretched, his left shoulder socket sore from his bench presses last night. "All that sumbitch was concerned with was we had him on the El Paso killing. He was definitely aware he could get the hot shot for it."

"If it was me, I'd be crying to make a deal." Acosta tapped the accelerator, the car's well-tuned engine barely audible as they rode along. It was if they were in a chariot propelled by their willpower, aimed into the heart of the impending storm.

"Well, you know how these fools are. One second they're acting like Tony Soprano, and the next all of a sudden they get a flash of insight and realize what the fuck they're facing." Culhane laughed harshly. "I mean, it kills me when I hear plainclothes talk about solving crime like it was a chess game."

"How's that?"

"Like it's about thinking ahead, anticipating the bad guys' moves."

"Well, isn't it?"

"Take Westmorland up here then down Sunset Place. The Nines have a patch there where they sell to the law students over at Loyola," Culhane directed. Then back on the topic, "Yeah, sure, there's some of that, no doubt. But chess is about logic and pre-scribed moves, right? The bishop moves diagonally, the knight in an el, and so forth. But out here that kind of discipline, right-brain thinking or whatever it is, just don't apply.

"Too much emotion, pettiness, envy, paybacks, the *chisme*, right?" He swiveled his head, eyes and brain keyed to distinguish-ing the assholes from the civilians.

"That means *gossip*, but I get your meaning—the drama is heavy out here," Acosta agreed. The tableau outside the car's windows had changed. The contrast between the neighborhood they'd left and the one they were entering was readily apparent. Less than a mile behind them were the towering office buildings of mid-Wilshire housing law firms, doctors' offices, financial outfits, and the like. The denizens there strutted in name brands found in spreads in *Details* and *Vanity Fair*. But those people were transients; they worked in the area but went home to houses and condos in different zip codes.

The people Acosta and Culhane watched now also wore name brands, but theirs were Dickies and Dee Cee, and knockoff Silvertab jeans bought at the indoor swap meet on Washington and Grand, or La Curacao on Olympic and Union. This was their home, these women with the Indian faces balancing laundry baskets on their heads, and pushcart vendors in their straw *vaquero* hats selling roasted corn or fresh pupusas.

"I know him." Culhane pointed at a young man who took off walking rapidly west on Sunset Place upon seeing them. "That's Jamie Villar, a known associate of Harpy."

"Let's bounce on him." Like the tachometer gauge on the dash, Acosta could feel the needle of his energy level climbing into a higher range.

"That's okay," Culhane said, watching the gangbanger bolt between two buildings. "He won't know shit, and if we ride around
with him in the car everybody else will get scarce. This way, at least
we keep them guessing. Too bad the slot car tip was a bust."

"Yeah." They'd ridden west on Wilshire out of the Heights, to a
three-story strip mall at the corner of Wilton in Koreatown. Large
blue letters in Hangul, the Korean script, announced the place as
the Tehan Shopping Plaza. Upstairs there was an arcade that included an old-fashioned slot car track. The manager of the place
recognized Harpy from Culhane's description but had told them
he hadn't been in for a week or more.

Back on the hunt, where Sunset Place ended at Hoover, Acosta
took a right, then swing down Eighth at Culhane's suggestion.

"Four-L-thirteen to Four-W-fifty, come in," the radio crackled.
Acosta had to check himself from involuntarily goosing the gas
pedal.

Culhane caught the movement and smiled slightly. "Control, W-
fifty, over," he replied into the mic.

"Suspect Harpy just entered Galvanez Check-cashing on Carondelet near seventh in the company of another male Hispanic."

"Fifty to Thirteen, I know where it is."

"Thirteen to Fifty, what's your location?"

"Two minutes, tops, Thirteen."

"Fifty, in one minute I'm going down the side—there's an entrance with a peephole on it. A couple of the employees know me
and I should be able to gain entrance."

"We'll be in front, Thirteen, roger." He replaced the detachable
unit as Acosta stepped on it. Soon they were in front of the check-
cashing place as Harpy and another Crazy Nine were exiting the es-
tablishment on the run. The rookie cranked the wheel hard and
brought the vehicle to a stop halfway on the sidewalk and inches
from a telephone pole.

"I'll get Harpy," Acosta yelled, wrenching the key out of the ignition.

"We're on his partner." Culhane was already on the sidewalk and
joining the uniformed officer, Jayford Reynaux, the one who had
radioed them. The two gangbangers had split in opposite directions on the screech of the Impala's tires.

Please let this be nothing complicated, Acosta prayed as he took off.

The sun was bright, he could see clearly, and *please, God, don't let this young fool reach for his waistband.* Acosta ran after Harpy, who was heading north on Carondelet. He assumed the gang member would break right at an angle across Seventh and try to lose him in MacArthur Park.

Named for the famous general, the large park, bifurcated by Wilshire Boulevard was Crazy Nines territory save for the southwestern corner, which the Maratruchas claimed. There'd been several shoot-outs between the two rival gangs until the Baja cartel stepped in and engineered a truce. Now it was relatively safe for workers in the shops along Seventh or Alvarado to come and sit on the grass and enjoy their lunch. Even a few of the gang members whom fatherhood had snuck up on occasionally brought their toddlers to the lake there to feed the ducks.

The bucolic scene of the fowls quacking amiably evaporated in the cop's head as he, too, jetted across Seventh, which was wide down this way. A Volkswagen Beetle smoked its back tires as the driver halted to avoid creaming Harpy. But as he crossed the double yellow in the middle of the street, an Isuzu with oxidizing paint, going west, also had to come abruptly to a stop. But this vehicle was going fast enough that Harpy collided with the front quarter panel.

The lanky cholo was stunned but unhurt and sliding toward the front of the vehicle when Acosta leaped. Like Warren Sapp, he brought his quarry down. They landed roughly on the asphalt, Acosta on top of Harpy's back.

"Bitch!" the Crazy Nine wailed.

"Hey, you two all right?" a woman's voice asked.

Acosta had his nightstick in its sheath and wasn't inclined to use it now. After the shooting last week, he didn't want anything suggesting he had overreacted.

"Help me, help me, nice lady," Harpy pleaded as the two wrestled. He tried to bite Acosta on the wrist, and the cop punched him.

"You're not hurting him are you, Officer?"

"No, I'm trying to give him a gum massage, lady, please."

She was the driver of the Isuzu. Acosta was on a knee, and Harpy on his back. The banger tried to sit up, and the cop drove an elbow into his sternum, knocking the wind out of him.

"Was that necessary?" the driver went on. "Aren't you trained better than that?"

Shut the fuck up, he wished silently. He got up, pulling the coughing Harpy with him. He slammed him against the hood of the Isuzu.

"Hey, be careful," she advised. "It was washed yesterday."

"This will just take a moment ma'am." He got the cuffs on Harpy. This was how it was supposed to be: a good, clean bust. Less than twelve hours ago he'd been cleared by the shooting team, though he knew that McGuire was still looking into the incident. Why the hell had he let Culhane use that throwaway? He should have said something. But he was in it now, and what could he do?

He tugged on his prisoner. "Thanks for stopping him."

She was about his age, twenty-five or -six, blond, and pretty though on the chubby side. Her sunglasses were crooked on her face, and she was setting him straight, taking in Acosta. "You need me for a witness or something?"

"Who knows?"

Harpy made an inarticulate sound.

After they exchanged cards, Acosta marched his prisoner back to the check-cashing place.

"I like 'em big like that, too," Harpy volunteered cheerfully. "Gives you more to hang on to." He made a motion of grinding his hips.

"Quiet." He liked them like that, too, but no sense telling this shithead.

Reaching the spot, Culhane and the uniform had already captured their man. He was sitting, head down, in the back of the patrol car—a Caprice Classic with the police interceptor package for a mill. Culhane nodded quickly at Acosta's success. The younger cop got the back door of the cruiser open and noted the other prisoner's profile. There was a bruise on his cheek, and a gash under his eye.

"Usual," Harpy snorted.

Acosta got him secured and closed the door. Then he stepped close to Culhane. "He give you some static?"

"Yep," he said tersely. "Me and Reynaux had to subdue him."

"Call an R.A.?"

"Said he didn't want one."

"Did he, now?"

Culhane looked off in the middle distance, as if gathering himself to talk with an obstreperous student. "You know how these locos are, Double A. They have to show how tough they are when their audience is around."

Gathered on the street people watched them from in front of the check-cashing place, the open windows of the *Noticería* office above that, and the doorway of the Red Scorpion Bar, where cumbia music poured forth. Next to the bar was an electronic-gadgets store. Out of the massive speakers the store had placed on the sidewalk, a Los Tigres Del Norte number played without distortion.

"Uh-huh," was all Acosta could give it.

"Let's get them over to the station," Culhane said.

"You and Reynaux gonna interrogate Harpy?" Acosta hadn't moved yet.

Culhane had opened the passenger door but stopped. "Why don't you? Hell, you can ask either one of them anything you want." He flashed a bright smile and got into the car.

Driving back to Temple Division, Acosta made a right on Rampart Boulevard heading north off Third. He knew it was a challenge from Culhane. Would he be an asshole and ask Harpy's homey had he been beaten after giving up? Or would he only ask both of them the questions pertinent to the Villa case, thus giving the signal he wasn't interested in any other kind of conversation?

Acosta was still debating what to do by the time he pulled into the station's parking lot.

CHAPTER 7

"Oh, man, what's her name? I need to know her name," Will Aarons, host of the F/X cable show *Stuff* cracked. The audience roared in approval. "Can somebody please get me this honey's number, 'cause I need a submariner like her quick." Again there was more laughter and a sprinkling of applause. On the large screen behind Aarons's set, designed to look like a bachelor swing pad circa the seventies, the muscular prostitute who called herself Hyacinth was bobbing her head between the legs belonging to Jayford Reynaux.

"See, I always wanted to be a fireman when I was a kid, but obviously the LAPD has got all the perks. I mean, some serious oral benefits—damn!" Aarons cracked up along with the rest of the audience.

There was scratchy sound, and Reynaux could be heard through his moaning, saying, "Oh, Gawd, I love it when you do that, baby."

Aarons did a silent bigmouthed laugh as the camera cut back to him for a take.

On screen, Hyacinth was now back on her feet, grabbing Reynaux's very rigid member and easing herself down on him. The lopsided angle provided by the hidden camera enhanced the lurid quality of the homemade porn. And their dialogue was even cornier.

Hyacinth said, "Thanks for the ride, Officer."

"We're here to serve, ma'am," Reynaux responded through his grunting.

The cinema's salacious tape had surfaced, two days prior to its re-airing on *Stuff*, in an only slightly less goofy venue than the pop culture show. The segment had been part of the ABC news program *Undercover*. Cynthia McFadden and John Quiñones sat at a raised horseshoe-shaped table, their attire and setting black and beige and muted. McFadden, wearing a particularly muted green eye shadow, introduced the tape with a warning that this was rough fare.

Quiñones intoned that the following had come into their possession through a circuitous route, and though some may find it offensive, it was important that this sex on duty by a uniformed cop be viewed.

"Indeed, this is not simply a matter of a policeman while on the clock stopping by his girlfriend's apartment to be intimate," McFadden added, interlacing her fingers on the desktop. "As you will see in the opening scene, and as will become evident in what these two talk about, this is a complicated matter. That as the woman who's obviously a prostitute services him, after smoking crack allegedly supplied by the officer, he asks her questions about an ongoing case. So here we have the Los Angeles Police Department, already rocked by various scandals, once again in the eye of the storm."

Cut to Quiñones. "But rebuild for better or into something that still has officers who can't tell right from wrong?" And he could barely contain the smirk forming on his face as the tape of Reynaux and Hyacinth played on millions of TVs across the nation.

The damning first scene popped on, the two of them in the bedroom of the Playpen. McFadden, in her voice-over, mentioned that the location of the duo's coupling remained unidentified.

Reynaux's hand rubbed Hyacinth's packed backside, and as they pressed together, she asked in a little girl's voice, "Can I have some candy, Daddy?"

Reynaux laughed and told her, "Maybe."

"Can I see?"

"Sure you can."

Hyacinth was sucking her thumb and used her free hand to reach into Reynaux's pockets. She took out a packet of rock cocaine. "You're so sweet," she said. Reynaux unbuckled his gun belt, and she walked toward the camera.

"The woman you're seeing in this video," McFadden continued," was willingly carrying a surveillance camera and mic—a nanny cam, if you will—in her large messenger-style purse."

There was a jumble of the picture as Hyacinth lifted her purse to take something out of it. She then placed the bag back in position on the nightstand, giving the disguised lens an unobstructed view of the bed and a reclining Reynaux. She lit the crack pipe she'd removed from her purse, and inhaled deeply. The narcotic fumes escaped her nostrils as she handed the pipe to Reynaux. Thereafter, given this was a network show, the sex scenes were partially obscured by pixelation. The overnight ratings for *Undercover* were good. And for *Stuff*, which could show the tape unexpurgated, the ratings were spectacular.

The effect of the initial broadcast was immediate. The morning after the tape aired, Mayor Fergadis held a press conference at ten in the hallway linking City Hall with City Hall East. He used his fist to pound the lectern with the city seal on it. "I can promise you that Chief Hidalgo has assured my office that this is an isolated incident, and that the officer who's been identified in the tape will be dealt with accordingly. But let me reemphasize that this is not"—and he thudded again against the podium—"a replay of the past. There will be no obfuscation nor any stonewalling. We will handle this rogue officer and any others in the Department who had any hint of this activity going on."

The mayor finished and, with his flak-catcher Gordon DeMarco by his side, took questions from the gathered media.

"Has this Officer Jay Reynaux been suspended?" A woman from KCAL blared above the din.

DeMarco leaned over to Fergadis's ear to whisper something to him, and then the mayor answered. "The process is, he's been placed on administrative leave pending an investigation by the inspector general's office."

"The same office you sought to understaff?" another journalist asked.

Fergadis clamped his jaw, counted a quick three in his head, and answered coolly and efficiently, as DeMarco had rehearsed him. After another ten minutes of grilling, the press conference was over and Fergadis and DeMarco retreated to the mayor's inner office.

"That fucking devious bitch," Fergadis fumed, tossing his prepared remarks across his desk. "McGuire wired that broad up and sat back and let the fun unfold. I'm sure of it."

"Reynaux, not surprisingly, isn't saying anything." DeMarco plucked two Calistoga lemonade coolers from the minifridge. "The goddamn Police Protective League has given him Glassman as his lawyer."

"Figures," Fergadis snorted, taking one of the offered bottles and twisting off the cap. "That bastard will try to convince a jury that his client was suffering from delayed stress and sleepwalked his way through his blow job."

He sipped some of the cooler and sat heavily in his chair. "I can just see the mailers she's going to put out. Goddamn grainy shot of that asshole with his dick in her hands and the words, 'This happened on Mayor Fergadis's watch.' Fuck."

"The more you can turn up the heat on the chief, the better it will look in the eyes of the electorate." DeMarco slipped off his Prada coat and perched on the arm of the couch in the office. "This has to lay squarely at his doorstep."

Fergadis was leaning back. "But I'm the one that endorsed his selection by the commission."

"And gave lukewarm support when the council affirmed his appointment. As I recall, the night his appointment was announced, you said that you were happy that the process had been successful, but there was still work to do to restore a-hundred-and-ten-percent confidence in and among our men and women on the front lines."

"You should—you wrote those words." Fergadis tipped the bottle in the other man's direction.

"My point is," DeMarco said, "that gives us plenty of wiggle room as the pressure increases." He finally had some of his sparkling juice. "Do we know who this whore is in the tape?"

"Let's call Connie and ask her," Fergadis said, smiling for the first time. "Maybe we can catch her in a lie, then really barbecue her self-righteous ass on the evening news."

"I shall make the appropriate inquiries," DeMarco replied.

"I bet," Fergadis began, "if she's got half a brain, the whore will make like Casper and not be on anybody's radar."

"I don't know, this is her fifteen minutes of fame. *Playboy* or somebody is going to offer her big money to do a spread—to use the term in a technical sense—and I'm sure all kinds of producers are running around right now to find her and get her to do an interview."

"And maybe TRASH puts the squeeze on her. Culhane, the prick that wears those ostrich-skin boots, is friends with Reynaux."

"Interesting," DeMarco allowed, nodding his head. "All the more reason we need to get a line on this woman fast—force McGuire to cough her up."

"Then get to it."

DeMarco reached for his cell phone in his inner pocket. "On it." He walked as he talked and left the office.

Fergadis waited a beat, then opened the bottom drawer of his desk, the one he kept locked. Extracting his one lone pack, he shook loose a Camel, unfiltered and unadulterated, and lit that guilty pleasure, drawing the fumes deep in his chest before exhaling. His office windows were, at his direction after the retrofitting of City Hall, fitted with windows that opened. He had the top panel canted outward, and consciously stood near it so the smell was not too blatant. How would it look, particularly at a time like this, for the mayor of the great and populous City of Los Angeles to get busted for illegally smoking indoors?

"Politics," he grumbled, sending smoke into the morning breeze.

CHAPTER 8

"**F**ree cell phone, free cell phone," Linda Delarocha announced, mimicking with her thumb and little finger like she was making a call.

"Your number on speed-dial in that celly, sweet thing?" one tall young man in sagging jeans asked as he strolled past with his boys.

"You wish," Delarocha remarked, and resumed her efforts to lure potential customers into the Radio Shack in the Baldwin Hills Mall on Crenshaw. The store was having a special sale on a service package in conjunction with Verizon phone service, and the employees could get a 5 percent cut for anybody they signed up. She'd gotten more men flirting and trying to "push up on them digits, girl," than those signing up, but that's why this was a shitty job. Like most jobs were, as far as she could tell.

An old man with stained dentures pestered her about whether this deal ensured that he could call his sister in Kansas City anytime, anywhere, for ten cents a minute. She could feel the headache start in her right temple. Fortunately, the pensioner shuffled inside, and the manager, Jim Morris, got him "enrolled," as he liked to refer to the process.

But the headache kicked in again as three chumps she could do without walked up.

"Look who it is, Chavo."

"Is that her? Naw, I thought she was livin' out there in the sub-urbs with her porker boyfriend, Prick Santián."

"Yeah, that's right, the third one piped in, a beefy individual in khakis and a black cutoff sweatshirt. "She got to be the maid and clean up his crib and suck his dick." The three Crazy Nines laughed loudly, Chavo slurping on a drink from Orange Julius.

"Why don't you broke mothafuckahs roll on out of here, be-cause you ain't doing nothing but taking up space."

"When the last time you seen your old man, Linda?" the middle one, lanky with a wispy mustache, asked unpleasantly. "I mean the father of your baby, you know?"

"I know who the fuck you mean, moron."

"Talking all big like you something," he said, getting in her face. "You better show some respect, eh? Like the respect you should be showing Hector while he's down." He glowered at her with red-rimmed eyes.

Delarocha put her hands on her hips. "Like the respect he showed me, Flaco, by knocking me around and putting my head into the refrigerator door? Or threatening to stomp Frankie for ru-ining his life when he was high and shit?"

"You bitches need to be put in check some time, that's all," Flaco said dismissively. "But he's loyal, for the cause, you understand. Something you ought to learn from, understand?" He poked her hard on the breastbone.

She slapped his hand away. "What I understand is, you're an idiot."

"Problem, Linda?" Morris, an earnest young man with fashion-able spectacles, had stepped out into the mall's thoroughfare. Without waiting for an answer, he went on. "Why don't you fellas move along and let Linda get back to her job?"

"Who the fuck are you?" Chavo shook his drink cup at the man-ager.

"Somebody who's going to get security on you, fool."

"I got you, fool." Chavo threw down the cup, the top popping off and the ice sliding across the slick floor.

"Leave, stupid," Delarocha hollered.

A security guard had already noticed the escalation of the vol-ume in front of the Radio Shack and had radioed her partners. Four were now walking fast toward the grouping. The service they worked for outfitted them with trooper-style Smokey hats, and with their heads tilted down, they looked like models of UFOs moving through shoppers in tight formation.

"Hoota," one of them warned.

"Fakes," Chavo said, his mad-on focused on Morris.

"They can still arrest your stupid asses," Delarocha reminded them.

The guards had arrived. "Need a hand, Jim?" the woman who was a sergeant asked. Her hand was on the Taser Velcroed to her belt. She'd been eager to try it since seeing what it did to malcontents on the training video.

"Gentlemen?" Morris said.

People started to gather to watch. Flaco responded, "I'll make sure to tell Hector you've been thinking about him." He turned, and the other two took the cue and followed.

"Fuck you, too." She hoped she was long gone from the neighborhood by the time Hector Reynoso got out of Mule Creek. Long gone.

The security guards escorted the Crazy Nines from the premises.

"I got dudes I used to go to school with at Dorsey like to drop by and fuck with me, too," Morris said by way of commiserating.

"Thanks, Jim."

She got one more sign-up before her quitting time at 5:30. Out in the parking lot on the second tier, she stood by the used Civic Santián had given her the money to buy. As she watched some people enter the Magic Johnson Theater to catch a flick, she dialed her mother on her cell.

"What's going on?" She could hear music in the background after the line connected.

"Just a couple of my girlfriends from school over, that's all," her mother answered.

"Frankie asleep?"

"He's bouncing in his walker, having a good time with us."

"You ain't smoking dope around him, are you, Mom? That's not good for babies to be breathing in that shit." Her mother was so immature.

"You don't need to get that tone. I know better than that. We hit the blunt on the back porch landing."

"God. I'm on my way home."

"Stop and get some chips and salsa, 'kay? And some beer."

At their home, Linda was introduced to her mother's friends Lettie and Sara, whom she'd heard about previously since her mom loved to gossip. Sara was in her mid-thirties and was taking construction courses at Trade Tech.

Lettie was older—older, in fact, than her mother—but dressed younger in a short skirt and hoop earrings. She was holding on to the last illusion of youth. She was divorced and on stress leave from a county job. She didn't seem to know what she wanted to do with her life. At the moment she was taking a few fashion design courses, but not with much enthusiasm.

"Your son is a cutie," Lettie remarked, nibbling on a freshly dipped Dorito.

"Yeah, he is," Linda Delarocha smiled. Frankie was now asleep in his walker, having propelled it into a corner of the living room. His chin was on his chest, and he gurgled softly.

Sara said, "You know, they're probably going to open up the apprenticeship program; you ought to think about getting in it."

She had a brother who worked for the international construction firm SubbaKhan. And SubbaKhan was on tap to erect the new football stadium, and he could secure her a laborer's slot if she completed the requisite classes.

"Me?" Linda said, shaking her head. "I can't hammer a nail."

"You can learn. And don't making twenty-five to thirty an hour sound better than that chump change you getting now?"

"Of course, but shit, you got all those men making fun of you, staring at you."

"So," Lettie put in, "What's wrong with that? The staring part, you know?"

"Oh, please," Lucía Delarocha chortled. "You not that hard up for a man, are you, girl?"

"Nothing wrong with men."

"Or women." Sara winked.

They all stared at her.

"I go both ways, if you really want to know."

"See, that's why I can't be in no construction," Linda said. "I can't have everybody thinking I'm a dyke—damn!"

Sara made a V with her fingers in front of her mouth and wagged her tongue through it. "You don't know what you're missing."

"Oh, you nasty girl," Lucía Delarocha laughed.

"That's right."

They all cracked up. They munched some more and drank some more and turned the TV on.

"Look at that," Lettie said, pointing at the screen. On it a news copter was broadcasting yet another live police car chase along one of the Southland's flexuous freeways. This newest version was a late-model Ford pickup doing its best to stay ahead of three Highway Patrol cruisers. "Some fool probably held up an In-N-Out, and now thinks he's going to get away. Like, where's he going to go?"

"Stupid," Sara said, shaking her head in disgust as she rolled another blunt in a vanilla-flavored wrap. She finished, then asked, "Who wants a little?" She held up the finished blunt.

"I'll partake," Lucía Delarocha said.

"Be cool, Mom."

"I've been smoking ya-yo since before you were born, girl."

"That's what I'm talkin' about."

Frankie, who was awake again, started crying, and his youngish grandmother reached for him where he'd scooted in front of the sofa. On the TV, the pickup was blowing sparks out of the rear fender, riding on its rims. The Highway Patrol personnel had laid down some road spikes and had partially disabled the vehicle.

Lucía Delarocha made funny faces at her grandson, but he wasn't having any of it. His mother reached for him and put him to her shoulder.

"He probably needs a change, Mom." She cooed soothing sounds at him, walking toward the bedroom.

The older Delarocha and Lettie went out on the back landing to enjoy their blunt.

"I don't know, Lucía," Lettie said after imbibing some narcotic, "this school thing sucks, you know?"

"Yeah, but what choice neighborhood girls like us got? You don't know all the bullshit jobs I've worked." She took the offered marijuana and had a toke.

Her friend leaned in close. "Hook it up with the Nines, *¿que no?*"

In the bedroom off the back porch, Linda Delarocha threw out her son's messed Huggies and got some wipes out. The voices of the two women floated in through the window with its sash partially raised.

Out on the back landing Lucía Delarocha said, "Hook what up?"

"My cousin Nino. He runs the Bella Donna nightclub down in TJ for the cartel. He said they can use me in this shit the hoota's been sniffing around here about. He's got it wired."

"Twin Towers is full of fools who had it wired, Lettie."

"This shit is real, the other woman continued. She puffed more on the blunt.

Linda Delarocha got her son cleaned and happy. She crinkled her nose and tickled him. He kicked his legs and giggled. She got the new ready-made diaper on him.

Lettie was still talking. "Nino said the Nines are finalizing business with the Del Fuego brothers and some East Coast gangsters. Said that they've been buying up businesses and local city councils all over Southeast L.A."

"And what you gonna do, Lettie, be one of their hoes?" Lucía asked, the doubt evident in her tone.

"I got A's and B's in math at Roosevelt," she proudly said. "Nino said they can use someone with my skills." She coughed harshly.

Linda Delarocha returned to the front room carrying Frankie. She sat next to Sara on the couch. Her mother and Lettie came back in shortly afterward.

"Shit," Lettie retorted, "I know what I'm talking about. I'm going to get a split-level in Montebello before I'm too old to enjoy it."

"Uh-huh. How's my baby doing?" The grandmother took the baby and swayed with him cradled in her arms. On the TV set, the pickup had slammed into a sound wall. The desperado was on his stomach, handcuffed on the ground as the cops completed his arrest.

Sara yawned and stretched. The chase on Fox TV over, the scene had switched back to the studio, where the newscaster, an aging blond surfer named Kelly Drier, announced an upcoming debate between the mayor and the woman perceived to be his only viable contender, Assistant DA Constance McGuire.

"Who wants pizza?" Lettie asked, her munchies full on.

The following morning Santián was pouring coffee in his breakfast nook while his wife, Nicole Scott, did their daughter's hair.

"When can I drink coffee?" Monica, the eleven-year-old, asked, pumping her legs as she sat on the stool at the counter.

"It'll make you blacker, short stack." Her father chuckled as he poured milk into his cup and swished the mixture around.

Santián's wife loudly kissed the little girl on the forehead. "You're just too sweet like you are, honey. Don't listen to your ol' chucklehead daddy."

On the top of the fold of the *Times*'s California section was an article about Reynaux and the prostitute. Santián sipped and scanned the piece lying on the kitchen table.

"He's been over here for your little clubhouse barbecues." Nicole elicited a yelp from her daughter as she tightened her braid.

"You sound like McGuire—guilt by association. He's not a member of the squad."

"Just observing," she said none too innocently. "You want Creme of Wheat or Rice Chex?" she asked her daughter.

"Creme of Wheat. Daddy, can I be a cop like you?"

"You can be anything you want to be. Last week it was a doctor."

"That's a good choice," Nicole said, getting the cereal ready. "Helping people get better is a good thing."

"Daddy helps people."

"Doggone skippy, I do." He bonked Monica lightly on the end of her nose with the tip of his finger.

"You've got plenty of time to figure out what you want to do, sweetie. You just make sure you keep getting good grades so you can go to college and be able to make a choice about what you want." She put the bowl of ingredients in the microwave. "Me and your papa didn't." She tapped the keypad, and the machine binged.

"We have a big house."

"We both work hard," Santián said, eyeing his wife over the rim of his cup. "But that's not what counts, Monica. You want to do something where you feel . . . alive, you know?"

She frowned. "No."

Santián got a perplexing look on his face. At a loss for words, he said, "Now who's a chucklehead?" He put down his cup and tickled his daughter, to her delight.

The microwave bleeped, and Nicole opened it to stir the food.

Santáin had his arms encircling his daughter. Standing over her, he noted the time on his Baum & Mercier. "Shouldn't His Lordship be rising about now? That bus gets down here in about twenty, don't it?"

His wife said, "I think you should have the honor of getting him up since this is the first time in two weeks you've been home this time of the morning."

"It hasn't been two weeks," he mumbled, heading out of the kitchen. He went up the stairs to his son Curtis's room. Of course the door was locked. Santián kept a key in their bedroom, but he chose the more audacious route.

"Yo, let's hit it!" he bellowed, rattling the door with the flat of his fist. "Get up, rise and fuckin' shine." There was no response save the not-so-quiet lyrics of the music his son downloaded every night from the Internet. Every other word seemed to be "fuck this," or "bitch that."

Santián knocked again "Come on, Curtis, time to join the world." There was an unintelligible response from inside the room. Once more his father rapped on the door. "Aw, don't you miss us?"

"Hell, no," was the answer.

"Now, that's not pleasant."

"I'm up."

"No, you ain't. Get up."

There was a growl, then the rustle and creak of his body on the bed.

"Open up." Santián rattled the knob.

"I'm naked."

"You beatin' off?"

"Dad!" his son yelled, then unlocked the door. "Be cool." He was dressed in SpongeBob SquarePants boxers and an athletic-style undershirt.

"Let a brother in," he said, without waiting for a response, stepping past his son. On the computer some woman was moaning lustfully while a flute played. Santián turned the volume off.

"Hey, I need my tunes in the morning."

"You need to wash your funky ass and clean this shit up." He kicked at one of the numerous heaps of clothing littering the floor. The smell in the room was a combination of stale maleness and remnants of incense. Santián wondered if the latter was to hide the stench of marijuana. Looked like he'd have to toss the joint when his son wasn't home. And the good thing about it being so sloppy was, his son would never notice.

"What time is it?" Curtis Santián was already six-one and muscular. On the dresser his dad had bought for him ten years ago at Goodwill were trophies attesting to his lettering in basketball and football. He wasn't the best, but he was a starter at Ben Franklin High in the San Fernando Valley.

"What?" his son said, digging at sleep in the corner of his eye, aware that his dad was staring at him.

"Nothing, man, get ready; I'll drop you off."

"Yeah? Can we stop at Yum Yum so I can get my grub on?"

"Just get dressed. And put a belt on, so your middle-class butt ain't saggin' and pretending like you from a set." He turned to leave.

"When you gonna get me a car?"

"You gotta be eighteen until you get your full license, fool."

"I know," he said, stooping and darting his hand through his piles of clothes, like an archaeologist on the hunt for old bones. "But if you started saving now, then you could get it for me when I'm a junior this fall. You can sign a paper that lets me drive it to and from school."

"I could sign a lot of things, Sonny Jim, but—"

"I know," his son said, cutting him off, "grades, grades, grades."

"Sure, you right," and he went back downstairs. Twenty-three minutes later, the two were in the Malibu heading out of Simi Valley on the 18 Freeway.

"You mind?" His son was already punching in a music station on the after-market digital radio.

"I do, Santián answered, adjusting the rearview mirror as he drove. "Put the news back on so you can learn something about the world."

His son made a sound but finally switched back to KNX on the AM dial. "This is just the weather," he complained, grimacing at the dash.

"Relax," Santián said, downshifting as they hit a pocket of traffic. "You need to turn that cacophony off now and then and don't be in such a goddamn hurry all the goddamn time."

"Right."

Santián could hear the eyes rolling in his son's sockets. There was an announcement on KNX informing the audience that they would broadcast live the debate between Mayor Fergadis and candidate Constance McGuire.

"I can't miss that," Santián said, chuckling softly. "They should just go on Celebrity Boxing and get it over with."

"She's the one out to get you, isn't she?"

"You do keep up."

"It's hard not to, when everybody knows who your father is." A combination of resentment and pride lay behind those words.

"It gets to you, huh?"

His son didn't answer immediately, gazing out the window at the other cars. "Some of them say we live in a mansion 'cause you and Cheese and the rest have ripped off all this money from the gangsters in the hood. That you sell dope out of the back of the squad car, shit like that."

"All of them say that?"

"No, not all."

"What do you think?"

Curtis Santián laughed nervously. "I don't know."

"Yes, you do."

His son looked evenly at him as they drove along. "Did you and Cheese bury a man behind a chrome-plating place in North Hollywood? Where he used to work summers when he was in high school."

"What?"

"He was supposed to be this member of the Del Feugos and y'all were supposed to have some kind of falling-out with him."

"Think about that," Santián said, grinning. "If I had done that, would I be walking around now? You know the Del Fuegos don't play."

His son shrugged his wide shoulders. "I'm just telling you what goes around."

"But what do you say? Think your old man is as bent as all that?"

"Nobody's any this or that."

"Now you sounding like Cheese with those philosophy books Madeleine's got him reading."

"You mean like situational ethics?"

"That means you do what you need to do to survive."

"Not exactly," his son said. "Joseph Fletcher, a religious guy, came up with it as about the greater good, not like it's been used to excuse doing wrong."

"Ah-ha, Professor. You mean if you're the captain and you have to order a few overboard in the lifeboat so it doesn't sink, to save the others."

"Yeah, you gotta do a little evil to do the right thing."

Santián considered a comment.

His son finally asked, "Is that you, Pop?"

Santián was contemplative as he guided the Malibu off the 18 and onto the 134. "I grew up in the Heights; I wasn't hardly anybody's idea of a model schoolboy."

Curtis Santián was nodding his head. "Grandma told me."

"Yeah, and she got tired plenty of times yelling at me, trying to make me see the left from the right after the old man skipped out on us."

"So whatever you do to get out or get over is cool?"

"I'm not saying that." I am saying that you use what's at your disposal to achieve your objectives, your goal." He tapped his chest with his blunt fingers. "But it's gotta come from the heart, see? It ain't about money or pussy, 'cause both of those things will make you lose sight of the shit you better know about. It's about why you get up every morning."

"Damn, Pop!"

"Hey, you ain't no kid but you just ain't full grown yet, though I know you think you are. I've been where you're walking, youngster." He exited the freeway and got on Chandler to swing by the doughnut shop. "You want to know about a man's world—what a man has to do to make things safe, make them right—then this is what I'm telling you."

"You ain't feelin' guilty about anything, are you, Pop?"

Santián caught his own off-kilter smile in the rearview. "You breathe, you're bound to collect some sins, Curtis. Otherwise, you haven't been living." They drove on, neither saying anything but each weighing his next words.

Curtis broke the silence. "So what are you saying? You have to be willing to do what it takes to what? Make the old neighborhood like it used to be?"

"It wasn't paradise when I was growing up in it," Santián shot back. "But why can't the Heights be like, you know, not a storybook, but clean, ordinary? A place where you can raise your kids and send them to the store without worrying about are they gonna get jumped into a gang or caught in a drive-by. Where your grandmother can be out on the porch talking with the other *viejas* and not have to see crack hoes out on the stroll prancing around in front of their house. What's wrong with that? Ain't this America?"

His son looked at his father, wide-eyed. "Dang, Pop, maybe you ought to be running for mayor. All that gee-whiz."

"That's all right, smart-ass, you just hit those books as hard as you press on the court and you'll do all right."

"There's no guarantees; you told me that."

"I'm just talking about evening the odds in your favor, 'cause it's damned sure not a fair world." The Malibu turned into the tiny parking lot of the strip mall off Ventura Boulevard where the Yum Yum Donuts was located.

"So what's the answer?" Curtis Santián said as they stepped from the car.

Santián sucked at his teeth as they walked together toward the entrance. "You can't justify everything, because that means you'll eventually try to get away with anything." He held the door open for a woman in pink pumps. "But if you aren't willing to do what's needed, nothing will get done."

Curtis Santián frowned. "You're saying it depends on the situation."

"It depends on the man," Santián said, giving the teenager a light poke in the chest with his finger. The two went inside, his son smiling awkwardly.

Less than eight miles north and slightly west of where Santián and his son enjoyed warm French crullers and mediocre coffee, Judd Ahn and Barbara Reno were indulging in another pleasure.

"Baby, I love riding your dick. It fits me so good," she murmured as she straddled him in room 11 of the Starlight Motor Court, a clean and quiet two-story affair on Havenhurst.

"Not bad for an Asian," he cracked, fondling the stiff nipples of her large breasts.

She bent over and they kissed as he climaxed inside her. She eased off him, then slipped her head beneath the covers and licked his balls and took him in her mouth, making sure to make a lot of noise as she did it. Al Roker, on the muted *Today Show*, guffawed from the TV chained to the floor.

"Jesus, Barbara!" Ahn exclaimed.

"I love to have you in my mouth after you've been in my pussy, baby." She knew talking dirty turned him on, made him all the more willing to do what she wanted. She finished and got out of bed. Idly she noted, and not for the first time, the difference, in taste and texture, of Ahn's balls versus Red Dog's. There was something about a man who bathed regularly and wasn't always farting beer fumes.

Ahn propped himself on an elbow and turned the volume up on the set using the remote. "Your old man been doing like I ask him?"

"What, about the piece?" She sat on the toilet in the small bathroom, leaving the door ajar. "You know him, J. A.—he's like my nephew who's got ADD. You tell him to do X; he does Y and will swear later that's what you told him to do."

"This is important, Barbara. This ain't just bureaucratic bullshit. I need you to keep him on task—subtly, of course. His general distrust of everyone keeps him sharper than it seems."

"I know, I know: your boss wants a new job. And what do you get if she wins?"

"I'm not about working in City Hall."

"But you've thought about it." She flushed, washed up, and gargled with some water.

"Is that what you want?"

"Wouldn't nothing be wrong with a civil service job," she said. "Shuffling papers or spending my day Xeroxing this file and that. Give a little tail to my supervisor so I can get a raise." She got back into the bed, grinding against Ahn. "Have a pension to look forward to other than winding up in the old biker hags' home. Shit."

Ahn caressed her back. "I'm going to make sure you come out of this all right, Barbara. I want to get you away from the Vikings—you must know that."

Reno nuzzled his neck. "Will you, baby?"

He put her face between his hands. "I promise." They kissed passionately as a Mylanta commercial assured the viewers of easy and fast constipation relief.

Later, Ahn walked through the third-floor hallway of the Foltz criminal courts building in downtown Los Angeles. He'd just picked up a copy of the sentencing report from the clerk's office. It was a case involving a man he'd helped gather evidence against who'd smothered to death his twelve-year-old daughter, and he had a particular interest in seeing that the man was punished accordingly. Rounding a near corner was Phenias Washington, talking to a casually dressed woman who set off a bell in Ahn's head. Getting closer, it hit him why.

"Don't say a word without your lawyer present," Ahn joked, recognizing the Channel 5 reporter.

Christie Yamaguchi glared at the newcomer. "Mr Ahn, maybe you'll be more forthcoming than Mr. Washington here. It's fairly obvious it was you guys that got Norma Dietz, who goes by Hyacinth, to use that hidden camera to gather evidence against officers operating out of Temple Division."

"Oh, yeah?" He looked at Washington.

Washington said, "I was just telling her that I have no knowledge of Ms. Dietz being approached by our office or by us."

"What about Ms. McGuire? Why isn't she returning my calls?"

"Maybe she doesn't like your Q ratings," Ahn said.   .

"Maybe you ought to stop screwing around and answer my questions," she charged. "Where's Norma now? She's hasn't been at her apartment."

"That's not our concern, Ms. Yamaguchi," Ahn retorted.

"It will be if you want to bring Reynaux to court."

"Then that's when we'll worry about it," Washington said.

"Your lack of cooperation won't play well on the nightly news."

Ahn said, "We can't tell you what we don't know. Can't you understand that?"

"I know when I'm being stonewalled."

"Well, Ms. Yamaguchi," Ahn said, "the First Amendment and the laxness of the FCC allows you so-called reporters to make all manner of unsubstantiated allegations."

"That's your statement for the record?"

"Take it as you wish. Come on, Phenias, we've got the people's business to attend to."

"Like hell," she blared as the two walked away. "This isn't going away, you know."

Out of sight of her, the two stopped to talk.

"Connie's stunt could bite us in the ass," Ahn said, leveling his colleague a stern look.

"Let's not get carried away here, Judd. She didn't do anything illegal. It's just politics. It'll blow over."

"That's my point, Phenias. As the race gets hotter, she's going to listen to us a lot less, and to that Pastor a lot more."

"I know campaigning will take her away from her duties to some extent, but that's to be expected. I don't see that as drastic. If TRASH is to be sacrificed on the altar of the almighty vote, than that's not so bad, is it?"

"I just don't want her ambitions getting her so blinded she rationalizes that if need be we can be fed to the shredder of the press."

"You're being melodramatic, aren't you, Judd? Connie's always been an overachiever, but I've never found her to sacrifice integrity for her goals."

"Maybe the prize has never been big enough."

"If I didn't know better, I'd say you were a cynic."

"Or a realist," Ahn retorted. The two walked off together, continuing their conversation.

A short walk from the courts, at First and Alameda, Cheese Cortese and Madeleine Jirac were having lunch at the Señor Fish restaurant. On the north side of First was the sweeping facade of the Japanese American Cultural Center.

"Are you serious, Bruno?" She smiled while chewing her grilled Chilean sea bass.

"Why not? This style is always good for laughs and people remembering who you are." His index finger tapped the postcard that was a reproduction of a 1940s photo. "What do you call this again? Ono something?"

"Onomatopoetic. But it's not my word; it was in that book you found on my shelf, *A Short History of Los Angeles,* and it's not accurate how he defined the term. It really means the formation of a word, say, like *boom,* by imitating the sound of what is being referred to. More accurately, it is referred to as vernacular architecture."

"I like his better, a building that looks like what they sell or do. Like that giant tamale for a joint that sells tamales, or a giant hot dog." He gave a self-satisfied nod. "That's what I want for my place," he said. The image under his fingertips was a tint of a building done up like an overgrown beer keg, complete with spigot on the roof leaking cloudy suds.

There were steps and a door slotted in the bottom of the keg, and a small window on either side. Naturally, the name "The Keg" was suspended in neon in one of the windows.

"Of course, my version will have the keg on top of some books stacked at angles, you know?"

"You're goofy but sweet." She leaned over and gave him a kiss. As she pulled back, the serious look on her face was revealed. "What about this Reynaux business?"

"Baby, that's his lookout." He ate his catfish heartily. "They didn't catch me bending you over a table in the Playpen, your dress hiked up, doing you doggie-style, now, did they?" He smiled broadly.

"Don't change the subject," she whispered, "even though I enjoy it when we do it like that." She puckered her lips at him and said, "I'm not one of your partner's hoochies, Cheese."

"Don't I know."

"My point being"—she pointed the fork at him—"you can't take anything that happens at Temple lightly, playing it off like we're all suckers. The garbage men are not the Teflon cops, to coin a bad phrase."

"He knows what to do." Cortese swallowed, his eyes following three office workers who entered.

"I just want you to be careful, honey. As you would say, you better not get your dick caught in the wringer. You've got too much at stake."

He laughed. "I won't, sweetie." He adjusted his large frame on the chair and ate some more. "What I need you concentrating on is getting some of those geek freak students of yours to do up some plans of my dream bar and bookstore." The cell phone clipped to his belt hummed.

"That better not be some nineteen-year-old named Irma with big titties." She had more of her fish.

"That mouth," he tisk-tisked. He grabbed the instrument and squinted at the number on the screen. He then clicked it off and returned the device to his side.

"Running off?"

"Not me, I've got plenty of time. "Too bad you've got that after-noon class, huh?" His tongue lingered on the tines of his fork.

"My, my."

After saying good-bye to Jirac in the parking lot, Cortese turned off his cell phone for the third time it had hummed since their meal together. He should ignore it, but then again . . . Standing next to his Camaro, he punched in the number of the person who'd been calling him.

"What is it?"

"I want us to have a talk, just me and you, Cheese," Constance McGuire said.

"I'm not giving you shit about Reynaux, or even telling you how many letters there are in the alphabet, McGuire. You want to de-pose us, do it. You've tried it before."

"How long, Cheese? It's about nineteen months, isn't it? Nineteen until you hit twenty-five years and that sweet pension?"

"You better call your pals up at *20/20*, Connie. Maybe they can give you a job when you lose the mayor's race."

"I appreciate your concern, but really, you should be figuring out how you're going to hide that lease for the Playpen I'm going to find."

"Gotta go, slick; when I talk to you I always seem to feel the need to take a dump. Know what I mean?"

"You can't laugh this away, Cheese. Santián is going to sink you and your plans for that idyllic retirement in Montana."

"Go fuck yourself, McGuire."

"No, fuck *you*, my friend."

He stared at the instrument for several moments after she'd clicked off. She was playing with his head, worming into his brain. Even if—and it was a big if—even if Reynaux did give up the loca-tion of the Playpen, so what? DNA, sure, but there was a lot of traf-fic in the joint, and they did regularly have the sheets and bedding changed. If need be, they'd use bleach to scrub the place down.

Cortese got in his car and fired it up. It wasn't about the Playpen—that was just her opening move in this latest round; he knew that. The landlord of the apartment building was in debt to Santián for saving his daughter from being gang-raped by some wanna-be Nines who'd doped and slapped her around in a basement laundry room. The crime wasn't reported since he, Santián, and Ronk had adjudicated the rambunctious young men over by the old Taylor train yards in Glassel Park. And he was paid each month in cash, so, so much the better.

No, he mused, pulling onto Alameda heading south, the weakest link was that muscle-bound bitch, Hyacinth. He was about to call Santián on the cell, then reconsidered. Could be, the good counselor was tapping their phones. It was doubtful, but why press it if he didn't have to? Getting the phones scrambled wasn't that big a deal—they'd done it before through a hookup with an electronics geekazoid Big T knew. Time to be stepping lightly for a while, anyway. There were land mines ahead.

CHAPTER 9

The late-model Grand Am crested the dirt rise. Beneath the car, in a valley of metal, the stroke arms of automatic oil pumps rose and fell. It was if the end of the world had come, and only these machines remained as a testament to human consumption. The car was parked among some others, the engine off.

Big T Holton alighted from his vehicle, jamming his porkpie onto his nub of a head. His size fifteens splayed across loose gravel toward music lilting from a darkened structure that in a former life had housed county maintenance trucks and equipment.

Getting closer, he could distinguish the unmistakable blare of Fred Wesley's horn as the JBs cut it up on "Pass the Peas." He bobbed his head as he knocked on the metal door.

"Who is it?" a voice deeper than Shaq's asked from inside.

"Stop playin' and open this motherfuckin' door, man."

A bolt slid back, and a blue-lit cavern was revealed. The owner of the voice was a man in a wheelchair, his spindly legs encased in chaps and his expansive midsection encased in a fringe buckskin vest. A pump shotgun lay across his lap.

"You got the best hand," he said. The two knocked their fists together. The JBs bumped through the speakers.

"Slim Chance, you lookin' like a stud."

"Don't I?" The man wheeled back to allow Holton to come through.

Holton looked out over the people dancing to the beat. Mostly it was young folks, though he spotted some cats in his age range. Dudes on the wrong end of Father Time's measuring stick who were stepping out on the old lady or had recently been through a divorce. They still could move and groove and hoped against hope that they might catch some young, firm thing who might ignite lost memories in them at least for one night.

"Niggas love to be fucked up," he ruminated aloud.

"Aw, man, E parties are the best," Slim Chance said. None of that thug shit like on crack or back in the day fools trippin' out on PCP. Ecstasy is progress, Big T. It's peace and love, baby."

"That's what I've always liked about you, man—you see the good in everything."

"Don't I?"

Holton moved off, staying at the periphery of the partiers. He made his way to a set of stairs near one of three bars that had been set up in the hollowed-out building. Club Cognac was the happening scene among middle-class college-aged and twentysomething buppies. Given that the venue existed in a location that you had to know somebody to find, let alone get in, and the strict policy of no wave-cap wearing, OutKast-humming roughnecks rolling through kept it bourgeois with an outlaw veneer.

Because Club Cognac was really about one thing, and that was selling records. Sure, the DJs spun a mix of sounds from various labels, but the heavy rotation was on tunes from Silk Cut Records. And the label belonged to the club's owner.

The bartender, a large, pretty woman named Glenda, nodded at the cop as he gave a brief wave to her and ascended the stairs. Sitting on an upper tier of the steps was another man with another shotgun across his lap, the red dot of a burning cigarette glowing in his mouth.

"What it be?" the guard said.

"Horace."

Horace rose, taking the cigarette from his mouth, blowing smoke above Holton's head. His starlight vision goggles were off, suspended around his neck by their elastic band. "I told you Kidd would come up short, didn't I?"

"Please." Holton sniffed, taking the folded twenty out of his pocket and handing over the wager. "Sunday'll be different."

"Double up?" Horace asked hopefully.

"I look lucky, don't I?"

"No doubt." And he moved aside to let the big man through.

At a door painted lavender, Holton knocked and was told to enter. Inside the room with subdued lighting and an Ahmad Jamal piano number playing, there was a mood-indigo feel going. Sylvie "Silky" Richards, in a Donna Versace pantsuit, was pacing and talking on a cell phone. She was somewhere around fifty-plus but still had her shape and her looks. Her straight, long black hair was highlighted with reddish touches, and her omnipresent ivory-inlaid cigarette holder was clamped between her fingers. She'd quit smoking four years ago, but the holder was part of her persona. He shut the door to the soundproofed room.

"You just make sure my five points are covered," she said into the phone while also acknowledging Holton's presence. "Fuckin' Iranian fucks think they can fuck someone just 'cause it's a fuckin' habit with those people. I can read a motherfuckin' contract, Barry, and I goddamn well know that I better be getting my cut off the gross of this album and not the invisible net."

She listened, then said, "Okay, uh-huh . . . Gotta go, too, but let's talk by Friday. . . . Yeah, yeah . . . All right, bye." She clicked off and marched to her desk, where her laptop was open and its electronic dinging was telling her she had incoming mail. "What do you think?"

Holton had been looking at one of the framed posters on her wall of one of the acts Richards was producing. This was yet another trio of sweet young things with pouty, wet lips and flawless bronze skin, in feathers and leather. This group called themselves R-90, whatever the hell that referred to.

"These girls got pipes, or is it some whale of a chick who you keep hidden behind the curtain and they lip-sync to her?"

She was chewing on the cigarette holder in her mouth. "A little of both. It helps that their asses jiggle like sculpted Jell-O."

"I guess," Holton said, sitting opposite her. "You ain't doin' our business on that thing, are you?" He pointed at the laptop. "I know they got ways of digging up shit from the hard drive even after you think you dumped the information."

"They got erase programs, Big T."

"The only permanent erase is when you've stopped breathing, 'cause I don't believe in seances."

She smiled. "The answer is no," she tapped her forehead, "I keep all really important business where it belongs."

"Good," he managed. "So what you got?"

She pecked at her keyboard, then turned the laptop around for him to see the screen. She leaned back in her ergonomic chair and looked across at him. "Mercury, as you might suspect, is extended like the circus rubber man." On the screen he was viewing, Holton could see it was an article she'd called up from some archive. "This is from *Fast Company* magazine four months ago," she explained.

Holton had on his reading glasses, having pulled the screen closer. "They link him to the Del Fuegos and something called Escapade. Who's that?"

"Escapade Enterprises is a legitimate company headquartered in New Brunswick, New Jersey. They own copier outlets, building security services, and the El Taco Rojo chain."

"What the hell is that about?"

"Twenty-first-century diversification. You have sewer companies buying film studios—why not? Now the visible hand says it has no knowledge of the other, the invisible one." She sat forward and scrolled down the screen. "Here's a part with Tom Gardner, the CEO of El Taco Rojo, who swears that these rumors about Def Ritmo being beholden to gangsters doesn't have him worried. The record label passed their inspection, and their line of credit is solid."

Holton's finger impatiently tapped the screen. "But what good does that do me to know? I can get that from the *Wall Street Journal* or whatever."

Silky Richards laughed huskily. "You never ask anybody anything, Big T, without six reasons to Sunday behind it."

"Say what?" he said flatly.

"Negro, please. I know you. You want the lineup. You want to know who the players are, their strengths and weaknesses."

"So about this Escapade connection . . ."

"The real deal is that Escapade is a front, too, probably Red mafia."

"The Russian mob? An alliance or a power struggle?" Something got bright behind his eyes.

"More like a shotgun weddin'. The deal with Escapade is, while the Del Fuegos are directly involved in the businesses they buy into,

Escapade was created to be the corporate face of Russian capitalism." She looked as if there were really a cigarette in her holder, the way she held it in her mouth and sucked air through it.

"You're losing me here, Silky."

She set the holder aside, wetting her bottom lip. "There's a lot of intermingling of what used to be dudes in the KGB who didn't get absorbed into the new intelligence apparatuses. So naturally they used their skills at spying and intimidation for something."

"Extracurricular black market activities," Holton said.

"Right—take them and add the coming up of street gangsters who now had the chains of Big Brother Communism off; then it was on; it was all about the bling-bling, Russki-style."

Holton cracked his knuckles. "So Escapade is a money-laundering operation?"

"No, it's an investment group. Some of these boys have got smarts and used the profits from the underground shit, smuggling cigarettes, whores, what have you, and plowed that into things like Escapade—ventures that make high-risk loans or buy-ins—'cause at the end of the day, you damn sure won't be filing Chapter Eleven on their asses."

Holton smiled slowly. "Can you dig it?"

Silky Richards didn't say anything; she knew he'd put the pieces together.

"Okay, Mercury needs cash flow like a big dog needs his Alpo. I know the connection to the Del Fuegos was through that lawyer, Heckman. It has to figure she hooked him up with Escapade, too."

"That I don't know, but my educated guess is, they probably came to him. Unlike the Del Fuegos, who are on the list here in the States, the Escapade's crew are not wanted for anything. The music business has always been a magnet for the sharks, 'cause you can make money so many different ways—the manager's cut, the studio costs, fucking with royalty statements, and so on—and a lot of it goes unscrutinized."

He judiciously didn't mention that silky was known to have double- and triple-dipped on an artist's fees if they blinked. "Then Mercury has got to be very uptight about the Gargoyle hit. It could be a warning to him from either one of his partners that he better not fuck up."

"You're the detective. I'm just a lonely businesswoman trying to do the best she can."

"And maybe scoop up a few of those hot Def Ritmo artists should our boy August trip and not get up."

"The majority of accidents do happen close to home." She chewed on her cigarette holder.

Holton rose; now it was his turn to pace. Over by a mirror-and-marble wet bar, he looked down at his shoes, then back at her. "Mercury's got to be feeling froggish about now. He's worried about his alliances."

"And his company," Silky said.

Holton frowned. "A company that might be ripe for the plucking, I imagine."

Silky Richards said languidly, "I also imagine we have some tradin' to do, as my grandmother used to say. You're right, I sure could fill out my roster with a few prime selections. And if I could know when the hammer is going to drop on Mercury, well"—she spread her arms—"that could be a blessing."

"Granny use to say that, too?"

"She had a lot of foresight."

Holton ambled back toward her desk. "Then we better get to tradin'."

Silky Richards turned the laptop back around and began to work the keys again.

Holton bobbed his head slightly to the rhythmic tap-tapping of greed.

Afterward, he left Club Cognac, on the perimeter of Signal Hill, and took the 710 north then the 60 back to the 105. He went west toward the airport and got off at the Century Boulevard exit. He snaked around beneath the overhead tangle of crisscrossing freeways until he was on Ninety-eighth and Inglewood. On the northwest corner was a four-story brown-and-beige-colored box of an apartment building, devoid of style or character.

After parking and activating his LoJack, Holton went up a flight of concrete steps.

"Breezy," he said softly, knocking at the security screen door of apartment 5. The inner door opened, and the heavier door was unlocked. Holton stepped inside as a woman with wide hips in tight jeans walked back into the room. She had medium-length black hair filtered with gray, and a squat tumbler in one hand.

"I'm fine, dear; how are you?" Holton cracked, tossing his hat and coat onto a Barbara Barry Paris couch.

"Yeah, yeah," she said, waving her free hand listlessly in the air. She walked into the kitchen, and there were sounds of a cabinet opening and closing, glass scraping across tile, and ice clinking in the glass. She returned with a drink for Holton. She handed it to him silently.

"Thanks, baby."

Bressy Tabon was a middle-aged Filipina with oversized glasses and a generous mouth. "Whatever." She flopped onto the couch and glared at the big-screen TV in the corner. Joan Crawford and Eve Arden were doing some grocery shopping in "Mildred Pierce."

"What crawled up your butt?" He stood to the side of the couch, hand on his side, trying his drink.

Over her glass she took in the doings on the screen. The glass came away and she said, "I called you twice today and you didn't call me back."

"I was busy. Shit, when you're doing double at King-Drew do I bug you?"

She chewed on ice loudly. "Danny came around work and started with that shit of his, Big T."

"Shit." He stepped closer. "Honey, I'm sorry; you didn't say that in the message you left, so I just figured whatever it was, I'd take care of it when I saw you."

"You better listen to me," she said, "I'm not one of your little tricks you clowns go around poking in the hallways of the Heights then run off to compare rings around your dicks."

"Breeze, come on—I fucked up; I admit it. You can't find it in your heart to forgive the Teddy man?" He set the drink on the floor and eased down beside her, putting a hand on her stomach and rubbing.

She touched her glass to his nose. "You take me for granted."

"No, I don't." His hand was moving up toward one of her large breasts. You know I'm crazy for you. I can't keep away."

"I know what you can't keep away from." But she didn't remove his hand, which was now massaging her nipple through the material of her sweater and bra. "I'm serious, Theo; I'm serious about us, but if this is just about when you can make time kind of thing, then I don't need that again."

"Damn, girl, I'll have a talk with your meth-head brother."

"It's not about Danny, though I would like you to tell him he can't just show up begging for money like he does, looking like he's been sleeping in his goddamn clothes for the past week, smelling of piss and—ugh . . ." She waved a hand between them as a way to ward off the bad karma of her brother.

"He gets to you; I know that. That's 'cause you still care for him despite all the bullshit he's done, what he put your mother through. I know about disappointment, Breeze."

She took his large face in her hands. "You just better not break my heart, or I swear to God I'll cut your balls off."

"You're such a romantic." They kissed, and his hand went under the sweater.

Later, in bed, Holton got up as his girlfriend slept. He snugged into his robe hanging in the walk-in closet. He strolled across the Berber rug and down the short hall, then through the Moroccan-style archway they'd put in. From the outside, the bland apartment house was like many other places in Lennox, a low-to-moderate-income community near the airport. A lot of the workers who were housemaids and waiters for the big hotels along and off of Century Boulevard lived here, out of sight and out of mind of the world travelers who came through L.A. on matters of commerce and pleasure.

But his old lady's crib, his home away from the drama, was a point of pride for the big man. When he first met her she was living in one of the standard breadboxes that passed for apartments in this building. She made okay money as a nurse at the hospital, but her useless brother and the medical bills Medicare wouldn't cover for her mother were draining her something fierce.

So the Teddy man stepped in. He worked out a deal with the owners, a Chinese national couple who lived in Cerritos, and had the walls to two adjoining apartments knocked out. Then he had the larger space redone to make a large bedroom, redone kitchen with a nook, a retiled bathroom, a good-sized living room, and a spare room, too. Yeah, Big T knew how to take care of his woman.

In the spare room there was a loaded built-in bookcase, an open rolltop desk with bills on it, a small couch, and a couple of mismatched chairs. If you pressed the number button on the TV remote in a specific sequence, the section of wall with the attached bookcase swung open.

"Just like the fuckin' Shadow," he murmured approvingly. The secret compartment was well designed. It had been installed by a retired safe peeler Holton knew, who'd written a few scripts for *Adam-12* in the '70s. If the apartment got tossed, only pry bars and sledgehammers would reveal its presence. He knelt, clicking on the light. Inside the compartment were a number of handguns arranged on one wall, two rifles, one with a scope, a jeweler's case, and bound stacks of cash—some $220 grand.

Holton perused the guns, then settled on a rebuilt CQB 1911 .45 with a Bomar sight. He sniffed the gun, and it was good. Then he clicked the bookcase and wall back into position. He carried the pistol into the bedroom and put it inside an equipment bag on his side of the bed.

"Hey," Tabon said, moving under the covers.

"Hey yourself." He took off his robe and got back in the bed. He set the alarm for 3:15 A.M., and using another remote control unit, he thumbed on the CD on the dresser. A Kurt Weil song, "Pirate Jenny," came on. It was sung by Nina Simone. Holton loved his Weil; his stuff was so sad and so true.

Tabon snuggled up next to him as he lay on his back, his fingers trilling his sternum as Simone wrung all there was out of the lyrics.

She got one of her legs on his body and started grinding and kissing his neck. Holton's other hand was splayed across her wide butt, kneading the flesh as she moaned. Soon they were making love again, their large frames sweating with effort and lust.

His breath cycling in short bursts and his hips pumping steadily, Big T Holton climaxed inside her as her legs clamped him. And as he drained himself, Holton imagined that nothing, absolutely nothing, was going to mess up his good thing.

CHAPTER 10

"Pick your end up, beeyatch," Culhane groused as he angled the awkward mattress into the hallway.

"Don't worry about me; you just put your back into it." Cortese was on the low end as the two wrestled it down the flight of steps.

"Damn, we need to throw this thing out," Culhane said, referring to their load. "Who knows how many body fluids have been absorbed into it?"

"That's why we're moving everything out, then going to burn the mattress, sheets, towels—whatever could be used to hold DNA trace evidence." Santián was at the top of the stairs, carrying the nightstand.

"I think this is overkill, man," Holton added from inside the room. "Reynaux is stand-up; he ain't gonna tell nothing. For what? Like McGuire's tight ass would cut him slack if he did? Shit."

Cortese spouted, "It is the bright day that brings forth the adder, and that craves wary walking."

"Whatever the fuck you just said, Professor, shut the fuck up and keep working." Culhane lifted, and the two got the mattress to the bend of the stairwell and around the corner.

"I had to leave my warm bed—"

"And warm pussy," Santián cut in.

"Exactly," Holton replied, carrying a box containing the microwave and coffeemaker they'd used in the place. "To do this shit."

"Like Cheese just said, man, the snake is out to get us—we have to be cautious." Santián continued to descend.

"In that case, we should have just torched this rattrap and Manny could collect on the insurance," Holton huffed, following his sergeant out to the truck at the curb.

Because there was only basic furniture and no personal items in the Playpen, it took the four less than an hour and a half to get it cleaned out. The only thing left was the refrigerator.

"What about it?" Culhane asked the squad gathered in the kitchen.

"We wipe it down with solvent and bleach like we do everything else in this joint," Santián said. "I got the mops and jugs in the closet."

"You better get Florence or Weezie for that," Holton squawked.

Santián answered, "Think, Big T—we can't leave prints, and as much as possible, we need to remove hairs, oils, and what have you."

Holton made an impatient face. "Damn, Saint, even if Reynaux rolls over on us, what do they have? Our snatch patch, that's what. You the only one of us still married. You the one got to explain your little eightball hoochie to your wife and the brass."

Cortese said, "That how it is, Big T? Every man for himself?"

"You know that's not what I mean."

Cortese pushed off the counter he'd been leaning on. "Prosecutors make their cases like building a wall, one brick at a time. If McGuire gets the pad and can link it to any of us, then that's just one more piece of that wall she's looking to topple on us—all of us."

Holton looked at Culhane, who didn't give away anything in his return glare. "I'm cool, Cheese; we're cool. I know we run this thing together or that mothafuckah ain't running at all. I don't need the Three Musketeers speech."

Santián had let it play out, electing to remain silent. As the leader, there were times he needed to insert himself, and other times when his instincts told him to let the men work these flareups through. "We also know Hyacinth hasn't given up the location to McGuire 'cause she must see that as her hole card. But we get on that, too, once we get this scrubbing done."

The men got back to work. And though grumbling while they did it, the crew sanitized the place. As dawn started to filter over the apartment-dense rooftops of this edge of the Heights, the former Playpen was returned to a pristine, if tiny, apartment.

"Of course, the first thing we have to do is get another crib," Culhane noted. "I don't know about you Girl Scouts, but I've gotten rather fond of 8th Street skank."

The men laughed and departed, following Santián in the U-Haul truck out to an empty dirt lot tucked under an overpass of the 5 Freeway off Mission Road. There they set fire to the mattress and bedding and drove off.

At the unopened Code 7, Santián, who with Cortese was a silent partner in the bar, used his keys to let the men inside. He unlimbered a bottle of Bushmills from the rack and poured out the doses.

"We run these fuckin' streets," he toasted.

"You damn right," Holton chimed in, taking a quaff after they'd clinked their glasses.

"We've got to get in high gear on this Gargoyle thing," Cortese said. "We ought to take another run at Mercury. He's the weak sister."

Holton poured himself another brace of Irish whiskey, pointedly saying nothing of what he'd learned of Mercury's business connections.

"I agree," Santián said, "but we also need to shake the trees in the jungle. Otherwise, the Del Fuegos will take out Mercury in a heartbeat, and we'll be stuck holding our dicks like a bunch of Kansas City faggots."

"Exactly." Cortese shook his glass in the direction of Culhane. "Gargoyle didn't give anything? Something we could use?"

"He clammed up; you know him—knew him," Culhane corrected. "He was playing hard as they come when we had him in the docket."

"But he liked to brag, to show he was the cock of the walk."

"Tell me something I don't know, Cheese," Culhane shot back. "Me and Big T leaned, and he clamped up. Got that shit-eating grin on his mug and dared us to slap it off him."

"We've been doing this a while," Holton said, reeling toward Cortese. "Ronk and me ain't no rooty-poot amateurs. Shit."

"Nobody's saying that, chief, I just want to make sure we cover every base. We have a lot riding on it."

Holton, who'd downed half his second drink, scratched at the stubble on his chin. "I know that, too." He breathed traces of whiskey into the other man's face.

The two men did a stare-down, neither desiring to be the first to break contact.

Santián popped his glass onto the bar top. "Let's remember who the enemy is and what our objectives are, shall we?"

Holton and Cortese slowly nodded their heads and took their respective positions, like prize fighters awaiting the next bell.

"You two listen. Now more than ever we need to be operating like we were joined at the hip. No freelancing, no 'I'm going to get mine and fuck the rest of you.' We are a unit within a unit, and that's how we proceed. I ain't no goddamn Phil Jackson, so I don't have no Zen words of wisdom to lay on you. But we all are aware that we've got a lot of eyes on us and we need to be smart, think ahead of the others. We're a team, and we act like one and shit like one. If one sinks, the rest get sucked under. Now, that you do know."

"Yeah, you're right, Saint," Cortese said.

"Big T?"

Holton tipped his hat back. "That's why you're the sergeant." He stuck out his fist, and Cortese knocked his against it.

"That's what I'm talking about," Santián beamed. "What about Acosta—is he gettin' right?"

Culhane jerked his head from side to side. "He got broke in raw, dog-style, but he's solid. He's stand-up."

"But we're going to have to depend on him in the crunch," Cortese said. "We don't have time for a full courtship."

Santián squinted an eye. "You don't think he's Internal Affairs, do you?"

"Naw," Culhane said. I can smell those bastards blocks away. Look, I got some informants to run down in the next few days. I'll take him around with me and see how he jumps."

Santián considered that and said, "Okay, it's your call, but if he's feeling angelic, we Siberia him."

"Understood, *mi jefe.*"

"All right, gents, light, tight, and we get home at night." He poured out his unfinished booze, and the men left. After returning the rental truck, Santián drove his Malibu back to Temple Division.

To his surprise, Mayor Fergadis and Chief Hidalgo were holding a press conference on the front steps. Cortese, who'd gotten back before him, was off to one side with a few other cops, watching the proceedings.

"The fuck is this?"

"Never hurts to do a little grandstanding," Cortese observed. "Especially when you've taken a dip in the polls because of that video."

"Is he roasting TRASH?" Santián asked.

"Not directly. He's assuring the natives that any improprieties will be dealt with swiftly and . . . well, you know."

"And he's got Hidalgo there to cosign."

"Wouldn't you? The debate with McGuire is tonight."

Santián's cell rang, and he unclipped it from his belt. He could tell who it was by the number displayed on the screen. "What up?" he said. He winked at Cortese. "Cheese says hi."

Cortese made a face as Santián listened.

"This might surprise you, girl, but I actually have police work to do." Santián walked a small distance from Cortese,

"Don't be shy," the other man said, making a puckering sound.

Santián kept talking to his girlfriend, then clicked off. "She says she has something that may be of value."

"Oh, I bet."

"Claims it might be a line on what the Nines are up to."

"You know, for such a smart guy, you sure like to get led around by your other head a lot."

"Nothing worse than a convert," Santián replied. "Before you and the mademoiselle took up, you'd be standing outside of the YWCA just hoping you could get a sniff."

"Can I help it if I've matured?"

"At any rate, Linda ain't like these other chickenheads running around out here. She's pretty steady, what with a baby and all." He looked off at a point beyond the press conference and the station house.

Cortese said evenly, "Okay, Saint, okay."

The press conference ended, and the mayor and the chief took questions and answers. Cortese and Santián, along with the other personnel, filed back inside or left in their patrol cars. In the Aquarium, Santián checked messages on his desk phone, and Cortese read through a file on the Jensen case, which had been kicked to him by Kubrick.

Seven months ago Serain Jensen had been on her way home from Morningside Lutheran Middle and High School, in Culver City, walking on Culver Boulevard on a sunny day. She usually walked with two of her friends, but that day one of them was home sick and the other had to do detention for talking back to Pastor Reynolds, the principal and English teacher. She was last seen at 3:42 that afternoon, stopping to buy a soda and chips at Majid's Mini-Mart.

As Culver City was its own municipality, naturally its department investigated. But since that time, after a tearful mother's plea on TV for her child's return, a $25,000 reward offered by the city council, and several leads that never panned out, the mature thirteen-year-old hadn't been found—either dead or alive. There were two separate reports of her being seen in the Heights and North Hollywood areas of town. To make sure the Department didn't get accused of being slack, particularly in this period of scrutiny, her file had been assigned to Temple and Devonshire Divisions. Kubrick had given the case specifically to Cortese because before he'd come over to the unit, he'd worked vice. And he'd been responsible in busting up a pedophile club where some sick bastards, including a priest from his high school, St. Brigid's in the Valley, traded thirteen- and fourteen-year-old runaways like baseball cards.

Recalling that priest, Cortese studied two different pictures of Serain. One was the pubescent kid in the official picture-day shots, with big teeth and lustrous cornrowed hair to her shoulders. The other was an instant shot taken with her friends goofing and carrying on in a mall. One of the girls carried a Yellow Bus shopping bag. Serain was dressed in a skirt he knew wasn't allowed at the school, and a spaghetti top with a black bra strap showing. He turned the photo over, but it wasn't marked. He looked at it again, working out ideas in his head.

"Hey, Cortese, I got something for you."

Cortese looked up slowly from the photograph at Rod Gates, a uniform cop. He was some kind of relation to the infamous former chief of the LAPD, Daryl Gates. The man who once opined in front of live mics that the reason black suspects died from the choke hold—the baton pressed against the carotid artery, the main supply line of blood to the brain—was due to their not having veins like normal people.

"What's up?"

The cop lowered his voice. "I might have a line on your whore."

Cortese pushed the young teenager into another compartment of his mind, but he silently promised her he'd be back. "That right?"

"Yeah. We pulled in a couple of working girls last night near the Staples arena, working the johns after a Kings game. We get 'em back here for booking, and this one called Jade says she has something for trade. She knew Hyacinth had gone scarce, and we'd want to find her."

Cortese held up a finger and got Santián's attention at his desk. He hung up and walked over. Gates filled him in, adding, "Jade and her partner bailed out this morning—I guess their pimp came through."

"I know him—Antoine something, goes by Trey Mack," Santián said. "But she didn't give up a name?"

No, her pal, ah, Ling-Ling, gave her the eye, and Jade shut up. Could be nothing, but figured you'd want to know."

"Ling-Ling?" Cortese chuckled.

"Blacker than midnight, she is."

Thanks, Gates."

"Sure. Always good to do a favor for the garbage men." And he went back upstairs.

"Couldn't hurt to see if she was bullshitting or telling the truth," Santián said.

"I'm gonna let you ride this one solo, *hombre,*" Cortese replied. "I want to see what I can hunt down on the Jensen grab."

"Okay," he agreed, "I'll hit you later if I turn up anything." He started to turn around, then stopped. "You feeling all right? You look preoccupied."

"It's this kid, that's all. I hate motherfuckers who do this."

"Righteous."

Santián returned to his desk, and Cortese made a call to records. He requested they pull the files on the pedophile club.

Forty-five minutes later, Santián was driving toward the second hangout where he hoped to find Trey Mack. He knew finding girls like Jade was hard when the sun was up. They had no set addresses—in some threadbare apartment one day, a motel room the next. Sometimes they ran off, going to another city to try and make it and get away from their pimps. Some stayed gone, even finding they could get out of the life altogether. But most wound up returning, caught up in the twisted cycle of codependence they had with their "daddies."

On Centinela near the Westfield Fox Hills Mall was a café called the Quality Diner, on the south side of the street. Santián pulled the Malibu into a slot and got out.

"Sergeant," an older man in sunglasses and a floppy hat said. He was sitting on the bench out front and greeted him. He was perusing the *Racing Form*, pen poised to make his picks for the upcoming races at nearby Hollywood Park.

"What's a good one?" Santáin said, reaching the door.

"I like Fenway Flier in the fourth and Gertrude's Earring in the seventh."

"You always were lucky." He gave the man two twenties and stepped inside. Moving his head from the counter, he spotted Trey Mack and two others in a booth. He squared up and approached.

"You smell something?" the pimp said very loudly. He was dressed conservatively in an off-white linen shirt-style jacket, matching pants, and Polo golf hat. He was somewhere in his thirties, but his lined face reflected his crooked soul. "Something don't smell right. Smell like somebody's got shit on their neck." The other two guffawed. One of them spit out particles of food, he was having such a good time.

"If you're not too busy, Mr. Trey, I'd sure appreciate having a word with you." Santían held his hands down in front of him, one over the other.

Trey Mack put a hand to his ear as if he couldn't hear. "What was that? Somebody hear something?"

"Must be some flies buzzing around that shit," one of the other men joked. "Might need to get some Raid up in this mug." They laughed again.

Calmly and deliberately Santián took hold of the man and yanked him out of the booth, onto the floor.

"Bitch, I'm going to—" was all he got out of his mouth before Santián whacked him over the head with the side of his Beretta. "Shut up."

Trey Mack and his remaining companion glared malevolently at the cop. The pimp pointed a manicured nail. "This is the 'Wood, niggah; you can't go 'round pulling that shit over here."

The man he'd hit was starting to rise, and Santián kicked him in the face, knocking him into the table, upsetting a glass of water. "File a complaint," he said, reholstering his piece. He slid into the spot formerly occupied by the man groaning on the floor. "But you know why you won't, Trey? 'Cause you know goddamn well if you do, we'll continually round up all your fillies. See, I know your predatory self specializes in intimidating and turning out broads fresh up here from Honduras and whatnot, with no family, no friends. I'll have 'em all deported, and the only job you'll have is working at the fuckin' checkout of the Smart and Final."

When you applied the squeeze, it was important to allow the mark to retain a modicum of dignity. Otherwise, you were only adding to the list of clowns that would be only too happy to ambush you. "A simple conversation, that's all I'm asking."

Trey Mack made a pretense of considering the request, then said, "Okay, five minutes is what I can give you."

"Oh, that would be smashing."

Trey Mack got up, and the two walked into the parking lot. The man reading the *Racing Form* was still there, still studying the horses.

"I need to talk to your girl Jade."

"She ain't in my crew anymore."

"You bailed her out this morning."

"That was for old times' sake," he said, looking away. "Broad is too flaky—too much on the pipe, feel me? I can't have no bitch that is unreliable, man. I got a business to run."

Santián said, "You make some kind of deal with McGuire? She tell you her office won't prosecute your girls? She convince you you're going to get a book deal or something out of this?"

"You trippin', Santián. I got to go." But he didn't move, he knew what the cop was capable of doing, and wasn't going to get sucker-punched.

"We'll have this talk again," Santián decided. There was no sense escalating anything until he was sure what the game stakes were.

"It's been real." And the pimp strolled back inside the diner.

Santián got in his car and drove away. It bothered him that Trey

Mack was more in fear of McGuire than of him. But it probably was greed more than safety on that fool's mind. What kind of golden carrot had she dangled before him? He could pull the chump in on any number of charges and sweat him that way, but that required too much exposure. Though taking him way out to the jail in Sylmar and booking him under a different name was a possibility. It had been done before with others you wanted out of circulation so you could give them your undivided attention.

He smiled at the notion of making that overgrown punk whine and plead, but checked himself. That wasn't what was called for here. He had to outmaneuver McGuire if he and the team were to come out on the other end of this intact. The reality was, Trey Mack still had to earn a buck, so that meant his girls would still be out on the stroll. He'd move Jade to another location, but there were others in his stable who could provide some link to Hyacinth. There had to be—these chicks were as hungry for a dollar as their daddy was, and at any given time, one or two of them was looking to make a break.

Santián took Sepulveda north until it split off where Overland merged into the thoroughfare. He took Overland north, then eventually wound his way to Pico, then swung east. It was time for a stop at the bank.

Just past a street called Carmona, in what was midcity, he slowed and parked at a meter. This part of the avenue was populated by the likes of liquor stores with hand-painted signs advertising sales of Remy Martin and beer in Hangul and Spanish, auto body shops, and lawn mower repair shops. Next to a quick-print shop was Leeds' Lock & Key.

He could hear the grinding wheel whirring beyond the heavy-gauge screen door facing the street. "Tommy," he said through the grate.

In a moment the door was unlocked by a middle-aged Latina bulging through her dress.

"*Con permiso,*" he said, stepping inside the cramped quarters. "No problem," she replied.

Beyond the glass counter with its array of locks—some of them relics from the 1920s and '30s—Tommy Leeds made a set of keys for his customer. He was a handsome dark-skinned black man who could be forty or a young-looking sixty. He was medium-sized but had forearms like a stevedore's. His long apron was smeared with grease, and there were faded red splotches on it, too. Leeds loved his Red Rooster hot sauce on his chicken and fish.

The locksmith finished the job while Santián leaned on the counter, leafing through a recent copy of *Low Rider* magazine. The woman was handed her old and new keys now on a cheap ring. She paid and left, she and Santián exchanging a nod. He relocked the screen door after she'd stepped out.

"What's goin' on?" Leeds knocked fists with the cop.

"Got to make a withdrawal," Santián said, already moving around the counter.

"Then, like Shultz used to say in *Hogan's Heroes,* 'I see nothing; I know nothing.' "

Santián went to the rear of the shop and, after moving some parts on a shelf, lifted free a fire-safe box. He dialed the combination and opened it. Inside were two neat stacks of hundreds. He extracted a couple of thousand and replaced everything. All across the city and parts of the county, the TRASH men kept such banks tucked away.

Santián stepped back in front as Leeds busied himself cleaning the spindle of one of his disassembled old locks.

"Everything cool?" Santián asked.

"If it wasn't, you'd have heard it from me. Why you ask?" He sprayed some WD-40 on the shaft and rubbed it with a shop cloth.

"Let me know if somebody that sticks out comes around—trying to be on the sly, particularly."

Leeds looked up. "Should I be worried about something?"

"Always," he said jocularly, and quit the shop. Eventually Santián wound his way over to Normandie around Hollywood Boulevard. He spotted a working girl he knew who went by the name of Roxanne, and pulled into an alley, tapping his horn. She came over, popping gum, and leaned down to talk to him on the driver's side.

"You want me to toss your salad, Saint?" Her front teeth had a wide gap, and one of them was chipped.

"You know I'll take that rain check, girl." He held out one half of a hundred-dollar bill that he'd torn apart. "The other half of this one and two other whole ones are yours if you produce."

She took the paper, then asked, "Who I got to gut, baby?"

"Get me a line on Jade, one of Trey Mack's ladies."

"That's easy, she—"

"Nope, she won't be at her usual station tonight. She'll be somewhere else—probably traded places with one of his others. You talk it up, and anybody who turns out to be on the square, tell 'em I got a hundred for them, too."

"Okay, lemme see what I can shake loose. Hit you back on your celly?"

"Yeah."

"Sure you ain't got time, Saint?" Lasciviously she waggled her tongue for him.

"I got work to do, girl." He copped a feel of her breast.

"Shit, what I'm talking about?" She straightened up, and he backed out of the alleyway and righted the car. A little later he was eating lunch at the Tommy's on Beverly and Rampart when he got a call.

"Hey," he said, recognizing the phone number in his display window. He swallowed his food.

"You busy fighting crime or want to commit some later?" Linda Delarocha said.

"I should say no. I do have a big case, after all," he responded, sipping his soda. "Plus, what are we gonna do for accommodations?"

"I'll treat, cheap-ass. How about the Olympiad? It's been a while since we were there."

"Six?"

"Make it six-thirty; we've got inventory to finish up today."

"Okay, but I really shouldn't be so weak-willed."

"What you better be is ready." She hung up.

He shook his head and had more of his chili burger. He really shouldn't be such a victim of his own vices. This shit was going to bite him in the ass for sure one day. But damn if he could get over her, even though he sometimes felt he was orbiting ever closer to the fire of the sun.

After lunch he tried to reach Cortese, but his cell phone was on *Message*. Heading into the Heights proper, he prowled about, but nothing stuck out. On the northwest corner of MacArthur Park he spotted a chucklehead Maratrucha slanging rock. The son of a bitch even waved at Santián. He knew TRASH didn't concern itself with these nickle-and-dime chumps. But there was something about the car, an old Ford Fiesta with sporty rims, pulling away after the sale, that made him frown. He called it in.

"I need a plate run," he said. "Ocean Victor Edward, one-five-nine, copy?"

"Copy."

The Fiesta was three cars in front of him, heading south on Alvarado. Soon they got to where the street made a bend by the old church and became Hoover. And Hoover dead-ended at the USC campus before continuing again at King. Given the alternate rock station KROQ bumper sticker on the car, it wasn't hard to guess that a college student had just purchased a little rock to help with his or her studies. Or maybe there was a frat party tonight and this clown was bringing the door prize.

The radio fuzzed, and the voice said, "1-W-fifty, do you copy?"

"I'm here."

"Car is registered to a Madeleine Jirac; insurance records indicate it's driven by her son—"

"Jakob," Santián finished. "Copy that. Thanks, Hilda."

"Anytime," she said, putting honey in her voice.

Santián turned off to circle back the way he'd come. His son and the older boy had met at Madeleine Jirac's house when she'd had a "little finger-pointing soiree," as Cortese liked to call them, and Santián and the family had been invited. She knew about Linda but certainly wasn't going to have him bring his girlfriend—she wasn't that liberal.

And Jakob had picked up Curtis to go to a party last weekend. Jakob was older, a freshman in college but not particularly athletically inclined. Santian's son was physically bigger and already being scouted on his high school team. Now, just because Madeleine's kid was sucking that rock didn't mean he should shake down his own son. For all he knew, the youngster could have been buying it for some girl, since young men were known to do such foolish things if there was a chance of getting some head or poontang. Still . . .

Swinging past the Gothic Revival church again, which was now the central location of the Seventh Day Adventists, Santián was reminded of being younger than Curtis and hearing his grandmother go on about the services she'd gone to there given by the infamous

Jim Jones. He was part American Indian and would talk about being an outsider, a minority, someone who understood what it was not to be accepted by white society, and how such injustice would not stand. In those days, before the madness took hold of him, before the murders and suicides he oversaw in Guyana, he made a lot of sense. He preached about how the Lord's work was changing the conditions of unfairness, about how we all, no matter our color or creed, had to work together to make a better world. Jones was involved in charitable and social-activist efforts. Hell, Santián recalled reading, he even spoke at an ecumenical rally at the Shrine once with Farrakhan and some Baptist preacher.

Fortunately, his grandmother didn't follow Jones back to the Bay Area, partly due to her daughter, Santían's mother, who argued with her and convinced her she was needed in their home. Which was true, given that even then Santián was starting to cut up. So, was the parable that he needed to be doing some intervention of his own?

Santián had stumbled into fatherhood. He hadn't done any deep soul-searching about kids other than that it was expected, the way he was raised, that when you got married, you had kids. His mother was happy he'd managed not to get any girl pregnant before he was eighteen. But once you had those kids, a man's duty was to feed them, clothe them, make their asses go to school, and hope to God they didn't grow up to be serial killers. Or at least if they did, be the best goddamn nutzo killer there ever was.

He chuckled at this. What he did know was, he at least could do a better job than his old man had. When the bastard was around, and off the booze, he was okay. He was a near-illiterate Dominican immigrant who hadn't worn hard-soled shoes until he was twelve. Pops, like a lot of kids he grew up with in the rugged Los Charamilos section of Sosua, played *beisbol*, baseball. And like those kids, they all hoped they'd get drafted and play for the Yankees, the Cubs, any club, like their heroes Roberto Clemente, Orlando Cepeda, and the Alou brothers.

And like a lot of kids, he had a decent swing and better than average fielding skills, but he didn't set scouts' hearts on fire. He hustled as a shoeshine boy, worked for a cab company as a tire changer, and even managed to get a gig as a doorman at one of the big hotels in Santo Domingo. By the time Santián and his sister came

along, the old man, who was only twenty-five, was working on a lifetime of disappointment. For even in America, even though he'd
consciously chosen the West Coast rather than New York because
he didn't want to be living in some slum building with all the other
poor fucks just like him, he had to hustle. And he never did get
over.

The old man was more negligent than abusive. Santián vividly
recalled one particular memory of his father walking into their
apartment after boozing it at the El Papagayo Bar on Olympic.
He'd spent part of the tip money he made on the weekends at the
car wash, and smelled of some broad's Thrifty brand perfume. Like
the typical Latino male, he dared his wife to give him any static and
pushed her hard enough that she fell against the one club chair
they owned.

To her credit, she got up and slapped the shit out of the drunk
fool. He knocked her for a loop, but like Larry Holmes before he
went goofy, she poured it on. Santián was glad the old man was getting his. At one point he tripped his dad, and he fell on his ass sput-
tering beer and obscenities. His sister Flora, always the peacemaker,
got the combatants separated by the time the uniforms arrived.

It was a white-and-Chicano pairing, and the white cop was a
woman, all butch and bristly. Massaging his leg where he'd bruised
it in the fall, the old man naturally addressed the man in Spanish.
The other cop just gave him the look while Amazonia kept her
hand on the hilt of her sheathed baton. Those were the days before
the alloy T-handle, and her nightstick was a scarred piece of work
that you knew she liked knotting heads with—especially drunk fool
men.

The female cop interviewed his mother out in the hall while the
old man kept trying to get a modicum of understanding out of her
male partner. Watching this, the young Santián was bathed in the
emotion of satisfaction of seeing his father have to be humble in
the face of a power greater than the iron hand of order he tried to
impose on their household. The male officer finally allowed a
human response on his face, a slight grin at something his dad
whispered to him. But he then held up a finger for warning and
told his father in the command tone that "Men have a responsibil-
ity to set the example for their children."

Doing his best to look contrite, his father, Felipe, reached out for his daughter's hand to show that he was a good and caring parent. Flora wanted to be nice and came and stood beside him, hugging the clown. He glanced over at Rafael, and his wet eyes said he knew better than to ask such a favor from his son, but that in return he better not volunteer any information, either.

Rafael played the dutiful son and remained silent. He kept remaining silent when his mother came back in the room, holding on to a kitchen towel she used to dab at her bloody mouth. The woman cop, her wide shoulders straining the material of her shirt, motioned to the other one. Those two went into the hallway to talk, and Rafael smiled at his dad. He made the symbol of a gun with his index finger and the thumb clicking away like it was the hammer. His mother shook her head, a stern look on her face admonishing him to stop. The old man alternated between anger and wariness as the cops came back into the room.

The dyke spoke directly and forcefully to his father. She told him if they had to come back to this address because of fighting, they'd arrest him and he would go to jail. Bad enough that it was this muff diver telling him off, but she pointed at him and raised her voice when he tried to say anything. The capper was when she asked him did he understand. Did he know how serious this was, and that if it were up to her, she'd drag him over to Temple Division right now?

His father seethed, his clenched fists held tightly at his side. He looked at the Chicano cop, who wouldn't—couldn't at that point—provide any kind of indication that he was on his side. The woman got in his dad's face and made him say yes, that he understood what he'd done and wouldn't do it again. As they turned to leave, the female uniform turned around and said that he was on her shit list, not a good place to be. They left, and the four of them stood for a few moments doing nothing except breathing and taking up space.

And though it would take several years and puberty for the import of that day to crystalize for young Santían intellectually, it began to flower in him that day. Men like his dad, men whom life shortchanged but who could only figure out how to be bitter and narrow-minded, stomped all over the goddamn city. But you showed them a badge or a piece of paper that had power, had force behind it, then that was a different story. He determined he wasn't going to wind up like his pops.

Sitting at the traffic signal, Santián was brought out of his reminiscing by the honk of the UPS delivery truck behind him. He looked up and the light was still red, but the truck honked again. He looked back, ready to set this civilian straight, but recognized why the driver was honking at him. The light changed, and the two went through the intersection, then pulled to the curb.

"What's going on, Benny?" Santián said after getting out of the Malibu.

"Same old shit," Benjamin Orozco smiled broadly. He was a large man with a shorn scalp, wide hands and feet. He hugged Santián briefly as the two stood beside the open door of his truck.

"Look, *ese*, we got some wide-screens gonna ship to Circuit City first of next month. You interested in getting in on this like before?" As he talked, Orozco kept shifting on his feet and looking around, like a man doing his best not to make himself too much of a target.

Santián had his arms folded, leaning against the truck. When talking about criminal behavior, he found it was best not to advertise you were doing so. "Sonys, Philips?"

"Naw, this is knockoff shit: Goldstar, Bandline, Korean and Chinese versions. But they'll sell in the Jungle if not Beverly Hills, right?"

Santián nodded. "We talking off the trucks?"

"Uh-huh, these are coming in from the port down the Alameda rail. But because of time schedules they have to sit in one of those cargo containers for a few hours. But they figure since it's unmarked and at night, no need for extra security. That's when it goes down. And that's why we need to backup."

"Okay, you get me the time and location and I'll let you know up or down."

"This is what I'm talking about." Orozco climbed back into his truck and honked one more time as he drove away.

Santián checked the time and called Cortese. He got him and talked. "Where you at?"

"Ran down one of the fucks that was in that sick club."

"He's out?"

"You believe that? He got a deal 'cause he rolled over on the other motherfuckers, including that shitbird Father Olson."

"The justice system truly sucks."

"Damn straight. I'm at his place, a goddamn halfway house for these assholes out here in Glendora—oh, my bad, I mean morally challenged," he snickered.

"Jesus, somebody ought to torch the joint."

"I got to talk to this guy first. I'll call you back."

"Right, right."

Cortese clicked off and walked along the stone path laid across a front yard landscaped in desert plants. This led to a converted three-story Craftsman. He rang the bell, and a lean man in a baseball cap and overalls opened the door. He had a claw hammer in his hand at his side.

"I came to see Preston Goode," Cortese said, not showing his badge.

"Does he know you?"

"I arrested him."

"Then you're L.A. and this isn't. And since you ain't his parole officer . . ." The man started to shut the door.

"If I have to come back, it won't be quietly," Cortese said evenly. "I'll make sure that whatever homeowners' groups are around here know that a registered sex offender is now living among them."

"Our neighbors know this is a halfway house, Officer. This is an older community—retirees and even a couple of former policemen, too."

"People get funny about child molesters, champ. You can understand a thief, even a murderer, but a lowlife scum bucket who harms kids—now, that's different."

The man sighed heavily. "Wait here."

"Sure, I'll just hang out in your lovely foyer."

The man was going to object but curtailed a comment and retreated up a set of carpeted stairs. From where he stood, Cortese could see down the length of the house, past the propped-open swing door of the kitchen. Several people were inside, going about the tasks of preparing meals for the household. After a moment, a woman in a business suit came down the stairs, the handyman behind her.

"I'm Mrs. Whitney, the director." She didn't offer her hand.

"I'd like to talk to Goode about a matter he might be able to help me with."

"This an official inquiry?"

"Why else would I be here, ma'am?"

"To harass Mr. Goode, who's done his time."

"He's on parole; therefore, technically, that isn't so. Don't you think it would go a long way toward his rehabilitation for him to aid in this case?"

"He's"—she looked toward the flocked wallpaper—"he's a man who very much regrets what he's done."

"Mrs. Whitney, I'm sure the only way the court would remand him here is because he wants to make restitution of some sort. All I'm asking is to talk with him about—let's face it—his expertise about an area he has some familiarity with that neither you nor I do . . . I assume."

"I don't legally have to allow you in."

"That's true, but like I told your man here, I'll make it uncomfortable for you if I have to come back."

"That's police misconduct."

"That's being a good citizen, lady."

"I'll want to be present."

"Why don't you let Goode decide? He doesn't need anyone holding his hand."

"You certainly need some lessons in your people skills."

"Don't I, though?"

She went through the back, trailed by the man in overalls. Presently, the handyman returned and motioned for Cortese. He stepped into a well-tended garden that was a mixture of the front xeriscape with edible plants including tomatoes and pumpkins. Preston Goode, who was thinner than the last time Cortese had seen him, was brushing dirt off the knees of his khakis. His hair was thinner, but he was tanned, and his glasses the same design the cop remembered from the past.

"Goode," he said.

"Cortese." There was no inflection in his voice.

"Shall I remain?" Mrs. Whitney said, standing near the detective along the path of square pavers inset in the earth. The handyman had drifted off to return to his chores.

"That's all right, Mrs. Whitney. I can stand his questions. I have nothing to hide."

"Very well, but at any time you don't want to talk to him, you tell him that."

"I know."

She lingered and then went to another part of the garden to provide the pretense that she was supervising three other men who were working there. That didn't matter to Cortese, nor would it have if she had sat in Goode's lap during their talk. He'd been making a point about his authority, and he was damned if this broad who got all wet over civil liberties was going to crowd him.

"How's it hangin', sport?"

"Cut it out."

Unfazed, Cortese proceeded. "You hear about this Lutheran middle school girl getting snatched?"

His body tensed despite his efforts to remain relaxed. "No."

"Yes, you have, because it's been in the news off and on during the last six months. And the Culver City Council has offered a twenty-five-grand reward for information about the girl's kidnapping."

"I may have seen something in the papers," Goode allowed.

"And as you know, there's some facts about this case that bear some similarities to that association you were involved in several years ago."

"I know nothing of the kind, Cortese, and you know that, too."

Cortese went on as if he were discussing the case with a colleague. "I've had a talk with the investigators from Culver City, and reviewing the file raises several interesting points for me. There's a photo of Serain taken—I guessed and the CC cops confirmed—at the Fox Hills Mall. One of the girls is holding a Yellow Bus shopping bag."

Goode crossed his arms.

"One of the runaways you and the boys had your way with was picked up at that mall, isn't that right?"

Goode adjusted his glasses, his hand betraying a slight tremble. "You know it is."

"Serain is also mixed-race, half black and white, the kind of caramel-colored little girl that Olson had a real weakness for, isn't that right, Preston? The kind that like to dress sexy, like one of those singers they're always watching on BET?"

"Ask him."

Through a small stand of corn stalks, Cortese watched Mrs. Whitney. "Well, he's still in the joint, Preston. But check this out. This picture I'm talking about is one of those instant ones, like a Polaroid does? The cops I talked to said they interviewed the two other girls in the shot, and they said this old man, beard and hat and all that came hobbling by on his cane, this old-school Polaroid around his neck."

Goode looked over at the corn stalks. "You're reaching, Cortese. You never were much of a cop."

"Time will tell, Preston. See, the old man giggled with the pretty young girls, and they mugged for him and he took their pictures, giving each one of them a snapshot. Now, one of the girls did say the cute old guy took a few shots that weren't any good and threw those out in the trash can. Interesting, huh?"

Goode put his hands in his pockets. "So what, Cortese? That doesn't mean anything."

"That was your technique, Preston. You were a bit-part actor who did street theater and worked with one of those troupes where you had to do all your own makeup and getups."

"This is Hollywood, Cheese; everybody's something else around here."

"Don't you use my first name, you freak. You'll never know me well enough to do that."

Goode had taken a step back as Cortese leaned into him. This brought the director walking briskly around the stalks, her crisp stockings swishing. "That's it, Officer. That's enough."

"Oh, it's not enough with this bastard; it's never enough," Cortese bellowed. "Serain Jensen disappeared less than three weeks after this shit got to your little wonderland here."

"Get out!" she also hollered, and pointed toward the front.

"You're making a mistake, lady."

Goode had backed up farther, into the plants, his head down and body drawing in on itself.

"No you are making the mistake by wearing out your welcome, Detective. Now get out of here."

Cortese jabbed a finger at the sex offender. "Ask him about the razor cuts he'd slit in his dick, then sprinkle salt on it while he jerked off to girls' pictures in teenager magazines. Ask this freak about that," he yelled.

"Get out," Mrs. Whitney repeated as if addressing one of her obstinate charges.

"When I come back, if this twisted shit isn't here, I'm going to have you arrested for being an accomplice."

"Get out of here, you idiot, or I'll have you arrested."

"Your mama's an idiot." Cortese left and headed toward the 210 Freeway, contemplating his next moves. He'd like to toss Goode's room, but the problem with halfway houses was that somebody was always around. Mrs. Whitney no doubt went home to the suburbs— well, hell, Glendora *was* the fuckin' 'burbs—but he'd give odds that the handyman lived on site. According to what Goode's PO had told him, the fuck had a part-time job at a bindery in South Pasadena. He could follow him around, but Goode wasn't a fool— he'd know that Cortese would be shadowing him.

Lining up to get back on the freeway, Cortese kept running over scenarios on how best to go at the bastard. For the next few days, Goode wouldn't do anything but play solid citizen. For Cortese that meant he had to work the evidence, follow up leads and build the case. He checked his cell and there was a message. Cortese navigated the car into the middle lane as he listened to the playback. An answer to his intra- and interdepartmental queries had brought back a result. There had been an abduction a month ago of another mixed-race girl from Redondo Beach, according to the police there.

He checked his watch, made a return call to the RBPD. It was going to be a bear getting way the hell across town to the South Bay via several freeways and traffic snarls. L.A. was getting to be one big perpetual conveyer belt of cars and trucks. But if it all added up to his locking Goode back in a cage, or better yet, sending him on the line to wait for the hot shot while Cortese grinned from behind the glass, then any effort in that regard was worth the expenditure of energy. This was why he had become a cop.

CHAPTER 11

Linda Delarocha bit hard on Santián's biceps as the two climaxed together. They kissed, and she licked his glistening chest. "Not bad, old timer; not bad at all." She kissed him again.

He then nibbled her neck and got off her, breathing hard. "I know you're trying to give me a heart attack, but what would you do with my body?" Santián lay on his back, looking at the Olympiad's water-stained ceiling.

"I'd have to have the trash taken out, now wouldn't I?"

"That's cold, baby."

"Who taught me?" She got out of the bed and headed for the bathroom. "Who is that?" She asked on her way, pointing at a painting on velvet in a bronze, gnarly frame.

"Steve Reeves," he said. "He played Hercules in these crazy Italian flicks I used to watch on Channel 9 on Saturday afternoons with my sister when I was a kid." In the painting, Reeves, as the legendary hero, was battling a lion up on its hind legs, and his powerful arms bunched as he kept the beast from devouring his head.

From the can she called out, "I think you'd look cute with one of those—what do you call 'em?—on."

"Headband?"

"No, around his waist," she chortled.

"Loincloth."

"Loyne?"

"As in 'covers.' "

"Then why ain't it called a crotch-cloth?" she giggled.

"Think how that sounds."

"Whatever." She finished and snuggled into her black thongs. Santián watched her through the doorway. Like a lot of women her age who were graced with natural beauty, Linda assumed she'd be forever shapely. But her hips were starting to get heavy from the junk food she consumed regularly, and Santián knew that in five or six years, as those pounds spread, she'd get wise that she couldn't just eat anything and not exercise or watch her diet—indulgence had its price.

She exited the bathroom, which was framed by Ionic-style columns that appeared to have been cut in half. In reality, the columns were convex plaster mounds that had been fluted and topped with capitals to match the Greek style. The furniture—what there was of it—looked like it had been stolen off the set of a grade B sword-and-sandal epic of the early sixties. And the walls were made of some material imitating Mesoamerican block, like the stuff Frank Lloyd Wright used. The whole of it was a comfortable tackiness meant for conventioning Slurpee-machine salesmen and guileless philanderers.

"Miss me?" she leaned onto the bed, her hand massaging his balls.

He reached out and put his hand between her legs, and they kissed. "You're something else."

"You just remember that, Sergeant." She stretched across him, her breasts dangling over his face. As his mouth played with her nipples, she retrieved the remote buried in the bunched blanket. She sat cross-legged and turned on the box.

"What's this crap you're watching?" He got up, stretching, and padded into the bathroom, too.

"It's called *DigiDate.* In this one, when the couple are out, people can go to the show's Web site and send messages to both of them that they receive on their Palm Pilots."

"So it's live?"

"Yeah, the man and woman are followed around by two camera-women."

"Women?"

"They figure if it's good-looking women doing the shooting, that clubs and what have you won't object as much if it was two dudes."

"Fascinating," he monotoned, picking one of her pubic hairs out of his teeth as he walked back into the room. "This shit is for simple minds, don't you think?"

"It's fun. That's what TV is supposed to be."

He got into his boxers and lay next to her on the bed, his back against the headboard. "What about stuff like the Discovery Channel, where you learn about astronomy, or the History Channel?" He gestured at the set. "I mean, there was a great one on the other night about Ho Chi Minh. This cat was a hell of a leader—never gave up on his goal of his country, his people, no matter what it took." He shook his head in admiration. "Say what you want about him—he was one bad mothafuckah."

Delarocha stared blankly at her boyfriend. "Who?"

"See? They didn't teach you none of this in school, did they?"

"Easy, Pops, easy." She patted his leg. "What the fuck does anybody need from history and something that happened in China?"

"He was Vietnamese," Santián corrected. "And history tells us something about the future. The past shapes who and what we are, Linda. What we all are. How we got into the mess we're in."

"Ho Chow Mein did all that?" A commercial came on, and she flipped through the channels.

He pushed her playfully. "Damn, youngster."

"Careful, or I'll have to kung fu you like your boy Ho." She grabbed him by the wrists, forcing him down on the bed. "And what kind of name is that for a man?"

"Are you deaf? It's Vietnamese, fool."

"Oh, right." She shook her dark hair as it cascaded onto his chest. "He was your personal hero, huh?"

"I don't know about all that, but yeah, I guess he was somebody to—you know—study." He flexed and got his arms around Delarocha. Simultaneously, he twisted his body, putting her under him. "My point was, you need to be doing more than watching *Soul Train* for fashion tips and this mindless shit."

She kissed him. "Now you gonna take on the education system and bust them, too?"

"I'm just saying there's a lot out there, and you need to be checking it out." He kissed her back. Their mouths parted, and the two lovers gazed at each other.

"What time do you have to be home?"

"It better be sooner than later," he sighed. "Nicole has been all up in my ass lately."

"You poor, poor married man. You got to leave that young pussy alone." Her nose crinkled as she laughed.

"Temptress," he said, getting off the bed.

"You the one that's hypnotized me with your dick." She reached over and pulled his boxers down.

"Girl, you better stop." But he walked toward her, his boxers on his thighs as he held his legs apart. His stiffening rod was in his hands, and he waved it in front of her.

"See? I said you were a nasty dog." She took him in her mouth, her fingers kneading the flesh of his butt as she slid him in and out until he came again.

"That ought to keep you until next time."

"You are going to stroke me out for sure."

That's my plan, and then collect on the insurance policy I took out on you." She stood on the bed and started bouncing up and down.

"You're a nut."

She leaped onto him, bringing him down as he attempted to get his pants on. "Goddamn it, you about to get on my last nerve," he laughed.

Grappling on the floor, Delarocha started to tickle him.

"I ain't no fuckin' baby," he stammered, slapping her hand away from his sides.

"You're my big, dangerous baby." She tried it again, and when he grabbed her by the wrists this time, he applied pressure. "Damn!" she squealed. "Ugghh, I like it when you get rough, Saint."

"Nut." He got up and resumed dressing.

Delarocha lay on the shag, taking him in. "I got something for you, Sarge."

"As much as I'd like to pretend I'm good for a third round so soon, even one with as mighty a loin as I have needs to recharge, young lady." He buttoned his shirt over his athletic-cut undershirt.

"I'm talking about a goddamn clue for your ass, Steve McGarret."

"Yeah?"

"Ever hear of a club called the Bella Donna down in TJ?"

Now she had his full attention, and she related to him what she'd overheard the other evening. She finished by saying, "So this makes me your little snitch bitch, huh?"

He slapped her butt. "You're just doing your civic duty. You ain't my CI." Seeing her quizzical expression, he elaborated: "Confidential Informant."

"That's right, I'm your confidential fuck." She, too, got up and started dressing.

She was at the window overlooking Olympic Boulevard, and he put his arms around her waist, snuggling her from behind. "You know it isn't like that with us."

"Do I?"

"I won't lie to you, Linda. At first, yeah, you were just a *hina* I could bone when I felt like it, one of the perks of being a Trashman." He nuzzled her neck, and she responded. Out in the street a car alarm went off, and a baby cried.

"And now?" She had her hands over his. She liked his strong hands and enjoyed them when they touched her body.

"And now there's the neighborhoods you live in, that I grew up in, and what you've told me may help give this place stuck between the downtown developers and cold-shoulder Koreatown a chance to be—I don't know—like it's supposed to be. Normal, or whatever the hell *normal* means when anthrax can be sprinkled on your cereal and knuckleheads with exploding shoes are running around."

She kissed him on the cheek. "And TRASH can make all that happen?"

"No, but there's got to be cause and effect, Linda. If you do the civilians righteous, that's got to add up to something." He stared out the crack of the curtains onto the gray evening. "I know what I am and what I've done." He gave her a squeeze. "I lined my pockets—yeah, I've done that. But I didn't do it knocking up some woman working housekeeping at one of the airport hotels with three little mouths to feed and clothe."

He turned her around, the intensity tightening the muscles in his jaw. "The money we've confiscated from the ya-yo-slangin' Nines and middlemen? Hell, half those ducats we keep in circulation because we've got to grease the machine, or shit'll grind to a halt and we wouldn't get any busts to go down. None that mattered, anyway."

"And you want what you do to matter?"

"You goddamn right I do." He grinned at her, then put his shoes on. After the two said their good-byes, Santián checked his message and played one from Cortese. He called him at Madeleine Jirac's house, where he said he'd be that evening.

"Hey," he said to Cortese after pleasantries with Jirac.

"What up?"

He told him about the possible lead.

"That might be something to that. I don't know that Kubrick is in the mood to let us romp down there. Especially with McGuire crawling all over us with a microscope."

"He wants this shit cleaned up like we do, Cheese. We could sneak down, but for sure your girl would get our nuts in a vise and twist."

"Okay with me if we do this on the up-and-up. You just better hope he doesn't press us for you to ID your source."

"Don't remind me." He hesitated, then said, "Hey, ah, Madeleine and her son getting along okay? I mean, you know, as good as it can be with a goddamn teenager."

"They argue like cats and dogs—that is, when she sees His Lordship. Fact, he came over tonight for dinner. Why? You playing marriage counselor?"

"I'm just delaying telling you this, 'cause it means I got to deal with it, too."

"What?"

He told him about spotting the car at MacArthur Park and the rest.

"Fuck," Cortese issued quietly. "I knew that moody little fuck was doing something, but I hoped it was just weed. Or he wasn't getting enough—something normal."

They shared a burst of gallows laughter the way cops do.

"So how you going to tell her?"

"If I was honorable, I'd tell her just as soon as we hung up. But that means I don't get none tonight, and the lizard needs to get milked."

"Come on, man, you gotta get real on this."

"Oh, Lord in heaven, why me?"

"Look, I can't stand any more of your *Father Knows Best* angst. I got my own problems."

"Fuck you."

"Yeah, uh-huh. I'll leave you to handle the domestic front and let me get on Kubrick and see what he says."

"Right." Cortese hung up and returned to the front room, where he and Jirac were watching a program about Tom Paine on PBS. She arched an eyebrow. "Going out? A chippie call?"

"What," he feigned. "Can't a man talk to his partner without you getting all suspicious?" He snuggled down next to her on the couch. Jakob, a medium-sized, serious type with unruly hair and worn jeans, tromped through with an armload of clothes toward the service porch.

"Mom, can you put these in the dryer when they're done?"

"Certainly. Hot date for you, too?"

Jakob made a grunt and went to put his clothes in the washing machine on the back porch.

"You're giving him your X-Ray, Joe Friday," Jirac observed.

"Sorry," he said. "It's nothing."

Jirac slowly moved her gaze from him back to the screen as the late Howard Fast, author of such fare as *Spartacus* and various detective novels, discussed his seminal play, *Citizen Tom Paine,* and the man's progressive politics in relation to the capitalist bent of the other founding fathers.

Cortese compartmentalized what Santián had told him. Sooner rather than later he would bring it up, or maybe take the end-around route and ask Jakob straight up. He owed it to his mother, and to the boy himself. Experimentation was one thing, but he couldn't have the kid wind up like too many clowns he'd encountered over the years, who swore they weren't hooked on that pipe. No, if for no other reason, he couldn't have the boy fucking up just when he was trying to get out with the woman he wanted to be with for a long time to come.

Santián was also headed home after he'd clicked off talking to Cortese. As the car powered along the freeway, somewhere in the mountains beyond his cracked windows there was a fire some-where, and the evening smelled like dying embers.

Back in the city, on a darkening patch of a street called Onacrest, in Windsor Hills, Ronk Culhane also noted the peculiar charred aroma. At that moment, he and patrolman Alvaro Acosta stepped across a well-tended lawn. A late-model silver-gray Audi TT roadster was in the driveway next to a Rav 4.

"Want me to hit the back?" Acosta peered through the gloom at the ranch-style house.

"*Tranquilo*, baby. This is a friendly call, trooper." Ronk pointed the way and went lightly up a set of flagstone steps to the door set with leaded glass. He rapped lightly. "It's Ronk," he anounced.

The creak of hinges was apparent, accompanied by the sound of a thumping yet subdued bass. "What up, my man?" A voice said jocularly, imitating a frat boy trying to be street.

"We got to palaver," Ronk said, hands on his hips.

The heavy screen clicked and popped open. Ronk entered, Acosta behind him.

The inside was not the typical gangsta Ghetto Fabulous decor Acosta expected. The man was supposed to be an Ace Deuce Swan of some standing. Therefore, Acosta expected some brother in Sean John gear replete with the customary wave cap, its flap hanging over the back of his neck like it was a legionnaire's havelock cap.

This young man wore designer glasses, pressed and cuffed twill trousers, and a loose, elaborately designed print silk shirt. He had on Docksiders, and there was a goblet of wine on a smoked-glass-topped table. There were Warhols and Beardens and a few other prints on the walls. Acosta halted his inventory of the signatures he could make out on the pictures and stood and observed while Culhane started the talking.

"Rene, this is a new member of the squad."

Rene extended his hand. "Good to meet you."

Acosta hoped for a signal from Culhane, who had an expectant look on his face. He firmly and quickly completed the shake.

"Can I get you anything?" He'd picked up a remote control and turned down the volume on the Mary J. Blige CD he'd been playing.

"I could use some of that bomb-ass Glenfiddich you keep stocked," Culhane replied, "but I wouldn't want to give Double-A a bad impression of me."

"Naturally." Rene made his way to regain his seat at the glass table, and Culhane followed. Acosta remained standing.

Rene pushed his glasses tighter on his face. He crossed his legs and clasped his hands together, a professor discussing the events of the day. He waited.

"The Swans seriously pushing into Nines territory in the Heights?" Culhane sat opposite. There was a maplewood cigar box on the table, and he helped himself to a thin cigar.

Near the cigars was an open laptop, and the young man tapped some keys on it. "That wouldn't be prudent. You know the Swans have diversified into meth. That's been rather lucrative in the out-lying colleges in Riverside County and the hub cities. Those stressed-out housewives in Agoura Hills do like to have their blast, too." He chuckled.

"No side-door deal with the Del Fuegos?"

"That would be precedent-setting, Ronk. A black street gang and a Mexicano cartel." He looked beyond the room but didn't elabo-rate further.

"You've got big dreams, Rene."

He spread his hands in a mild gesture. "I merely do what I do; I don't set policy."

"You advise and the shot callers listen."

He made a self-deprecating nod.

"There's plenty Swans ain't too happy about their corner of the market getting smaller and smaller, forcing the move to the hinter-lands," Culhane pointed out. "Nobody made a move on Gargoyle to fuck up a potential deal just on the GP? Just to show they could-n't be messed with?"

"There's always hotheads, I suppose."

"Anybody you care to put a name to?"

Rene mused, "I could say Little Ce-Ce, but then, you must have had a talk with him by now."

Culhane nodded. "No, but I will. Who else?"

Rene's brow creased. "The more we talk about it, the more it doesn't fit. That was a sophisticated hit, Ronk. There's not a whole lot of dudes that could have pulled that off to begin with." He paused, considering his next words. "As far as I know, this bunk about the Ace Deuces behind the killing is just that. Why in hell would anyone want to bring that kind of heat? Especially if the Nines are supposed to have the hookup. Everybody's looking to make a deal with them, not create a squabble."

"There was another drive-by on some Swans over on Forty-eighth two days ago," Acosta said.

Rene shrugged. "That don't make it Crazy Nines shooting, Officer."

Ronk got up. "But like you said, there's always somebody who will act a fool even if it doesn't make sense. So Little Ce-Ce was making noise?" He lit the cigar.

Rene shrugged. "Yeah. About a month and a half ago him and Gargoyle got into a beef."

"Over what?"

"What else? A chickenhead. A hottie named Hillary, if you can believe that. She's part black and Latino, like your boy Saint."

Ronk grinned at Acosta. "Where can I find this sweetie?"

"On the theory she leads you to Ce-Ce?"

"I can't ask Gargoyle, now, can I?"

Rene breathed heavily and opened a file on his laptop and read the screen. He gave them an address in the 3600-block of St. Andrews.

"You're a man of many talents."

"People say that."

The two cops left. As they walked toward their car, Acosta asked? "Who the hell is that dude?'

"You ever hear of Meyer Lansky?"

Acosta shook his head in the negative.

Culhane beeped off the lock. "The young," he lamented. "Don't they teach you-all nothing these days?"

"So who was this dude?" He got in the passenger side.

Culhane started the car. "You never saw the movie *Bugsy*?"

Acosta was getting tired of this game. "The one with—what's his name?—Bulworth?"

"Yeah. Beatty." Culhane backed up from behind a dented Tahoe and, clicking into drive, pulled away from the curb. "Well, anyway, you remember the guy in the film that is this smooth talker, quiet, but is the one Bugsy has to convince that he needs the money to build the Flamingo out in Vegas?"

"Sort of."

"My point is, that quiet cat was Meyer Lansky. He was this Jew but he was the mob's money man."

"An accountant."

"Yeah, I think he might have had a degree or something, but he didn't just crunch numbers—anybody could do that. But what he had was vision. He was the one that got them into other kinds of businesses and not just, you know, pussy and dope. Shit that brought in money from the civilians."

Acosta worked a thumb in the direction behind them. "And that's what this Rene does for the Swans?"

"Exactly. He's some kind of math whiz and reads *Forbes, Wall Street Journal,* and whatnot and applies that expertise to moving Swans money around."

Acosta absorbed this. "And he does this why?"

Culhane laughed. "Why do some people go on national TV so they can tell the nation how big a ho they are or that they've been sleeping with their aunt or some such madness? People do all kinds of shit in this world, man. Logic would say Rene could be pulling down six figures in some gig at a Century City high-rise, but clearly that ain't what floats his boat."

"And why is he your snitch?"

"That's cruel to call him that."

"What? You getting sentimental now?"

"I'm just saying, there's snitches and then there's other kinds of people."

"So how is it that he's other kinds of people?"

"He's a considerate citizen." Culhane headed east on Slauson.

"Because he owes you?"

Culhane hummed.

Acosta watched cars out of the windshield. "The question is, what does he owe you? Huh, Ronk? And what do I think about that?"

"What would you do to stop crime, Alvaro? What does it take to really make a difference?"

"Like the alley?"

"Like the alley. A rude introduction, but there you go."

"You must know enough about me to realize I won't say anything."

Culhane regarded him. "Of that, I had no possible worry."

"I wish I was a better Catholic."

"That's cold, *ese*. You saying I'm the devil?"

"It's the temptation you're putting in front of me that's having me losing sleep, Ronk. You should have let me take the blow, whichever way the shooting team concluded it went down with Serenade."

Culhane negotiated a turn onto Crenshaw. "How bad you want to do your thing, kid? How bad you want to make the bad guys, the real motherfuckers that are bringing down our way of life, pay?"

"At any cost, you mean?"

Culhane rubbed his thin hair on his scalp. "Short of murder, yeah."

"That don't separate us much from them."

The veteran cop stared at the newbie. "Sure it fuckin' does. We stand for order; they stand for chaos. When we drop one of those two-thousand-pound satellite-guided bombs on some mud huts in Afghanistan and that rascal goes off track, blowing apart some orphanage, what's that?"

"Collateral damage."

"But those kids, who didn't have nothing to do with anything but wanting milk from their mama's tit, are dead now, aren't they?"

"Yeah, but that's different. Those are accidents."

"But acceptable deaths." Culhane jabbed an index finger toward the front window. "We're on a crusade, man. The civvies want their barbecue grills and two hundred channels on the dish. And they don't want some bandanna-wearing cholo coming over the fence and peeing in their pool."

"If we're on such a righteous cause, then why the—"

"Manipulation," he cut him off. "Because we didn't make the rules, Alvaro, but we have to know how to roll with them or they ream you for sure. Anyway," he continued, "it's not like that asshole was an honor student."

"But he wasn't armed."

"He just as easily could have been. And let me ask you this way: you want to be part of busting this thing wide open—and yes, getting beaucoup props in the process—or you want to watch us from where you're sitting behind a desk?"

"Acosta let the sound of the roadway occupy the space, then said, "You know goddamn well what I want."

"That's right." Culhane raised his fist, knuckles out, to the younger man.

A slight hesitation, but he knocked, gave him some pound.

"That's right," Culhane extolled.

Arriving at the address, Culhane slowed the car on the street, rolling past the address. They both craned their necks.

"No lights on," Acosta remarked.

"Let's see what we can see." The senior officer parked and the two walked toward the abode. It was a single-family early-'40s-era California bungalow typical of the style still prevalent in South Central. There was no car in the driveway.

"Your boy wouldn't be having one up on us, would he?" Acosta's hand had settled on the butt of his holstered semiauto.

"You worry too much, son." Culhane trudged forward. "No TV or stereo sounds, either," he whispered.

"This time the back?"

"Why not?" Culhane answered. The other man jogged around the corner of the cement porch. Waiting a few beats, he knocked. "Hillary," he announced. "Rene asked me to stop by." There was no response, and no movement in the house as far as he could tell. He repeated the action, and again nothing. He called out for Acosta, who came around.

"Guess we have to come back tomorrow."

"Or wait. What if she shows up later with Ce-Ce in tow?"

"Man, I don't know." Acosta blew air audibly.

"You got a hot date tonight?" Culhane took in the front of the house.

"No," he lied, "but this is a slim lead to begin with, Ronk." He'd been out once with Nan Chambers, the chunky blonde whose Beetle Harpy had run into while being chased by Acosta. She was studying painting at Art Center College of Design, in Pasadena, and liked to hit the clubs late. That worked well, so far, with his erratic schedule.

"Then you know who popped Gargoyle?"

Acosta held up his hands. "I take your point." He stopped himself as a car's engine could be heard approaching. The two jumped down on either side of the porch and crouched low. Sure enough, a fire engine red Suzuki Samurai pulled into the driveway, Eminem blasting on the CD unit. A woman was at the wheel, and a tall man with a knobby knee poking out the open side, wearing baggy shorts, was in the passenger seat.

"Look, I'm sure it was Busta Rhymes all up in that mug," the young man said as he unfolded from the seat. He was at least six feet five.

"Uh-huh," she replied in a Minnie Mouse voice. "That was Usher in Halloween Nitro."

"Naw," he replied, gaining the top of the steps in a brief leap. "That was fo' sho—"

"Can we have a few minutes of your time, Ce-Ce?" Culhane stood up, his flannel shirt open, the gun on his belt at the ready.

The long man turned and saw Acosta on his other side. The girl had her arms folded in contempt.

"Ain't y'all got some carjackers or pickpockets you can fuck with?" She was tan-skinned with big green eyes, and her black hair was combed to her waist. There was a silver stud piercing the area below her bottom lip.

"Yeah, fuck you McNabs. You always got to squash a brother's good thing. Can't you see me and my lady got plans?"

"This ain't gonna take but a few ticks, Ce-Ce, we promise." Culhane was coming up on the porch, and the Ace Deuce Swan pushed him, causing him to tumble backward. He then grabbed the young woman and shoved her at Acosta, who was also getting onto the porch.

"Hey," she protested, careening toward him.

Acosta sidestepped her and leaped as she fell on her side, skidding some. Airborne, he collided with Ce-Ce.

"Back the fuck off me," the Swan hollered.

Acosta didn't respond but concentrated on handling the suspect. The taller man braced his big feet against the front door and pushed, trying to grind the cop under his broad back. Culhane was hurtling over the lip of the porch. "Comin', partner."

Hillary was up, too, and she charged him. "Why don't you-all leave us alone?"

He went low and inside her praying-mantis-style grasp. He clipped her solid on the point of her chin.

"Bitch," she said, still on her feet and swinging.

Culhane was slugged alongside his jaw; her blow had heft behind it.

Ce-Ce and Acosta wrestled, each trying to get a fist or other part of his body on the other one. Acosta blinked tears after the Swan caught him under the ribs. He followed with an elbow he dropped into his chest like it was *Smackdown*. Acosta choked, trying his best to get free to get his own shots in.

"Fuck this," Culhane bellowed. He sent Hillary onto her butt hard with a short, chopping right that rocked her jawbone.

"Mothafuckah, hit my woman like that," Ce-Ce raged, rising. He made to twist loose from Acosta as he glared at Culhane.

"Shut up." Culhane swung the flat of his now unlimbered piece dead across the tall man's face. His head hit the door as he collapsed, groaning.

"Get up, honey; the dance ain't over." Culhane took him by the front of his Phat Farms and slammed his head into the door for safety's sake.

Acosta, breathing raggedly, turned to cuff the young woman.

"Get these off me and I'll kick your ass up and down Western, *pendejo.*"

"I'm scared." Acosta yanked her to her feet, starting toward the car.

"Hold up, Double-A," Culhane called. He'd gotten the stunned Ce-Ce on his stomach, and his wrists cuffed behind his back. "We got probable cause."

"What the hell are you talking about?"

Culhane jerked his head toward the house. "Get her keys. She was carrying them when they got out of the car."

"You ain't got no right," she said.

"See if we don't." Acosta spotted the Lakers basketball fob and tossed them to Culhane.

"I'll sue the shit out of your country asses."

"Quiet." Acosta thrust his finger at her, and she snapped at it like a piranha.

Culhane got the front door unlocked. He dragged Ce-Ce across the jamb. "Bring loudmouth inside."

"Hey, hey," the woman started saying loudly. "These porkers are trying to fuck with us. Hey, hey, goddamn it, the fuckin' cops are up to some shit," she broadcast.

"Shut her up. You want the whole neighborhood down on our heads?"

"How?"

Gag her, shit." He tossed him a bandanna that had been in Ce-Ce's back pocket.

"Aw, hell no, asshole. I'll have your mothafuckin' badges for this; I'll—"

Acosta got it tied around the struggling woman's mouth. He hoped to Jesus that no one was lurking nearby with a video camera. He pushed and pulled her into the house and closed the door.

Culhane, who'd gotten a light on, pointed at the floor. Hillary knew the drill and sat down cross-legged. Ce-Ce was coming around, but they left him prone on the floor.

"Don't you move," Culhane ordered his captives.

"Look at this stuff." Acosta indicated a bookcase in the living room filed with rows of CDs, bobble heads of rap artists and singers, models of customized cars, and all manner of hip-hop gewgaws.

"Yeah, so?" Culhane said.

"It's all kind of Def Ritmo gear," Acosta pointed out.

"You watch them." And Culhane stomped off to search the house. He pulled out drawers, felt behind cabinets, tapped on the kitchen floor for hollowness, and so on. All the while the young woman kept making muffled protests.

"What in the fuck?" Ce-Ce rolled over, his eyes refocusing. He got in a sitting position, noting Acosta's piece out and at his side.

"You just relax," Acosta advised, feeling the rush of control.

"Well, lookie here," Culhane called from the bedroom. He reappeared holding a multiround street sweeper shotgun. "Now, you know this thing is illegal, right?" he said, addressing Ce-Ce. "Or what will happen when we run the gun's numbers through the big, bad criminal index?"

The man built like a b-ball forward remained silent and sullen.

"You know what's next, big fellah." Culhane placed the firearms on the ground and reached for his cuffs.

"Can't we work something out?" the young man asked.

"This is a murder investigation, son." Culhane stepped over to where the Swan gang member was now sitting up, and put the bracelets on him. "You ain't got nothing to trade, anyway."

"This about that Gargoyle hit?"

"What if it is?"

"What if I know something?"

"Like what?" Acosta piped in as Culhane helped the tall man into a standing position. The young woman made more noise.

"Look, I got an alibi, aw'right?"

"Her?" Culhane jerked his head at the bound Hillary. "What crackhead jury is gonna believe her belligerent ass?"

Hillary garbled a "Fuck you" through her gag.

"Naw, look," Ce-Ce said as Culhane tugged him toward the door. Acosta had the woman on her feet, too.

"Mercury, that sneaky mothafuckah August Mercury did it, man."

Culhane opened the door. "How do you know this?"

"We got a deal?"

"What you and your hoochie got is an all-expense ride to the station house. Let's go."

"This is on the real, man. Tell him, Hill."

Hillary glared malevolently at the cops. Culhane nodded, and Acosta undid the bandanna. "I'm not telling you no-dick bastards anything until we talk to the DA."

"Girlfriend," Culhane began, "you've been watching too many episodes of *The Practice* on TV. The DA don't give a fuck about talking to you. We're the ones that can give or take away your freedom."

Acosta looked uncomfortable but remained quiet.

The pretty young woman named Hillary put a hand on her hip. "I work at Def Ritmo, chumps."

Culhane and Acosta exchanged looks, and everybody got comfortable as the cops asked several more questions of the couple. Then they left.

"Smart," Acosta said as they drove off.

"Yeah," Culhane agreed. "These two got their own little espionage thing going. Hillary works at Def Ritmo, picks up this and that tidbit of information about Mercury's operation."

"Probably looks in the files, too," Acosta said. "But does this mean that the Swans capped Gargoyle? It seems more like what Rene told us: why fuck with this deal now if the Swans were looking to get some side action? Especially if they have Hillary on the inside to tip them if something's up. And those two sure it was Mercury because he was afraid Gargoyle was going to edge him out."

Culhane said, "Or one of the other black gangs—like the Rolling Daltons, for instance—who wasn't going to be part of the new urban order stepped in to show their displeasure."

Acosta said, "So now what?"

"We keep on the prowl, *hombre.*"

"And maybe come back to ask Hillary more questions?"

"There you go."

CHAPTER 12

"That's it, baby; you know Mama loves it like that." Ferris Heckman closed her legs and ground the sartorious region of her inner thighs against the sides of August Mercury's face. He was buried in her muscled and tanned flesh. A cut from Alicia Keys's *Jane Doe* issued from the radio beside the bed. She bowed her head and back and shuddered to a climax, her hands firmly gripping the back of his head.

Mercury came up for air, gasping. "Damn, Hec, that's some potent stuff."

"And it's all yours, sweetie." She fingertipped his cheek and puckered her lips. There was a patina of sweat on her brow.

"And my ass belongs to the Del Fuegos." He plucked the snifter of V.S.O.P. from the flat headboard and had some. The stuff had been sitting there since last night. Heckman marked that he was drinking before ten in the A.M. Mercury's chest expanded and contracted; then he lay across the bed. "What are we going to do, Hec?"

She rubbed his back. "We're not going to give in to panic or paranoia, right?"

"I'm not suggesting that; I'm not a child."

"Far from it." She slapped his butt and fiddled with the setting on her radio. When their bodies shifted, the reception got fuzzy.

"We have to have a meeting." He had more of his drink.

She elevated a perfect eyebrow. "Go down to the ranch in Mazatlan and have a little face time with Rosario and Felix?"

"Why not?" he fumed. "This is serious shit. Though if Felix's not there that wouldn't hurt my feelings. He's so fuckin' touchy."

"To recap," a newscaster declared over the radio, "there was a large turnout last night at Trade Tech College near downtown for the debate between Mayor Fergadis and main challengers Assistant DA Constance McGuire and former Assemblyman Baxter Graham." Over the woman's voice the canned whoops and jeers of the audience could be heard.

"Punks. All of them useless as etiquette lessons for Allen Iverson," Mercury sneered.

"Shush," Heckman said, pressing a finger to his lips.

Part of Mercury's face knotted up, but he merely let his eyes swing toward the ceiling as he scratched his wrinkled, cooling balls.

"I'll give the mayor credit for one thing," McGuire was saying. "He did oversee an economic upturn for our city." She paused for maximum effect. "But that was three years ago, and he promptly oversaw a series of management blunders resulting in red ink flowing from a hemorrhaging City Hall."

This got some clapping that rose and fell like oscilloscope blips as the announcer came back on live. She reminded the listeners that the primary was Tuesday after next. Then a commercial for a miracle joint cream came on.

"So you going to see if we can talk with Rosario?" Mercury was at the closet and had pulled on his robe. It was a conservatively cut silk number with piping from the last collection designed by the late Bill Blass. Mercury liked the understated elegance of the classics. He felt wearing and surrounding himself with such fare projected to the public, if only on a subconscious level, that though he trafficked in what some derided as urban jungle music, he was a man who understood taste. And it looked good on him, too.

"It'll seem peculiar if I try to insist that it's only him," Heckman replied.

"No, it won't." Mercury turned halfway from perusing his appearance in the full-length mirror built into the closet door.

"Felix sees his murderous self as the original *vato loco*, baby. He hates to handle subtleties or details about a goddamn thing. All you have to do is send word via our boy Nino in TJ, the one that's tight with Rosario. He only likes to deal to that brother, too."

"Still," she allowed, "I'm not going to be blatant about such a suggestion. Each of them considers the other one their lucky charm, you know."

Mercury rubbed the back of his head. "But if we can work out a strategy with Rosario, Felix will go with what he tells him. If he gets wound up, that thin-skinned *idiota* can go off over, you know, the sun is coming in wrong through the blinds or some shit. But if Rosario thinks something is good for business, he can choke the chain on his brother." Mercury ambled about the room like a stranger who'd awakened in an anonymous city. He picked up the snifter and finished the brandy.

"I'll see," Heckman said. She was also up and getting a towel off the dresser.

He came up behind her, pressing himself close, his mouth fooling with her nape. "Once we get past this, we should take a vacation. Get over to London and Paris like we did that time." He kissed her as one hand fondled her stiffening nipple and the other massaged her clit.

She widened her stance and swayed against him. "There is something we can offer if Felix is there, too." She pulled on his rod, which was gathering strength.

"What, raw steak in a bowl with a side of bull's blood?"

She chuckled. "That and a target."

"Who?"

"McGuire."

Mercury started to shrivel. "Why?"

"Why not? You see that poll in the *Times* last week? She's inching ahead, up three to four points over Fergadis."

"But that's just now, before the runoff shakes out, Hec."

"Like Graham is gonna do anything? This is a one-woman and one-man show, honey boy. Kinda like you and me." She tilted her head back and gave him a love bite along his jawline.

"Let me say it again: why?" Now the two were facing each other—he in his unbelted robe and she naked with the towel draped over her shoulder.

"Imagine what would happen."

"Fuckin' chaos," he exclaimed. "A mayoral candidate shot down? The cops and the feds and probably the squareheads in black overalls from the office of Homeland Security will be swarming all over this town. Everything would be locked down."

She went on in a composed voice, the plan taking on a three dimensional quality as she did. "The brothers have their hooks into all kinds of people. It wouldn't be that hard to pressure some guy that owes them a debt to be the trigger man. Then, as the search for him intensifies, he's killed. Or better: it's during a public event where he shoots McGuire; then the killer of the killer knifes him as the crowd goes wild."

Mercury gaped at her. "Are you actually serious?"

She started to march off to the shower. "Anything is possible if you want it bad enough, August."

Hypnotized by her glorious backside, he could only wonder if he was the only sane person left in the city. He took a deep breath, then sneaked more brandy from the kitchen. Forty minutes later, the couple left Heckman's two-story Mount Washington abode perched atop Cazador Street and wound their way down to Silver Lake Boulevard. There, they parked and queued up for brunch at the Purple Foot, a popular eatery. Directly in front of the record exec and the lawyer were two older women in their sixties, in matching bright orange skirts too tight and with hems too high for women their age. Behind them was a six-four tat-draped, yard-muscled homeboy in a flowing guayabera shirt.

"Going to be hot," Mercury observed, squinting into the air as he broke out in a layer of alcohol sweat.

"Let's take a drive up the coast later," Heckman said. "Get our heads clear and we can work out our next moves."

"Sure, sure, that sounds all right. But I have to be back around seven. I have to catch this new rapper at the Rim."

"What you need to catch is a case," a new voice said.

Heckman speared a finger at Bruno Cortese's face. "And you should know better than threatening my client."

"Just expressing my First Amendment rights, champ."

Madeleine Jirac had a hand on Cortese's arm. "Come on, Bruno." She attempted to guide him away from the restaurant that they'd just left.

"Where's that bitch of yours?" Mercury blared. "Wait"—he snapped his fingers—"I bet he's down on Skid Row picking some drunk's pocket."

"Fuck you."

"It's you that gets fucked."

"Keep feeling frisky, Mercury. Shit's gonna rain down on you soon."

"I'm not the one that McGuire's got by the gonads. Of course, you'd have to grow some for her to have a grip, wouldn't you?"

Heckman interceded. "Okay, you both have dicks, all right?"

"Bruno," Jirac repeated.

Cortese sucked at a front tooth, then went away with her. "Can't even have a bite to eat without drama," he said.

"You started it."

"He's the asshole, Madeleine."

Jirac patted his arm, as one might with an overbearing teenager. The move wasn't lost on him.

"Yeah, I get it, Mom." He put a hand around her waist and tugged.

"You don't want to do anything to hurt your case in the event you get him in the docket."

Cortese snorted. "Like that refugee from a law library would have a chance of getting this chump off? Please. She's so deep in this, McGuire's going to wind up indicting her after she's disbarred."

"You hope." They crossed the street to where her car was parked around the corner on Micheltorena. She beeped the locks and shut off the alarm. "You still going shark hunting tonight?"

Three willowy Asian young women, all shimmering dark hair, giggles, and clunky open-toed platform shoes, came past them. Cortese waited until he was in the car before he answered, "I've got to solve this goddamn thing."

"But there's the risk." She pulled away from the curb.

"That's what makes it exciting to know me. 'The beauty of the act is in its expression.'"

"Hmmm, corrupting Jean Genet, if such a thing is possible." She leaned over and kissed him. She placed her hand on his upper thigh. "Don't get too full of yourself, darling."

"Oh, I know what to fill you up with." He pinched her breast.

"You're not worried about being followed? You know, other cops, I mean?"

"Followed, no. Bugged, yes. Saint's got a buddy from his Marine days who's the shiznit with the electronics, and has him sweep our rides and houses routinely."

"Including your pussy palace?" She drove east on Sunset.

"I don't know what you're talking about."

"You just better not be sticking your one-eyed monster where it doesn't belong."

"Ah, jealousy, thy name is—"

"Shut up."

"Okey-dokey." He turned the radio on and tuned in to the oldies station. Smokey Robinson sang "The Tears of a Clown."

"What if one of the women in your division used the ho hotel to take some male hustler there for a quickie?"

"*¿Cómo?*"

She curled her lip. "See? If it was a woman, you and your merry pranksters would be all atwitter."

"Baby, I'm for everybody getting all the slap-and-tickle they want. But as you must know, such a place you describe is not in existence."

"Until you find a new one."

He let a block roll by, then said, "Want to do it there when it's set up. Wear your black thongs?"

"Or nothing under my dress."

"There you go."

"I am not a slave to your dick." She lasciviously waggled her tongue at him.

"We're all just suckers for love, Madeleine."

"The question is, what kind of love, Bruno?"

"You worry too much." He patted her knee.

"I just want you to be careful."

"You mean as my golden years approach?" They stopped at a red light, and a man in a biker's leather coat, with a tattered pink chiffon dress over his black jeans, went through the crosswalk. He had a peacock on a twinkling leash. The couple barely noticed him.

"Something like that." The light changed and she proceeded.

"That's not going to happen; the sky isn't going to fall on me or you."

"It's not about me," she clarified.

"Sure it is. You wouldn't be honest with yourself if you didn't get that pause now and then about what us being together translates into among your little Jacques Derrida–lovin', bow tie beanie heads on campus."

She let a silence descend, then said, "You just like to fuck with my head."

"Don't I?"

"Bastard."

"Uh-huh."

She turned on Scott, the car rising and the Code 7 to their right. She drove her rebuilt classic Triumph GT, her fuck-my-ex-I-got-this-car, up past Dodger Stadium, then on around Elysian Park. Out on the lawn, a group of cholos in baggy shorts and athletic tees rode around on their tricked-out bicycles, all flashy chrome components and reflector disks. They were playing soccer Frisbee, and more collisions of bikes and spilling of beer took place than any actual game. She went on toward Griffith Park, a massive land trust bequeathed to the city by the self-proclaimed Colonel Griffith Jenkins Griffith in 1896—land that the city fathers originally didn't want but, because of water rights, accepted.

She went up a winding path that took them around part of the perimeter of the park, then finally past Roosevelt, one of its four public golf courses. She parked near a path paralleled by a dry gulley. They then walked up the path, the start of a hiking trail. Stopping at one of the trail's plateaus, they looked down on a bridle trail. A lone rider, a woman in wheat-colored clothing and sun hat on a gray stallion, went along it. Cortese and Jirac held hands as they gazed down at her.

"You know I don't give two shits about my position on the academic ladder," Jirac said, looking off. "When we got together, I knew perfectly well about the reputation of TRASH."

"But you figured you could tame the beast?"

She lightly slapped his cheek. "*Taming* is such a sexist notion."

He knew she liked the ride, like an adrenalin junkie who couldn't get enough of the sheer drop at an amusement park, or who took up skydiving because the jumps were just so exhilarating. She liked to hear about his escapades in the underbelly of a city she longed to experience more deeply than just in slapdash crime novels and half-assed TV cop shows.

At first he hadn't been very forthcoming in details. But as they spent more time together, he began to open up as he came to understand that she was his intellectual and emotional anchor. She was his sound board and his sister confessor. And he damn sure knew that if Santián or the others found out, they would not be what one might call ecstatic. Still, pointedly, he hadn't told her about his call from McGuire.

He put an arm around her shoulders, drawing her closer. "Baby doll, all the tough guys are dancing with shadows up at Corcoran."

"Keep being cute. But you might have to make a choice: this door or the other."

"If you're trying to spook me, Elvira, you can quit. And besides, you hip to something I'm not?" He didn't want to think about it, but turning a man's girlfriend on him had certainly been done before. Maybe all her talk about not being that protective of her career was all smoke and cinnamon.

Now they were walking through an expanse of oaks and patches of emerald. On the ground among the rocks and wild grass were broken vials, used condoms, and discarded Rolling Rock and Corona bottles. "I know about ambition and about drive, Bruno. And I know you can't let this business about the child molester go."

"I'd love to nail him to the wall," he seethed. "It would be good and clean. No ambiguity, no two sides to this."

"Unlike your role as TRASH man?"

Cortese dredged up a weak smile.

Jirac stepped around a sodden blanket becoming one with the earth. "Then you have to be where he is."

"He'd spot me for sure, the crafty fuck."

"I mean, there's plenty of chat rooms where these types hang out."

"Wonderful. Hi, I'm a little-boys'-underwear-sniffing, chocolate-speedway-stuffin' freak like you; can we talk?"

She lightly tapped him alongside his head. "You know what type of girl he stalks. In this racial smorgasbord of ours, bet there's a few sites designed for interracial kids to talk. Now, I'm sure they have some sort of security measures, but what if he lurks on one of these posing as a mixed-race girl. I'm sure he can imitate them exactly, given it's his obsession."

Cortese mused, "You might just got something there, Professor."

"Fuckin' A."

They kept walking. "So your take on McGuire is, she'll do anything to get over?" They'd halted by the side of a boulder, and Cortese leaned against it. She leaned into him.

"She's already done that *Twenty/Twenty* stunt. She's got that girl—what's her name?"

"Hyacinth."

"Yeah, she's got her secreted away. She's building her case, block by block."

"I don't want to be arrogant, Madeleine, but we know what a full-court press looks like. We've been doing this for a while now. We're not going to let her end-around us. At least not without one hell of a fight."

"I don't want to lose you, honey." She ground against him, kissing him deeply. "You and I have come too far, understand?"

"I know." They kissed, his hand slipping inside her pants as he held her close. He'd planned to mention the business with her son, but it seemed inappropriate to do so now. It could ruin the mood as her hands explored the familiar territory of his body and his finger worked its way around her sheer panties and into her crack.

CHAPTER 13

Hours past sundown, Cortese and Santián walked along the main line of Tijuana, Avenida Revolución in the Zona Central section. Saturday night was the bacchanal bebop as far as the college kids and their crew-cut counterparts in the U.S. armed services were concerned. Tijuana was on the border, twenty minutes from San Diego, but this was Mexico, and the drinking age was eighteen. And that particular fact, coupled with the primordial desire to activate and elevate hormones, couldn't help but make for uninhibitedness.

"Smell my motherfuckin' finger, bitch; smell it!" a tanned blond-haired girl in cutoffs and sandals bellowed at her friend, gesticulating with her digit in no particular direction. Both women laughed so hard, aided by their obvious inebriation, they crumpled to the sidewalk, helplessly spasmodic.

"Ladies." Santián saluted them as the two cops in civilian clothes stepped past.

The blonde called to him, "Come here, sweetie; come over and help me up, big Papa. Damn, you fine."

Cortese said, "No matter how blitzed the chick, man, you make them short of breath."

"Can I help it if you're jealous of my power?" his partner said flatly, intent on their destination.

Dashing in front of the two was an older woman in a peasant

dress, browner than the vapor curtain of smog that perpetually hung over the city. She was pushing a cart of grilled corn and *yuca* sprinkled with chili powder for sale. A young man in a USC sweatshirt who looked like a lineman stumbled into the woman and her wares. Her cart tipped over, and her foodstuffs skidded along the concrete.

"Watch your self, Granny," the big boy blustered. "You ought to put some blinkers on that fuckin' thing."

The woman knelt, assessing what she could save.

Cortese said to Santián, "Just keep stepping, man. It's not our concern, and we don't need to attract attention."

But then the kid had to show off in front of his buddies. "Say, Mama, here's five bucks; how about you give me a blow job? You know, el sucko." He made the motions with his hand and his mouth. His friends nervously giggled.

"Oh, fuck it." Cortese clasped the flats of his hands together in supplication as Santián wheeled around.

"*Con su permiso, señora,*" Santián said to the vendor. Then, to the younger man, who was some three inches taller than he was: "Tell her you're sorry and give her fifty bucks to replace the damage you've done."

The lad's pinprick pupils constricted further. "Who in the holy fuck are you?"

"Miss Manners. Now apologize." All around them the carnival swirled. A barker in a chalk-line three-piece suit and a sombrero from which dangled lit dingle balls hollered for the potential customer to see the smothering-titty wonders inside his strip club. People laughed and gawked, and a kid with blue spiked hair bent over and vomited onto a broken plastic hubcap lying in the street.

One of the big man's friends spoke up. "Hey, man, we're just having some fun, okay?"

"I'm all for it. Apologize and make it right."

Naturally, the larger man was defiant. "Fuck you. Maybe you'd like to take a suck, huh? You cute ho, you." He glanced back at his companions, but they weren't joining in on the fun. They recognized the look in Santián's dead face.

The cop drove the side of his forearm quickly into the younger man's solar plexus. This caused a retching action on his part, and with seemingly no more emotion than it took for him to breathe,

Santián followed that with a blow of his heel against the spot between the kid's brow. He went over in his pressed khakis. None of the partiers stopped their pace for an instant.

"What I asked you is so hard to do?" Santián was crouching down, like he was helping his sloppy-drunk pal to his feet.

The collegian merely blinked at this intruder into his revelry. "Look, man, I—"

Santián wagged a finger in the space between them. He then brought his nose closer. "Think about what you're going to say."

Cortese was positioned between them and the young man's friends. From the way he had his hand pressed to the side of his loose flannel shirt, the outline of his belt-holstered gun was apparent to them.

The footballer on the ground took this in. "Okay, sure, whatever."

Santián beckoned to the woman, who'd been standing off, unsure of what to do. "Go ahead; she'll get your meaning."

"I'm sorry," the athlete said softly. He was on his side, looking away, Santián hovering nearby like a stern coach.

"The money. Hand it to her."

"I don't have that kind of dough on me." He couldn't keep the spoiled-brat tone out of his voice.

"Give her seventy dollars or you'll think shoe leather is a new Jolly Rancher flavor."

The USC student's jaw tightened, and he briefly considered his options. He then rose and got his wallet out. He counted out four twenties and handed them to the woman. She took the money at Santián's urging.

"Enjoy the rest of your evening." Santián and Cortese continued on their mission. The woman rolled her cart on as the young men slunk away.

"Don't say it, Cheese," Santián said.

"I ain't saying shit."

Between Second and Third, there was a venue billing itself as Club Gladiator. As the name implied, it was a bare-knuckles emporium where patrons paid forty-five dollars for the privilege of going three rounds in a raised ring with some guy, or girl, who might be nice as pie or a two-time felon just out on parole. But that was just part of the fun. There was a second floor—canopied roof, actually—devoted to exclusive lap dances by women in diamond-studded thongs, or so the posters outside the club promised.

Down that same stretch, hemmed in by a squat twenty-four-hour tattoo parlor and lighting fixture emporium and a sea food restaurant, was the narrow three-story building, the Club Bella Donna. Live music pulsated from its interior, and Santián and Cortese got in line just like any other civilians. Once at the door, the bouncers gave them the sweep since they were on the other side of the age curve.

"If you're looking for your daughter," a beefy black man with orange crownrows said to Cortese, "you best not go off if she's in here, understand me?"

"Yes, thank you," Cortese managed neutrally.

Santián joked. "We just trying to get our swerve on, man."

"Old nasty bastards," the bouncer grumbled as they paid to enter.

The two headed toward the bar. On the dance floor, people bumped and shook and gyrated while the band played a combination of ska, metal, and classic rock *en español* on the florid stage. Somebody had taste and had done it up with scaled-down pilasters and scalloped cornices that had an overhang of copper and gold leaf. How it was outfitted reminded Santián of those days as a kid when he and his friends would sneak into the Orpheum or The Tower on Broadway to catch a double feature. Invariably it would be a kung fu flick with Sonny Chiba fighting Nazi zombies in the Amazon, and a horror feature with fanged buxom English babes.

"Let me glom those shots of Nino again."

Santián produced the digital prints. The photos revealed a handsome individual with hazel eyes and a build like a middleweight, in an expensively cut suit.

"He's the manager?"

"Yep. According to Vogel from the task force, Nino's been a fixture around here for a year, year and a half."

"But not a member of the Nines?"

"No—street kid, grew up on both sides of the border and was always working this hustle or the next. Just a dude doing his best to get by who got lucky.'"

Cortese frowned. "You know him?"

His partner motioned for the bartender. "Somewhere in his adventures, he and Linda's ex, Hector, were crime partners for a while."

"That ain't that surprising."

"I guess nothing is." He sounded reflective but adjusted into his usual demeanor when he ordered two Pacificos. "This being the busiest night during the week, my understanding is, Nino's usually flitting out and about here."

Cortese lifted his head toward the ceiling partially dotted with spotlights. "What's upstairs, in case I didn't know?"

The beers had arrived, and Santián tried some of his. "Second floor is supposed to be rooms that you can rent on the half hour for whatever. Each one is done up in a different theme like that place—what's it called?"

"The Madonna Inn."

"Right. Past that, on the third, are the offices and a storeroom. It's the store room that the task force has been very interested in."

"They got it bugged?"

"Vogel wouldn't say, so that means yes, but no doubt without that troublesome matter of getting it okayed by a judge."

"Yeah, the Constitution can be so pesky," his partner agreed.

Next to Cortese, a sailor downed another glass of Adios, Motherfucker. AMF was a concoction of vodka, gin, tequila, and rum in varying percentages. He yee-hah-ed like a drugstore cowboy. Leaving their beers unfinished, the two split up and moved about the first floor, hoping to catch a glimpse of their boy.

The band had taken a break, but there was no stopping the music. Canned techno reverberated from suspended speakers, and the dancing and attempted coupling continued. It was if the Bella Donna's patrons had all received the same message on their cell phones that the Apocalypse was nigh, and the only response was to amp up the hedonism.

In front of Santián, two pretty Latinas lifted their tube tops and rubbed their breasts together to the pleasure of the men and women around them. Reluctantly looking elsewhere, he spotted Nino, snaking through the crowd, holding onto a lit cigar. Santián shadowed his steps.

As he proceeded, there was a knotting of people, and he had to halt. He was going to push through, but the bunch untangled to reveal three people engaged in a free-for-all wrestling match.

"Shit." Gazing over the heads of the feisty revelers, he saw Nino signal to a couple of the bouncers, who went into motion. He tried forward motion, but a tall redhead slipped and collided with him.

The club goons were almost to the mini-event. Now the redhead was tangled up on Santián's ankles. As the focus was on the wrestlers, no one noticed when he kicked her loose. Nino went around a corner of the stage. One of the wrestlers, a big-shouldered kid out of an Archie comic book, upended one of his opponents. In turn, this person crashed into part of the crowd, causing drink glasses to shatter.

"That's enough," one of the bouncers in a leather vest said. He collared the corn-fed youngster and marched him toward the exit. The other two were helped up, and they, too, were removed. Santián made it near the stage and could see that there was a stairway back there. And there was a guard there, too. Watching, he saw couples and threesomes come up to this man and present tickets. Thereafter, they'd be allowed up once he talked into his two-way. He went to find Cortese.

"But they'll hardly let us look around," Cortese said after Santián explained the setup.

"It gets us closer."

"You got some hot mamas in your back pocket?"

"This is TJ, Cheese. And money is the universal lubricant."

"Colorful way you put that, mate."

Not a half hour later, the two escorted a high part-time college girl in hip-hugger jeans toward the stairs. She only hooked when she needed tuition money, she'd told Santián, but because there were two of them, she was going to give them a discount.

"*Aquí está,*" Santián said to the guard. The ticket, which verified he'd paid the rental fee, was for an hour.

He casually took in the trio and radioed to the bar where the tickets were sold. After a moment he received confirmation, and they went up. As they did, Cortese had to keep their shill from tumbling backward and cracking her head. They got to the top and were stopped by two more guards.

"We need to search you for drug paraphernalia," one of them growled. The big word escaped from his lips smoothly; he'd had a lot of practice saying it.

"Nino said everything was *tranquilo.*" Santián produced two fifties.

Without argument the guards each took their tribute and indicated a room midway along the north wall. The trio went forward,
their third leg shaky.

"You ever been to Muscatane?" She had one eye closed and the
other bleary one trained on Cortese like he was a suspect.

"No, baby."

"You sure?"

"I've been to Connie Romita's House of Steak and Pies in Queens;
that count?"

She made a sound through her nose. "Where's that?"

"Here's our stop." Santián got the door open, and they went in.
The decor was not as tacky as the two cops had expected, given the
floor's function. The theme was Roaring Twenties and included a
phone from that era, an ice box, and photos of Bogart, Cagney,
Sylvia Sydney, and Pat O'Brien along the floral wallpaper. The part-
time prostitute spun and flopped onto the bed, preparing for her
event. "Come on," she slurred, lying on her back and cocking her
legs open like barn doors. "Which one of you guys wants first,
huh?"

Ignoring the alluring come-on, Santián and Cortese went to the
curtained window. It was painted shut, but at least it was on the side
of the building and not facing the busy boulevard.

"Let me see what I can do." Santián bent down and started to
work the blade of his Swiss Army knife into the sash and the ledge.

"Hey, how about we order some drinks?" their companion said.
"And some fish tacos. You like fish tacos? Who doesn't like fish
tacos?"

"Yeah, baby, sure," Cortese said, "only let's keep it on the down-
low, okay?"

She gave him her Popeye bit again, sitting up on an elbow. "Fuck
you mean telling me to be quiet, Pops? I'll talk anytime, anywhere I
feel like it." She snapped her fingers, diva-style.

"Handle your woman, dude." Santián continued digging between the crevices.

Cortese sighed heavily and went to stand over the girl. "What's
your name?"

"I told you my goddamn name. Goldie."

She looked about as well suited to the name as Jason Kidd did to
being a marriage counselor. "Well, look, Goldie, how about you just

be cool and let me and my friend do our thing, then we take you back downstairs and we'll buy you dinner?"

She pushed her chipped nail into Cortese's chest. "What about the three hundred bucks you promised?"

"We don't want sex."

"What? I'm supposed to watch you two go at it? That's what this is?"

Exasperated, he looked over at Santián, who was now using the flat of his fist to knock around the edges of the window frame. He resumed what he knew to be a losing conversation with the young woman. "How about I give you a hundred to just lay there and shut the fuck up?"

Her blue eyes widened. "Say, who the fuck you talkin' to like that, huh? You think jus' 'cause you buy a little twat that gives you the right to say any damn thing you want to, huh?" She tried to get off the bed but couldn't coordinate her feet with her legs.

"Keep her quiet, Cheese." Santián pushed on the window, trying to make it budge.

"Hey, come on; we're all on the same side, right?"

She slapped his hand away. "Fuck you guys. I'm leaving."

Santían came across the room to the woman, grabbing her arm and shoving her back on the bed. "Sit still."

"You like it rough, big and tan? Well, come on, then." She stood on the bed and started bouncing up and down like she was on a trampoline.

"This fuckin' broad." Santián and Cortese reached for her, and she started to scream. "That's enough of that." Santián got her prone on the bed, his hand over her mouth. She started to beat at his arms, but the alcohol she'd soaked up had dulled her reflexes.

"Good plan," Cortese lampooned.

"You're a big help." To the young woman he said, "You don't get your money unless you keep your loud mouth shut." She made sounds and tapped his hand with hers. He looked at his partner.

"You must listen," Cortese said, like a stern schoolmaster admonishing one of his stubborn charges.

She made a motion with her head that could have meant anything. Santián took a chance and removed his hand, though it hovered close to her face.

"So what's the deal, fellas? Wha's the haps?"

Cortese declared, "Great, now she's all Nancy Drew on us. Look, we're after some tough *hombres*, okay? This is big. I mean like, we have a chance to bust this racket wide open after months of undercover work."

Slack-jawed, she glared at Santián. "You mean like in that movie?"

"That's right"—as if he knew what movie she was talking about. "That's why you have to help us."

"Okay." She started to unzip her pants.

"No, no, not like that." Santián had to look away from Cortese to keep from busting up. "Here's the thing, Goldie."

"Ashley," she said. "I use that other name when I'm . . . you know."

"Smart," Cortese contributed.

"So, what do you say, Ashley? Can you help us out here?"

"I can," she said proudly. "You want me to keep watch?"

"No, don't go out in the hall. We don't want the guards getting suspicious, know what I'm saying?"

"Sure." She nodded her head vigorously, the ends of her damp hair flailing like alien antennae.

"Good. Just be still while me and my friend do what he gotta do."

"You do what a man's gotta do." Cortese patted his thick, solid gut. "I've been having too many lemon bars while Madeleine has her macchiato at Starbuck's"

"Fine, you keep homegirl company and keep a listen. But help me with this sash first." Together they got it open, Santián having knocked loose the paint. On the bed, their date was flat on her back, gasping like a goldfish out of water.

"What a lady." Cortese stuck his head out the window and looked up, then across at the wall to the other building. By extending his reach, he could easily touch that wall.

"Don't you take advantage of my girl while I'm gone," Santián gibed. He got a leg through the opening.

"Me? How can you say that?"

Santián started up the wall.

"You know," Cortese began, "this shit works great in those old episodes of *The Wild, Wild West*. But Robert Conrad was smaller and lighter than you."

His partner said with effort, "What are the alternatives?"

"Nino might be getting his wick wetted in his office."

"Maybe," he huffed, "but we still have to see."

The building next door was close, and Santián was using that wall to brace his back against and inch himself upward.

"We could get our heads blown off for this."

"I'm trying to climb here, Cheese." Santián exhaled forcibly as he moved up. "Fuck, I'm scraping the hell out of my elbows."

"Don't be such a crybaby," Cortese said. "Careful, there's a window above you.

"Don't you think I see it?" Santián kept his steady ascent, but then his foot slipped, and dust and loose pieces of brick dribbled down. He had to get his footing and his breath back.

"You all right, man?" Cortese was leaning out the window, his butt propped on the window frame.

"Just give me a second."

Cortese wasn't sure, if his partner should really slip, whether he'd be able to halt the fall, but he'd do something. Out on the boulevard, someone shouted and a bullet singed the air. It got quiet for a brief moment; then the steady hum of the revelers rose again.

"I had Vogel draw me a diagram. Nino's office is to the left, about in the middle of the third floor."

"So where does this window above you look into?" Cortese asked.

"Uggh. Fuck I know. Vogel just showed me the main sections." Santián continued until he'd hoisted himself below and across from the window. A weak light filtered through it, but he couldn't hear any words or movement.

"Well?"

"Well . . ." He had his feet positioned on the window's ledge, huffing and tasting salt on his lips. "I got to see about getting this up or something."

Cortese chuckled. "How you plan on doing that, champ?" The drunk woman made noises on the bed.

Santián shifted along the wall, the scraping of his jeans against the brick making a dry, sandpapery sound. "Why didn't you mention this?" Since Santián had to press his back and shoulders to the wall to keep from sliding down, there was no way he could bend forward enough to reach the window.

"I didn't want to spoil your good time, seeing as how you wanted to play Spider-Man. Didn't you bring your web shooters with you?"

"Kiss my ass."

"Hey," Ashley who went by Goldie when she hooked said in a syrupy voice from the bed. "When we getting dinner?"

Cortese laughed. "You better get back inside, son. It's obvious even to you that we need a new plan."

Santián started back down. "This ain't the Heights, Cheese. We don't know all the back alleys. We're on Nino's home court."

"Maybe your girlfriend can help us on that score," Cortese said.

"She couldn't give a blow job away to a man two minutes from the electric chair." There was more brick dust and some skidding as Santián lost partial purchase and started to come down too fast.

"I got you." Cortese grabbed his shirt and arms and hauled him through the window. Both men fell to the worn industrial carpet.

"Yeaaaah," Ashley clapped and bounced, sitting up on the bed.

Santián clapped his friend on his arm and they both stood. "If we trail him, then we're going to have to waylay the dude," the sergeant announced. "If he gets to the crib, no telling what kind of firepower he's got or who's staying there."

"That means we would need to take him someplace where we can sweat him."

Santián brushed himself off. "I might have the answer to that, homey."

"You guys are funny," their new pal said.

They allowed some more time to pass so as not to give the guards any reason to believe they weren't using the room as intended. They got Ashley to cooperate, with the promise of a meal, now that she was part of the team. Cortese left with her to feed her while Santián remained in the club. His patience was rewarded when Nino reappeared on the ground floor in less than half an hour. He stopped to say something to one of the bartenders, a cute brown-haired woman in a leopard-print top, then left the club.

Out on the *avenida* he walked briskly, and Santián assumed he might be going off the crowded thoroughfare to retrieve his car. He and Cortese had parked some distance away, but there were plenty of cabs of lesser or greater degrees of legitimacy jockeying about. He called Cortese.

"You should see this chick attack a plate of tamales and ceviche," were his first words.

Santián put him on alert.

"We're on Constitución, between Sixth and Seventh; sounds like you two are parallel and heading in our direction."

A man in an unreasonably long trench coat tried to sell Santián carved stone heads on a card table, claiming they were authentic Maya. The TRASH man waved him off. "He's stopped to get an ice-cream cone and gab with this little mama at this stand. Either he's swimming in trim or he wishes he was."

Tailing someone with plenty of people around allowed you cover, but it also made it too easy to get put off track. You had to zig and zag around lost couples, arguing couples, amorous couples, and the drunk and the high. Santián kept his distance but kept his man in sight. Near Sixth, Nino Cruz took a right and scooted down a passageway cut between a building and a fence made mostly of corrugated metal sections and plastic sheeting. Santián approached the corner cautiously and peered around it.

"Damn it," he groused, turning and scanning the street. He trotted over to three women about to get into a '93 Oldsmobile Delta 88 taxi.

"Sorry, ladies," he said, bulling his way through them and toward the rear door.

"Oh, hell, no," one of the women with a raspy cocktail voice blared. She put a hand on Santián, and there was muscle behind it.

"Police business." He flashed his badge and a twenty. "Catch the next one, froggy." He handed the tough one the money and dove inside.

She and one of her other adventurous pals flipped him the bird, but they accepted the compensation. In Spanish he barked, "There's a Mercedes coming out up there," he pointed, "follow the goddamn thing."

"Not a problem, bro," the cabbie replied in English. He was a young man with long curly hair and a crucifix for a lone earring. He wore a baseball cap backward with a Mavericks logo on its brim. "This something heavy, man?" He got the car around a pothole as Nino's vehicle slowed because a women in a purple sarong had tipped off her Vespa right in front of him.

Santián called Cortese back to fill him in while they idled three cars behind the Mercedes.

"You need some heat, bro?" The cabbie smoked and dispensed clove-scented vapors against his cracked windshield.

"I'm cool." He clicked off. Cortese was to call him back in fifteen if he didn't hear from him. "You know who we're following?"

"No, bro." Miss Sarong, with the help of three stout lads, got her scooter out of the way, and the traffic resumed its pace. "You from San Diego?"

"L.A." He sat forward. "Nino Cruz is the man, right?"

"Who's that, bro?"

Santián assumed the driver was just naturally being closemouthed until it was clear how he could make money out of whatever it was that his passenger was up to. A fifty was laid over the top of the front seat, held in place by Santián's two fingers. The cab driver kept his eyes forward, both hands on the wheel. But he could have a white cane and a hustler like him would have smelled the money.

"The faucet doesn't just run once," Santián told him in Spanish as he let the bill flutter from his fingers.

The driver left it on the seat beside him. In English he replied, "He makes moves; that's for sure. He's in tight with the Del Fuegos."

"The first one was just to break the ice," Santián said. "But to earn the other four I'm holding, you got to give me something I don't know, bro."

As Santián had surmised, Nino was heading into the hillsides, the upmarket area of the border city. There were two- and three-story houses of designs ranging from understated to ostentatious in a way that only new money—illicit money—could manifest. Here the tailing would be more obvious.

"Don't follow him to his crib." Santián also switched to English.

"He's got some pussy up this way." The promise of more had primed his greed—everybody liked money. "Good pussy, too—connected, know what I'm sayin, homey?"

"He don't live up here?"

"No, bro."

"Since you know where he's headed, let him get there first."

"I've never taken him there direct, you know. But my boy, another driver, told me."

"Hang back anyway." They were now south of the Playas region, the Pacific Ocean adjacent. The car slowed and went to the curb near a Calimex supermarket. The Mercedes made a light then turned left up an inclined street. "How many ways off that hill?" he asked.

"There's a side road out, but if he's not worried about anything, he's likely to come back this way."

"What your name, man? They call me Ray," Santián said, extending his hand. Like a lot of the operator-owned taxis in TJ, it had no ID card fastened anywhere.

"Umberto," the other man answered.

Santián weighed that Umberto could be bullshitting him, knowing he was eager to keep on Nino's ass and therefore playing him like a mark.

"Can you call your buddy?" Santián asked.

"Who's that, bro?"

"Come on, you know I'm good for it."

The cabbie produced a cell phone and, after calling two numbers, located his friend. There was a haggle over price, but the man on the other end produced the address at the assurance of seventy-five dollars for his knowledge. Everything, Santián reminded himself, was negotiable.

They waited. Santián went into the market and got some beers—Budweisers, the king of brew on both sides of the border. He and Umberto sipped until Cortese, summoned by Santián, arrived with Ashley in another taxi. Cortese paid off his cab, and he and Santián conferred by themselves.

"That ain't much of a plan, Saint," Cortese said after Santián talked. His lips were cracked, and the crow's-feet at the corners of his eyes were more pronounced.

"We've hummed mothafuckahs standing on shakier ground than this. What the fuck?"

"Don't go getting all indignant with me." An olive-colored Tahoe with tinted windows drifted past. The two were tight-lipped until the vehicle was gone. There were law enforcement branches of the Mexican government into big SUVs, therefore no sense taking a chance. "If we get jammed up, that's it—we're cooked," Cortese resumed.

"We ain't going to get caught. We're the TRASH men, baby."

"You're starting to believe your press just a little too much, Saint. We keep pushing it, somebody's bound to push back harder."

"But not today. Nino surely has some local cops in his pockets. But we shave the odds in our favor. Like we always do."

Cortese could keep arguing, but to what end? He'd come along like he always did—the corner man, the stand-up partner who had his friend's back. But a man just couldn't always run in the same direction, always chasing the same thing over and over. He'd done his time on the squad and in the Department. Yet here he stood on a humid Tijuana street about to put in more work. What the fuck?

Umberto ferried them past the house. Like a lot of the upscale *colonias* in TJ, the house had a high wall with shards of broken glass embedded along the top. There was at least one dog, a Doberman they spotted through the grill of the front gate, and an octagonal decal announcing the alarm service. The taxi then parked down the hill.

"You're not fucking with us, are you?" Santián leaned into the driver's window, the payment in his hand.

"How can you say that, my brother? Specially since you and your beefy Italian friend are strapped. They still say 'strapped,' yeah?"

"Oh, yeah." He let go of the money as Umberto took hold. The taxi clunked into gear, and he drove off. Santián went over to the others.

"You can do this." He clasped Ashley by the shoulders, a coach bolstering the Little Leaguer who'd yet to shine.

"Damn straight," Cortese rah-rahed.

"You ready, Goldie?" Santián said.

She nodded her head animatedly. "Shit yeah," she affirmed, dropping back into her hard-girl persona.

"Let's do this," Cortese said, pushing the woman in the small of her back toward the intercom they'd noted on the wall next to the gate. She stared at the box.

"Easy, baby, easy." Santián could tell she was starting to get agitated. Of course, from what he'd observed, either of her identities was easily set off. "You'll be great." He had his arm around her like the prom queen's escort.

"I like you."

"I like you, too, Goldie. You're the best."

"Jeez," she giggled.

Maybe she'd been skipping her meds, he speculated. "You remember what to say?"

"I've taken acting lessons, you know."

I bet you have. "You're going to be the next Angelina Jolie, I can see that." He maintained a straight face.

"After this, you and me can discuss other things I do."

"We'll get to that. One thing at a time, right?"

"Yeah." She bussed his cheek. She reeked. This chick was perfect. The young woman sashayed to the squawk box and made a production of leaning over and pushing the button. She must have seen it in some movie, Santián figured. He rejoined Cortese.

"Ready?"

"I'm good; let's hook and book." They knocked fists.

"Tell him it's Goldie, bitch," the temporary third member of their crew was yelling into the intercom. "Tell Nino he better get his useless self out here so I can get this money for the abortion. This is serious, *¿comprende?*"

"Go away," a woman's voice said. "See him at the club, not tonight. We can't be bothered by your problems tonight."

She smiled at the two, and Santián made motions for her to continue. "This is your problem when I go to the newspapers. I'm American, señorita."

There was no answer, and for all they knew, the woman had tired of Goldie's tirade and had unplugged the box. Or the hand was overplayed and she was calling the cops on this crazy woman at her door. Presently there was a sound of high heels on concrete. The dogs barked happily and trotted beside their mistress.

"You are drunk and stupid," the woman behind the gate announced upon viewing the stranger. She was in her forties, handsome, with Indian features, in a red kimono and smelling of expensive perfume. "Now, go away before you get hurt."

"No," Santián said, stepping quickly from their spot beside the wall. Quickly, he grabbed her hair, mashing her face against the wrought-iron bars. "Take us in to see Nino."

The woman glared defiantly at him. "You think if you step inside my property my beauties won't chew your balls off?" Her English was clear and concise. On either side of her leg, her disciplined Dobermans sat and waited for the signal. They didn't pant.

"I believe you are as smart as you are pretty," he answered in

Spanish. "You didn't get this house by doing foolish things. Certainly not for someone like Nino." Who he figured was her boy toy, a passing lustful fancy. At least, that was the rationale he needed to get him through this.

Cortese came into view, gun in hand. "This is business, that's all. No one gets hurt if we get what we want."

Ashley who went by Goldie breathed through her mouth, watching the negotiations unfold.

"You just remember who I am," the homeowner warned. She unlatched the gate, and Santián still gripped a fistful of her hair as he walked backward, letting one side creak open. Cortese pointed his gun at the dogs, who were standing, their bodies trembling with anticipation.

"Ma'am," Cortese began, "If you don't tell your beauties to stand down, there's going to be some messy results."

Despite the fact that the woman had her face pressed into the bars of her own security gate, she was still collected. *"Genet, Márquez, esperen,"* she ordered.

"You named your dogs after writers?" Cortese asked, impressed.

"Why not? Writing's a dog's life, isn't it?"

Santián released her hair. His gun was aimed at her. She had to assume that if she flicked her finger and the dogs lunged, she would be shot.

"This way." Her robe had come undone, revealing satiny underwear. Unhurriedly she tied her sash back in place. Ashley was motioned inside by Santián, and the gate was clicked back into place. The handsome woman started up the walkway of irregularly shaped flagstones, the dogs, her four-legged centurions, on either side of her. The landscape inside the walls was verdant with transplantings from the border region. There were fiery salvias, sprays of antique rose bushes, plumeria, trumpet vines, and more.

"Where the fuck is Nino?" Cortese whispered to Santián as they walked up the path.

"You ain't never lied." It had been a while since the woman had gone out to see about the crazy *chica* at the gate. Why hadn't Nino followed her as they'd expected? Was he lying in ambush? "If Nino jumps out with a goddamn machinegun like he's auditioning for the remake of *Scarface,* you know what will happen." Santián pressed the muzzle into her side to underscore his point.

"You always talk so tough with women? Does it make you hard?"

The swish of the material around her legs and the scent of her mingled with the flora could give a man pause if he didn't keep his mind on straight. "I'm not a kid like Nino."

"Oh, I can see that."

"The door, madam."

She undid the latch to a heavy medieval-style portal, all rough wood and heavy metal brackets. The intruders followed her into a kitchen, where indirect lighting gave its hard surfaces a warm, soft glow as if it were prepped for its pictorial feature in some home decor magazine.

"Come on," she said, as if taking the others on a tour. She was too relaxed and that made the cops' nerves tingle. Her dogs had also trooped into the house.

"Those bruisers stay in the yard," Cortese said.

The woman was in an archway leading to the rest of the house. The dogs were stationed between her and the two cops. She was clever.

"I think not." She was about to utter a command until Santián put a round in the microwave. It flew off the counter and clattered onto the ocher-colored pavers.

"We told you what this is. We told you we weren't kidding."

The muscles on the dogs' hindquarters were rigid, tensed to spring at the attack word they longed to hear their owner say. The woman stood very still.

Ashley was standing at the back door, comprehension seemingly elluding her. "We going back to the club?" the party girl inquired. "I'm hungry again."

"What's it going to be?" Santián didn't know for sure which dog had what name, but it seemed to him that the larger one would be named Márquez. The damned beast looked like a Márquez.

Resigned, the woman said, "Very well. She told the dogs to retreat, and they headed toward the outside door. The one Santián had in his mind as Márquez looked back at him. And as humans tended to project their traits onto man's best friend, it seemed to him that the dog had a twinkle in his agate eyes, as if he were communicating to Santián that they'd settle this matter later. Then the dog turned its head and followed his companion back into the yard.

"Lead on." Cortese shut the back door.

In the spacious living room there was a big screen TV with a frozen image of Guy Pierce battling a slouching apelike being with long hair and whitish skin.

"The Time Machine," Ashley said, plopping onto a heavily cushioned chair. She was enthralled by the big faces.

Nino Cruz was also clad in a red robe, with slacks and no shirt. He had his head back on the couch, a smoldering Monte Christo cigar between his manicured fingers. Ash was on the carpet, and several small open bottles, poppers of amyl nitrite, spread across the coffee table along with a bottle of Cuervo Gold. He also had a raging boner going.

"I told him not to mix the shit with tequila." The handsome woman moved off to one side, the impresario making way for the main event. "He likes to get the rush before we have sex." She folded her arms.

Santián stood next to the blissed-out man. He tapped his cheek with his pistol. "Wake up, slick; we got something we need to ask you."

"Yeah, Yolie," he drawled.

"I'm not your honey," Santián replied, tapping the man again with the gun. "Wake the fuck up; this ain't no time for beddy-bye." He plucked the cigar out of the narcotized man's hands and dabbed the lit end against his forehead.

"Fuck," Nino Cruz swore, sitting upright in a flash. "The fuck's wrong with you, woman?" He blinked rapidly, looking around the room. "I know you?"

"We're friends of Gargoyle's."

He scowled. "You *putas* better step."

"Why? Rosario or Felix coming over?"

"Man, fuck you." Cruz started to rise, but Santián pushed him down.

Cortese crowded closer, too, keeping the woman in sight. He wouldn't be the least bit surprised if she produced a Glock from her crotch and started blazing.

Ashley had gotten hold of the remote and had the DVD going again. A bestial growl bounced around the living room. Without cajoling, she muted the set and became absorbed in the doings of the time traveler.

Nino Cruz snarled, "Do you know who the fuck I am?"

"Everybody likes to remind us of just how bad they are up in this mufuh," Santián cracked. He bonked the top of Cruz's head with his gun. "Now, I know you're a for-real gangster and all that goes with it." He winked at the handsome woman, who stared back at him. "But we got a real interest in getting a line on your silent partners."

"Ain't nobody but me, *carnal.*"

"Oh, *¿sí?*" Santián was on one side of him and Cortese on the other. "Now you trying to clown us." He grinned at his friend. "I told you he wouldn't be straight with us."

"Yeah, yeah, you did." No sense half-stepping or Cruz would see them as candy-asses. When you asked a question, you better think long and right on the answer.

It wasn't always right, but that's the way things were. Cortese's blow to the man's mouth was so sudden, the two women in the room jumped.

"Shit," he exclaimed, and let go a bloody wad of spit onto the coffee table. "What, you two Border Patrol? That it? Tired of making five hundred a week and want to play on the big boys' court?" He wiped his mouth with his hand. "How much you small-dick motherfuckers need to go away, huh?"

"We are not interested in going away, Nino. What we want is a line to the Del Fuegos."

"What you need is a bath, bitch."

"Tough guy."

"Absolutely," Cortese said. His kick to the man's midsection doubled him over. He gagged and dry-heaved. Ashley remained absorbed in her movie. The other woman said nothing.

"Whatever you think you can do to me," Cruz wheezed, "it ain't shit to what would happen to me if I told you anything. So once again, fuck you."

Cortese didn't appreciate a chump taking him lightly. He raised his fist to strike him again, and Santián stopped him. The sergeant pulled him away from Cruz.

"We actually might have to employ some detective skills, old bean. Or take this to a level we can't have these ladies around witnessing."

"Are you stopping?" the handsome woman asked. Her hand was pressed against her flat belly, the veins blue in her dark hand.

"Freak," Cruz said.

Santián looked from her back to Cortese. "If you were making big ducats with a hook to the Del Fuegos crew, wouldn't you have a number for them on speed-dial?"

"Yeah," the other man agreed.

"You keep our guests cozy, and I'll take a gander upstairs."

"Righteous." Cortese could feel the heat cool in his body, the taste return to his mouth as his head cleared from the haze that enveloped it when he got like this.

Santián went up the tiled stairs with the hand-carved banister. The master bedroom was tastefully appointed in somber hues, complemented in a mix of modern and classical art in sculpture and painting. There was a print of a comic-book-style World War II fighter plane Santián had seen once on the cover of some magazine.

He searched and found some videotapes that, judging by the labels, featured the woman of the house and Cruz—and, it seemed, a few others, too. More nosing about and he found a cache of U.S. money and a few handguns. Where the hell was Cruz's cell? They might have to beat the man senseless after all if he couldn't produce the instrument. He kept looking, but it wasn't to be had.

Going along the hallway, he passed the bathroom and spotted a cell phone on the ledge of the sink in there. He thumbed the settings on and got a series of numbers to pop up. He went back downstairs and showed the readout to Cruz.

"You ain't getting shit from me; didn't I make that clear to your simple mind?"

Santián shrugged and wrote the numbers down. Then he started dialing.

"Hey, dude . . ." Cruz attempted to get off the couch, but Cortese put his gun on him. "You can't just call those people, man. That's my business you're messing with."

"So?" He dialed the first number and got the answering service for a limousine company. On to number two.

Cortese said to Cruz, "How's it gonna be when some *gabacho* is calling the number only you and a few of the special people are supposed to have, huh?"

"Who you calling a *gabacho?*" Santián asked. The second number was to the phone behind the bar in the club.

"Cut it out," Cruz said. "What the hell do you two want? You want a line on a shipment, that it? I can break you off some, okay, before the money goes across."

Cortese said. "A little money-laundering detail you supply for the brothers?"

"Put the fuckin' phone down, hear me?"

"Number three might be the charm." Santián began putting in the number.

Cruz chewed his lip while, on the big-screen TV, Guy Pierce swam through a massive vat of human stew in the city of the Morlocks. Ashley watched, quietly chewing a cuticle.

"No," Santián announced after listening to a recording on the other end. "Some other chick's pad." He glanced over at the woman in the corner. Her robe had come undone again, but she made no effort to belt it shut. Her hand was pressed hard against her stomach.

"Let's see what's behind door number four, Monty," Cortese said.

Cruz held up a hand. "How much?"

"How much. . . ?"

"How much you want to stop fuckin' with me?"

Santián didn't hesitate. "Two hundred grand."

Cruz didn't balk. "We have to go back to the Bella Donna for it."

"Let's roll."

"I gotta get dressed."

"My man will help you."

"Fuck I look like—Alfred?" Cortese complained as he followed Cruz up the stairs.

Ashley was now mouthing the dialogue to the movie.

"How many times have you seen this, girl?" Santián stepped over to the other woman. "Yolie? Yolanda, is it?"

"Uh-huh." She looked up at him. "You going to kill Nino?"

"Nothing that drastic."

She smiled. "Just some more fist work?"

He smiled back. His hand touched her thigh, and she guided it between her legs, rubbing her wet mound. They were flicking their tongues together when footfalls clacked on the tiles. "Maybe you should come back here later and show me how rough you can get," she whispered.

"Maybe I will, Yolie."

The three drove back to the Bella Donna in Cruz's Mercedes, Santián at the wheel and their prisoner in the back with Cortese. They'd left Ashley enjoying her movie. At some point Yolie would either kick her out or put a blanket over her if she fell asleep.

The streets were jammed with bodies and cars and bicycles and pushcarts, all of it overhung with a pallor of excess pheromones and exhaust. They got within five blocks of the club and parked in an alley, this after a traffic stop wherein Cruz paid the cop a crisp one hundred American. When the cop had pulled them over, recognizing Cruz, and leaned into the car, he'd appraised the other two, hand on his holstered gun. He'd rested a steady gaze on Cruz. The club owner had played it right, and they'd departed, unperturbed.

Santián said, "Don't give your boys the high sign when we get inside, understand?"

"Sure." He'd used a wet washcloth and cleaned his face and chin. In the murky lighting that was the perpetual condition of Tijuana by night, his bruises weren't too apparent.

At the door Cruz got a cursory nod from the bouncers, and the trio were let in. Inside, they had to move slowly because the first floor was packed like a cattle car.

"The stairs are over there," Cruz said, pointing.

"Okay." No sense letting him know they'd been in the Bella Donna before. Neither of them believed for a second that he was really going to take them upstairs and pull out wads of cash from the safe. But whatever he was going to try, he'd still want to play along to get them off guard.

With Cortese in the lead and Cruz sandwiched between them, the men pushed their way toward the stage area. The band was laying down a slow number—something about the bad flower—so this helped since people were coupled off and not whirling and jerking about. They went up, and as they rose, Cruz's body tensed. Santián was right behind him.

"If you yell out, after the bullet I'll put in, you'll be lucky if you have to use a colostomy bag for the rest of your life."

At the second floor landing, the guards stood on duty. They frowned at the two cops, recalling their faces.

One of them said, "What up, boss?" Through the door to one of the playrooms, a man could be heard pleading for the woman to swat him harder.

"They're guests of mine, homies from the big city." The three continued up to the last floor. Here were two more who let them pass.

"You know," Cruz said softly as they walked to his office, "once you put your hands on my money, you won't get three feet down the street."

"You should learn when to hold that mouth in check, son," Cortese said. "Yolie isn't around; you don't have to be the mack daddy with us."

"I'm just trying to help you out. You guys are messing with the wrong people."

"Come on." Santián motioned toward the man's office. It was fronted with an oak door inlaid with a frosted glass pane.

Cruz unlocked it and stepped inside. Crowding into the room, Cortese closed the door. Cruz turned to speak, and Santián casually rapped him on his head. Dazed, he sank to the floor like a sack of soggy towels. Quickly Cortese pulled the cord from the drapes and hog-tied Cruz. Using one of Yolie's slips that he'd filched from her house, Santián gagged the man, too, after sniffing the material.

"How much time you think we got?" Cortese asked as the two put Cruz off to one side. "You can breathe, can't you, champ?" Cortese patted the man's sweating cheeks. "Don't want you stroking out on us."

The trussed-up man with bugged-out eyes could only shake his head at the temerity of the two. He twisted his body from side to side, making unintelligible noises. But he'd get tired of expending the energy soon enough and settle down, because it wasn't as if they were paying him any mind.

"He probably does have a safe somewhere around here." Cortese stood in the center of the room, hands on his hips.

"Nino's an orderly man," Santián said. He was using a letter opener in the shape of a miniature sword to try to get the locked middle drawer of the desk open. "But he's also smart, ain't that right, Nino?"

Cruz's head bobbed as he cursed them, making muffled sounds.

"So he's not going to have a little black book lying around."

Cortese moved Santián aside, and after a couple of well-placed kicks with his heel, the drawer was loosened.

"Brute."

"I'm going to have a drink." He took his large frame over to the wet bar and poured himself a dose of Johnny Walker Black.

Santián rummaged through the desk. "Here's something." He flipped a color print over for Cortese to see. "If I'm not mistaken, I believe that's Felix." The shot was of Cruz and the younger Del Feugo brother at a celebration. Each man held a glass of liquid, and each had the look of one who had imbibed too much. Felix had a flashy gun tucked in his waistband.

"Not enough background to tell us where it was shot." Cortese sat near their captive, crossed his legs, and tasted his drink.

"You want it that easy," Santián groused, and continued to go through the contents of the desk. There were a few more photographs, including a few with two women in bikinis jerking off a horse as Cruz, Felix, and others—men and women—cheered them on. He got up from the desk and kept looking.

Cortese swirled his whiskey and ice in its tumbler. "What about the keys?"

"What?"

"The keys he dropped when you slugged him."

Santián took them off the carpet and looked through them. There was a small one on the ring that got his interest. "You are good for something."

"Ain't I?"

"Let's find out what it fits."

"I was hoping to learn by watching you work." He drank more.

"Exercise will do you good."

"If you insist."

Fifteen minutes later, using a screwdriver from the desk, they'd pried open a panel in a lower part of the wall behind the bar. A hidden strongbox was removed, and the key opened it.

"Nice. At least we get something out of this trip," Cortese remarked. He removed two bundles of cash, twin stacks of thousand-dollar notes.

"Of course they're no longer in circulation, but I suppose we can trade them in for smaller denominations," Santián remarked absently, concentrating on the other contents of the box. Cruz made more noise and shook to demonstrate his objection to their prying and thievery.

"Check this out." Santián produced an unmarked CD in its jewel pack. He put it in the computer on a side desk and booted it up. The drive came on, but a password was required to access the disk's contents.

"Everything all right, Nino?" one of the guards asked through the locked door. He tried the knob.

"Yeah," Santián said. He and Cortese had their guns in hand.

"Okay," came the tentative reply.

"We better bounce," Cortese said.

"He's got to have a back way out in case of a raid." Calmly Santián crossed to a door that led to a small washroom.

There was a window and, outside on the wall, a fire escape. "Come on."

"It's been a blast, baby." Cortese patted Cruz's head and joined his partner in the bathroom. Together they descended the ladder that led to the narrow space between the club and the adjacent building. He'd just put his foot on the ground when the sound of the office door being forced open reached them. Hurriedly they got to the street and took off in the opposite direction from the way they'd come. Two blocks away they hailed a cab and told the driver to take them back to the maquiladora section, where they'd left their car.

"You like this shit too much, man." Cortese grimaced as the cab frequently had to slow down due to vehicular and pedestrian traffic.

"It keeps us young. I'm just sorry we don't have time to swing back by Yolie's crib."

"Do you ever listen to what comes out of your mouth?"

Santián laughed, and Cortese couldn't help but chuckle, too. Santián knew him too well—too well for his own good. Once they were outside the tourist area, the normal Tijuana took over, and they arrived unfettered at the factory part of town. The maquiladoras were light-to-heavy manufacturers maintained by foreign companies, who could assemble their super-soaker water rifles, the latest-craze tennis shoe, or components for prefab furniture for less, given the wage an average Mexican worker made. And there wasn't that pesky business about possible union organizing to worry about, either.

They paid and started to walk toward the car they'd stolen earlier for transport.

"Aw, fuck," Santián said as an Escalade whipped around a corner, bearing down on them. The license plate read, *Bumpy*.

"They did follow us. Some cops we are," Cortese complained as the two ran for cover. The SUV screeched to a stop, the passengers alighting.

Shots boomed as the two made the side of one of the factories. They were glad it was made of cinder block and not corrugated metal like some of the structures. What gave them less reason to celebrate was the security lighting dotted all over the place, which kept coming on as their bodies triggered the sensors.

"At least they only have handguns."

"It's so fucking wonderful when you manage to see the positive in the shit we step in." Just to show them he wasn't a chump, Cortese cranked off two rounds on general principles.

There was brief return of fire, then words in rapid Spanish until Cruz had his men talk quietly, knowing that Santián spoke the language.

"How many, you figure?" Cortese asked.

"How's four sound—five, tops? The two on the second floor and two from the door, plus our boy. Nino ain't gonna pull everybody away from the club—business is business."

Cortese poked his shoulder with his finger. "Over there." And he ran low for a set of bobtail trucks parked in a row. They made it without incident. One of the gunmen was running at a diagonal, and Santián popped off a shot. The man yelped but made it to safety.

"If we can make it over there, we got half a chance." Santián pointed to an area behind the trucks and the low wall crested by the cyclone fence they were up against. There were buildings with lights on. "Hopefully that means there's crews in there working."

"Like they'll be willing to get shot for us."

"Like Nino isn't the fucking kingpin, and he can't waste two *americanos* with a whole lot of witnesses around. Cheese, come on, brah, we've been in bad situations before. I need you sharp, man."

"Don't worry, I'm on it. Aren't I always?"

"We can get through this way." Santián kept crouched over as the two ran along between the rear ends of the trucks and the wall. They made it to a rip in the fence's links. Apparently it was used by the workers to cross back and forth on a regular basis. A bullet whizzed close, chewing into the dirt near them. Cortese let off some shots, driving back one of Cruz's men, who'd taken a chance to peep around the corner of a truck.

"Let's go." Santián went through, and Cortese was right behind him. They had to cross a large parking lot, but there were cars for cover and only two lamp poles, their anemic bulbs illuminating little.

Hunkered down next to a worn Ford Taurus station wagon, the two waited and listened. Scuffling footsteps moved across the asphalt.

"They know what we're trying to do, and will try to block us," Santián announced.

"You saying we should blast our way through? We'll never be able to smooth that over, Saint."

"That's why I'm the positive one. I'll bet"—he pointed—"those fancy SUVs and, if I'm not mistaken, a kraut car or two mingled in the bunch, belong to the management." The vehicles were parked the closest to the factory.

"Yeah, so?"

"And I bet McGuire's used Kotex there's a guard or two on duty at these all-night sweatshops, too." Santián crawled forward on his belly like a soldier through a combat zone. At the end of the station wagon, he used a two-handed grip to support his gun as he aimed. "The mothafuckahs in there might not give a shit about us getting capped, but they do love their toys." He fired into several cars near the entrance, setting off alarms that wailed and howled. One of the electronic guardian systems announced over and over, "I will cut your balls off," in Spanish.

Doors banged open in the factories, and backlit forms filled the spaces. There was shouting, and some of the forms started across the parking lot. Santián and Cortese ran doubled over around the rear of one of the buildings. Behind them they could hear Cruz yelling and somebody yelling back at him.

"Señoritas," Santián said as the two came to a group of women gathered around an open side door, the commotion an excuse to take a quick break. The two L.A. cops went in and sprinted across the shop floor. Women and a few men were busily assembling retro-looking table radios intended for sale at upscale mall stores in middle-class neighborhoods they would never visit. The two ran through an exit door and along hallways and eventually found themselves before a locked front door.

"Everything's the hard way." Cortese lifted one end of a steel-tubing-and-cushion couch next to the receptionist's desk.

"I know, I know," Santián commiserated, and lifted his end. Together they rammed the couch through a window, triggering yet another alarm. They ran away and hid until the cops had come and gone. No doubt Nino had distributed some money to keep everything quiet. He wouldn't want the Del Fuegos finding out about this little mishap—they might take their anger out on him.

"That was entertaining, huh?" Santián said as they drove north later in their car which they had left near the border. The roadway had light traffic.

Cortese brooded.

"We got away, like we always do."

"The cards won't fall our way forever, Saint."

"They just need to for this case, man. We're not only going to solve who killed Gargoyle, but we'll make McGuire look like the chump she is."

"I doubt that."

Santián frowned at him but elected not to make a remark. He was too tired to have an argument for the next three-and-something hours back to town. They were the goddamn TRASH, and they were an institution, not some rooty-poot John Waynes that slammed handcuffed suspects on the hoods of cruisers and got videotaped like goofs doing it. They were smarter than that. When they bent the rules it was because the rules were hamstringing them from achieving the greater goal. Yeah, they copped some extras for themselves, but who didn't? It was drug money, whore money, laundered money. They weren't taking food out of the mouths of orphans or widows. Hell, some of that money had been given with a wink and a nod to wives of guys who'd been cut down defending the citizens. Fuck, what else were they supposed to do? The bad boys didn't play, and neither could they.

"I wonder," Santián said, breaking the silence that had settled between them after they'd cleared the border check.

"What?"

"Which president was he?"

"Who?"

"Cleveland—Grover Cleveland on those thousand-dollar bills we got. Which number was he? Ninth? Sixteenth?"

And for a while the two rolled along, engaged in the kind of back-and-forth they'd always done and, Santián hoped, they'd always do.

CHAPTER 14

ugust Mercury reread the printout from the psychology site he'd found using the Google search engine on his computer. He particularly regarded the section on paranoia. The definition was *a mental disorder characterized by systematized delusions and the projection of personal conflicts, which are ascribed to the supposed hostility of others; chronic functional psychosis of insidious development, characterized by persistent, unalterable, logically reasoned delusions, commonly of persecution and grandeur.*

He had more brandy. Mercury certainly didn't have any delusions of grandeur. He wasn't some squirrely little bitch who went around ranting that he was Napoleon or Tupac. The threat of the Baja cartel was demonstrable. You would need a truck scale to weigh the bullets pumped into people they'd killed all over the Southwest. He hadn't heard from Hec since this morning. She was not at home, or at her office, though she sometimes worked there on a Sunday. And her cell continually rang over to her answering service. Had the Del Fuego brothers reached out and done harm to her? He could see Felix, who had never hidden the lust he had for Hec, waiting to ambush her, a knife in one hand and the panties he'd taken from her drawer and sniffed in the other.

He shuddered and poured more V.S.O.P. He had a gun; that was helpful. No, he had two guns; that was even better. But—and he hated admitting this—he'd gotten soft, gotten too used to expensed lunches on Montana and doing deals over vodka gimlets at the Sky Bar. That strutting cock Santián had known this when they'd bogarded into his office and he'd pushed his finger into Mercury's mushy center. Fuck Santían. If nothing else, surely he would catch a hot one in his swelled head. He smiled at the pleasing notion.

The jangling of his phone made him jerk, causing him to spill some of his drink on his lap. He snatched the handset free. "Yes!" he bellowed, his excitement cutting through the alcoholic fog floating across his brain.

"Sweetie, where you been?" Ferris Heckman said hoarsely.

"What do you mean? I've been trying to reach you all day."

"You have? I was at the office, then running errands. I didn't get any messages, baby. You drunk or something?"

"Stop using that tone with me," he said, realizing he sounded like a spoiled child.

"You left me messages?"

"Yes, I did."

She sounded concerned, and that put a chill down the center of his chest. "What's going on, Hec?"

"I'm not sure, but we should probably get off the phone."

"Fuck. Fuck me with a greasy *churro.*" They both laughed nervously at his gaffe. "What's going on? Did you hear from our friends?"

"That's just it," she intoned quietly. "I did."

The import of that descended like a shroud over the two lovers. "What should we do, Hec?"

"We better meet, honey, tonight."

"Okay, where?"

"I'll fax it."

"All right." He was scared and aroused all at once. His woman was so smart and so sexy. He was a lucky homeboy, and he was going to do everything he could to hold on to her and his lifestyle. He absolutely had to, because turning back was not an option. "I'll see you soon." And then he added without hesitation, just in case he didn't get a chance to say it later, "I love you; you know that, right?"

"I'm crazy about you, too, August." And she clicked off.

Mercury rubbed his face and got up from his desk. Looking at the clock, he realized he'd been on-line, checking out Web sites from porn to conspiracy to psychology, for some four hours. He dully noted the near-empty bottle of brandy, but he wasn't drunk; he was functioning. He started the shower, stripping off his robe and clammy pajamas. Even if his ass was in danger, he wasn't going to see his girl funky, like some lettuce picker straight up from Oaxaca. Damn that.

Making the water blast more cold than hot, he stood under it, trying to sort out what his and Hec's next moves should be. Going on the run didn't appeal to him, though if the alternative was taking that one-way express into the ground, then leaving town might have to be the answer. He finished, and as he toweled off, his head started to ache. The fax chimed from his den. He retrieved it; a tremor in his hand made the paper shake. Mercury ignored that and carefully read Heckman's handwritten note. She told him they should meet at the Banning Cultural Center and Gallery, out in Wilmington. The gallery was a series of converted World War I-era naval barracks that were now studios for photographers and artists. Perplexed, he read it again, then recalled that his girlfriend was on the board of the place and had handled their nonprofit incorporation paperwork. He crumpled the note, then lit it with his lighter. It wasn't paranoia, he reasoned—just being careful.

Mercury got dressed and left his condo on Wilshire. He stopped at a 7-Eleven for some coffee and got on the 405 south. Usually he drove with his music on, but he was too keyed up and too fearful that he'd become preoccupied. He regularly checked his rearview and made sure to switch lanes often to see if he could spot a tail. He kept this up until he reached the harbor.

The port, part of a massive infrastructure from nearby Long beach to San Pedro next door, operated continuously, and its streets were busy with big trucks. The smell of diesel, fish, and petroleum from the refineries was a heady mix that only those who worked around it could get used to. He got turned around but then went past a cement storage warehouse—a bloated, ash-colored and windowless structure like a forgotten vault left standing after the fall.

He then drove slowly along a narrow street between industrial hulks leading to the center. Mercury had his window down, alert for anything untoward. At his destination he stopped, shifting into neutral, letting his clean, original-parts restored mid-'69 big-block

Boss Mustang fastback idle. Fewer than nine hundred of these bad mammajamma 'Tangs with the gas-devouring 429-cubic-inch-displacement engines had come off the assembly line that year. It had taken Mercury many years of trolling various specialty publications, the Internet, and antique car shows to track down one that was authentic and worth the money and effort he'd poured into this machine to return it to its Detroit splendor.

Save for light spillover from the businesses behind him, there was no other illumination at the complex of studios. That was not surprising, though he understood that at least one of the artists was suspected of living at the facility, which was verboten. He drove slowly, parallel to the rows of barracks, and saw Heckman's car parked between two sets of the buildings. She was near Number 23, where she'd written she'd be. A light went on inside that studio, and his cell phone rang.

"It's me," she said.

"I'm coming in." He parked his car facing hers and got out. Not too far away a foghorn announced the imminent arrival of the gray mist that Mercury had noticed out on the water as he'd come off the freeway. He touched the Glock he'd placed in the pocket of his windbreaker and opened the door to Number 23.

He was in a smallish area with black-and-white prints of people tacked on the walls, and a detritus of several mismatched chairs from different eras scattered around. Through an open window came diffuse lighting that cast amebalike globs of shadows where he stood. "Baby?" he called, his hand near his coat pocket.

"In here," Heckman replied from the other room. There was a scuffing of a chair's legs across the studio's linoleum, and the figure that filled the door frame could have been a woman—but not his woman.

"What the fuck?" Mercury said as he backpedaled into a low-slung canvas chair. Fear and gravity tangled up his legs, and he went over as a bullet creased his chest, searing the cloth and his flesh. Like in a scene from a Woody Allen film, Mercury was on his back, his legs draped over the toppled chair, looking at the killer between his two spread feet.

"Fuck . . . fuck!" he sputtered, bile pumping into his throat. Fearful, he fired the gun through the material of the windbreaker even as the other one shot at him again. Rounds blew holes in the jacket, and damned if he didn't almost blow his own toe off. But one of his hurried shots made the looming figure react as if it had been hit flush by Lennox Lewis.

The man made a gurgling sound and stumbled backward, as if doing an imitation of what Mercury had just done.

"Hec . . . Hec," he called, rolling on his side, then getting to one knee. A lancing pain shivered through his leg, and he realized he'd been shot on the inside, meaty part of his thigh. He touched it and recoiled at the throbbing this brought him. But there was no time for a Band-Aid or whining, so he got to his feet and shakily but steadily went forward, gun in hand. He kicked a wooden folding chair out of his way.

"Baby?" he said, his back against the wall at the open doorway like he'd seen on so many *Cops* shows. A .22 could send rounds through the sheetrock, but what the fuck was he supposed to do? She didn't answer, but there was a sound—something sliding across the floor. His sphincter felt like letting go, but he hung on for Ferris. He took a breath, asked Jesus for mercy, and dived through the doorway. Mercury popped off four rapid shots that punctured the acoustic tiles in the ceiling and destroyed the fluorescent light fixtures.

Sucking in gallons of air, his leg hurting like it had a hot knife shimmed in it, he lay still in the dark, trying to figure out what to do next. He was about to call her name again when somebody moaned. Shaking, Mercury strained to make out shapes but couldn't tell anything. There was that sliding again, and Mercury groped before him; his hand touched a shoe, and he pulled his fingers back as if he'd encountered a snake's fangs. He waited and listened, and there was that gurgle like a drain emptying of standing water.

He readied himself and moved forward, his gun at the end of his extended arm as he dipped it to his left, to his right, up, then down; then he smacked into a solid form. The phlegmy rasp continued as Mercury put pressure on his wounded leg. He got into a kneeling position over the figure he'd seen between his feet. His eyes had become adjusted to the murk, and he could now see the man who'd shot at him, lying on his back on the floor, his hands at his throat. This was where one of his wild shots had landed.

He looked from the man, an Asian—Chinese, he concluded, in his twenties—along the short hallway and could now distinguish

that there was a side door, partially ajar. The damp night washed
across his body, and he knew there was no sense exploring the rest
of the studio for anyone. "Where is she?" Mercury shook the dying
man. "Come on, you fuck, get straight with God so he'll let your
crooked ass into heaven," he said.

"The man's eyes registered his presence, but speech was lost to
him. He gripped Mercury's arm, like he was trying to not slip from
this world; then he expired. On each finger of his right hand, save
for his thumb, he wore an ostentatious diamond ring. Mercury had
never seen a man die, and even though this one had tried to take
his life, it rattled him. But his old lady was in trouble, and he was
hurting, so pity would have to happen some other time. He got
into a sitting position, letting his legs stretch out, which eased his
discomfort and let him breathe.

Momentarily recharged, he then went through the man's pockets. There was no wallet, but he did have a set of keys that had one
of those electronic key tags for Blockbuster Video on it. Mercury
transferred the item to his pockets. He took off the man's belt and
used it as a tourniquet around his own wound.

He rose, groaning, aware that his blood was on the floor—and
probably on the dead man, too. He could run, but they'd catch
him, and what was the point of that, anyway? He needed to get
Ferris back, not fuck around. He found a desk lamp in the other
part of the studio and clicked it on, his hand trembling again. He'd
half expected to see his lady-love lying with her head bashed in on
the floor, and was relieved that he was wrong.

Mercury started to call for an ambulance, then reconsidered. If
he went to the hospital, that meant questions from the police, and
that might mean jeopardy for his woman. But he damn sure had to
do something about the bullet; letting it stay in his leg and fester
and turn gangrenous was not smart and would only lay him up further.

He evaluated several options, then made a call using the studio's
phone. Ismael Lorenzo, called Peacock, picked Mercury up and
took him out to a clinic in Santa Ana serving the burgeoning
Latino community down there behind the Orange Curtain—this
after they'd dumped the body near one of the piers and closed up
the studio.

One of Def Ritmo's acts had donated money from a charity concert to the clinic, and the staff knew Mercury. It was late, and Dr. Martinez would have to notify the police about his gunshot wound, but they'd let him rest after the removal of the bullet. That way he'd be fresh and on the road to recovery when they came to question him in the morning. But they worked out a plan, and Peacock, who was seeing one of the night nurses, was able to get into his room at four in the morning to help Mercury sneak out and drive him away.

"You sure you gonna be all right, Merc?" As usual, Peacock was dressed in warmup togs, beige and black Karl Kani wear. He smelled of his favorite, Emperio Armani, and he'd splashed on a fresh amount before driving out to retrieve his boss.

"I'll make it," Mercury said, groggy from the surgery and the overdose of the man's cologne. He removed the IV and, with Peacock steadying him, got up from the bed. Peacock had brought him more clothes, and he got dressed. The wrapping around his wound chafed him as he got his pants up, and he had to regroup after getting his shirt buttoned up. He felt like an old man, he was so winded. Old age was going to be a bitch. But he certainly intended to make it that far.

"You look pale, man." He handed him his shoes.

"I've been shot, Peacock. What the fuck, huh?"

"Just saying, maybe you should sleep and we leave tomorrow. When the hoota comes in the morning, just pretend you all doped up and, you know, you ain't right in the head and they got to come back later. I come get you and we zoom away."

"Or the mothafuckahs that tried to cap me send more Y-Tang boat boys to finish the job while I'm nodding."

"Oh," Peacock drawled. "Wasn't that dead dude Korean?"

"Chinese."

"You sure?"

"I know my Asians. And I know the Baja cartel has a distribution relationship with the Y-Tangs out of Alhambra, who sell shit to those parachute kids in San Marino."

"You hungry, Merc, you want to stop for a cheeseburger?"

"Let's just go, okay?"

"Absolutely," Peacock said, masking his disappointment. It was going to be tough going, and a man sure needed his nutrients.

"Where to?" They were in the car, heading away from the facility.

"I was going to say in my cabin up in Big Bear, but the brothers would know about that place. And anyway, I need to be close, because I'm sure what they'll do is want me to come for Hec and then drill both of us."

"Then I better get some homies together—we gonna need a crew that can put in work."

"Not too many—I can't have anything getting back to the Nines."

"Yeah, but . . ." Peacock began, "this beef seems to be between them and the Del Fuegos. Seems to me there's a war breaking out."

"Still, we don't know who's on what side yet. I need a day or two to rest up; then I have to make some moves."

They went along in silence as Peacock headed toward the 5 freeway. "Hey, what about that chick—what's her name?—the one I hooked you up with that you hired to fuck Kid Chili when he got out of jail on the domestic abuse thing."

"Who?"

"You know, the dark one with the big titties who said she'd do anything to be in a music video . . . get her career started." He snickered. He'd lost count of how many whack chicks with bodies and no talent had hit them up looking for their big break. "The one that sucked your dick in your office."

"Oh, Jade."

"Yeah, her."

"I don't know, man; hoes ain't trustworthy."

"You ain't moving in with her, just bunking for a day or two, right? Plus, she won't cross you, 'cause she wants to be a star and you're her ticket."

"Where's she live? If it's a fuckin' motel, forget it."

"She stays near Inglewood, and most people don't know that. She's smart like that 'cause she don't want them other whores dropping by with their drama."

"Give her a shout?"

Peacock got on his cell and reached her. "Yeah, I know you just getting in, baby, but me and August need a favor. . . . Just a little while, understand?"

"Tell her I'll pay her a thousand," the record chief said.

"Hear that? A grand, and he'll see about getting you in a video."

Mercury was going to protest, but a begging man had little choice.

"That's right, girl, you getting ready to be hotter than Jenny Lo-Lo." Peacock listened, then said, "About forty-five minutes." She talked, and he added, "Then tell that bitch she better get used to it, shit. And wash up, huh? We don't need that fish smell stinking up the joint, you know what I'm sayin?" He laughed and hung up. "It's set, Merc."

"What about this other broad?"

"I don't know; she said something about a temporary room-mate, another stupid ho. But she'll treat you like a goddamn king, man. It's cool."

"Just as long as I got a phone and my own room."

"It's cool, Merc, no problems."

In the lane ahead of them a tanker truck suddenly slammed on its brakes, and the two men lurched forward as Peacock had to react. A van on their rear also screeched to a halt. Peacock's eyes were wide, and his hands tightly gripped the steering wheel. For his part, Mercury was calm. He'd already beaten calamity once this evening, and he felt in his bones that the karma that had taken him from the streets of the Heights wasn't done with him yet—not by a long shot.

CHAPTER 15

"The Rigby angle is cold," Constance McGuire pronounced, picking at the coleslaw on her plate. The lunch crowd at Langer's, an old-fashioned deli across from MacArthur Park, included city hall denizens of various echelons.

"Damn thing was part of a crate of them stolen from a federal armory in Topeka." Phenias Washington had more of his pastrami sandwich. "A militia group was suspected, but none of its members got convicted for the crime . . . the idea being they sold the rifles for fund-raising purposes."

"The right-wingers are always very entrepreneurial." McGuire chewed.

"But we do have the fresh corpse of Joey 'Diamond Jim' Hong in the morgue." Judd Ahn munched on one of his steak fries. "He's Y-Tang, and they have ties to the Del Feugos."

McGuire said, "So they're looking to cap Mercury to keep him from talking?"

"But it can't be about Gargoyle," Washington said, "unless the brothers think we have more on this than we do."

"Image is everything," Ahn said.

McGuire dabbed her lips with a paper napkin. "After we eat, since we're in the area, let's stop by Ferris's office. See what she has to say about her boyfriend getting shot at and his disappearance."

"I like that," Ahn agreed.

Laughing effervescently, Pablo Pastor came through the entrance in the company of a man and woman in dark suits. He spotted McGuire and came over to lean on the table. "Gents. Connie, I've got a great spot my people put together this morning. Can you get on the phone at three to hear it?"

"I'll see."

"Come on," he urged. "You're rising and Fergadis is going down, lady. Time to go for the soft underbelly."

"We do have this latest killing to look into," she responded.

"That's Hidalgo's lookout. You get to be mayor, you get to skewer him and his merry TRASH men."

"That's not why—" she began.

"We want the same thing, Connie," he placated. "You were a litigator, and this is no different. We present the best case we can to the public and let them decide."

"A few well-placed attack ads helping them get the picture," Ahn added.

"What is this, a choir meeting?" Pastor's smile was captivating. "Three," he repeated, touching McGuire's shoulder and moving off.

"Don't say it," McGuire told the other two.

Washington and Ahn exchanged grins and had more of their food. Later they went by Ferris Heckman's office, but her receptionist said she hadn't been around for the past two days and no, she had no word as to where she might be. And yes, it was unusual for her to be gone without leaving word.

Alvaro Acosta was glad that Ronk Culhane was busy with Big T Holton. The man didn't bother him, really. He was old-school and not what could be called enlightened about women, but he was straightforward and, if he was on your side, would go down swinging for you. But it was the way the man did his job that gnawed at the edges of Acosta's psyche. Acosta damn sure wasn't going to be acolyte of the year, but still, if you cut corners all the time, warped the rules to fit your objectives, what did that say about you as a cop at the end of the line when you pulled your twenty?

Then again, he reflected, scanning the file copy again, police work wasn't for pussies, as Culhane would say. You had to square up

with the bad boys if you wanted to get results. He shoved such ru-
minations aside for now. Too bad he wasn't like Culhane, a man
who had mastered the technique of nonreflection. He was like one
of those robot toys you turned the switch on and set in motion, dis-
regarding the hazards and immune to being tripped up by subtleties.
But Acosta's doubts would not evaporate so easily and would invariably wend their way back into the front of his brain.

That's why he'd submerged himself in his current pursuit of the
culprits since the presumed attempted hit on August Mercury. A
dispatcher for the ILWU, the longshore union, had been going to
work and had spotted the body of Diamond Jim Hong near berth
147. The area was cordoned off, and it was quickly determined that
the young man had been shot through the throat elsewhere and
then dumped. Fortunately, a smattering of a blood trail took the investigators back to the nearby artists' studios and eventually to
Number 23, where Diamond Jim's precious body fluids were in
abundance.

According to the extensive file on the young but criminally mature Mr. Hong, there were at least seven unsolved murders associ-
ated with the youthful malefactor. He was an enforcer for the
Y-Tangs, originally a Chinese immigrant set, which now included
their American-born brethren. Diamond Jim Hong had come of
age in Alhambra, in the outer ring of the San Gabriel Valley, and by
the age of twelve had assaulted two of his teachers, which led to a
stint at the California Youth Authority's El Paso de Robles Youth
Correctional Facility, in the northern part of San Luis Obispo
County. There he graduated from misanthropic punk to cold-blooded
hood under the tutelage of some of the incarcerated older members of the Y-Tangs.

But now he was just one more statistic of "gang-involved" deaths
that weekly were tallied up in the Southland. The regular citizens
were nearly inured to these numbers and to the Herculean task too
many parents and single moms went through on a daily basis, not
only making sure their kids did their homework, but keeping them
away from lads like Diamond Jim.

Once the criminalists had gone over the studio, the other blood
found on the scene was still being traced when a bulletin from the
Sheriff's Department had gone out about August Mercury splitting
from a clinic in Orange County without waiting for questioning.

Elementary mathematics said he was the man they were looking for. A check by the Santa Monica PD at Def Ritmo confirmed he wasn't there, and no one, including his cologne-drenched factotum, knew where their boss had gone in the last two days.

And while obviously there was a concentration on searching for Mercury, Acosta had decided to take another track and look into the Y-Tang hookup. He knew from a high school friend of his who was now a sheriff that the Y-Tang was the face of the Del Fuegos in several Asian communities. And thanks to his buddy, he now had a file on the recently departed Mr. Hong that included known associates. The late Diamond Jim was indeed a child of the hip-hop era, having crossed the racial divide as far as who he partied and committed antisocial acts with over the years.

Indeed, the fine Latina *hina* with the tube top, in the glaring Polaroid picture from a party busted by Acosta's buddy and other deputies, had been draped all over the very drunk Hong. Diamond Jim also had male friends of the Latino swing of things mentioned in the file. And that was the part of the puzzle Acosta was going to peruse in solving the equation of the missing Mr. Mercury. His friend the deputy had alerted him about this because one of the dudes Diamond Jim Hong rolled with was Quintano "Fiver" Morales.

And in the six-degrees-of-separation department, Fiver had been the starting running back when Acosta and his friend the deputy had also been on the football team at Garfield High. Like an updated east-side version of one of those Jimmy Cagney and Pat O'Brien Depression-era flicks Acosta got a kick out of on TCM, two of the neighborhood boys stuck to the straight and narrow, more or less, and the third one had gone on to be a crook after graduation. More correctly, once it became clear that there wasn't a four-year all-expenses-paid scholarship to a college in the mix, where Morales could, in his own words, "score some blond sorority trim," school held no more interest. He dropped out of school before the end of that last semester.

But now Acosta had a reason to look up his old teammate, whose name he'd seen surface now and again on this field report or the other. He'd run what he wanted to do past Kubrick, who said he'd give him three days to produce the tangibles. Acosta closed the file after reviewing it for the tenth time and rose from the bench seat in the locker room. He put the folder away in his locker and put some items in his gym bag.

"What you all looking all cholo for, Acosta?" Dresen, a uniform who liked his jelly donuts asked as he walked around a bank of lockers.

"A little undercover, son—something you can only hope to do one day in your otherwise hopeless career," Acosta replied. He was pumped and primed.

"You TRASH prima donnas get to do any goddamn thing you want, don't you?"

"You're jealous of us crime fighters," he chuckled.

"I got your jealousy," he said, grabbing his crotch.

"I'll put it in my memoirs how you inspired me." Acosta checked his look in the mirror. He was dressed in paint-spotted khakis, worn work boots, a loose cotton shirt, and a bandanna around his head. On second inspection, he removed the rag from his head and stuffed it in his back pocket.

"You do that, hot dog. Good hunting."

"Righteous." And they knocked fists as Acosta walked out.

Kubrick couldn't authorize an unmarked, as the plainclothes had first dibs and all those cars were out. He could get reimbursed for mileage on his car, but if he had any accidents or bullet holes, than he'd have to square that with his insurance company. Acosta hadn't checked, but he didn't think he had a rider on his policy for slugs.

There were several places that his friend the deputy had given him as usuals for Fiver Morales. One of them was a day-laborer site in Pacoima, in the Valley. It wasn't that Morales picked up occasional work like that—he had worked as a body-and-fender man—but he made scratch selling fake IDs to the undocumented. Acosta's car, a late-model Nissan Frontier pickup, was too clean and too new for that of a day laborer, so he'd make sure to park some blocks away from the site. That was a liability should Morales show and Acosta have to give chase, let alone be recognized by him, but there was no way around it.

As usual, it was ten degrees hotter out in the Valley by the time Acosta was on San Fernando Road, along a stretch of auto body shops and salvage yards. It was in areas like this where you realized how much the Southland was dependent upon the car and its upkeep. Acosta had no idea how many vehicles were in greater L.A., but no matter what magazine or newspaper you picked up, there was a car ad. He'd heard somewhere that cars accounted for the bulk of TV advertising dollars, and that had to be true given that people still came here searching for the golden dream in California, and the only way to pursue it was by car or in even larger SUVs. He realized he was starting to bitch like his father.

Acosta found a parking spot at a meter and locked up his truck. He put on his Dodgers baseball cap and went the long way around the block to make it appear that he'd walked or hitched to the location. The day-laborer site was alongside a taco-and-burger stand next to Arturo's Primo Arts Body Shop. He got a root beer at the fast food stand and stood about. Clearly there were some men who knew each other. There were at least two who were in the same soccer club and were discussing the new goalie who'd recently arrived from Oaxaca. Fortunately, given the transient nature of this end of the labor pool, several of the men standing around or whistling at trucks laden with ladders and tools were new and unknown to one another.

"Where you from?" a man with a thick accent Acosta couldn't place asked him in Spanish. He was wearing a T-shirt with a large full-color decal of the comic book character the Flash streaking across its front.

"I'm from here," he replied. There was no sense trying to fake like he'd just got to town from Sinaloa or some other Mexican state, since he would invariably run into someone who was from there and this person would know his phrasing was not authentic. "I was working at the beer plant in Panorama City until I got laid off. I got a wife and a kid. I'm good with my hands, and I gotta do something."

"Hey," his new friend said, "if I was you I'd get on welfare or unemployment or something."

"I want to work. I'm not a woman."

The other man, a short, stoutly built man with powerful forearms, nodded his assent. "You're right, of course; work is good. Last week I got three days digging out a pool for these two blondies in a big house up in the hills." As he pointed toward the north, he grinned like a kid who found a box of candy. "They were doing each other, you know what I mean?" It was hard to tell due to his complexion, but Acosta was pretty sure he was blushing.

"Did you get to watch?" Acosta sipped his soda.

"I wish, man." They both chuckled. "My name's Oscar," he said and stuck out his hand.

"Rubén," Acosta said, shaking the man's hand. That was his middle name, and he wouldn't have to rack his brain trying to remember it should someone yell it out. Just then a Mercedes rolled up, and several of the laborers pounced on it.

"Two weeks ago," Oscar began, "there was this actor; he was on this show—Peruvian, I think he is. Anyway, he came around looking to hang out with us because he had a part in a movie where he had to pretend to be a day laborer."

"Yeah." Acosta had some more root beer.

"So he did, and you know, he got work because he's handsome, and I think those rich people are saying to themselves, 'This guy sort of looks like this guy in that show, right?' "

"Is he coming back?"

"I don't know," Oscar frowned, "but one of the men here may have a small part in his film. Man"—he shook his head—"is some country where something like that can happen."

The driver of the Mercedes pointed his index finger at two of the men, and they got in the backseat of his car and drove away to paint the guest house or install tile in the newly remodeled kitchen— this so the big homeowner could save money on what had no doubt been a project that had gone over budget. And the money he'd pay these men for a few days' work was less than what he probably spent on getting his Mercedes tuned on a regular basis. Yes, Oscar was right, it was a hell of a country where the haves always had the have-nots by the short hairs.

Enough of that radical thinking, he jokingly warned himself. That's what he got for having an aunt who had worked her ass off for La Causa for decades. She'd been an organizer for the United Farm Workers in the fields up north and would always have plenty of colorful stories to tell during Thanksgivings. She knew the low-down behind the public demeanor of Cesar Chavez and his inner circle, and told how she and her brave comrades had faced down the Teamsters, who made sweetheart deals with the growers during that nasty period in the '70s.

Oscar introduced Acosta to some of the men, who gave him the once-over. A new man meant the odds of getting work decreased, so any new addition was welcomed warily at best. And, like in any group where there were established associations, there were cliques among the men, though this was somewhat fluid since the competition for a day's wage all too often meant each man for himself.

After an hour he was getting into the rhythm of studying the faces of drivers as their cars and trucks went past—how to spot that expectant look, or what was the best angle to zero in on a vehicle that might stop at the far corner. He even had to pretend to come up with a reason for not taking a job installing light fixtures at a restaurant, because he wanted to get a line on Morales.

The break came later that day. One of the soccer players was a motormouth, and though he wasn't talking to Acosta, he was enamored with the sound of his own voice. He was talking to another man about the money he'd won wagering on a cockfight. Acosta butted in.

"I know about fighting birds," he said. He'd learned from his background information that Morales was into the sport, and he also figured if he asked where the matches took place around here, he'd be frozen out. But saying just enough should get the blowhard hooked.

"Is that right? I haven't seen you around."

"In Palmdale, back of that radio station off Quartz Hill was a grove of apricot trees—they fought there. There was a champion called Popeye; I won on him." He then stuck his hands in his pockets and casually walked away. There had been a gamecock named Popeye—several, in fact—and Acosta knew from his deputy buddy that matches had taken place where he'd said.

The soccer player let this sink in as a battered truck pulled up. Several of the men went over to it, including Acosta. He couldn't seem too anxious, and his instincts told him a new man asking about who sold fake drivers' licenses would mark him as a possible INS snitch, or worse, get him jumped. As much as possible he had to blend in, be part of the scene. The contractor who was driving the truck needed three men for hauling, and Oscar and the soccer player were two of the ones chosen.

Acosta had allowed himself to get jockeyed to the rear and did his best to maintain a neutral expression as the laborers went off with their temporary employer. He checked his watch. His car was going to have a ticket on it, but how would it seem if he walked off, then came back in a few minutes? He could say he'd gone to pee, but for fifty cents, the owner of the taco stand let the men use the facilities. And it was understood that everybody put in a dollar to cover rest room costs. He wasn't sure Kubrick would reimburse him for the parking infraction. Well, he might if he got a solid lead.

The one that the soccer club guy had been talking to was still around, and Acosta tried him for information. "You bet on the birds?"

"When my wife doesn't catch me."

"I know what you mean. When I was working steady, I didn't have much time to go, but now . . ." He shrugged his shoulders. "Any way I can make some money I have to try. And I miss going, too."

"You know how to pick them?" The other man, a lanky individual with a boxer's nose, took in Acosta.

"I'm not an expert, but I've done all right. I put my money on what I talk about."

The man looked off in the middle distance. "There may be something coming up. Two weeks ago a empty house with a pool and no water was used off of Roscoe."

"You're kidding."

"No. They even pass out flyers sometimes, you know, at the dance halls and the lunch trucks that go around."

"You going? I mean, if they have a new match?"

"I was thinking about it. I've seen some of the roosters fighting before."

"Let me know."

The man didn't commit.

It took another day and a half of Acosta hanging around the site, but Julio Gomez, the man who was considering going to the next fight, had made up his mind. There was a fight tonight. Acosta had played it smarter this time and had taken the bus to avoid his car's being spotted. If he was desperate for work, he would have sold it for the money.

Oscar, whose last name was Herrera, was also going, and together they and two others rode in the back of a Dodge van with expired tags to a North Hollywood neighborhood of World War II–era clapboard houses, many with noncode additions.

Down a narrow alleyway, then around the rear of a yellow stucco apartment building, the men arrived for the *corralera* as the evening turned humid. Admission was two dollars, and preteen youngsters circled about on their BMX bikes as roving watchdogs for the law. This venue had a rectangular pit with rough-hewn cement walls constructed about four feet high and at least eighteen feet long by half that wide.

This was the battleground for the Kelsos, the McLeans, the Denizilis and other species of cocks bred to be contenders. Already several men, a few of whom who had brought their girlfriends, were gathering around, the pit, laughing and talking. There were several street vendors about, doing steady business in roasted corn, jicama sprinkled with chili powder, and homemade tamales.

There was also an area with pens for the birds, where several men were injecting their gamecocks with various vitamin mixtures to boost their chances of victory in the blood sport. Acosta wandered around, hoping to spot Morales. The sharp odor of animal anxiety—from the birds and humans—was pronounced. He passed a fifty-five-gallon barrel, which one of the kids was stocking with pieces of wood and newspaper. Later the kindling would be lit, and if the looser of a match was too torn up to be healed, he was consigned to the funeral pyre.

Acosta settled in, recalling similar outings as a kid with his dad and uncles to the cockfights here in L.A. County and in the Central Valley, where his extended family lived—and where they still engaged in this ritual. Much more than a hobby, this brutal undertaking was to some a calling. Apart from the terror of the corral, they could be loving fathers and sons—men who had regular jobs and paid the bills and fed their kids but who, worse than devotees of boxing or football addicts, just had to be amid the heat and the feathers.

The dirt in the pit was hosed down to cut the dust, and bets were placed on the first match. The fight was between a black-and-red rooster with a deep scar along one flank and a bright orange bird called, appropriately, Sunset. Acosta grinned, imagining the look on Kubrick's face if the sheriffs should raid—him having to explain how one of his cops happened to be here. Particularly since Acosta had just put some money on Sunset.

The yelling and cajoling started as the owners stepped onto either side of the corral, holding their contenders. One man, in his Sparklets Water delivery uniform, spat a stream of water across his rooster's head to cool him down. The other one inserted his bird's beak between his closed lips to accomplish the same result of calming the fowl before it struck. Each gamecock had gaffs—curved hooks—fastened to its legs to enable it to rend and maim better.

Acosta had a good position near the rim of the pit that allowed a panoramic view of the gathering. Next to him an Anglo woman who had to be in her mid-fifties, with too much makeup and gin-for-lunch breath, sidled up. She had on a mass of costume jewelry, and there was wetness to her eyes.

"This is great, isn't it?"

"You bet," he said. Her Spanish was good.

"I haven't seen you here before." She took him in as if he were a new rooster in the hen yard. In one of her ringed hands she held a rolled up copy of *Steel,* a magazine that covered cockfighting.

"I didn't have this kind of time before."

She had a hand atop her rounded, gravity-defying breasts—the obvious result of recent plastic surgery. "I see."

The fight was on, and she refocused on the pit as a blur of colors exploded in midair. Sunset raked with both its legs, and the one with the scar got scratched along its throat. But the weathered rooster was tough and recovered, leaping over Sunset and taking a chunk out of the other bird's head with one of its gaffs.

"Oh, my!" the woman exclaimed.

Sunset flapped his wings and whirled around, causing his attacker to rear back momentarily. As the scarred one did so, Sunset suddenly lunged, his beak hooking toward the other's exposed belly. Part of the crowd remained silently stunned while others yelped in excitement as blood now dotted the floor of the pit.

"Come on, Sunset," Acosta said, getting caught up in the fight. "I got twenty riding on your sorry slow butt. You don't want to wind up at KFC do you?"

Sunset was dancing and hovering and squawking over the scarred one which lay flapping on the ground. But he wasn't done, and a sweep of claws embedded a gaff in Sunset's taut leg muscle. The brightly colored rooster crowed. Acosta felt the bird's pain, a twinge working its way through his body. The cloying air and his anxiety level had his shirt wet from sweat.

"Don't give up yet, honey," the older woman advised, her hand gripping his arm. "These birds got more piss in 'em than any of my three exes." Her laugh was rumbling and contagious. She, too, remained locked on the match.

Sunset and the scarred one had separated, hopping about each other, circling, heads twitching and beaks pecking, each taking the measure of the other.

"Sunset, move, thrust; move thrust," his owner kept repeating. Mimicking his champion, he would lift his leg at the knee like a chicken as he pranced back and forth on his side of the corral. His head dipped and swiveled as if, through telekinesis, he were sending these moves into his bird's head.

The scarred rooster rose and dove at Sunset, its claws leading as it was trained to do. The orange fighter responded, and the two came together in another flurry of feathers and flesh.

"I love this!" the woman screamed. "Come on, baby, come on; get him, get him." It wasn't clear which bird she was urging on, or maybe it didn't matter to her as long as there was a contest.

Sunset was trickling blood from his head, and the other animal lunged for him, trying its best to peck at the wound that had opened. But as it did so, Sunset slammed his body against his challenger and knocked the other bird off balance. Sunset plunged his head, then tore his gaffs into the other bird's side with determined ferocity.

"Enough, enough!" the scarred one's owner yelled, throwing a grimy shop rag onto the dirt floor of the corral.

The man who owned Sunset stepped forward and, sweeping his leg, got the birds separated. He then plucked his barnyard gladiator aloft, and a cheer went up from the winners.

"My sister likes baseball; can you believe it?"

Acosta laughed along with the woman. "I know what you mean."

He looked for the banker, to collect his money, and came across Morales. He was on the other side of the pit, head closely shaved, heavier than in high school, but Acosta had seen recent shots in the file his friend had lent him. Morales was wedged behind a grouping. Acosta guessed he must have arrived in the past five minutes.

The scarred rooster was carried tenderly from the ring by its owner. He sucked the blood from his bird's wound, and the creature twitched in pain. Tears ran down the man's face as he spit the blood and gore out, and he said soothing words to his fighter.

"You will get better; you will be stronger, my brave one." He took him away to do his best to repair and replenish his gamecock for another day, another battle, one more round in the pit.

"Crazy," the woman commented, watching the owner, his shoulders hunched over in concern as he cradled his damaged charge and walked toward the pens.

"A kind of love," Acosta commented. "They breed them from hatchlings, feed them right, keep them from disease, then train them to keep at it till they are shredded or victorious."

"Yeah." She nodded, pointing her cone of a magazine at other combatants being shown to the throng to get the second round of betting going.

"Know anything about these birds?" he asked.

The jeweled woman indicated the black rooster with the red-feathered neck. "Enrique, his owner, knows his gamers, and I'm pretty sure I've seen that one fight before." She leaned forward to squint. "Yeah, that's the one I saw take down this mother of a cock—must have been seven or eight pounds of muscle and gristle. That's one tough *gallo.*" To prove her faith, she held up some bills for the banker to collect.

The banker came over, trailed by a kid who wrote the bets down as the banker, a robust fellow in a straining shirt, took the money. By this time, the new fighting birds were held in the middle of the corral and pushed at each other, then pulled back by their owners. This was called flirting, to get the gamecocks' senses alert and, as they say, get the blood up.

Outdoor floods were turned on, offering maximum illumination of the corral. The shapes of the people around the pit took on an undulating, bloblike quality as the individuals seemed to blend into one another. The clatter of the chickens coming together rose from the pit and echoed off the surrounding stucco walls. In the bowels of the city, the primal instinct of survival was in full effect.

"I want to get a better look," Acosta said to the woman.

"This is a good spot, handsome."

"I'll be back." He wasn't going to get sloppy and lose Morales now. He went the short way around the corral as a man in canvas shorts and new Yao Ming tennis shoes leaped up and grabbed his head, screaming for the bird he had bet on to do better.

"Come on, you bastard," he wailed.

Given that both roosters were black, it seemed like a miniature storm cloud was suspended over the floor of the pit as the gamers went at it. Acosta went behind a big woman in a quilted vest with arms like a stevedore's. In front of her, pressed against the wall of the corral, Morales was edging sideways through the knot of people. He was looking ahead and didn't notice the cop keeping tabs on him.

"You fucking need something?" the giantess growled, turning her head sideways and glaring at Acosta. An earring in the shape of a penis pierced with a lance dangled from her lobe.

"No, ma'am." He touched the brim of his cap like some cowboy in a three-reel oater.

"Then step the fuck away."

The interlude gave him the space he needed to reverse gears, and he trailed after Morales. He was now sipping on a bottle of Tecate and talking with some other men at the corner of the pit. Walking around them, he made sure not to pause in his steps as he passed them. But he heard no useful snatch of information, though Morales did give him a second, I-know-you-from-somewhere glance. Acosta inserted himself near the jewelry-laden woman again.

"Peck his guts out," she hollered, her clenched fists pumping the air in adulation. "Nail his ass."

Acosta made noises, too. The gamecock with the red plume sank a gaff into the eye of his opponent nine minutes into the fight, and that was that.

"Shit." The jeweled woman slapped her magazine against the corral.

"There's, what, three more matches?" Acosta asked.

"That's right; a winner is always around the corner."

"It wouldn't be exciting otherwise." Morales, who hadn't been paying much attention to the recent match, was now talking with an owner holding one of the next contestants, a brown-reddish bird with shiny feathers. He lovingly stroked the rooster's head.

The woman leaned her perfumed hair toward Acosta's chest and said quietly, "Why are you keeping watch on Morales?"

"He owes some money to a friend of mine. Am I that obvious?"

"Not really, particularly since he don't give a shit about you." Which meant she was noticing him. "You know Morales?"

"Seen him around. Know his rep. Know you better walk light, as I hear he's got some serious friends."

"I've been told. What else you know about him?"

"Buy me a drink after the matches and I'll tell you all, honey boy." She gave him a swat with the rolled-up magazine.

"Bet." He felt like a low-rent James Bond, gigolo-ing loopy middle-aged women looking for cheap thrills in order to get the information he needed. But hell, what was being a garbageman if you weren't willing to do the dirty work?

By the last match, Acosta was freely moving about, indistinguishable from others who were also roaming around. The crowd had thinned, and only the hard-core fans and the owner-trainers remained. Morales was smoking a cigar and talking about an upcoming derby, that is, a series of elimination rounds in cockfighting, that he was going to be participating in later this month in the San Juaquin Valley. By then, he'd walked to his car, a restored '70 Dodge Magnum. It was an XE model complete with the hideaway lights and factory fender flares. The damned thing had only been produced for two years, and this was the best version of the vehicle. It was the last echo of the muscle car era, and Morales's also had aluminum rims and smoked windows. Acosta had followed him at a discreet distance and memorized the license plate number.

"You ready?" his date asked him after the fight. The battle had ended with a flourish as the winning rooster had destroyed its opponent with a spin that buried its gaff in the other bird's neck. The loser was kicked by its owner, an older white man in overalls and run-over boots. He stomped off in disgust, and one of the kids whose job it was to clean up the ring tossed the dying gamecock in the barrel.

"Sure," Acosta said, nervous.

She hooked an arm in the crook of his as they walked away. The fire had been lit in the barrel, and the wounded rooster gave a last crow as the flames consumed his body, a sacrifice to the gods of futile pursuits.

Natasha Morehead, the costume-bejeweled woman, lived in a small but clean house in Lawndale on a cramped street choked with older cars, broken pavement, and unkempt lawns. She had a roommate, a Teamster retiree named Hickey who had slowed down due to a couple of strokes. Hickey spent his days reading technothrillers or clicking through the 130 channels their satellite dish afforded them. The drink she had in mind was from the two-liter bottle of Old Smuggler Scotch she bought at Costco every other Thursday.

"You know how I got my name?" Morehead said, pouring more Scotch in her tumbler.

"Please tell us," Hickey said, sitting nearby in his worn Barca-lounger in the tidy living room. On the wall behind him was a velvet rendition of Elvis, standing in the middle, an arm around Cesar Chavez and the other around Muhammad Ali in his boxing trunks.

"He hasn't heard it," Morehead said, clapping Acosta on the knee.

"But I could tell it," Hickey shot back, winking broadly at the third member of the party. "I could tell him all about your grandpa in vaudeville and how you were supposed to be the next Ava Gardner and—"

"He's my guest," she retorted.

"Oh, please, my bad, as the kids say." Hickey, a large man gone to blubber, took a dainty sip of Old Smuggler from his plastic cup. Just a little jolt for the heart muscle, he'd said. "Don't let me spoil it."

"That's right." She swept her hair back with flair, exposing gray-ing roots. She proceeded to tell the story, lubricating it with several pulls of Scotch along the way. The tale wasn't that inspiring, but the drinking and the occasional kibitzing from Hickey made it enter-taining. She concluded with laughing loudly and slapping Acosta on the knee again, this time letting her hand remain for a few sec-onds.

"That was something, all right." Acosta also had more booze. What the hell—she wasn't bad for an old girl, and he'd never been with a mature woman. Even being the newbie in TRASH got him reorienting himself in all kinds of odd ways, he reflected. He should be concerned with his developing relationship with Nan rather than fantasizing about Natasha's chest. Jee-zus, did hanging around with Ronk and the rest mean you figured you should be able to get trim like ordering pizza? He had more Old Smuggler, contemplating such a worldview.

"You ain't much of a laborer, are you, son?" Hickey had returned from the kitchen with a bowl of sour-cream-flavored chips, which he slid onto the coffee table.

"I had a regular job until recently."

"That right?" He squinted.

"Stop bothering my guest," the jeweled woman cautioned. "He's plenty strong." It was her turn to take in his chest.

"I didn't say he didn't work out; I said he ain't used to working with his hands. Those calluses along the ridge of his palm are from weights, not digging. I know."

"I had an inside job, Hickey." He didn't really care if his cover was blown—it wasn't like he was moving in or anything. "I was a shipping clerk—brake parts at the Tycor factory in Burbank." *Roll with that, you nosy bastard.*

"What you got to say to that, Hickey?"

"There's still something about you." He swirled the contents of his cup around as if the answer might possibly be forming in the shallow bottom.

"Shit," Morehead declared, "you all the time hoping to jump-start that book you've been threatening to write since I don't know when." She turned to Acosta, grinning. "That's why he's always reading 'em, keeping his notes and starting and stopping on his own thriller—gonna make a million when Harrison Ford plays his hero."

"I got thirty pages done, woman. You'll see."

"Yeah, yeah. Hey," she blared, jumping up, "let's put some music on."

"Anything to keep you from yakking," Hickey said.

Over at a produce crate of vinyl, Morehead retorted, "That's what I get taking pity on my ex-brother-in-law."

"Soft touch, soft head." He smacked his lips as he finished his drink.

"You two go at it like this every day?"

Hickey cackled. "Just for you, stud." He munched on some chips.

Nat King Cole began singing "Mona Lisa" over lofty strings in the way only he could. The scratchy LP, the cheap Scotch, and the ticky-tacky home spoke of inarticulate wants in a part of the city where you lived and grew gray and few if any marked your passing.

A web of melancholy clung to Acosta. Would he be Hickey in decades to come?

"Come on," Natasha Morehead said, standing before him, her hand outstretched.

He looked up at her, momentarily puzzled. Then he rose, his hand going to the middle of her back as they started to dance. She rested her head on his chest, and her hair smelled of off-the-shelf shampoo, but he found it reassuring, pleasant. Acosta wasn't even self-conscious when the older man had to make polite and look away.

"Just for tonight, let's believe you and me are in our own movie and it's been like this for a long time, okay?"

"Sure, Natasha, sure." And he held her tight as King Cole's voice soared on the song's outro.

In her room they committed noisy and desperate lovemaking and didn't fall asleep until well into the early morning hours. The next morning, she had to get up and ready for work at the Home Depot in Carson, where she was a cashier. But sitting on the edge of the bed in her teddy, with Acosta propped up against the headboard, she told him what she knew, remembered, or guessed about Fiver Morales.

CHAPTER 16

Northwest Las Vegas was minutes from the Strip, but it might as well be another city altogether. This was where the showgirls, the janitors, the maids, the change cart pushers, the pot washers, sign maintenance, workers at the Ocean Spray plant, and the guards who walked the floor made their homes. They were the often invisible yet indispensable parts of the ever evolving entertainment complex, who kept the wheels greased and the neon lit that drew the suckers from all over the world to the adult playground that was modern Las Vegas. Or at least the Vegas sold to them.

Now, this was not the place of mile-high sparkling towers and misplaced Venetian canals, but of boxy apartment buildings and frame houses with ten-year-old Honda Civics parked in front, dripping oil and sporting mismatched tires. And this was where Judd Ahn had come based on information Red Dog had obtained about the piece in the Serenade shooting.

He noticed the numbers on Bonanza Road were going down, and could tell he'd passed his destination. He turned around in a strip mall and soon parked in the tiny side lot for the Community Action Foundation of Vegas Valley. Inside the converted building were several people of various colors, going about their work.

"Can I help you?" a young woman with numerous piercings

asked as she edited copy at a desk that looked like it was a prop in a 1940s private eye movie.

"I had an appointment with Carver Edwards." He gave her his name and she asked him to wait. Not too long after, Edwards, the executive director of the CAF, appeared. He was tall, with an easy gait and the mobile eyes of a man who missed nothing and assessed everything.

"Come on in," Edwards said after shaking Ahn's hand. "Janis," he addressed the young woman who'd fetched him, "you get a hold of the good reverend for the town hall?"

"He's set."

"Good. What about Miguel from the Culinary Union?"

"We've traded calls, but I've got to go by there later."

"Most excellent." Edwards proceeded along a short hallway with framed posters recounting various organizing and social movement efforts, including a stark black-and-white one decrying a police shooting in West Vegas a few years back. He led the way to a small office jammed with file folders and a new Apple computer. He sat his rangy frame behind the crowded desk and motioned Ahn to the seat opposite.

"So you've come to excoriate me on my past sins?" Edwards smiled broadly. "Oh, where's my manners? Coffee, juice, or water?"

"I'm fine, thanks. And I'm here to ask about the past only because it has bearing on a case now."

"Involving me?"

"The gun you used, the Dan Wesson thirty-eight."

Edwards tilted his head. "You know good and well it was taken into evidence. The last time I saw that bad rascal was at my trial, with a tag on it. And also, as you well know, ex-felons can't own a firearm. Legally, I mean."

"But because of your exemplary work, turning your life around after prison and all that, Mr. Edwards, you petitioned and were granted a pardon last year by the governor of Nevada."

"You've come prepared, Mr. Ahn."

"I didn't come to jam you up, Carver. I'm here about the gun because I'm interested in what happened to it after you caught a case stemming from the 'ninety-two riots in L.A."

"Ask the court or the LAPD. That stuff goes back into the evidence room or storage or something, right?"

"Yes," Ahn agreed. "Do you remember the cops that busted you coming out of the stop-and-rob?"

Edwards snorted. "I remember a big chick shoving a shotgun barrel upside my head, and blues hollering for my black ass to hump some pavement. That was a lifetime ago, Mr. Ahn. I was a high school dropout existing on forty-ouncers for energy boosts, and visions of honeys draping my arm after I stole enough money to get some product then turn that profit into the rap label I was gonna start." He looked off, blinking. "I'd actually written up what I figured was a business plan outlining this shit, man." He shook his head.

"So do you remember any of them?"

Edwards leaned forward. "You trying to get something on one of these cops? From way back then?"

"Would you mind just answering the question?"

The one called Janis appeared in the doorway. "Excuse me, but I just e-mailed you over the revised draft of the flyer and need your comments back by this afternoon. Before I go out, okay?"

"On it." She went away and Edwards said, "You know who was there; they keep the records, log, whatever y'all call them."

"Sometimes the reports aren't as complete as we'd like them to be. Particularly when you have cops on riot detail suddenly converging on a robbery in progress."

"Look, man, I was buzzing on crack and Olde English, and I'm thankful I had enough presence of mind to drop the piece and do what they said or they would have blown my head clean off." The reformed community leader shrugged his shoulders. "It was the big woman, Nakorski, who testified at my trial. Her I remember clearly. Why don't you ask her who-all else was there that night?"

"I did." Edna Nakorski was now a detective on the Seattle PD, and she'd told Ahn via telephone whom she recalled of the officers there that night. But the chain of possession of the gun first used by Edwards in that robbery of a 7-Eleven during the riots, to Serenade through Macklin, a white-supremacist gun dealer, was a puzzle waiting to be deciphered.

"What about this guy?" Ahn produced a photo of Ronk Culhane in civilian clothes.

"Can't say I know him," Edwards mused. "He's a cop, isn't he?"

Ahn showed him a grainy reproduction of Macklin from a surveillance done at a gun show in Pomona several years ago. He was in his fifties, in shape, and had a banner with a swastika hanging in the back of his booth.

"Nope," Edwards said, leaning back from the printout. "But I'll tell you this 'cause you're gonna ask it. I got the gun from a dude once named Smokey, but they buried him with his real name, Keith Davis."

"How'd he die?"

"Believe it or not, heart problems. He died when I was in the joint in the early nineties. He was only in his twenties, but it was some sort of hereditary thing. If his father had been around, the doctors might have known about it and done something to help him before his condition got worse. But like all us young fools, he maintained a diet of drugs, malt liquor, and Popeye's greasy-ass chicken. Damn." He shook his head again and added, "Your picture made me think of him, though."

"How do you mean?"

"He was a gun nut and loved to frequent those shows with everybody from the Nazi low-riders to the vatos running around all excited over their common love of firearms." He elaborated more on the late Smokey Davis and his short, unproductive life, but whose antisocial comings and goings were part of what the then incarcerated Carver Edwards had reflected on, ultimately leading him to seek a productive path upon release.

Ahn mulled that over as he said his farewell to the man and his organization. Could it be that Macklin had originally sold the piece to Smokey, a Four-Trey Rolling Dalton? Wouldn't the white supremacist gun dealer be afraid of supplying one more potential killing tool to the mud people? Or could it be that Macklin was a bit of a sociologist and assumed, given the rate of black-on-black crime, that he was only hastening the demise of the dark race he so despised?

But what Ahn really wondered was, how did the weapon get from police custody for one crime, more than a decade ago, back into Culhane's hand in the Serenade shooting? Assuming, as he and his colleagues did, that the shooting was hinky. And then there was Red Dog. Fucking Red Dog. He really hadn't given him shit in the way of a lead to Macklin. The most he'd come up with was that the guy had been seen at a biker rally in Tahoe, or maybe he was on the run from some dudes he'd burned. What the hell? Was the Dog fucking with him just to be fucking with him, or was he too scared of exposure to find out something useful?

In his car, Ahn was looking for a place to have a late breakfast and burning up gray cells on how he could make any of this tie together. Even on the face of it, even if he gave Culhane a pass, the goddamn piece wound up in Serenade's hands. In the past, the Crazy Nines had had loose connections with the Aryan Resistance Movement and the Vandal Vikings in the California and Pacific Northwest prison systems. This was due to the black gangs' dominance in some prisons, given the disproportionate number of African-American young men busted in drug sweeps. Was he looking in the wrong direction? He knew from the records that Culhane had been working out of 77th then and was in the thick of things as a uniformed cop. Nakorski, who'd been credited with the arrest of Edwards, couldn't say if he was or wasn't there at the bust, as some cops merely passed through, stopping to help, then going on to respond to other calls. By his written accounts, which Ahn had gone over and over, Culhane was in the vicinity that night, but so were hundreds of others—some of whom had gone on to TRASH and beyond.

It could easily be that some other cop had lifted the piece from evidence and it eventually came into Culhane's hands. He'd have it ready to use in just the right emergency, at least from his perspective. In this case, he'd used the throw-down to bind Acosta to the fraternity. Ahn spotted a Denny's and pulled into the parking lot. All of his speculation was just so much educated guessing. He needed conclusive links; otherwise, he was just wasting time and city money on fools' errands.

Inside, he sat at a back booth and ordered. There was an electronic slot machine mounted on the table in place of a juke box selector. Ahn put some money in and played a few rounds of poker against the machine while sipping his coffee. He got three jacks against the house's two pair and stared openmouthed at the screen. He got out his cell and dialed a Los Angeles number.

"Phenias," he said after the line connected. He listened to the other man's response, then continued. "Go over to the Code 7 and look at this picture up against the back wall. You know, like you're heading through that archway to the can, and to your left is this booth with photos tacked above it . . . Yeah, uh-huh, that's what I'm talking about. Well, if memory serves, one of them is of a poker game or tournament they had there, and Ronk Culhane and some other cops are in that shot."

Ahn nodded thanks as the waitress set his food down. "That's right; see if you can ID the cops in that shot, man. I'm on my way back to L.A." He ate heartily.

CHAPTER 17

Red dog awoke with the usual beer-and-meth malaise that soaked familiar aches in his body. They'd been calling him by his nickname since he was in junior high and would cut class to hang with the older kids, to swig some brew and pop red devils. His face would get all flushed and, well, there you go. He scratched himself and looked over at the clock radio. It was past ten, and he was hungry as a bear. He was always hungry for something.

"Barbara," he called. Not that the odds were such that his old lady would cook for him, but she had on more than one occasion actually stood at the stove to do up some eggs and Spam. He liked his Spam. "Barbara," he called once more, and again got no answer. That dizzy dame was off somewhere. *Fuckin' modern women*, his old man would grouse. *All them overeducated Jew bra-burners are to blame for this*, he'd go on. *Used to be women knew their place and kept to it—no back talk, no trying to show you up and make more money than you.* As if that fuck were good at anything but staying one step ahead of the bill collectors and furniture repossessors.

He got his jeans on and went into the front room, surveying the accumulation of a life spent as best he could. It didn't take long, and as a trickle of disappointment went through him, he traipsed into the kitchen. There was beer, of course, a partial block of cheese, some grapes turning to raisins in a bowl, a half bottle of some shit called chutney, and one egg. Quietly he closed the refrigerator door, then stretched and yawned. He'd finish getting dressed, get on his bike, and tool down to that Norm's over in Sylmar. There were a couple of all-right-looking waitresses there. He fondled his johnson, a twinge of a chubby coming on as he fantasized about these two young women at the diner with their white tennis shoes and firm coed titties. Used to be, Barbara would wake him up in the mornings by sucking him off. When the fuck was the last time she'd done that? Red Dog returned to the bathroom to complete the scene playing out in his head of him doing the two and them doing each other.

Afterward he was buttoning his shirt when the phone rang. This was the one he kept in the closet in its own hideaway that Ahn didn't know about. He got the floorboard out of the way and picked up the cordless.

"Uh-huh."

"Roy, it's Tony. I've got tickets for tonight's game."

"You have the wrong number, my friend." He hung up, satisfaction widening his mouth. He finished getting dressed and even brushed his teeth. Nothing like earning some scratch on the side. Especially—and that fucking trickle had been occurring more lately—especially given the Dog was convinced he needed to make a move soon.

That business with Panhead getting popped by Ahn had rankled the Vandals leadership, and it wasn't like he was on their A list to begin with. And he had to do some fast and fancy lying to account for the slick gook coming to see him. He'd told them it had to do with a warrant on some tickets, and that seemed to placate them. The Dog had been angling for a lieutenantship for some time, but the Ring, the inner circle, had made it pretty clear he was only as useful as the remote location of his place was useful to them—this last incident reconfirming his low-level position. He was, he admitted to himself, a glorified watchman.

After all he'd given and sacrificed for the cause . . . Shit, Panhead only did two days in the pokey and was now out on bail. If Ahn hadn't had him arrested, that would have looked too funny, and Red Dog would be served his balls for appetizers.

"Fuck," he swore. He was getting squeezed from both sides and had better get his shit together. The question was, what about Barbara? There was a time there would have been no hesitation about her. She was his broad and she'd stand with him no matter what fell. But now? He just wasn't sure.

Was it just the sex? It wasn't like he'd been counting the number of blow jobs she used to give him a month, yet they'd sure slacked off. Could she have some other dude's tool dangling from her jaw? Somebody in the Ring? She was an ambitious broad.

This played on his mind as the thick-bodied man guided his Harley along a narrow footpath paralleling the Santa Susana Wash before it branched off into a thick bunching of trees and brush. He had to park his bike and proceed on foot to where he kept his stash. Red Dog was loyal but not a complete goddamn fool. This secret cache of drugs was his personal 401K. The Vandals knew nothing about it, nor did Barbara or Ahn, and he planned to keep it that way. The coded call had been from one of his steady distributors, a hustler who went by the handle Trey Mack. Those niggers sure liked their colorful names. But hey, times were changing, and if the darkies and meskins wanted their speed high too—wanted that tang that was different from crack—who was he to deny them? A market was a market, and the farther it was away from this end of the Valley, the better.

Red Dog came to the spot and, wearing his gloves so as not to leave prints, removed the already loose ground covering to reveal the lid of a buried fifty-five-gallon drum. Inside, cocooned in foam peanuts, were small boxes of pale yellow pills. He got out two boxes, each weighing seven ounces, and covered up his moneymaker. The Dog wasn't foolish enough to skim from the Vandal Vikings meth supply—well, not more than was reasonable. Plus, since his place was just the way station for the raw chemicals, he only made his trips out to the lab in Lancaster when he was ordered to do so on transport errands. Therefore, whatever he filched from them amounted to pocket money. But his side business of the "new coke," as some called the pills, was his retirement money.

He remounted his bike, backed it out with leg power, got it turned around and rode back to the asphalt road. The Dog marveled that no matter how many smart bombs and talking computers the pencil-necks built, everybody from the crap-in-his-pants street bum to the $650-an-hour lawyer liked to "get their buzz on," as Trey Mack would say. And now that the first generation of Ritalin kids were finishing college and entering the workplace, methylphenidate was getting to be as common as the other kinds of speed for the masses.

Those nice attention-deficit-disorder middle-class sons and daughters, some of whom had grown up on Ritties or one of its like drugs such as Adderall or Concerta, were used to taking the shit, so naturally they had prescriptions for it when they were away at their little fancy colleges. For the ADD crowd, speed worked in a kind of opposite way and helped their hyper brains function in a more focused manner.

But for the regular ones looking for the next cool way to get fucked up, this stuff was ready-made to be abused. Motherfuckers would snort roach powder if they saw it would get them a blast. And invariably it would have to be somebody's job to supply them with their methods of flight. The Dog had a source in Tijuana, Nino Cruz, a connection established from a brief and strained alliance between the Vikings and the Crazy Nines. That was when there was a push in Venice and Santa Monica from keeping the Shoreline Crips and Rolling Daltons, the city's two large black gangs, from gobbling up rival drug territory. The turf battles had always simmered, but as more black and brown types got more into meth, naturally their gangster cousins smelled a moneymaking venture and wanted a cut of that trade, too.

But as always, greed had a way of putting aside bad blood for the common goal of generating profit. So Red Dog, through Barbara and her hagged-out sister, who loved banging the brothers, put the word out that he had what the college kids wanted—some of whom were willing to pay five dollars a hit. And there were plenty of places like USC and UCLA in and around the urban and surrounding areas that the inner-city slangers had inroads to that the Dog didn't. And as long as the well in TJ didn't run dry, he'd keep his end up till those honeys with the volleyball-sized tits and coifed muffs stumbled on to the next cool drug to snort or smoke.

Traveling into boogietown on the freeway, his Harley's pipes blaring, the wind cleansing his hungover head, Red Dog was glad he was an American. Where else could you get over like this?

* * *

Trey Mack took the stairs two at a time. That bullshit with that bitch-ass Santián was the wakeup call he needed. Sure, you couldn't stay in shape solely by getting some twice a day. You worked up a sweat; it felt great as hell, but clearly he needed to get back to the gym, since pussy was only good for one kind of muscle. And now that he was getting close to thirty, he definitely couldn't afford to be going soft. He carried a pill bottle of his freshly acquired Ritalin. Jade had acquired a taste for the shit, and he was a good daddy to his bottom bitch. She had a couple of regulars, rich boys with trust funds who pictured themselves as hard—thus his way into the campus action for sales.

He was at the top of the second-story outdoor landing and, from his vantage point, saw a mark standing at Jade's open door. He hung back, staying in the recessed stairwell, scoping out the scene while laying in the cut. It paid to know what your hoes were up to, because you needed to stay ahead of their deviousness. By chance he'd come up the rear way. Jade stepped aside, and a dude came out of her apartment. Trey Mack recognized August Mercury right off. What the fuck?

Then it clicked. The mark, whose heavy dose of cologne carried to him, was Mercury's boy, Peacock. His girl had met the label-head at a Def Ritmo album release party he'd also attended. Trey Mack had encouraged her pretending to dig him to bank future favors. Jade and some of her friends, in and out of his stable, had been used to sex down some of the Def Ritmo artists, and even picked up some change by shaking their rumps in a few music videos. But she hadn't mentioned that she was servicing Mercury on the regular.

Trey Mack watched as Peacock now entered the apartment. The front door was left ajar. He waited. Sure enough, the two men came back out and headed toward the front stairs, the closest way to the street. The door was pulled shut from inside, but Trey Mack was sure he heard two female voices in the apartment. Things were definitely getting very interesting. He could just charge into her place and start a whole lot of drama with Jade to find out what was going on, but his better sense told him to be sharp, not violent just to be violent. He went back through the complex's security gate, which the kids tended to leave unlatched during the day.

Back at his car he sat and worked through what might be going on. He knew that Mercury was in with the Nines and had been getting sweated by Santián and his crew since Gargoyle Villa's killing. He also knew that homeboy hadn't been around his office in the past few days, since the listserve, the Electronic Urban Report, ran a piece on the rumor that Mercury had disappeared after an attempt on his life. Trey Mack was a big believer in the Internet. He advertised his girls on a Web site. So this meant the mufuh was on the run and looked like he'd lighted in Jade's place, Peacock being the intermediary, as a hideaway.

Trey Mack laughed and rolled a chocolate-wrap blunt. He then took a deep drag of the kronik as he formulated how best to take advantage of this development.

CHAPTER 18

"**Y**ou get to take out on account of your advanced years." Curtis Santián tossed the ball to his father.

"Gee, thanks." The older Santián dribbled forward, his right eye stinging from the sweat trickling steadily from his forehead. His son stood, legs apart, scooting backward as his father advanced toward the basket. The old man pivoted with his hip, his son reaching in for the ball; Santián then did a back step and bounced the ball between his son's legs. The teenager adjusted, turning around as his father ran past, catching up with the ball, then shooting a three. The ball circled the rim and fell through.

"What's up, huh?"

"Lucky." Curtis Santián took the ball out. He came in fast, causing his father to move crablike to keep up on his flank. He stopped abruptly, took the ball behind his back, faked left, drove right, and was posting up as Santián jumped to block. The older man's fingertips grazed the ball just enough to make the shot veer off.

The younger Santián made a sound in his throat, then got himself set as his father trotted past the imaginary boundary line then circled back, slowly dribbling the ball on the curve of the cement in front of their two-car garage.

"Looks like you got school all damn day today."

"Come on, Grandpa."

"My pleasure." Santián did a crossover, but his son got a hand in, and the ball careened off their blue recycling bin.

"That's on you."

"I know who it's on," Curtis Santián said testily.

His father chuckled while he retrieved the ball. Feeling sporty, he dribbled in quickly, set, and shot. The ball went off and his son rebounded, evaded his dad's block, and laid the rock in.

"Ain't no thing," the older Santián snorted.

"Let's go."

Santián charged, but his son was on him tight. He backed up, looking for a break, then dipped his shoulder into his son's breastbone, steadily moving forward. He faked like he was going to hook his shot, then spun, getting a second of space and shot. The ball bounced off the backboard but went wide off the rim.

Both of them went for it, and the youngster snagged the ball. But he couldn't get clear as his dad pressed and forced him to take an off-balance shot. The ball banged off the top of the backboard and rolled down the driveway.

Santián was bent over, hand on his knees, sucking in air.

"That's yours."

"Bullshit, you're just tired." Curtis Santián went for the ball.

Santián straightened up, flexing his shoulders. "I got your 'tired.' "

His son came in hard, and both of them grunted upon contact. The older man got his arms out from his body, his tennis shoes squeaking across an oil stain.

" 'Zup now, huh?" the father taunted.

"We're gonna see who's in school, son," the teenager said.

"Bring it, if you can."

Curtis Santián spun and, in the same movement, reached around his father's legs with his dribble to get the ball past him. Santián sought to block this maneuver, but his son's speed and handling were such that he was getting away from his block as Santián twisted his torso and brought the side of his hand down on his son's wrist.

The younger Santián ignored the foul, and as his father rushed to get in front of him, he hooked the ball and it swooshed through the netting.

"That's right," Curtis Santián boasted, tapping his chest with his fist as he scooted backward effortlessly.

The older man didn't say anything as he focused on his next attempt at the hoop. He dribbled the ball in bounds, keeping his upper body hunched over, using his head as a way to batter his way toward his goal.

His son laughed, staying on his old man like paint. "What's this? Some old-school shit like Wilt Chamberlain used to do?"

His son slapped at the ball, nearly knocking it loose.

Santián huffed and drove, huffed and drove.

"Look out you don't lock up your knee, Pops."

"Your pops is dangling, fool." Santián gave him a chuck, but his son wouldn't be forced back and remained stationary.

"That Bogart shit don't play here, junior." Curtis Santián anticipated his father's next move as he suddenly stopped short, pulled back, and took his shot. The younger man was already off his feet and got part of the ball as it arced upward. The Voit Kobe Special plummeted to the ground, the son's last basket going unanswered.

"Fuck," Santián muttered, running to retrieve the ball.

"Indeed," his son said as he set again.

Santián came forward slowly, then broke into a fast charge. His son closed the gap, and the two bodies rattled together as the older man sweated and exerted effort to get in range. He used his shoulder to cleave into his son and try to wedge his body out of the way.

"Be careful—you might blow a blood vessel," his son warned.

Santián scrambled, gave it all he had, and dribbled to the left to find clearance, but his son wasn't having any of it. Curtis lurched into him, and Santián elbowed him, causing a moment's hesitation. He took his opportunity to shoot and the ball sunk through the rim.

"That's how you always win, huh? Cheating."

"No blood, no foul," Santián remarked, breathing through his mouth. "Can't take it?"

"I'm just getting started." The younger man bounded forward, feinted one way, then got through going the other way. He did a layup, the ball skying then dropping through nothing but net. He bounce-passed the ball to his father. "What's that, sixteen-ten?"

"Don't worry about the score, youngster."

"Oh, I'm not." Curtis Santián had his legs apart, arms spread, leaning forward, his upper body rocking slightly from side to side.

It surprised Santián that he hadn't noticed of late how developed his son had become. He went in straight, then angled off, but his son wouldn't commit. Curtis Santián knew that the old man was less likely to take a shot from that far back and would save his energy for crowding him if he tried another burst of speed.

Santián jerked forward, looked up, then jumped and shot, the ball thudding against the rim but falling away impotently. His son effortlessly got the rebound, but the old man wasn't going to let him get his two that easily.

The father was on him and backing him up, making him duck and dribble, marching him back against the garage door. But at the last second, the teenager triple-timed and scooted by the barest of openings. He went up, turning in midair, and finessed the ball in. He landed like a big cat, on the balls of his feet. "That's how the ballers do it, Super Fly." He grabbed his crotch to underscore his dominance.

"Game ain't over yet," Santián said, circling back in with the ball and moving purposefully, gnawing on his bottom lip. He couldn't let this kid, barely old enough to hold his dick by himself, make him the goat. Naw, it didn't go down like that. He faked one way, then tried to charge the basket in the other direction. But Curtis had too much board experience to fall for that and stayed on him. You'd think, Santián reflected, that listening to that goddamn rap music all the time would have scrambled more of his brain cells.

"Ugh," Santián exhaled, using his upper body to try and dislodge his unwanted shadow.

The younger Santián responded by extending his torso to bump his father back. No way was he going to let his old man get over on him. He'd faced down all-city players and showed them that just because he went to school in the Valley, he wasn't no punk.

Santián stepped up his pace, blatantly using his free arm to try to hold his son off.

"What's up?" The younger man said, tapping his hand against that flagrant elbow.

Santián worked his arm like a rooster flapping its wing to ward off an enemy.

"That don't faze me!" Curtis Santián bellowed. He also pressed, and now both of them were bunched up under the hoop, their bodies shoved against each other like bucks enraged by the scent.

Santián peddled sideways, looking to get a shot. But his son wasn't giving him any slack and matched him step for step, grinning mischievously.

"Too much heat for you, champ?"

Santián was too pissed and too winded for a smart-ass comeback. He threw the ball against his son's knee, letting it rebound away. "On you."

Derisively his son said, "That the best you can come up with?"

Santián was already back in play and stood on the boundary of the imaginary sidelines and took his shot. The ball went home.

"Don't get all excited. I ain't through giving you your lesson." And his son proceeded to sink another basket, then get a steal off his father and send it through yet again.

"Twenty-twelve, if I'm not mistaken."

Santián's cell phone rang from where it had been placed on the porch steps.

"You better get that so you can get yourself a little break," his son chided.

"Don't need it." Santián bulled toward the hoop, running smack into his son, who'd planted himself. The younger man stumbled and went over; the older man, ignoring his flagrant foul, continued to make his two points.

Curtis Santián got in his father's face. "It's like that, huh? What's crackin', then?"

"Come on."

The two glared at each other, their flared nostrils nearly touching. Whatever their respective disappointments or hopes for each other, the contest was now injected with preening maleness as they entered an elemental state where the categories of father and son evaporated, and the only relevance was in which one had the upper hand.

"Let's finish this," Santián said.

The younger man picked up the ball.

His son clamped his mouth shut in determination and put his feet in motion, going at his father. At the same time, he crossed the ball from his left to his right rapidly, turning his body, too, to throw his father off as to which direction he was going to take.

"Showboat," Santián said, his hands all over his son.

"Bam!" the son hollered after a clean pullup shot that banked the ball off the backboard and through the net.

Santián's cell rang again, and he went to answer it as his son stood, ball held on one lean hip, a satisfied smirk blossoming across his face.

"Yeah," he snarled into the instrument.

"Saint," a female voice said.

"Who's this?" His mouth hung open and sweat dripped from the top of his head.

"Roxanne. I found your girl."

For a moment, his head still in the game, Santián was disoriented; then it clicked into place. "Good work, baby. Where can I find her?"

"Her place is on Ivy, near Market and Arbor Vitae." And she gave him the exact address of Jade's apartment. "You know how I found her?" she asked pridefully.

He didn't give a shit how she found her, but why piss her off unnecessarily? "Sure, Rox, how?"

"We gonna finish?" his son challenged, bouncing the ball. "Or would you like a return engagement for your ass-whupping?"

"Who's that?" asked Roxanne.

"Just some pipsqueak. So how'd you find her?"

She proceeded to tell him in the most elliptical, nonconsecutive narrative manner how she'd been foxy, operated on the down-low, but essentially kept asking around until she got to a working girl who had to loan Jade money for a phone bill last week and had seen Hyacinth over there, too.

"So what if I scoped the place out for you?"

Great, now she was going to be a thong-wearing Nancy Drew. "You've done your part. I don't want you anywhere near her crib."

"Aw, Saint, I ain't stoo-pid, shit. It don't take no talent to peep the apartment."

"You looking for a career change?"

"I just want to see that ho gets what she deserves. She's always acted like her shit smells like Chanel, like she was just trickin' until something fabulous came along. That the rest of us was lucky to be sniffing old men's balls for a living."

"Look, I'll tighten you up. I gotta go, but you did good."

"Prove it," she teased. "We ain't tumbled in a while, Saint. You suddenly don't like stank?"

"You know better than that. I gotta bounce."

"Uh-huh. You better call me tomorrow, nigga. Have my money and that sweet dick of yours ready."

"Jesus," he chuckled, clicking off.

"We gonna do this? Or you want the excuse you got to go hold the hands of one of your little snitches?"

He should chase down the lead, because who knew how long Hyacinth would be holed up with Jade? But then, it was early evening and the girls would be out and about. There was time. "Let's go, youngster. I'm through taking it easy on you."

"Damn, I'm scared."

At thirty-five to twenty-four, they called it quits, the older man stomping away as the younger one guffawed. After toweling off, Saint Santián aimed his Malibu back into the city. On KNX, the all-news radio station, there was a report about the largest city employees' union, SEIU 347, coming out with an endorsement of Constance McGuire in the mayor's race. This announcement had newsworthiness because the County Federation of Labor, the confederation of the various unions, had come out for the incumbent.

"Oh," Julie Butcher, the head of the union, opined in a sound bite, "it's not that unusual in this city's politics for unions not to be all of one voice when it comes to the candidates. After all, we have a strong tradition of fierce independence, and I'm about expressing the wishes of our members. And in this case, they feel that Connie McGuire is one of them. Her father was a janitor, a member in good standing with this union for some thirty years. He cleaned the courts building where, as a little girl, she'd go with him sometimes and marvel at the halls where justice took place. She's now going to bring a fair shake not only to our sisters and brothers, but to the whole city, too."

It was all the self-control Santián could summon not to put his fist through the radio. So far, his day was turning out to really suck big-time. And as the sun started to disappear over the horizon, he hoped his night wouldn't be equally shitty.

*   *   *

Red Dog rode onto his driveway and parked his bike next to his old lady's car and killed the headlamp. Inside he could hear her raised voice, barking at somebody on the phone. Dusk had descended, but the lights weren't on as he stepped onto the porch, the aging floorboards creaking. He was surprised that the door was locked and he had to use his keys.

"Hey," he said, entering the front room. Reno, in profile, stood looking at the window, her hands on her hips. She didn't respond. "Barbara, what's up—static with your sister?"

"What? No, no, nothing. How'd you know I was on the phone?"

"The whole goddamn neighborhood knows, the way you were going on."

"We don't have a neighborhood," she mumbled.

"Where have you been?" she added, her mood suddenly softening as she moved toward him.

He was about to tell her the truth, but that gnawing doubt put the lie on his tongue. After his business with Trey Mack he had looked up some old buds in Hermosa Beach. And time passes when you're bullshitting about the days when you rode together and drinking beer in the heat. He just told her some jive about having to run Vandal Viking errands, about how this would help show he was a stand-up guy.

"Hey, why don't I make us some burgers and homemade fries." She rubbed his stomach and nuzzled his neck. "I'll mix the meat up with chopped green onions and chili powder like you like, baby."

"Sure, baby." Maybe he was worrying for nothing.

"Why don't you shower up, huh? For later, you know?" Her hand went lower.

"Hell, yes." And he kissed her deeply and longingly.

After dinner and doing some crank, they coupled like they hadn't in at least a year, Red Dog reflected. It was if Barbara had picked up his vibes and was doing everything sexually to erase any and all second-guessing he had about her and their relationship.

Without any prompting or wheedling on his part, she willingly and effervescently went down on him. Hell, went down was mild—she devoured him and then nibbled and licked his balls until he was about to blow. She then scooted up until her legs were smothering his head. Red Dog didn't admit this to his buddies, but he loved to eat out. And his woman jerked him off as he did so.

Later they lay exhausted in bed, and the Dog listened to her un-cluttered breathing as she slept. Quietly as he could, he got out of bed and went into the front room. He star-sixty-nined the phone, but only a one and three came up. She'd obviously picked up the handset when he was in the shower and redialed to get rid of the number of whomever she'd been talking to when he'd come home. He should leave it alone, but her sudden turnaround was just too fucking good to believe. What was wrong with him that he couldn't embrace happiness when it came his way?

Rifling through her purse on the kitchen table, he found her cell phone. There were several numbers stored in its memory. A few of them he recognized. But there was one with a 213 area code and a prefix he knew that gave him dread. Using the house phone, he called the number, and even before the recorded voice on the other end announced his name, he knew it was Ahn. The number was his inside line in the DA's office. He didn't have that rice-cake-eatin' motherfucker's line; why did Barbara?

His first impulse was to tear into the bedroom, bounce the cell phone off her skull, and see what she had to say. But he calmed himself; this one he had to play close, not go off—not just yet. If she was talking to Ahn, she must have made her own deal. But it couldn't just be about the meth, because Ahn certainly had the goods on him if that was what he wanted. So what was it? What the fuck were his two-timing girlfriend and that conniving slope up to?

The Ring, Red Dog concluded—that must be what Ahn was after. There wasn't anything else that it could be, only the joke was, after that business with Panhead, those bastards weren't about to elevate the Dog into the inner circle. He laughed hoarsely as he got back into bed. Reno shifted her body, draping an arm around him as she snuggled close. He patted her hand, working out what he needed to do next. If he worked it right, he'd show the Ring he was valuable. Of course, he had to be careful, lest they blame this shit on him for letting Reno get away with it. He had to make sure they understood he was the one who was betrayed, and so that meant them, too, and wasn't it smart of him to find out before the cops swooped down.

Reno adjusted her head on her pillow and mumbled something that the Dog didn't process. Through the partially open slit of the blinds, the three-quarter moon shone brightly, as if coated in luminescent paint. He was mildly surprised that he was sleepy again—not at all too rattled given what he'd discovered. He guessed it was the not knowing that had had him all knotted up. Now a kind of detachment soothed him, and if things got out of control, he had nearly forty grand in his kitty. That wasn't much for two, but it was enough for one on the run. Yeah, just enough.

CHAPTER 19

Staring at the three-quarter moon, Santián rubbed his hands together and stifled a yawn. He lowered his vision from the heavens
to more earthly concerns. He'd been staking out Jade's apartment
on Ivy and was bored doing so. Conversely, Cortese could watch a
place like he was autistic—just stare and wait. The corpuscles in
him needed to be in motion, the electrons colliding and sliding
along his arteries and nervous system. The only excitement he'd
gotten for hours of nothing was a homeless man pushing his shopping cart past with a plaster statue of Serena Williams in her butt-
hugging Lycra outfit.

Checking the time—it was 3:17 A.M.—he had the queasy feeling
he was going to have to be cramped up in the Malibu the entire
night. He hunkered down, curious how his wife would interpret
the basketball game between him and Curtis. That was going to be
one more tussle they'd probably get into. It was getting so he didn't
know what was worse: the stress of the streets or the stress of his
home life. She hadn't directly stated anything about his extracurricular poontang, but he knew she must suspect something.
Women had their ways. She'd busted him years ago over another
twist when Curtis was nine and Monica—what—two? He'd had to
endure sessions with the department shrink, but he had to admit
that both of them had come out better for it. But shit, could he
help it if Linda practically crawled into his lap?

Not that he flaunted his exploits to belittle his wife. And in his own way, he did love Nicole. They'd been through a lot, and it was more than just the financial entanglements, though he knew plenty of cops, male and female, who stuck it out because of that. The preachers might be right that money wasn't everything, but who the fuck from Compton to Kandahar didn't need those pesos to put some grub in their belly and give them someplace to lay their head?

But was his marriage now merely of convenience until Monica was old enough to understand that Mommy and Daddy had grown apart? The idea made him colder than he already was. Pondering that, Santián was dully aware of a car pulling into a space at the curb a few yards in front of him. The driver then crossed to the prostitute's apartment building. Santián had sat up, suddenly very awake. It was August Mercury.

Santián had his hand on the door handle and was about to light into the street to tackle him, but he decided to learn more first. Santián shook his head. "Fuckin' Trey," he muttered. That forked-tongued bastard had to be the connection between the hoes and the runaway record exec. Everybody had an angle to play in this town. He got out and noted the plates on the car, a late-model Saturn. He walked around to the front and saw the Enterprise sticker in the lower left-hand corner of the windshield. The door was locked, but his lock-picking tools got it open easily.

He found nothing of value in the glove box or digging around under the seats. He popped the trunk, and except for the spare in its well and the tire iron, the space was empty. Closing it, he heard voices, and sure enough, Jade and Hyacinth were rounding a far corner. He kept the lid up to better obscure his face, since both women knew him. The two were laughing and recounting their night's adventures with their various "dates." Jade was holding a can in a paper sack, and Hyacinth was munching on a burrito in its plastic wrap.

After they, too, entered the complex, he closed the Saturn's trunk and got in his car. He went home to his bedroom community. He was on such a roll, his wife woke up and they made love with an intensity he hadn't experienced in months with her.

"Am I the king of the streets, baby?" he grunted as she inserted

him from behind, on her knees and holding on to the headboard.

"I'll nominate you for king of the sheets," she laughed, then
moaned while the headboard creaked as she gripped it tighter,
rocking back and forth.

He laughed, too. He was the goddamn king of the streets.

CHAPTER 20

Some sixty miles from Santián's bedroom, Alvaro Acosta came out along the narrow passageway to the illegally converted garage behind the house in Compton on Ezmerlian Street. Because affordable housing was at a premium in the Southland, these types of dwellings flourished. Not because the owners were a magnanimous bunch, but because they had a constituency of immigrants locked into low-end jobs and too often without proper documentation, who had to take what they could at exorbitant rates to keep a roof over their families' heads.

In Fiver's case, he was an American, but Natasha had told Acosta he maintained several places around town to keep below the radar of the law—and, she added, to help support at least two women he'd had babies by. Hanging out at the day laborers' site yielded some specifics in terms of locations. This garage was where Morales stayed at least three days of the week. His gun at his side, Acosta scanned his surroundings, hoping not to antagonize a pit bull that might leap from the gloom.

Fortunately, there was no dog, and he got to the front of the garage's double doors unmolested. This type of garage hadn't been built since the fifties, Acosta guessed—which made sense because the housing stock in this part of Compton was pre–Second World War construction. Where the lock's hasp and catch had been, there were now two holes drilled on either door at parallel heights. Through these, Acosta surmised, a chain would be inserted and Morales could padlock the doors closed from the inside or outside, depending on whether he was coming or going. The chain, Acosta could see by peering through the gapped doors, was on the floor inside the garage. He could make it out in the spill of light from a window in the front house. That was where he could hear the muffled droning of a TV. He brought the gun up, moved the door wider with the flat of his hand, and stepped in.

Even in the murk, he could see that the man had expended effort and resources to make his quarters comfortable. There was a big screen and music combo like the ones found at Best Buy tucked midwall to his left. The furniture, a couch that probably folded out and two overstuffed chairs, looked better than what Acosta owned. Moving farther in, he saw a microwave, camper stove, and minifridge clustered in one corner. Several electrical cords snaked in from a slot where the ceiling and roofline met, leading to the various appliances. The place was "laid," as they said. Too bad Fiver Morales wouldn't be taking advantage of it any longer.

Like a penitent, Acosta's quarry was on his knees, his head inside the open cavity of his minifridge. There was no light in the box, and it had taken Acosta several moments to reconcile the shape in his brain. Now, bending over the inert form, he could see the twin set of gaffs, the fighting hooks used on the gamecocks, buried in the carotid artery of his neck. Morales's hands had been duct-taped behind his back, as had his ankles, and a band of the stuff was wrapped several times around his mouth and head. He'd been beaten first, then left this way to bleed out. It hadn't been more than a day or two, for there was rigor but little smell. Decomposition was no doubt occurring but not yet apparent, though maggots could be seen wriggling past the edges of the tape around his mouth.

Acosta surmised that it had been a two-man job. Morales was a good-sized individual, with plenty of experience dealing straight up with fools. It would take two humps who knew how to apply the muscle to take him out like this. Somewhere—and he couldn't remember where—he'd read or heard that Styrofoam packed around a corpse preserved the body quite nicely. Funny he should remember that as he sat on the couch—there wasn't a butt print he was messing up, right?—and put in a number on his cell phone.

He severed the connection before it went through. Automatically, he'd been calling Santián. He redialed.

"This is Acosta, control, seven-oh-nine-twenty-two. I have a body, homicide, in Compton. Put me through to Captain Kubrick and then reroute a call to the Sheriff's Department. Here's the address..." And he recited the numbers and gave directions to the rear unit. Then he waited for Kubrick to get on the line. Whoever did this was on a cleanup mission, he concluded. Botching the Mercury hit by the second-stringers had brought the big hitters off the bench.

Hyacinth found the shy dark-skinned black guy kind of cute. He wasn't bad-looking, and thankfully he'd bathed. It was getting so the smell of musty, sagging balls was going to make her lose her mind. She hadn't been on the stroll that long, and he'd pulled over in his little pickup truck. She'd gone out early this morning, before Jade was up, because she needed to get some more money together to get her situation straight. And there was always some chump on his way to or from work who didn't mind a treat from a chick built like her. When there was time, she'd try to get her Web site up again with a photo of her, posing all buffed and flexing. Men and women had paid good money for custom shots of her. But the damned site had become infected with a virus, and all sorts of other drama had happened, so she hadn't gotten around to getting it fixed yet.

"Darling, we gonna have a good time," the muscular woman promised on her knees between his spread legs. His boxers were still on, and she'd grabbed hold of him through the slit. He'd paid two hundred dollars, so that earned him an hour and a room. Trey Mack had negotiated deals with several of the hotels in the Inglewood area, and she'd chosen the Bing Bong on Centinela because they kept the place respectable.

"Don't be nervous," she said, starting to work on him. "What's your name, cutie?"

"Tommy," the john said.

"That's a nice name," she replied, licking his shaft.

"Jesus..." The man shifted as he lay on the bed. "That feels real good."

"It's supposed to." She kneaded his thighs with her corded hands and got in better position.

"Haven't you learned that you should keep foreign objects out of your mouth, Hyacinth?"

"Damn it, Saint, did you have to break in now?" the customer complained.

"Come on, we need to talk." Santián had his gun pressed to the back of her head, one hand on her bare shoulder. When she was taking a pee, the big spender had unlocked the room's door as planned.

Hyacinth still had her head near Tommy Leeds's crotch, and she bobbed and latched her teeth onto his shrinking member.

"Oh, shit."

"Be cool, now," Santián said, jabbing the muzzle against her head. She applied her jaw muscles.

"Fuck, Saint, this chick is gonna emasculate me." Tommy Leeds squirmed and tried to sit up to punch her. But as he did so, she bit down harder.

"Lie still, Tommy. Don't give her no excuse."

"Do something!"

"I am, I am." Santián moved around from behind her to the side, keeping the gun on her. Hyacinth had her teeth bared and her mouth open to breathe. She watched the cop peripherally.

"This ain't gonna get you anywhere, Hyacinth. You can't back out of here with Tommy's wang in your mouth."

"This isn't funny, Saint."

"Sorry, man." Come on, girl, the only reason you're hiding out is because McGuire didn't live up to her end of the bargain, right?"

The woman let go with her teeth but wrapped a hand around Leeds's flaccid penis. "You mothafuckahs are all the same." She spit onto the floor. "Do anything and say anything to get what you want, and let the little people take it up the ass."

Santián put his gun away. You had to know when to use the sugar or the bat. "Then get even, Hyacinth."

She fixed Santián with a look, then let a relieved Leeds go, and he scrambled off the bed. Clad only in her panties, she sat on the edge of the bed and crossed her legs. "Give me my cigarettes, will you?"

Santián fetched her purse, designed to look like a miniature trunk, from atop her clothes. He dumped out the contents on a table and tossed an opened pack of Virginia Slims and a book of matches to her.

She lit up as Leeds got his clothes on. "I guess I'm through with my undercover assignment," he said, tucking his shirt in.

"I'll make sure you get a departmental commendation for hazardous duty."

"Gee, thanks. Next time let a brother nut, will you?" And he left.

"You talk to McGuire since the tape aired?" Santián sat on a plastic chair that creaked.

"Once, just for a hot minute." She flicked ash onto the carpet. "She said she'd do what she could for me."

"What was your agreement?"

"I do the thing and she'd see about getting my daughter back."

"So your kid was taken by Child Services?"

"Yeah." She didn't go on, merely took another drag.

Santián got up. "Lay it out for me, Hyacinth. Did McGuire approach you first?"

She glared at the glowing end of the butt as if the cigarette had gone sour. She ground it out on the bed frame and got another one going. "Look, that ruka is smart, ¿que no? A couple of years ago I got rounded up in one of those prostitute sweeps the city council likes to make you cops do to show how much they're cleaning up the streets."

"And Reynaux got you bounced?"

"Uh-huh. I called him and he put in a call to the watch commander. That was the first time they'd threatened to take my kid, so I was pleading, man. I couldn't have that bust on my record. I was on my knees half the night, damn!" She appreciated her own sense of irony. "You wouldn't think shit like that would be written down, but . . ." She shrugged and lit her smoke.

Santián mentally assembled how it had gone down. McGuire was looking for ways to get her hooks into TRASH. Therefore, she'd run down known associates through all sorts of cross-references. Reynaux frequented the Code 7, and he'd brought Hyacinth there on several occasions. In particular, she and a few other working girls had been brought in for a bachelor party on the flimsy excuse of celebrating a plainclothes cop's getting married for the third time.

That rowdy session of sex and booze had gotten out of hand, and uniforms had been summoned by neighbors. The *pinche L.A. Weekly* alternative paper had referred to it in an extensive article as the Cop Copulation Party. And he was pretty certain Hyacinth was referred to by name in that piece.

"McGuire's done with you, Hyacinth. She got what she wanted and that's that." He actually believed the assistant DA would keep her word, but it was hard even for one part of the bureaucracy to make another part respond in a timely fashion. And for all he knew, Hyacinth's child had been taken from her for very good reasons—not something McGuire could change with a wave of her hand.

"Tell me something I don't know, Saint. And I should be used to getting fucked."

"Like I said, you can get even. You held back telling anyone where the Playpen was, because you figured to get McGuire to hold up her end. And maybe parlay that into some coin with one of those supermarket rags, right? Tell your story for money?"

Now she stood, unself-consciously putting a hand on a hip as her large nipples pointed at him. "Have you been listening, Santián? That chick has got my cunt hairs in a vise, *carnale*. The only thing I can do is try and get some money together so I can get myself into some kind of training school. If I can show I have stable—you know—regular work, maybe my court-appointed can get my daughter back."

"Maybe I can help you. Long as no real damage was done."

"Fuck you, Saint. I'm no animal. They took her because of me being out so much at night, and a dried-up bitch of a neighbor who ain't had dick since Michael Jackson had an Afro dropped a dime on me to the County."

She made a derisive sound in her throat. "Anyway, you'll say anything to get that broad."

"That's right. And I'm willing to do anything, too. Like help those who help me." He sat on the bed.

"Like I should trust you, a bigger gangster than the Crazy Nines."

"That's why I'm dawg number one, baby, and intend to keep it that way."

She'd folded her arms. Standing there, her splendid body taut with frustration, she looked like a model waiting for a Henry

Moore sculpture. "I know every other ho swears to this, but I know in my bones it's not too late for me to start over."

Santián held his tongue. Sometimes you just listened.

She turned. "You better not be fuckin' with me about helping me with my kid, Saint. Or I swear to God, I'll slice your goddamn heart up."

"I'm not. But you got to do your part."

"Okay, what do you have in mind, Cisco Kid?"

"You want to be a star, Hyacinth? You want to get some mileage out of that video and turn it into Hollywood gold?"

"The fuck, you trippin'. How's whatever you're talking about get to your girl?"

"Them digits, girl. Them digits."

"Huh?"

"Don't worry, it's coming together." Santián had opened a gap in the drapes; the window was sweating from a humid front that had moved in. He touched the pane, his fingertips picking up the vibrations of vehicles traveling by on the street. People were on their way to somewhere or coming from something. Maybe they had to take the morning off to get the kid to the doctor or make that dental appointment they'd been putting off. Or it could be some poor schmuck, down to his last fifty bucks in his account, on his way in his sled of a car to interview for a job at the newest, sleekest Costco, stacking twenty-pound bags of pretzels. People were up to all manner of shit out there, and Santián could feel their energies pulsing through him.

"Hey, Santián."

"Yeah," he said without turning around.

"Want to use up the rest of that two hundred? It was your money anyway, wasn't it?"

He caught the reflection of his leer in the pane. "Why the fuck not?"

CHAPTER 21

Cheese Cortese unbuttoned the top of his shirt and flapped the cloth to cool himself off in the humid air. He headed west along Centinela, past storefronts of nail and hair salons, plaque makers, high-risk insurance brokers, dressed-up quickie motels, and home-cooking cafés.

This was his fourth stakeout of a perv Madeleine had helped him meet on-line. The Internet wasn't unknown to him, but its thousands upon thousands of permutations for every imagined niche of geekdom and fucked-up fetishes was mind-boggling. It had taken some doing and patience, but his old lady, being a woman and thus more easily able to imitate a fourteen-year-old girl than he, had got him into some chat rooms where mixed-race youngsters hung out. Chat rooms that, according to some informative bulletins from the DA's child abduction unit, they suspected predators also monitored. They had even identified some by their cyber handles.

The irony of the district attorney's being a help to him was an added bonus. One of the three bites had produced a teenage boy wearing the Limp Bizkit T-shirt he'd told "Chrissie," Madeleine's chat room persona, that he would wear. He was obviously just using that method to try to meet girls. The second one resulted in a meeting that was supposed to take place in front of a shoe store at the Glendale Galleria. That had produced nada. For all Cortese knew, the pedophile had shown up, but there was no one wearing the agreed-upon clothes for identification. These fucks were sneaky. He'd probably been scoping out the scene, too, wary of cops and entrapment.

But the third nibble had been a winner. He was a registered sex offender whom Cortese recognized from recent circulars he'd studied. There was no law against his being in a public place—in this case a boba tea joint in Westwood—but he was wearing the red shirt that "Mark" had told his fake Chrissie he would be wearing.

"You can't hassle me for getting a refreshment," this asshole had said when Cortese had sidled up to him on his stool looking out the window yesterday.

"That's where you're wrong," Cortese had said. "You haven't been out a year, you fuck, and here you are rendezvousing with an underage girl."

"Yeah, well, there ain't no girl, is there, cop?" he'd replied, chewing on a ball of tapioca.

"But there's enough probable cause to get your wick in hot water."

"Fuck you."

"We'll see. Things can get awfully uncomfortable for you unless you give me something useful. I'll make sure your picture gets prominence on the sex offender map that the county supervisors have put up. I'll make sure that whatever little job you got gets wind of this misadventure of yours."

"Mark," whose real name was Hal Lawson, pointed his straw at Cortese. "I'll sue you for harassment."

Cortese laid his hand on Lawson's arm. Measuredly he said, "But you didn't hear the best part, freak. I know where you live and will simply go to your house one night and beat you within an inch of your worthless life." He patted the arm and withdrew his hand.

"You can't threaten me." He remained still.

Cortese had lifted his broad shoulders. "This is just two guys talking here, sport. It will come down to my word against yours. And I'll make it look like one of your bunghole buddies did it. Really," Cortese added. "I can do that easily."

Lawson's expression signaled his acquiescence.

Cortese resumed. "Now, there's various rumors running around in your circles. There's word that there's a club of you types who dig that caramel flesh, like the man-boy-love fucks and their association."

"I'm not gay." Lawson interjected.

"I'm happy for you. Back to my question."

"There's no clubhouse," he'd said, and started to rise.

"I didn't tell you we were through."

Lawson sat down again heavily.

"Where's the site? Where is it you guys share tips on how to meet the girls of your wet dreams?" Cortese watched a quartet of UCLA coeds walk past outside. They were laughing and gesturing, their pace quick with the disregard of youth.

Lawson gave him the address and passwords into two such sites. Moreover, he told him the teenage sites he monitored, and gave him some glimpse into how he reached out to mixed-race girls, in particular those of black-and-white parentage.

"I'm not a freak," he'd said at last. "I'm not sick, man. That thing that happened before was a misunderstanding. I just . . . want to talk to them. They're special."

Cortese felt like shoving the man's head through the window. He leaned over. "You just make sure you appreciate them from a distance. I know it's a drug to you, but whatever meds you're supposed to be taking or counseling you've been skipping, I'll be checking to make sure you're back on track, understand?"

"Yeah," he'd rasped.

What Cortese didn't tell him was that he was going to make sure to report his chat room trolling to a pal of his over at the sex crimes unit in West L.A.

And now, driving into the Bridge, a shopping mall off Sepulveda near Slauson, Cortese felt a thrill. This new pavilion of commerce wasn't too far from the Westerfield Mall, which had been called the Fox Hills Mall for decades. That place was Goode's old stomping grounds. It would fit the quirks of his ego to return, not exactly to where he'd made his "conquests," but close enough. It would be his way to turn up his nose at what he felt was beneath him. But the detective would be the one delivering the punch line.

Using the leads from Lawson, Cortese, with Madeleine Jirac's help, had constructed a new identity of a bolder girl who let it be known on pervert-monitored cyber-chats that she was disobeying her black mother, who was not happy that she dated only white men. And that really, tee hee, she shouldn't be sneaking out dating at all, since she was too young. And this wild girl also let it be known she liked the older, more serious types because they appreciated someone like her.

With that and some other phrases they'd worked in—shaped to pique Goode's interests, from what Cortese knew about him—he hoped to draw him out. And on the freaks' chat sites, Cortese planted tidbits about this girl, like he was a fellow predator who'd chanced upon this find. If Goode was on the site—and Lawson figured it was a select bunch—then he'd seen the messages.

The tricky part was getting him to bite. He just needed enough to haul him in and get a warrant to search his room and the premises of the halfway house. Cortese put his car in the parking structure and walked to the location where his adventurous chick said she'd be hanging out—you know, just digging the scene. What loathsome pedophile fuck job could resist that come-on?

He stationed himself at a window in the Borders bookstore. This offered a view of the main circular plaza of the Bridge Mall and the entrances to several shops, including the Ben and Jerry's across the way. This was where his wild child said she'd be after school because she liked to lick sugar cones. Forty minutes at his post produced two men that Cortese was sure were there to meet, or at least check out, his "Dolly." These men sat and slowly drank sodas at the tables in the center of the plaza area, their chairs pointed toward the Ben and Jerry's. All sorts of people came and went at the ice cream store. In particular, one was a willowy young woman with flawless bronze skin and long brown hair. Both men glommed onto her, but she didn't linger and walked away with her girlfriends once they got their treats. One of the men, a stockily built individual in a flannel shirt, got up, and Cortese started to follow him. But he merely wanted a better look at the group as they left, and he sat again.

An hour elapsed. Cortese concluded that Goode was going to be a no-show. Not that he realistically expected him to troop over to the Bridge the first time he set out the bait. Still, Cortese was anxious. He felt as if a timer were clicking down, and his chance to nail this asshole was slipping away from his grasp. How long would Kubrick let him work the case if he couldn't develop any credible leads? And there was also the matter of Santián, who was of the opinion that this was a useless exercise to begin with. And though this was familiar territory for Goode, it could be that he was unable to travel easily this far from where he was staying. A man just getting out of the joint didn't have wheels, and without a car, using the several buses it would take to get here from Glendora was a mother, even for a motivated pervert like him.

Back in his car, Cortese tried to ignore the ball sucking the energy out of the middle of his chest. For a moment, he imagined he was experiencing the first stages of a stroke, and that his car would plow into some wide-eyed Guatemalan nanny trying to cross the street as he went code blue in the driver's seat. The ball had moved into his throat, all but paralyzing him. He pulled into the driveway of a parking lot, where a bar called the Tattle Tale anchored the end of a row of graying businesses.

Some of the shops had been rehabbed and restyled in accord with the changing times and demographics. One of the establishments, Cortese remembered from years ago, had been a Hoover vacuum repair and sales outfit. Now it was a boutique hawking precious outfits for the Gen Y crowd. Next week it would probably be a tattoo-and-piercing wonderland.

The Tattle Tale hadn't changed the sawdust on the floor since the Gerald Ford years. A roller derby queen of a waitress in a wrinkled jean skirt muscled past him, her garishly lipsticked mouth cast in a perpetual scowl. She, too, must have been a fixture since forever. He commanded a stool and ordered Maker's Mark neat.

"Bourbon is the only booze that originated in these here shores." The old-timer was two stools down on his right. His Teamsters Local 42 cap was pulled tight across his balloon of a head. His callused hand was around a pint glass of beer, a thin layer of foam residing midway. "Goes back to the eighteen-hundreds, yes, it does."

"That right?" The retiree had a pleasant voice, nothing insistent about his manner, just making conversation to a fresh face in the bar. "You make a study of this?"

His new buddy had more of his beer. "Most bourbons comes from Kentucky—damn near ninety percent." He tilted his head back, staring into the overhead murkiness as if confirming his facts. "Not so much that I read on it as I find it fascinating that here were are—we've made amphibious tanks, saved all kinds of ungrateful runty countries from the boot of the Reds and the towel-heads, been the first ones into space, but we've only got one true home-grown alcoholic refreshment."

Cortese was fuzzy on his high school civics, but he was pretty sure it was the Russians who first got to space—with a chimp. But we did beat them to the moon, so what the hell. "Fuckin' A," Cortese said, saluting the man and taking another blast of his Maker's.

"It's the wood, you know," the older fellow continued.

This might be the spiel he gives every day at this time, Cortese re-flected, *with or without an audience.*

"You have to char the barrels. See, bourbon takes its flavor and color from the type of oak barrel it's aged in. It's all about the wood, you see."

His apprehension burned away as the glow of the whiskey fil-tered through him. Cortese's large fingers scooped some peanuts out of a small container and munched on them. The terrible real-ity could be that Preston Goode wasn't his man. He could be en-tirely innocent in the matter of Serain's disappearance and likely demise. Still, he was a connection to his peculiar peers, so that had value. The problem, then, was getting him alone to see what could be shaken out of him.

"You know, we got a preacher man, Elijah Craig, to thank for perfecting the stuff," the other man went on. He would do a brief sideways glance at Cortese, then focus on the shimmering menagerie of bottles behind the bar.

Savoring his second round, it occurred to Cortese that if Goode was his boy, then he'd for certain have needed a vehicle to snatch the girl. Assuming he didn't rent a car—and that was incredibly un-likely—then where would he get one for use? The big cop closed his eyes, letting the Maker's float through him as he called up the courtroom image during Goode's trial. Was there a sister there in the third row, choking back tears as the DA built her case? No, he couldn't recall any such sibling. And he'd recently devoured Goode's file like an actor with a vanity project script. Whatever was on paper, he knew about Preston Goode.

"Vodka, of course, is another matter entirely," the leathery team-ster was saying. "You got to give those Russkis credit for that. Here they ain't got shit but spuds and snow, and they manage to make a decent libation. Yes, sir, I'll give them that."

"Want a refill, Rick?" the bartender, in red vest and pressed white shirt, addressed the resident spirits expert as he leaned his upper bulk across the bar top.

Rick checked the contents of his glass, turning it in front of his face as if examining rare wine. "Well, why not, Jamie? Why not?"

The bartender walked back to the taps, which were to Cortese's left. He tipped the pensioner's glass under the spout and filled it with more Miller. In a low voice he said to Cortese, "He's okay, just likes to show off for the newbies. Spends a lot of his days watching that goddamn Learning Channel." The bartender rummaged up a half smile for Cortese's benefit and, after letting the foam settle and topping off, deposited the freshened beer to the teamster.

Lifting his own glass to his mouth, it came to Cortese whose car Goode could have used. He would have told her a story about going on a job interview, and what with her being a limousine liberal, she'd have gladly loaned him the keys. One of the reasons Cortese had it in his head about Goode was that he'd immediately applied for a new driver's license upon release. He'd passed his written test, according to the DMV printout he'd read, and had been granted his temporary. The hilarious bit was, here was this convicted felon, this registered sex offender, who was even prohibited from voting for the lowly dogcatcher, but driving? No sweat. And because his license had merely lapsed while he was in the joint, and he'd previously had a near-flawless driving record, he didn't have to take the actual operating-a-vehicle part. Fuckin' system was all topsy-turvy.

He had another taste of his whiskey. Of course, that could simply be logical given the need for personal mobility to get to work, and the lack of comprehensive public transit in the Southland. But Cortese refused to believe that the first or even second item on Goode's agenda was finding a job. Cortese had a new approach to try. Hefting his haunches off the stool, he paid his bill and clapped Rick on the shoulder as he passed behind him.

"See you, huh?" There was eagerness in his voice.

"Sure. Next time you can tell me about the history of gin." Outside, the night bracing his warm cheeks, Cortese breathed deeply and worked his shoulders. It felt more than right to be chasing down this scum-fuck. He needed this balance of the shit that he seemed to be more and more mired in with Santián and TRASH. With Goode, maybe he could climb out of the pit on the bastard's back. But then what? He still was a garbage man, and he'd always be, wouldn't he?

Driving north on Overland, Cortese found himself again considering where he was, and how much he wanted to be somewhere else. Not just geographically speaking, but spiritually. Gawd. What the hell had Madeleine done to him? This wasn't the time for Zen and the art of policing. This was shake-and-bake time, baby. Time to cowboy up and knock the gold teeth out of the bad guys. He radioed in a request for the address of Ronnie Loraine Whitney, who ran the halfway house where Goode was staying.

CHAPTER 22

David "Sonny" Raymonds was so called because he had the most dour disposition of any biker in California. This was a man who, kidnapped by Baja cartel rivals after a tenuous alliance fell apart, barely let out a yelp as they worried his nut sack with a pair of Channellock pliers. He was the regional leader of the Vandal Vikings. His legs were crossed, his fingers interlaced in his lap, and his python's eyes steady on Red Dog. He sat in the Dog's living room, Panhead standing nearby.

"Everything okay, Wally?" When Sonny was blue, he called you by the name your mama gave you.

"Sure, everything is fine." Red Dog had lost the taste for his ever present brew, but he put it to his lips anyway. He had to put on the show that everything was normal, everything like it always was.

"And this nip that was here? This deputy?"

"I told you, Sonny, it's cool. He was up here harassing me about some unpaid tickets, that's all. Let's face it—it was Panhead that went off on him."

"He wasn't dressed in a uniform," Panhead said. There was a nasty laceration on his left cheek. "And if he was one of their detectives, why the fuck would they send him out on that kind of errand?"

"You now how they are," Red Dog whined. "They say that because what he was really trying to look around for was—you know—our stuff."

Sonny Raymonds bestowed a noncommittal look on Panhead. "And you'd never seen him before?"

"No, hell no, Sonny. But shit, you know the sheriff's been out here before on bullshit, and have they found anything?"

"You tell me."

"Aw, come on, man, I can't believe we're having this conversation." *Drink more*, he reminded himself. Could this be about Barbara? Did they know? It wasn't too much of a leap to assume that the Ring had connections to members of the Sheriff's Department. In the jails and small cities like Lynwood there had been cliques of deputies with homemade tats on their shins and who went by names like the Westside Whities and Cavemen. Men who'd adopted parts of prison and gang culture as a way of separating themselves from the rest of the pack. Men who didn't mind handing out an after-hours ass-whupping on a meskin or some sagger named Ice Your Mama, if need be. And some of those guys had been busted for drug stealing and dealing, like their LAPD counterparts.

Raymonds flicked his hand in a dismissive gesture. "Thing is, Panhead's now got an assault beef we have to deal with, and we want to make sure there's not going to be any more unwanted attention on this location. You see where I'm going with this? "Like I said, Sonny, there's nothing that I can't handle."

"That right?"

"Yeah, you know my life is the Vikings. There's nothing I would do to fuck that up."

"You'd lay down you life for the cause?" Raymonds uncrossed his legs.

"We all would, right?" Red Dog had to concentrate not to rub his hands together. He busied himself with the beer can to hide his nervousness.

Raymonds was on his feet, his superior height and rank to Red Dog, along with Panhead's smoldering silence, only adding to the discomfort of the other man. "If anything comes up that requires taking care of, I'll be the second one to know, right?"

"Absolutely, naturally."

"Panhead will be checking in with you regularly, Wally—just to

see if you or Barbara need anything." Raymonds had already
turned toward the door.

"Sure," was the best Red Dog could muster as the two men left.
"Fuckin' hell," he cursed softly after he heard their hogs fire up.
He tracked out some meth and snorted up two nostrils-full to cut
the edge. His desire for beer returned, and he popped the tab on a
fresh one for its liquid brace. By the time Barbara Reno returned
from grocery shopping, he was riding the rush. That sweet orgas-
mic twist in the base of his spine had his head back and mouth
open. Why couldn't it be like this all the time?

"Help me with the bags, huh, baby?" She carried one in each
muscle-toned arm.

He was at the kitchen table, the remains of his crystal appetizers
dusting the Formica. He didn't say anything but got up and retrieved the other bags from her station wagon.

"I'll make us some steaks and corn, okay?"

"Why not?"

"You so far gone you don't have an appetite? You're not tweak-
ing, are you?"

"I'm hungry enough." He shuffled into the bathroom, his nose
tender and nasal passages open and waiting. He was hard, and it
didn't subside after he'd peed. He took his member in hand and
began to work it, watching himself with a blank expression in the
mirror. What he ought to do was go back in the kitchen and spread
the old lady on the table there and get a before-dinner bang in.
Then, when she was coming, ask her about Ahn all lovey-dovey like.
She'd be stupefied, and he'd press his body against hers, his hand
on the big pulse in her neck. He increased his tempo, and soon
that pleasant flush hydrogened in him and he let loose into the toilet bowl. He washed up and returned to the kitchen.

"That smells good." He retrieved another brewski. He wished he
were good at planning, like one of those chess goofs you saw hanging out in front of a froufrou Starbuck's on Ventura. Because right
now, Red Dog knew he had to be thinking ahead lest he get himself
caught between Ahn, the DA's office, and Sonny Raymonds—and
whatever bullshit Barbara was up to.

"I'll clear off the other table," he said as Barbara bent to snort
some meth herself. He was fascinated by her backside. After all this
time together, he still found her a very sexy and desirable woman.

"You can't have all the fun," she teased, grabbing his shirtfront and kissing him, her frozen tongue working his and getting him aroused all over.

Taking the debris off the only other eating table in the house, Red Dog became sad. There was a science fiction paperback open on its spine on top of some newspapers, and a recent copy of *Rolling Stone*. None of these items had been read by him. He couldn't remember the last time he'd read anything other than a notice to appear from the court. Had he never noticed this before? How could he have his head that far up his ass? Barbara was smart and he wasn't. Meth had brought them together, but there was more to her than that. She wanted and he was content. That is, until this shit with Ahn. That motherfucker was not only giving him problems with the Ring, he'd inserted himself into his private life, too. And he better find out how deep, or else the next time Sonny came calling, it would be with a shotgun in Panhead's hands.

The steak was great, and afterward they snorted some more and zoned out listening to vintage Guns N' Roses. On the couch, blissing out as Axl Rose sang "Out ta Get Me," Red Dog's eyes were open halfway. Barbara was resting her head on his chest as Rose screamed his paranoid rant. He reached between the cushions and brought out the fork he'd placed there earlier. He had planned this far. It was the rest he was unsure of.

"Barbara, I need to ask you something."

"Hmmm," she murmured, and snuggled against him.

Don't think about it—just do it, man. Be strong. Be a Viking. He straddled her, poking the tines into the yielding flesh of her cheek. "What's up with you and Ahn?"

"The fuck?" she said, her right eye snapping open like a cornered cat.

"You know goddamn well what I'm talking about. I'm not fooling about this."

"Hell I do. Get off, Red." Now both eyes were wide and wary.

"This ain't no time for that." He pushed the fork into the side of her face.

She winced. "That hurts."

"Sonny's been out here, and not to congratulate me on what a good job I've been doing. And I called that number on your cell phone, the one right to that gook's office." Her face froze; then it hit him. "You fuckin' him? Is that what's going on? You suckin' on some yellow dick 'cause he can do shit for you I can't?"

"That's crazy; you know you're my man." Her hand was on his wrist, but he wasn't letting up.

"I don't know shit lately, Barbara. But I know I wasn't on a crank high and imagined that number I dialed. What I do imagine is, something's going on, and I better hear you tell me what it is." The end of the fork pressed farther into her flesh, and she yelped.

"Why are you doing this? It's us against them, sweatheart. It's always been like that."

She was getting under his skin, and he couldn't allow that. He couldn't be taken off task. "That's not an answer."

"Yeah, I've got Ahn's number," she said indignantly. "And you know why? Because he wants to fuck me. Does that shock you? A lot of men want to fuck me, including your precious Sonny. I almost had to take it to him when we were at that party Moonie had a couple of months ago."

This was confusing Red Dog. This was not going like he'd hoped. He didn't have a plan B. She was supposed to have stayed scared, and he was supposed to get the truth out of her—whatever that was.

"What are you saying?"

"He couldn't keep his hands off my ass; that's what I'm telling you."

"Ahn?"

"Sonny. But if I would have said something to you, would you have said something to him?"

"Sure, of course."

She snorted. "Right. You'd go up against Sonny."

"Barbara," he said, the will going out of him like a switch had been clicked, "just tell me what's going on."

She shoved him and he got off. "I had to take his number, you ever consider that? I mean, come on, he's got you hog-tied and I should just piss a horny man off?"

"So you and him haven't been—"

"Of course not. But I'll tell you something else." She was up, hands on hips and pacing back and forth. "Ahn's about to double-cross us."

"What?"

"That's why he was pressuring me lately. He said if I didn't go to bed with him, he was going to turn you in to the IRS. And after they got through reaming you, give you over to the ATF for those guns you got from Macklin."

"I knew he was up to something when he came out here to pawn that photo of the piece on me."

"Just trying to build a tighter case against you . . . against us." She stopped and stood over him. The fork was lax in his hand, resting on his leg. He was like some overgrown schoolboy who'd lost his way to the cafeteria.

"We need to take care of him, Red."

This was definitely not how he'd seen this going. "Are you serious?"

"What choice do we have?"

"We must have a choice."

"Yeah, stand still and let either Ahn or Sonny do us with no Vaseline."

"We can't run. We do that, then one of them catches us for sure." In the back of his head, he had the impression she could be on the go better than he. He was spoiled; he liked sleeping late and eating when he wanted to. He was glad he'd never been in the service.

"What if you got on Sonny's good side?"

"How?"

"Deliver Ahn. Get him off us for good."

Red Dog held the fork up as if it were an alien instrument. Frowning, he said, "Even if there was a way we could set Ahn up, how do I explain—you know—what I've done for him? If Sonny—or any Viking, for that matter—should get any hint of that, I'm dead."

"Then guess who's got to die?" She sat on his lap. "You knew it was going to come to this, now or later."

Red Dog tasted his dry lips. "But . . . you're saying that we kill him."

"That's right. We get one of those disposable cell phones smart guys like Sonny use, call Ahn, and get him out here on some pretext."

"We can't have him come back to the house."

"No, not the house. But if you tell him that Sonny and the Ring are having a powwow about moving on the Crazy Nines and the cartel, don't you think he'd come running?"

"Or if you met him at some motel."

"Then we'd have to do it at a motel, and who knows what kind of DNA evidence we'd leave behind? It has to be an environment we can control, honey." She was straddling him, grinding against him as she nibbled on his neck. "We plant dope in the drop box we use for information exchange—a box that only us and Ahn have keys to, but that's in his name."

Despite, or perhaps due to, his fear, he was getting aroused. He grabbed her and held her tight as they kissed. He gasped, "You think we can get away with it?"

"We have to, baby. We can't let them get us." She unbuckled his pants and released his swollen member. "You're my man. You know that, don't you?" She scooted down and took him in her mouth.

"That's right." And he smiled lustfully as she rode him fiercely until firecrackers went off in the back of his head, her hands propped on his sweating chest.

Afterward, as Red Dog got his grip ready, Barbara Reno made the call from her cell phone, driving in a circle in front of the house so she would pick up the right ambient sound. She didn't point out that she was speed-dialing Ahn's house, but pretended it was his cell phone in case the Dog asked. She was confident that he was sufficiently enthralled to follow her lead. But she had to play it right lest she get caught in the squeeze.

"Judd," she intoned with the proper amount of hurried trepidation. "Listen," she continued when he'd responded. "Sonny Raymonds found out about Red asking about that gun guy, Macklin . . . Yeah, but listen, he's cool for now, 'cause they don't know where he is, but he got all twisted up on a mountain of meth and went off to hide.

"But I know where," she said. "It's where he's gone before when he gets freaked. That place in Santa Clarita that used to be a kitchen. You know?"

He answered that he did. "Kitchen" was the term used to denote a cooking facility, a lab for making the meth. The location she was referring to was a now-empty trailer in a trailer park on a mesquite-covered plateau. The ideal place to spring the trap on both of them, she calculated.

"I'm already heading there," she added.

"No," she said hastily when he offered to come get her and then go for the Dog. "Sonny and that Panhead, the one whose ass you kicked, came by the house, but I played dumb. It's better if we meet out there, then deal with Red Dog. And, Judd," she said huskily, "we need to tell him, okay? We need to tell him about us."

She listened, grinning. Then, "I know, I feel the same way. See you soon." Reno clicked off and stopped the car, putting it in neutral. Red Dog came off the porch carrying his shotgun, and together they rode toward the rendezvous.

On his way to the trailer park, Judd Ahn juggled what was the best way to get Red Dog off his plate and out of his life. He was sure that Santián didn't have this kind of problem with his CIs. If they got to be too much of a burden, he was so coldhearted he probably gave them fifty bucks and a pat on the back and left them to fend for themselves among the hyenas. But then, he didn't have a woman like Barbara he couldn't let down.

Ahn missed the turnoff and had to double back. The time on his dash clock read 12:07 as he killed the engine after climbing the incline into the facility, then coasting down the entrance. Off to his left, the strains of a banda number came to him from one of the trailer homes. The one he wanted was farther in and off to the right. Getting closer, he could make out Reno's beat Marquis station wagon. The front end was aimed toward the entrance. She detached herself from the darkness and came over to him.

"Hey." She greeted him with a kiss. She tasted of Tic-Tacs.

"You talk to him?"

"Yeah, but he's way keyed up; he's worse than I thought."

Ahn looked at the mobile home with its leaning awning and rusting corrugated sides. He had a flash of a premonition that this was the sort of place he was going to wind up in, an oxygen tank on rollers and a stack of worn girlie mags for comfort. He shook the vision away.

"Is he strapped?"

"I think he took one of his pistols. Let me go first."

He grabbed her elbow as she turned around. "You better let me, Barbara."

"You're something, you know that? This is the modern age, Judd. Women can take a bullet, too."

"Not if I care about her." He knew better, but they kissed, like in some goddamn scene from a fifties flick on AMC. What the fuck was wrong with him? He wasn't Dick Powell and she wasn't Veronica Lake.

"Tell you what: you call out to him and I'll do the talking."

She had a hand to his face. "Okay."

They went forward, and she called out. "Red, yo, it's me and Judd, okay? He's going to get you out of this, all right? Just be calm." There was no reply, and she spoke again.

"Okay, come on," came his stilted reply.

Ahn put his hand on the doorknob; it was greasy from residue. He clambered up into the trailer; a light was lit on the built-in side table. Part of the interior had been blackened due to an electrical fire. There were power lines nearby, and it was an old cooker's trick to tap them for juice used in the cooking of the chemicals. Ahn looked at the accordion material separating the main part from the rear. It was partially open, and he could detect Red Dog's bulk beyond it.

"Hey, come on, you ain't gotta be shy with me," he chuckled, walking forward. The main room had been previously gutted and contained what was left of the meth-cooking lab. Extra vents had been cut into the ceiling because the buildup of fumes from the required chemicals was highly flammable and narcotizing.

Ahn stopped because the Dog hadn't moved. Was there someone else in here? And why hadn't Barbara tipped him if that was so? "What's up, homey? You out on your feet?"

"No, no, I'm cool." But he didn't move; the collapsing door stayed frozen in place.

"Then let's get going, man. I've got a safe house to stash your unwashed ass in."

"Sure, Judd, right away. The partition swooshed back, and the shotgun swung up.

Ahn bellowed as he let his right foot slip out from under him, like one of the Three Stooges doing a pratfall on a banana peel. The blast of pellets tore into part of his face and decimated a poster of a cat hanging on a wire that had been tacked to the trailer's thin wall. Down on his side, his pistol extended away from his body, he cranked off two rounds, catching the Dog high and on the side of his torso.

"Oh, God, sweet shit, oh, God," the other man screamed, tumbling backward, the shotgun still in his grip.

Ahn shot him again, and blood spurted from the side of the knee where he'd clipped him. Red Dog landed on his butt as if hit with a sledgehammer. The investigator struggled to his feet, a red haze having descended over one eye. Bile congealed in his throat as he took his hand away in pain after touching the raw area where his skin hung loose from his face.

Red Dog was heaving for air, one hand holding his leg and the other feeling around for the Mossberg pump. Blood had exploded over the front of his shirt.

Ahn stepped over him and kicked him twice in the head, then came around as the door to the trailer opened and a shocked Barbara Reno looked in.

"Judd, what happened?

"I was ambushed," he shouted. "What the fuck does it look like?"

"Let me help you, honey." She came more into the trailer, her gaze momentarily shifting past him and onto Red Dog. "Is he dead?"

"I don't give a fuck," he said, pressing the muzzle of his nine against her forehead, shoving her back against the rust-stained sink.

"What are you doing, Judd? I didn't know this was going to happen."

"There's a big difference between a pistol and a shotgun."

She was nearly crying. "I didn't know he had that here. He must have brought it some other time, Judd. You're hurt, baby; you need a doctor. I'm going to drive you to a hospital. You're not thinking straight."

A weakness had started in his thighs and was spreading upward, funneling into every vein and cell in his body. His brain was on fire, and salty sweat and blood dripped from chunks of his face and dribbled down the front of his windbreaker. He wanted desperately to let her take care of him.

"What's going on, Barbara?" He rested the gun at his side. It was a testament to the marginal life of the trailer park that there were no sirens so far.

"It's like I told you, Judd. Red was all worked up since Sonny found out about him snitching for you. He must have had this gun and probably more meth stashed up here. Who knows how much he snorted?" She sniffed and said, "You need medical attention, Judd. We have to go."

"Yeah, yeah, you're right."

She got an arm around his waist, and they were at the door when Red Dog moaned. "You ain't leaving me, are you, Barbara?"

"Shit, he's alive," she stammered.

"Fuck 'im," Ahn blared. "We can call an ambulance for that motherfucker from the car."

"What about us, Barbara?" Red Dog yelled, hacking. "What about you and me and the plan to cross up Ahn you snake-tongued bitch?" He reared up in anger, the shotgun at an angle across his wounded body.

Ahn wasn't sure if his face was working correctly, but he and Reno locked glares, and he could read the betrayal in hers. She pushed Ahn into the table and sprinted for the doorway. His bullet caught her in the back, and the impact punched her down the steps and into the dirt, where she mewed like a trapped calf.

Red Dog couldn't make his hands work right and instead scooted on his belly to try to get his arms around Ahn's legs.

"Get off me, you stupid sack of shit, Get off me," Ahn screamed as he beat at the man's hands with his gun, tears stinging his eyes. And then he, too, crumpled to the floor of the trailer, and that was how the EMTs and the sheriff's deputies found him fifteen minutes later. Reno was on her back, blinking at the night sky. She was making mewing sounds, coming in and out of shock, uncertain of place or time. But she was certain of one thing: she couldn't move her legs.

"The time on KNX is nine past midnight. And in the Middle East another—" Cortese killed the engine and got out. Ronnie Loraine Whitney's house was a modest number tucked into a cul-de-sac in La Canada–Flintridge. It was a quiet street in a tidy neighborhood, and Cortese had little trouble breaking into her Prius, one of those hybrid gas-and-electric vehicles. It was parked on the wide apron of the driveway, next to an older-model Accord and in front of an attached garage. She was such a tree hugger, he wasn't surprised to find her yoga mat and workout togs in the trunk. He also knew that anything he copped that implicated Goode would be inadmissible since he didn't have a warrant, but he had ideas on that, too. He tossed the car quietly and thoroughly. The benefit of poking around in someone's business in a bedroom community was that at this time of night, all the solid, hardworking citizens were tucked in their beds. He searched carefully and quietly.

Lifting the carpet lining in the trunk, his penlight in his mouth, he felt something down in the crevice of the car's frame. Gingerly he extracted a charm bracelet and turned it in the light, glad he'd had the foresight to wear latex gloves. The bracelet was a thin chain that had snapped at the catch and was knotted with things like a silver heart, a skull, a four-leaf clover, and so forth. There were brownish stains discoloring some of the ornaments. Cortese's heart rate doubled, and his hand visibly shook with excitement.

"There is a Jesus," he declared softly. "And he wears a blue uniform."

A light came on in the house, and his face went numb. The shadow of a figure moved past a window, cast against a shade pulled low. He quietly lowered the trunk. The hinges made a squeak as he slunk down. A car was coming down the street and he crawled to the rear side panel, drawing himself in as tightly as he could. The trunk hadn't clicked, but there was only a small gap between it and the car's body. Even as a sheen of panic washed over him, he had the presence of mind to put the bracelet in one of the shallow paper bags he'd brought along, just in case he got lucky. Plastic, because it sealed so well, sometimes sweated and could fuck up trace amounts of biological matter. But paper breathed and allowed circulation, yet also prevented contamination.

The car passed, and so what if they'd seen him? He'd struck black gold and was going to see that fuck Goode get the hot shot that he deserved. He rose up some and cranked his head around. The form moved back past the window, and then the light was doused—the bathroom run completed, he concluded.

Cortese reached around and eased the trunk closed until it clicked. He duck-walked away from the Prius and straightened up as he cut across the neighbor's lawn. Momentarily, the tang of cigarette smoke seemed to be in the air. He stopped and looked around. But there was no red dot of burning tobacco and no smell.

Nerves. He kept going. The big cop was back on the sidewalk and reached his Camaro. He got in, fired it up, and, for the hell of it, let his lights sweep past Whitney's house as he wheeled around in the cul-de-sac's circle of asphalt. He put on a Creedence Clearwater Revival tape, and as "Up Around the Bend" reverberated from his cassette deck, Cheese Cortese nodded his head and sang along with John Fogerty.

CHAPTER 23

Santián drove west up the slight incline of 6th Street, over the Harbor Freeway and past a retro clock that was like something out of a town square from the turn of the last century. The artifact had recently been planted on the corner at Bixel. The hands of the thing, matt black alloy bars against a luminescent cream background with Gothic numerals, were nearly atop each other as they registered 12:07. There was all sorts of downtown development happening as this part of L.A. went through more Manhattanization. Unlike the downtowns of many other big cities, the central core of Los Angeles was nearly a wasteland after seven-thirty at night. But with the advent of the Staples Center, home of the Lakers, Clippers, and World Wrestling Entertainment extravaganzas, renewed attempts in the form of upscale apartment complexes with names like Medici and Metropolitan—invoking the Old World and the New—had been erected to lure a fresh set of urban pioneers to roost.

By and large, the reality was that still only an intrepid few paraded about downtown at night, and certainly not at this time of the early creep of A.M.—that is, save for the invisible ones, the ones whose job began after the partners of mega law firms such as Gibson, Dunn & Crutcher returned to their gated communities and ponytailed, soccer-playing daughters. At this time of night, the cleaning crews were busting their asses with practiced flair, cleaning and vacuuming offices in the buildings that the lawyers had evacuated.

Farther west, Santián got lucky and found an empty slot on Ardmore. This was the start of Koreatown, and several karaoke bars and private joints, where various client services could be obtained, were going full bore. Pretty, lithe young Asian woman and men in blocky suits sauntered past; a melange of Korean, Mandarin, even Spanglish—the argot of English and Spanish peculiar to L.A.—circled in the air about him. He walked north on Ardmore toward Wilshire and its highrises. He didn't want to take a chance of his car being spotted near Ferris Heckman's office building. Before reaching the front of the Equitable Building, he cut through the parking structure and spotted Rosa Barbosa, a janitor and union rep with SEIU Local 1877. She was waiting just inside the open service door, as arranged.

"You better not get me in trouble, homey," she told him in her Guatemalan-accented Spanish. "God knows I hate this work, but I'd hate being out of it worse."

"That's not an issue," he said. "If I get caught, that's on me. You damn well know that about me, Rosa. I'm a lot of things, but rat-out punk ain't one of them."

She laughed briefly and kissed him on the cheek. "I sure owe you something for taking care of Benito." She shook her head ruefully. "My boy still has his head up his ass, but at least he's not in juvie." She looked at him, wiping at the sudden tearing in the corner of her eye. "You know it's not too late to—"

"Rosa, please, enough with that *la luz de Jesus* jive," he said, mostly in English. "I gotta get to work."

"And I gotta get to the next building."

She let him through, and the knobless door closed behind him. Santián slipped on supple leather gloves and used the stairwell to gain the floors and avoid the lobby security. He got to fifteen, breathing hard. He felt like he was back in high school, a starting end, and had those pregame jitters that always left him after the first hit.

He cracked the door away from its frame and peered into the darkened hallway. The lingering perfume and cologne of the office-dwellers hung heavy, like invisible smog in the corridor. He stepped out and made his way to Heckman's office. Rosa had left the door unlocked. The guards would be up in forty minutes, according to the schedule, to set the various alarms. He went in and went to work.

At one point, Santián recalled, Heckman was on her way to making partner at O'Melveny and Myers, one of the oldest and most powerful law firms in the city. Among its senior partners was Warren Christopher, who'd been a member of President Jimmy Carter's cabinet way back when. And the original O'Melveny, himself an immigrant, made his bones in the late 1800s, representing the Mexican and Spanish owners of the vast ranchos that would be knitted together as the sprawl of twentieth-century Los Angeles. Somehow, a lot of those lands wound up in whites' hands, and O'Melveny died loaded. Funny how those things happened.

He jimmied a file cabinet open. And as he went through her files, he remembered that McGuire, too, had been in the firm a little before Heckman's tenure. Fucking lawyers. They were on opposite sides now, but let McGuire win the election and she'd probably hire Heckman to be her in-house counsel. Who better than a crook to handle politicians? He found some juicy stuff on a few of her clients, including where exactly the former '80s movie sex bomb had hidden her burning joint the recent night she was busted racing along Laurel Canyon, but not the dirt he wanted.

He didn't expect to find the secret black book or any other smoking gun detailing her and Mercury's dealings with the Baja cartel. But with ten minutes left, he finally found something of value. In a handsomely made credenza there was another locked file drawer. In that he found an unmarked folder containing paperwork pertaining to something called Escapade Enterprises, LLP. Leafing through the file, he saw some lease agreements that Escapade had taken out for vehicles. The Cadillac Escalade seemed to be a particular favorite. The agreements listed the VINs and license plate numbers, and there was one listing a plate entitled *Bumpy*. That brought a grin to his face. That was the name on the Escalade full of Cruz's gunmen that had come after them in Tijuana.

"Fuck me," he said happily. He used her Canon to make photocopies of the lease agreements and other papers from the file. Time was up, and he returned the folder to its place and locked up. He went out the door and listened. There were voices in the hallway, and that meant the two security guards stationed in the lobby were making their rounds and setting the alarms after the departure of the janitors.

He wasn't worried about the light being on, as that was normal, but Santián hadn't turned off the copier, and he reached over and did so. The voices stopped, and he berated himself for being sloppy. If he had to, he'd hide in the office, then chance leaving later. The alarm would sound, but he could be back through that stairwell as the guards came up in the elevator. He was sure Heckman hadn't left word of where she was with the security crew, so her being immediately alerted wasn't a concern. But it was a matter of pride not to be caught fucking up.

Detecting no movement, he poked his head out. Across the hall, to his left, there was an office door ajar. Laughter came from inside that office. He assumed it was the guards, but he had to go past there to get to the stairwell.

Slipping closer, he heard one of the men say, "Damn, do you see that?"

"Man, that girl's fine and a freak," the other one said. There was then the slapping of palms. "Shit."

Santián should just flit past the opening, but he couldn't help himself. He peered inside and could see the two of them huddled over a monitor at a corner desk in the front room. It was obvious from their expressions and what they'd mentioned that the two were viewing an on-line porn site. The cop waited; the angle at which the men stood meant they simply had to look up and would spot him moving across the crack of the door.

"That's Tanya Toy, man," the one sitting down exclaimed, pointing at the screen. "I've seen her take two in the ass at the same time."

"That's impossible," his buddy added.

As the men continued their discussion of the anatomical abilities of the able Ms. Toy, their eyes lasered on her gyrating image, Santián sneaked by and went down and out of the building. Outside, as he walked to his car, a homeless man passed him pushing a shopping cart with a dragging wheel, filled with goods gleaned from his urban excavations.

"Got a date with Tanya, yes I do," the man mumbled as he went on.

Santián stopped, openmouthed, and stared at the man's back, at the body stooped over from pushing the cart for who knew how many years living on the dodge. The coincidence was too much for him to contemplate, let alone process. He got in his Malibu, and as he drove off, he heard the breaking report, over KNX news radio, about a shooting incident in Santa Clarita, involving a member of the DA's office.

He listened closely, then shook his head. If all was right in the universe, McGuire could have her tits in the wringer, and wouldn't that be so fuckin' sad? He turned the radio down while he used the police-issue to leave a message for that chubby chick in R & I, who dug him, asking for any information in the criminal archive she could bring up on Escapade Enterprises. Santián was pumped; this case was about to bust wide open, and he and TRASH would be grabbing headlines, too—only they would once again be the champs, and McGuire the goat.

Santián laughed heartily at that idea.

Three hours later, Peacock picked up August Mercury at Jade's apartment on Ivy.

"About time," the record label chief said, exasperated, as they drove away. "There's a reason hoes remain hoes, man. Those bitches are stupid. They both think they're going to get over with their silly ideas."

Peacock drove.

Mercury adjusted his body, sore from his wound. "Though that one, Hyacinth? She's had a smug look the last day or so, hinting like she was about to get over on McGuire." He chuckled. "These bitches spend their whole lives about to get over."

"Yeah," Peacock said dryly, aiming the car along the freeway for their drive to Palm Springs.

"What did she say?"

"You know Ferris," Peacock said. "Told me to get you and she'd set things up at this crib in Palm Springs that Rosario owns. Turns out, she told me, that there's some who're supposed to be loyal been doin' shit behind their backs, like this Gargoyle thing. But things are gonna get settled." He smiled weakly at Mercury.

"You look tired, man."

"Ah, you know, my mom's cancer came back."

"Sorry to hear that," Mercury said.

At a house not far from the air museum in Palm Springs, Peacock carried Mercury's bag as they mounted the porch. Mercury tapped on the door.

"Hey, baby," he said. The door opened, and the shock at who was inside made his orbs go saucer. "What the fuck," he stammered. He turned to run.

"Sorry, man." The semiauto in Peacock's hand shook.

"Traitor," Mercury yelled, throwing himself at Peacock.

The slug traveled through his open mouth and out the back of his head. August Mercury expired as his body slammed to the gravel along the walkway.

"Now, that's how the big boys play. Welcome to the winning side, champ," one of the men told Peacock as three sets of feet stood around him and they gathered up the body to dispose of it.

CHAPTER 24

"You've got to publicly excoriate Ahn, Connie. There's no wiggle room on this." Pablo Pastor walked in a tight circle, hands on his trim waist, artificial light glinting off the metal snaps of his suspenders. "It's been almost three days since the incident, and it's still headline news. You need to respond forcefully."

"It's obvious that he was sickened," the assistant district attorney offered as an anemic response.

Pastor had ceased pacing and was facing the window overlooking the downtown L.A. skyline from the thirty-second-floor conference room. Unconsciously his manicured hand touched his firm belly. He'd have that rigid six-pack inside a month. "He shot a woman, Connie. This may be the new age of male enlightenment, but that code of the West learned from movies means we don't cotton to back-shooters, especially when they leave someone a paraplegic."

Her campaign manager turned slightly from the window and the overcast sky. "Now, I grant you, a man with half his face torn off from a shotgun blast tends to garner a certain amount of sympathy. There's no getting around that, either." Now he turned fully, extending his upper body and arm to retrieve his coffee cup. "But Ahn is facing a host of charges, from dereliction of duty to possible attempted murder." He sipped soundlessly. "Surely the next mayor of this metropolis, which has risen stronger and healthier post-earthquakes, O. J., the power crisis, and the failed valley secessionist movement—surely she will stand with her citizenry against those who would bend the law for their own personal aggrandizement."

McGuire gripped the arms of the chair she sat in. "What's that about your speeches coming back to haunt you?"

"It's the platform you've run on, and why you've outpolled the mayor. Because, believe me, our buddy Walter Kane, who's handling Fergadis's campaign, has already written a hit piece emphasizing why it is you're unfit for the job, due to this sort of thuglike behavior going on under your nose. He's simply waiting for the right time to have it mailed. As we've blamed him for being asleep at the switch when it came to matters about the TRASH unit, they're happier than Republicans kicking welfare mothers into the cold to be able to reverse the tables on us."

"That doesn't mean at any cost, Pablo."

Pastor gave her a pop-eyed expression, as if genuinely aghast. "I'm sorry, what did you say?"

"Come on, how would it seem for me to kick him when he's down?"

"It's called the universe of plausibilities, as you well know, counselor. You had no knowledge that he was entwined with this meth-headed biker, did you?"

"Of course not." She began to feel how easy it was to slip on the mantle of impersonal distance.

"And you certainly did not authorize him to play the laconic Lothario and bed this woman, this Barbara Reno, for purposes that will certainly become even more murky after the tabloid TV shows have squeezed this for all the footage they can get out of it. Especially after they pay this, this—what's the genius, the shooter's name?"

"Red Dog."

"Gawd." Pastor arched his back as he gesticulated with his hands. "A moniker right out of an Ice Cube movie. Perfect," he sighed.

McGuire looked away as she drew in a breath.

"You see?" He scratched at the side of his temple. "Loyalty is a wonderful and endearing quality, and people know that about you, Connie. They respect that about you, and that's one of the traits that differentiate you from your opponent."

"I don't need to be sold on myself," she grated.

"Oh, but I think you need to be reminded, ADA McGuire." Pastor sat down at the side of the table where she was. "We can't have this turned into more of a soap opera than it is. Something that will allow Fergadis, or at least Walter, to play the race card just that much more."

"How the hell is that?"

"Yellow man, white woman." Pastor made motions with his hand as if arranging elements on a floating board. "And because his incompetent black boss let him lust after this loose woman, he's making deals with known meth dealers, allowing this white trash to run rampant in our parks and near our schools.

"And believe me," Pastor finished, "beyond the mailer with Reno on the cover in her wheelchair with the banner, 'Look What Constance McGuire Did to Me,' there'll be another one with some big, honking scary-ass biker on his hog, glaring out at the concerned Sherman Oaks homeowner who's been looking for an excuse not to vote for you, and this will give them, those latte liberals, the out they've been praying for—or whatever the hell they do when they go to yoga class."

"Isn't it enough that I'll keep my distance from him? Judd's been suspended pending the investigation."

"An investigation that's going to drag out past the election, Connie."

"I'll issue another statement."

"That goes without saying. But we're not going to turn this into one Trent Lott–like contrition after the other."

McGuire had been fighting her caffeine addiction, but it seemed so pointless, given this problem and the solution she was being prodded to accept—to act upon with vigor. She poured herself some coffee from the carafe on the table.

"But you're asking me to attack a man, a good man and solid investigator, that I've worked with for more than six years, all for the sake of political expediency."

"Correct. Otherwise, let's fold up our tents and cut off the phones and save the heartache, because there's no way to address this in a collegial manner. Your opponents won't."

She brought the cup to her lips and blew on it before sampling the brew. Across from her she projected her father sitting there, her mother standing by his side, her hand on his shoulder. Those two, like so many other black folk, had migrated from the South because the West offered at least a chance.

Not that they or any of their friends were fooled that somehow the white man and his laws and his mores were really that much different here from how things were practiced down home. For here in the sunny clime, along with the detached garages were housing covenants and a white street gang called the Spook Hunters, and Nat King Cole had had NIGGER burned into his lawn when he dared move into upscale Hancock Park. Still, this was where her parents had settled and where they'd sacrificed so their only daughter could go further, climb higher on the stepping stones they'd hewn and assembled in her path. She willed them away before their disapproval cut into her too deeply.

"I want to talk to him first."

"I don't think that's wise."

"Pablo, I'm not doing it to get Judd's forgiveness or even understanding. But if I'm going to knock the legs out from under him, he should at least know it's coming."

Pastor regarded a portion of the wall, then refocused on her. "Very well. But please don't promise him anything."

"If we win, I hardly imagine he'd want to come work for me in City Hall."

"I know your instincts are to do the right thing. That's why you need to maintain perspective as we go for the goal we set out for ourselves."

"I can see clearly." Her cell phone chimed, and she noted the number but didn't answer. The two went over more campaign logistics; then McGuire left the office and went down in the elevator to her car. It was there she called Phineas Washington back.

"I hope this isn't about another surprise," she said after he answered.

"There was a bust this A.M. of a man named Preston Goode, a registered sex offender, at his halfway house in Glendora."

"He hasn't been processed yet; how do you know about this?"

"Because the woman who runs the halfway house is on a first-name basis with our boss. From what I understand, she used to be a drug counselor at some private clinic."

DA Chris Stevens had three children. And as with a lot of people who put their career before kin, there were bound to be consequences due to inattention on the home front. In this case, his middle son, Erik, had a history of difficulties with drugs.

"So she probably helped the wayward son at one point. And Chris does reward those that keep the fissures from bubbling up to fracture his public persona," McGuire mused further. "What do the police have?" she asked.

"A bracelet such as a girl might wear, that has blood on it, and that the mother of missing teenager Serain Jensen has identified as hers. A mixed-race young woman. And Goode had been busted by Cortese when he worked vice, for raping and sodomizing another girl who was half-and-half. And this Goode, because I pulled his file, was—"

"I know," McGuire cut in. "I prosecuted that case. Goode was part of a club of these monsters who specialized, if that's the right word, in victimizing girls who were of black-and-white parentage. There was even a priest among these motherfuckers."

"Well, this Mrs. Whitney feels Cortese is behind this. He'd been out to the halfway house before, harassing Goode, she claims."

"And now this bracelet turns up."

"Based on the ubiquitous anonymous tip."

"The bracelet was found in Goode's room?"

"That I don't know."

"Stay on it, Phenias."

"I will."

She clicked off and put her car into the vestiges of the downtown morning traffic. She cracked her window; the smell of impending rain was invigorating. Constance McGuire wasn't quite sure where she was heading.

CHAPTER 25

A light and steady drizzle had begun around lunchtime, and now, at half past two in the afternoon, a handful of regulars, retired cops, and an ex-con or two, were bunkered in the dark confines of the Code 7. Cheese Cortese and Big T Holton held down a booth and glasses of Jack neat.

"You're bullshittin'," Holton growled, moving his glass around like the table was a Ouija board.

Cortese spread his long arms wide. "I'm just telling you what I heard, Big T. That joker Acosta found in the converted garage left a goddamn diary—well, notes, really. This guy fancied himself a songwriter. He was spinning these tales of *narcocorridos*—all the rage in those dance halls down in Bell and Paramount."

"And he was talking about the shit he'd done on behalf of the Baja cartel?" Holton's eyes narrowed.

"And their hookup with this Escapade Enterprises. How it was a joint business effort at money laundering and starting legitimate companies between the East Coast Russian mob as they've moved west and the Mexican drug lords. Just like the companies traded on the stock exchange," Cortese said, shrugging. "I mean, it makes sense, don't it? These bad boys are pulling in more than some of these Fortune 500 companies, and they've gotta do something with all that *feria* they're generating."

Holton regarded his drink. "These goddamn notes name names?"

"Fuck I know. I do know the DEA and FBI had a meet with Kubrick yesterday."

Holton stared wide-eyed at Cortese; then he leaped across the table, knocking the drinks over, shattering the glasses on the floor. "You Judas mothafuckah. You wired, aren't you?" he bellowed. "You carryin', Cheese?" He'd ripped at the flannel shirt underneath the quilted vest Cortese was wearing, exposing the graying hairs on his chest.

"What the fuck's wrong with you, man?" Cortese slapped the other man's hands away as he bolted upright, the table toppling over loudly. The patrons knew it was best not to interfere with TRASH men business. "What's going on, big fella? What's got you jumpin'?"

Holton had his fists balled and his teeth barred. "Who the fuck do you think you're foolin'? This ain't some nigga shit you gonna pull on me, Cortese."

"Man, you're—"

"Where's Saint?" he demanded.

"In my pocket, bitch."

Holton's hand darted toward his sidearm, and Cortese dove his hand under his shirt. Each had his fist around the grips.

"Now, how would that be, Big T? A shoot-out between friends." His face was devoid of color or emotion. "That would give the rummies here something to talk about for years."

"Fuck you and your head games, man. We're through." Holton turned and stomped off toward the rear, to where he'd left his Grand Am parked in back.

He cleared the exit, and Santián whipped the wand baton across the man's face. Holton poleaxed onto the ground, groaning. Droplets dribbled into his gaping mouth, and the gash across his features was a luminescent red.

"Jesus, Saint." Cortese had come up behind Holton according to the plan. He glanced over his shoulder but no one had followed them out. Short of their laying a body on top of the bar, those dudes in there would be cool; they knew the drill.

"Help me carry his big ass into the shed," Santián said, collapsing the telescoping baton and putting it in his back pocket. They carried the dazed Holton over to the small structure in the back that decades ago had housed city fire hydrants.

"Fucking Big T has been putting away those pork chops, that's for sure," Cortese complained as they carried him.

"It's that damn Del Fuego brothers money that's weighing him down."

They got him into the shed and closed the door. Santián had already made room and had stacked boxes of peanuts, Old Crow, and Cutty to one side. Using two sets of handcuffs, they shackled him to a metal-and-fabric office chair with arms.

Cortese hung back as Santián roused Holton. As if he'd have room for deniability should Internal Affairs suddenly rush into the room.

"Y'all have gone stone crazy," Holton spit as his eyes focused. He tried to rise with the chair, stumbling his way forward, and Santián pushed him back down.

"Guess who I followed going into your girl Breezy's apartment, Big T?"

"Fuck you," Holton answered.

"So it is true," Cortese said. "Saint said he got a line on Escapade and staked out an office, some kind of toy facility in Culver City leased in the company's name."

Santián went on. "Ferris Heckman had been laying low there since the hit went wrong against Mercury. But yesterday I tailed her to a meet with you and Ronk at your old lady's place in Lennox. There's no way I could follow one of you without getting tagged, but she wasn't hard. Particularly since she wasn't suspecting anybody to tumble. And laying in the cut, I watched Ronk roll up after she got there."

Santián poked Holton in the chest with a finger. "You and Ronk killed that stiff Morales, who I figure as the wheel man for the hit that his running buddy, that Hong dude, was supposed to complete on Mercury. They fucked up, and you two had to clean up their mess. You and Ronk probably went up to his place in Big Bear, but he wasn't hiding out there, was he?"

Holton remained silent and sullen.

"You two did Gargoyle, didn't you?" Cortese said quietly.

Santián looked from him to Holton, blinking rapidly. "Yeah, yeah, that figures, Cheese." He kicked Holton's knee. "Where's Ronk?"

"With ya mama."

"You're gonna burn, Big T," Santián gloated.

Holton looked at Santián as if he were a disease. "What you mean *me*, round eyes? If I'm jammed up, we all are. What the fuck? You think you ain't a member of the club all of a sudden?"

"That's different."

"Only by degrees, Saint," Holton said. "Think about all the shit the three of us have done over the years."

"That's not the same," Santián repeated, latching on to Holton's shirt and jacket. "What we did was what we had to do to make things right, set this shit straight. You can't knock heads with these assholes and be a ballet teacher. It takes guts and game to do what we do."

Holton guffawed. "Aw, that sounds so purr-ty, Mr. Saint. Gosh, please tell us on the jury how you and that Cortese fella were looking after our community when you stole money from drug dealers like that Phat Freddy fuck in Moreno Valley—the one that managed to buy his way out of a third strike." He smiled crookedly.

"A lot of that money we used to set other deals up, get around the red tape, and get the work done out on the streets where it counted."

"Nobody's gonna see it like that but us, Saint," Cortese added. "Big T's right. If he goes down, we all go down. We've done enough shit to fill a file cabinet."

"Two," Holton amended.

"We didn't commit murder," Santián said with brittleness.

"Again, that might be a matter of interpretation in a couple of instances," Cortese said. "Besides, who the fuck is gonna miss Gargoyle, Mercury, Heckman—any of them?"

The rain was coming down harder, beating a steady rhythm on the shed's grimy windows. "That's not the point, Cheese, and you know it. We never—never—were the handmaidens to the scumbags. He and Ronk crossed a line they can't go back from. Fine, we lined our pockets, but we also put a lot of bad guys out of circulation. But not because it was on the orders of some gangsters. We run them; they don't run us. What they did is different. They can't be trusted."

Cortese responded slowly, absorbing his friend's words and gauging his own. "You are right, Saint. But we, all of us, you, me, Big T, Ronk, and the others who've ridden with us—opened that door, man. It's like that busted-window theory. You let the minor infraction slide, then this thing or that, then soon it's all gone to hell."

"Bullshit," Santián said. "A guy punches you, you hit him back, you don't machinegun him. But that same guy steps on your toe, well, maybe you get hot or maybe you let it go. Each situation calls for a measured response, and that's what TRASH does, Cheese. We've been as ruthless as we needed to be. We bent the rules, but who the fuck in City Hall or the prosecutor's office doesn't? Their shit smells just like yours and mine, baby. But this mothafuckah"— he pointed at Holton—"has made a mockery of what we tried to do."

"Shut up, you goddamn hypocrite," Holton challenged. "Yeah, Ronk and me made a deal, but you tellin' me you wouldn't have if it was you two that had been approached?"

Santián had his gun suddenly out and right against Holton's face. "The difference is, I wouldn't have had my hand out, Big T. They wouldn't smell it on me."

"Saint," Cortese warned, "put the piece away; we've got to be calm here. Reasonable."

"What's reasonable?" he said hollowly.

"Saint, come on, man. Before this gets out of hand, we need to meet, all four of us."

Holton said, "You're going to have to let me talk to Ronk. He's gotta see where we're at with this. And he damn sure ain't gonna be too happy."

"Fuck him," Cortese said. "The point is, this can't go on, Big T. You make him see there's no room to shimmy or shake on this."

"Want me to call him?"

"We get this done in person, so there's no misunderstanding," Santián said. They undid Holton. Santián opened the door, and a bullet hissed into him, crimson erupting from his torso as he fell back in the room.

Holton clubbed Cortese on the side of his neck, having interlaced his fingers as one. The other man reeled, trying to orient himself, but nothing was working right. The gun he'd cleared from his belt holster skittered across the cement floor, and as he twisted his body to get it, Holton hit him again, solid and hard in the gut.

"Motherless son of—" Cortese yelled and leaped to tackle the beefier man. For his troubles, he got a swift knee to the middle of his face, and he rolled onto the floor. Holton pressed the gun he'd dropped to his temple.

"Huh, now what?"

"This is wrong, Big T. We hooked and booked too righteous for this."

"Sorry, Cheese," he said, genuine affection in his voice. "But like I told you, this is some serious funds you're fucking with. I have to consider the future."

"Come on, tough guy. We got places to go." The man who'd shot Santián, wearing jeans, a windbreaker, and a woolen mask, grabbed the wounded cop's arms and forced him to his feet. Santián gurgled in pain. Now another man with a mask and zippered windbreaker was stepping into the room. He smelled sweet.

"We dump these fucks up in Angeles Crest," the newcomer announced. Behind him the rain was coming down forcefully, the metal roof of the shed beating a symphony of bleats and pongs. As this man leaned in to help with Santián, who'd gone all rag doll, the side of his masked head puffed out in cloth and bits of bloody goo that clotted on the nearby boxes.

"Goddamn it!" the first masked assailant swore as he started for the door, holding Santián before him as a shield. But with Santián weighing over 220 pounds, the man found trying to prop him up with one hand while holding on to his gun was not easy. He halted, and Santián shoved the blade of his Swiss Army knife into the fleshy area below the man's jaw. He howled as Santián dug and tore into the muscle with the blade. The two stumbled and fell to the wet blacktop.

Holton had wisely remained stationary, keeping a groggy Cortese between him and the doorway. "Tell your partner out there I'll blast you if I don't get a free pass."

"I don't even know who's out there, Big T. For all I know it's Kubrick and a tactical team."

Holton snarled in his ear. "You brought them, didn't you?"

"Man, I'm telling you, this was a two-man effort with me and Saint."

Holton grabbed Cortese just as his masked compatriot had gotten to his feet and kicked the now still form of Santián. He put a another round into Santián and ran back inside.

"We better get," the masked attacker said. He was dripping water and blood and holding a hand to his wound.

"Take that off, Ronk. It's not like I don't recognize your voice," Cortese said.

The other man did so and used the mask to help stanch his flow of blood. "Too bad you and Saint decided to get religion, Cheese."

"How many are out there?" Holton asked.

"Shit if I know," he said. "Visibility sucks. But we can't stay in here. I know it's not a deployment; otherwise we would have heard somebody barking on the bullhorn."

"That's true," Holton said, pushing Cortese forward.

"When you kill me, then what? There's no way to cover this up," Cortese hedged.

"Don't worry about us, sweetheart." Culhane got behind Cortese, too, and they went out.

Just as it had begun, the sheeting rain was lessening. Cortese looked down at Santián, who was prone on his back, ragged gasps escaping his lungs. "This isn't right, you fucks."

"Come on Sister Mercy." Culhane had taken the lead and shoved Cortese hard in the back, eager to be rid of the place. They were heading toward the old stone steps on the hillock that led up to the brush and, beyond that, a path to Elysian Park.

"Be lookin', man," Holton warned.

"You don't need to remind me. Just keep our guest in front of us. Whoever shot Peacock has to be up there in the trees where we're heading. But as long as he doesn't have a clear shot, we're good."

Another shot echoed, and instinctively Culhane and Cortese ducked. It was a moment before they realized it had come from behind them. Cortese turned to see a shocked Holton wheeling to one side. Santián had shot him from where he was on the ground. The second piece had been strapped to his ankle.

Cortese jumped Culhane, but the other man's reflexes were just as quick, and he gut-shot his fellow TRASH man then ran for the steps.

Cortese had been shot before, but not like this. The pain was incredible, and he hacked up bile and fluids as he fell down the steps. He got up and staggered toward the rear of the bar. Cortese fell again somewhere on his way there and crawled the rest of the way. He slid through the sawdust inside the bar.

In the brush, Culhane used his hands and feet for purchase as he went off the stairs and climbed the incline of earth to make himself less of a target. He cleared the foliage and paused to look around. Seeing nothing and hearing no movement, and spurred on by the necessity of not being caught, he ran to the path that wound up and to the cutout where he'd parked. He and Holton had suspected something was up, because in all their times together, Cortese had never called Holton for a drink alone. Culhane was getting light-headed and knew he had to get sewn up before he left town.

"It's over, Ronk." Alvaro Acosta appeared from around the car, his gun extended.

In the Code 7, Cheese Cortese tried to hoist himself up on the bar, knocking chairs over. "Call reenforcements. Call an R.A.," he rumbled. "Call them, please." He slumped back to the floor.

Outside on the path, Culhane hadn't let go of his piece. "Come on, Double A, it doesn't have to be like this. They're all through but you and me. Man, we got a king's ransom waiting for us."

"Good for you. Put the gun down."

"Are you listening to me," Culhane pleaded. "You want me to tell what really happened with Serenade?"

"I'll take that chance, champ."

"Fuck you," Culhane responded.

In the bar, while Andre repeated the address to the 911 dispatcher, two more shots carried on the air to the patrons, as the others had. The bartender had already been on the phone after the first round of shots. One of the retired cops was pressing some dish towels on Cortese's wound to stop the flow of blood. And two other regulars went out back to see about Santián as sirens and the whoop of a helicopter drowned out the quiet that had settled.

CHAPTER 26

"Who you gonna vote for today?" The nurse asked her companion.

"I don't know," the other RN answered. "Fergadis ain't been all that bad; he did step in and help us during the last time we had negotiations with admin."

"Yeah," her coworker agreed, changing the IV drip going into Rafael Santián's arm. "That's true, but the city's in a budget crunch, and he's put out some funky mailers and radio ads on McGuire that, you know, turns me off."

Her friend adjusted one of the several needles inserted in Santián's arm and chest. "He's kinda cute," she observed. "He's a cop, right?"

"Uh-huh," the other one said, lowering her voice. "That's another reason I'm not so hot on our current mayor. This dude got shot up by one of his own, girl. What kind of department is it that's so out of hand—know what I'm sayin'? I mean, shit, if they're busting caps in each other, then what does that say about my and your safety?"

Her colleague let her fingertips linger on Santián's chest, which rose and fell, aided by the ventilator. "I hear you."

"And this one," her friend added, checking the catheter, "he must have been some player. One time it's the wife and son in here seeing about him, and then, like two nights ago, I'm passing by and see one of these little cholas all crying and shit over him and know damn well it's not 'cause he helped her younger brother out. Damn."

They laughed and continued on their rounds in the ICU. On the same floor and another wing, John Castillo, head of the police commission, once again put a question to Bruno Cortese.

"What is your relationship with Sergeant Gerry Davidson? He was in charge of the property room at Temple at one point. And we understand from Judd Ahn that he's the suspected link of the so-called cold piece that turned up in the alley that night next to the gang member called Serenade. This Davidson played poker with Barry Culhane—your pal, Ronk."

Cortese tried to laugh, but it turned into a cough, what with the tube hanging off the side of his mouth and running halfway down his throat. "He was no friend of mine," was his whispery reply. "I'm glad Acosta took him out of this world."

Castillo looked across at DA Christopher Stevens. "Might want to think about your tone, Detective. You want a jury to sympathize with you."

Cortese, on his back, breathed in and out, staring at the ceiling and thankful for the morphine cloud he drifted on. He'd been worried about his waistline as he got older. But not now. They'd removed more than a quarter of his stomach and told him that fried or rich food would surely punch a hole in what remained. It was great to be on a legal high and not have to worry about such earthly matters like eating and crapping.

He was happy, too, that Goode was going to get his. McGuire had come to see him last night, election eve. At first, he was confused. Was she there working the harried doctors and nurses for any last-minute votes she could wring out of the Green Memorial staff? But then he looked over at his mother, and she told him it was past two in the morning.

McGuire told him there was a witness, a neighbor who had insomnia and had been out on his porch smoking when he'd left the Whitney house. But, she added, bending over him, she, too, wanted to see Goode get what was coming to him. The witness, she assured him, could be isolated. The search of Goode's room had produced the old-man makeup and clothing. There were hairs and other DNA trace evidence that would convict him. The bracelet didn't have to be introduced.

"But what about the theory of fruit obtained from the poisoned tree?" he'd asked. But by then she'd left, and so had his mother. Except, he reminded himself, the flare in his abdomen bubbling through his haze, his mother had been dead some five years now. Had he hallucinated all that? Was he no longer sure about the difference between what was real and what the drugs and his desperate projecting manufactured for him?

He knew, though, that he'd seen Hyacinth with Trey Mack as her manager butting in, on that tabloid TV show on the set in his room. How she was going on about how she'd been screwed over by McGuire and that the ADA had used her child's situation to blackmail her.

"He's blissed out," Stevens observed. "Reminds me of that scene in *One Flew Over the Cuckoo's Nest.*"

"That's cold, Chris. He's not a vegetable."

"Maybe he's figuring on a diminished-capacity defense."

"Before we get him on the docket, let's go have another go at Holton. He seemed ready to pop last time."

"Right," Stevens said as they walked into the hallway. "That's why he threw the chair at us."

"Twenty says he will," Castillo said. "That's just Holton's bluster. He's mad at himself for getting shot and caught. And that Heckman, who set her old man up to begin with, to show she was a good girl to the Del Fuegos, left him to twist on the hook."

"Hell, she probably had it worked out where she'd take over Mercury's operation."

"Oh, we'll find her," Stevens promised. "Let's double the bet, 'cause I'm figuring she's gong to be found in a ditch, facedown, in Tijuana."

"That might be a sucker's bet," Castillo allowed.

Suddenly there was the rushing of feet as an alarm sounded. A crash cart went whizzing past them as they stood against the wall, pushed by a burly orderly as a nurse ran beside him. She hollered, "Code Blue, Code Blue. Cardiac arrest in the ICU, patient Santián. Move it."

Castillo and Stevens trotted behind the emergency cart, worry deepening the lines in their faces.